"YOU'RE STILL WEARING YOUR WEDDING RING," HE SAID.

"Yeah." She dragged some waxy pink color across her upper lip. "So? You are, too."

"I'm still married." Angela pressed her lips together, refusing to rise to the bait.

"That's probably why they chose us, you know," Bobby said. "It makes perfect sense. At least when Crazy Daisy catches on to the fact that we're agents, she won't think we're living in sin right under her nose."

"I'm not planning on living in sin," she said. "I'm here to keep some crackpot from hurting the President's mother. And so are you. That's all. We're just doing the job."

"Right. But part of the job is being married."

"Acting like we're married," she corrected. "There's a big difference."

"Oh, yeah. I forgot." His mouth twitched in a grin. "With one, you just fight and go to bed. With the other, you fight and then you go to bed and make love. . . ."

"A fantastic read. . . . Smart, sexy, sassy, and full of heart, Mary McBride knows how to hit every note, in just the right key."
—**Kasey Michaels**, author of *Then Comes Marriage*

> Please turn to the back of this book for a preview of Mary McBride's upcoming novel, *My Hero*.

STILL MR. & MRS.

MARY McBRIDE

WARNER BOOKS

An AOL Time Warner Company

WARNER BOOKS EDITION

Cover design by Diane Luger
Cover illustration by Mike Racz

Warner Books, Inc.
1271 Avenue of the Americas
New York, NY 10020

Visit our Web site at www.twbookmark.com.

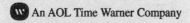 An AOL Time Warner Company

Printed in the United States of America

First Paperback Printing: September 2002

10 9 8 7 6 5 4 3 2 1

For Leslie
Again
Always

STILL
MR. & MRS.

PROLOGUE

For a moment it was oddly quiet in the Oval Office. President William Riordan could even hear the springs in his chair as he leaned back behind his desk. The sound was something like a sigh of relief. Enjoy it while it lasts, he told himself, just as Mrs. Kemp stuck her head in the door.

"I have your mother on line three, Mr. President."

So much for peace and quiet.

"Thank you, Mrs. Kemp."

He sighed, straightened up, and leaned forward for the phone.

"Mother, I'm glad you called. Are you still taking potshots at your Secret Service agents?"

"They're *your* Secret Service agents, William, and they're damned lucky I'm using BBs instead of live ammunition."

"You sound well," he said in response. She sounded heavy on the starch, as usual. Cranky. Irascible. It was her normal disposition, but she'd gotten worse since his father had passed away. They didn't call Margaret Riordan "Crazy Daisy" for nothing. "Sorry I haven't been able to get out there to see you lately."

The resultant silence on her end of the line was eloquent. It never failed to amaze William Riordan that he was president of the United States, and his mother could still make him squirm.

"You've been busy," she said at last, absolving him even as she deftly reaccused him in a mere three words. She might just as well have said, "You're not a good son."

He could have been better. He *should* have been better. But he *was* busy, for chrissake. Sometimes he just didn't know how to talk to her.

Then she said, "The Itos are abandoning me."

The president blinked. "Excuse me?"

"I said the Itos are abandoning me. My domestics, William. My housekeepers."

"Ah. The Itos," he said as she continued.

"They're going on a cruise. Mediterranean, they said. Leaving. Just like that. And the silly people seem to think I don't know how difficult cruises are to schedule. I'm sure they've had this in the works for months and simply haven't had the courage to confront me."

"Well, you can be intimidating, Mother."

"Only to the weak-minded, William." She sighed. "Anyway, dear, I wasn't calling to complain. Actually, I was wondering if you might have a cook and a gardener you could spare for a few weeks."

"From the White House?"

There was a slightly strangled quality to his voice, quite inappropriate for the most powerful man in the world. His mother, of course, heard it too, and proceeded immediately for his jugular.

"You *do* live in the White House, don't you, dear?" she crooned, which translated as, "Even a homeless bum would move heaven and earth to help his aging mother in a crisis."

As he was formulating a reply, Mrs. Kemp appeared in the doorway again, tapping her watch and whispering, "The director of the Secret Service is here for his appointment, Mr. President."

"Send him in," he replied without covering the mouthpiece. "Mother, let me see what I can do. I'll get back to you this afternoon."

"Thank you, William. I nap at two." She hung up, as always, without a good-bye, leaving her victim holding a dead phone.

The president returned the corpse to its cradle, sighed, and rose to greet the director.

Secret Service director Henry Materro had barely begun to describe the disturbing letter that had arrived at 1600 Pennsylvania Avenue late yesterday afternoon when the president suddenly stopped him with an upraised hand.

"Wait just a moment. Somebody wants to kill my mother?" William Riordan shook his head, chuckled softly, then added, "Other than me, you mean?"

It wasn't the response that the director had expected. The president received several thousand threats each year, a certain percentage of which were aimed at the First Lady or various members of the White House staff. The warnings—whether by letter, telephone, e-mail, or fax—streamed in on a daily basis, and each one required follow-up to a certain degree, but in the six years that Riordan had been in office, not a single threat had ever been directed at his mother. The agency was taking this threat, unprecedented as it was, very seriously. Very seriously indeed.

Thinking perhaps he hadn't explained the situation well enough, the director extracted a photocopy of the letter from his briefcase and slid it across the desktop.

"It's quite carefully done," he said while the chief executive perused the document. "No prints. The paper is generic, available nationwide. Same for the envelope, which is postmarked Tampa and not a great deal of help. Our forensics people are working on the sources of the cutout words, but for now the most they can say is that the person who cut them is right-handed."

"Doesn't narrow it down much, does it?" the president said, his voice now registering concern and his expression more appropriately grave.

"No, sir, it doesn't. The hope is that this will turn out to be just an isolated specimen from a crank who went to a great deal of trouble to create it and will get his satisfaction from the meticulous effort alone rather than carrying through with the threat."

"And if not?"

Henry Materro leaned forward. This, after all, was the reason he was here in the Oval Office on such short notice. "Well, sir, we've already put some things in motion, which is why I requested this meeting with you as early as possible this morning in order to keep you apprised." He watched the president nod, as if the man would be more than agreeable to and exceedingly grateful for any plan that would keep his elderly mother out of harm's way.

"You know, of course, Mr. President," Materro said, "that the Secret Service already has agents monitoring Mrs. Riordan's house from the outside. The arrangement has been adequate for her protection until now. But in light of this threat, that isn't the case anymore. Now we feel it's imperative that we have agents positioned inside her residence, as well."

William Riordan drew in a quick breath. The man nearly gasped. "Inside her house? My mother will never stand for it."

"I think she will, sir. Let me explain what we've already done, on the assumption that you would concur."

"The Itos," the president said, sitting back in his chair. "The Itos and their unexpected cruise."

"Yes, sir." Henry Materro smiled. "Exactly."

"Well, I'll be damned."

"We've arranged for your mother's domestic staff to take an extended vacation, and beginning tomorrow, their duties will be assumed by two agents, male and female." The director cleared his throat. "In order not to offend Mrs. Riordan and to avoid any possible hint of scandal, we've chosen agents who are married."

A small smile flickered across the president's lips. "To each other, I presume."

"Yes, sir. As a matter of fact, you know the male agent. It's Bobby Holland. With your permission, we're pulling him off the presidential detail and sending him to your mother's house in Illinois. Mrs. Angela Holland will be joining him there from California."

"Bobby's a good man," the president said. "The best. But I thought he and his wife were divorced."

"No, sir. It's my understanding that they've just been separated. A temporary thing."

"I see." The president cocked an eyebrow while he tapped a finger against his chin. "And now you're putting them, Bobby and Angela Holland, together under Crazy Daisy's—under my mother's roof?"

"Yes, sir. That would be the plan."

"God help them, Mr. Materro. God help us all."

Angela Holland was disgruntled, and she had a gun.

Of course, how she was going to conceal a semiautomatic weapon under a stupid apron was a mystery yet to be solved. This morning when Special Agent in Charge Dolph Bannerman had called her into his office and asked if she'd like to be reassigned to protective detail, undercover no less, Angela had leapt at the opportunity. She'd almost given her supervisor a high five and exclaimed "Would I!" before she bit her tongue and accepted the assignment with a proper and professional "I'd like that very much, sir." It was only after Bannerman had outlined the duty that Angela realized she'd made a big mistake. A real boner.

She was probably looking at weeks, maybe months, of wearing slacks and an itchy, cumbersome ankle holster. She was definitely looking at weeks, maybe months, in the Siberia of the Secret Service, in the musty armpit of the universe—Hassenpfeffer, Illinois.

"Hassenfeld," her roommate called out from the living room, making Angela realize that she'd been grumbling out loud while she trudged back and forth between her closet and the open suitcase on her bed.

"Hassenfeld," she muttered, aligning the sleeves of a

linen jacket, folding the garment carefully, and laying it into the already stuffed case. The black linen would be just right for September weather in Illinois. Her wardrobe would be perfect, in fact, as long as this September stint didn't stretch into late October or November.

The timing couldn't have been worse. Just when she was really beginning to enjoy L.A., dammit. Well, *enjoy* was probably a stretch. Tolerate was closer to the truth. Maybe she was just too uptight for the West Coast, where her colleagues all looked like surfers and tended to call one another "babe" or "dude."

"How long do you think this assignment will last, babe?" Special Agent Suzanne DiCecco, alias Surfer Girl, wandered from the living room to stand in the bedroom doorway, spooning yogurt from a carton, apparently amused by her roommate's rotten disposition. "Are there any leads on the guy who made the threat against the president's mother?"

"None that I know of." Angela was shoulder deep in her closet now, hunting for the scarf that went so well with her eggshell blouse. It wasn't where it should have been, in the top left drawer of the dresser, along with her other scarves.

"Any idea who you'll be working with?" Suzanne asked.

"Nope. I'm guessing that when Bannerman talked to me this morning, they still hadn't found anybody else dumb enough to do it." Like me, she thought.

The opportunity to work undercover had had an immediate appeal, especially when it involved protective duty with the president's mother. She'd been pleased, really gratified, thrilled as hell to be singled out for such an assignment. It was only after she'd agreed to do it that her supervisor had told her she'd be working undercover as domestic help. A freaking maid!

Aha! The sought-after scarf had been left threaded under the collar and lapels of her navy blazer for some odd reason. Angela yanked it out.

"Ask me how much I'm looking forward to playing house with somebody I don't even know in Hassleville, Illinois."

"Hassenfeld."

"Whatever." She smoothed out the wrinkles in the scarf, folded it, and laid it gently between the linen jacket and a pair of slacks. She wrapped the cord of her earpiece loosely around her radio and tucked it gently between several pairs of slacks. As always, her Kevlar vest went in last, although how she'd ever conceal it under an apron was another mystery. "That's it. I'm officially packed."

"So, how long do you think you'll be gone?"

"I don't have a clue, Suze. But don't worry about my half of the rent. I'm going to have them do a direct deposit of my paycheck, so I'll send you as many checks as I need to from Illinois. With any luck, it'll be just one, two at the most."

The buff little brunette shrugged and licked her spoon. "I wasn't worried about that. You haven't been late with your half of the rent since we moved in together. You're the best roommate I've ever had, to tell you the truth. Compared to you, all the rest were total slobs." She laughed. "Actually, compared to you, babe, everyone is a total slob."

Angela, aka babe, smiled as she closed and zipped her suitcase. It was nice, she thought, having someone appreciate her organization. Normally her attention to detail tended to irritate people, to really get on their nerves. Some people more than others. Her siblings called her Miss Prim. Her own mother had once suggested that they might have brought the wrong baby—the offspring of a CPA and a crossword puzzle fanatic—home from the hospital. And then there was Bobby. Bobby. As soon as he entered her head, she banished the thought.

"You might as well use my health club membership while I'm gone, Suze. I'll leave the card on the dresser. Right beside the lamp. Oh, and will you forward any mail that looks important or interesting?"

"Sure. No problem." Suzanne took another bite of yogurt, then cocked her head, grinning. "Can I also have Rod Bishop while you're gone?"

"Rod! Oh, my God!" Angela looked at her watch and swore softly. It was six-thirty, and Rod was sending a limo for her at seven. "I'm supposed to go to his premiere tonight. I completely forgot."

"*You* forgot something?" Suzanne laughed. "How could anybody forget about going to a premiere, especially when they're Rod Bishop's date?"

Angela shook her head even as she was frantically calculating driving times and distances, no mean feat when freeway traffic patterns corrupted every equation. It was another reason she didn't like L.A. Its sprawl of communities and tangle of highways struck her as disorganized, just plain messy. In her next life maybe she'd come back as an urban planner. Or not. Since this life wasn't working out so well, maybe she wouldn't even bother with a next one.

To the best of her recollection, the premiere was in

Culver City. Her flight to Chicago left LAX at 1:00 A.M. If she scrambled into her long black jersey dress and dragged a brush through her hair right now, she could do it. The last thing she wanted to do was stand Rod up on such an important evening.

No. The last thing she wanted to do was admit that she was really looking forward to seeing him, or confess that his sappy campaign to win her heart seemed to be making headway, or—worse—that part of the reason she had accepted the assignment to Half Ass, Illinois, was to put a bit of distance between herself and temptation.

She looked at Suzanne, who was perched on the bed, wearing not the standard-issue sober expression of a Secret Service agent but the fully glazed, semiconscious expression that always came over her whenever the actor's name was mentioned. Suzanne and a couple million other women, no doubt, all of them smitten with Hollywood's Hunk of the Year.

"He's just a guy," Angela said irritably.

"Just a guy." Suzanne sighed like a dopey teenager in the throes of puppy love. "That's like saying an AK-47 is just a gun." Her glazed expression turned slightly elfish. "Or that Rod Bishop puts his pants on one leg at a time, just like everybody else."

"I really wouldn't know about that," Angela snapped as she headed for the closet to get her black jersey dress.

"Oh, come on," Suzanne called after her. "You've been seeing him for at least three months now, Angela. The guy is absolutely gorgeous, and he's obviously crazy about you. Are you telling me you're not—"

"I'm married, Suze." She waved her left hand for emphasis before reaching for her dress. "That's a minor detail you seem to have overlooked."

"You're separated," the other agent said. "For an entire year."

Actually, Angela thought, she'd walked out on Bobby eleven months, two weeks, and three days ago, but who the hell was counting? She snatched the plastic hanger off the closet rod with such force that she broke its little plastic neck.

"Well, okay then, if you won't share Rod Bishop, how about if I take Bobby off your hands?"

"We're still married," she snarled, and immediately regretted the harsh tone that sent Suzanne scuttling off the bed and heading back toward the living room. "I'm sorry, Suze," she called to her. "I didn't mean to sound so abrupt."

"That's okay," her roommate called back. "Hey, divorce is tough. Been there. Done it. Believe me, I understand."

No, she didn't, Angela thought. How could her roommate understand when she didn't even understand it herself after all this time? She wasn't divorced. But then, in spite of what she'd just told Suze, she wasn't really married either, was she? She was just . . . well . . . separated.

"Separated? What the hell is that?" her father, the ex-cop, had exclaimed when she told him about her decision last year on the phone. "You're either married or you're not."

Her Little Limbo, as Rod kept calling her situation, much to her irritation. Her Current Confusion. Her Marital Mess. *You need to make some decisions, my love.*

Yes, she did, didn't she?

Angela drew in a deep breath and decided to get dressed for the premiere. At the moment, it was the best that she could do.

～

The red-eye flight to Chicago was on time and almost empty. For a woman who was a crack shot with a pistol and could take down a man twice her size with a few deft moves, Angela was a wimp when it came to flying. It had something to do with being at the mercy of an unseen pilot and a host of invisible, possibly incompetent mechanics. It had more to do with her tendency to be a take-charge person who knew she was out of her element, not to mention her league, in the air. Plus she just didn't like being cooped up with a bunch of sneezing, coughing strangers for hours on end.

Tonight, though, first class was empty, and she sighed gratefully as she settled into her dim little corner, buckled her seat belt, closed her eyes, and then finally—*finally*—got the big 757 into the air by fierce concentration while brutalizing a wad of strawberry bubble gum and saying half a dozen Hail Marys.

When the wheels came up, she opened her eyes and gazed out at the carpet of lights below. Dear God. An hour ago, somewhere down there, Rod Bishop had asked her to marry him.

He'd been waiting for her in front of the theater, smoking one of his long, thin cigars, standing just behind a police barricade that wasn't doing much to discourage a legion of screaming, camera-wielding fans. Rod was wearing standard Hollywood black—tux, silk shirt, and tie—clothes that fit his lean six-foot-two-inch frame as if he'd been born to wear Armani or Versace. Amazingly, the man looked just as good in faded denim and washed-out flannel. Maybe better.

His handsome, angular face was softened by the beginnings of a beard, and his dark hair grazed his shoulders, all in preparation for the western he was due to begin work on in Mexico the following week. Framed by all that dark hair and his perpetual tan, his lovely light blue, oh-so-expressive eyes had taken on a translucent, almost haunting quality.

"I'm late," she said, grasping his warm hand and climbing out of the limo.

"You're beautiful."

Ah. He made her feel that way. He really did. Beautiful to the marrow of her bones. It was just that Angela kept wondering how important feeling beautiful was to her in the grand scheme of things. Certainly not as important as feeling strong and competent at this point in her career. Certainly not as valuable a quality as skilled marksmanship or speed or upper-body strength. Beauty was nowhere on the list of requirements for a Secret Service agent. It just wasn't important to her, and yet . . .

When Rod drew her against him in front of the theater, when he whispered, "Don't fly east tonight, Angel. I need you here with me," and kissed her in full view of several hundred screaming young women, any one of whom would have worked a quick deal with the devil to be in Angela's sling-back pumps just then, she couldn't help but think that she didn't really appreciate her situation. Here was a man who needed her, who actually said so, out loud and in front of witnesses. Wasn't that what she wanted? Wasn't that one of the reasons she'd left Bobby, because he was incapable of such demonstrations of affection?

Then, after the premiere, on bended knee in the back of the limo, with tears in his aquamarine eyes and a diamond the size of a skating rink, Rod had asked her to marry him. Marry him! She hadn't even slept with him! In many ways, she barely even knew him. But to Angela's utter amazement, she hadn't told him no.

She hadn't said yes exactly either. What she said was, "I'll talk to a lawyer."

"When?" he asked, quite unashamed of the rough little catch in his throat, of the tremor in his hands as he held the diamond ring she'd just declined to wear *for now,* of the tears shining in his eyes.

"I don't know. As soon as I get back from Illinois."

"Promise me."

"I promise."

She'd promised. God. Had she meant it?

Out the window now, far below, the twinkling lights of L.A. had disappeared. Everything was black, opaque. It matched her mood.

The proposal wasn't supposed to happen. Rod Bishop was meant to be a fling, a distraction, a Band-Aid for her wounded ego, and—yes—even a way to make Bobby jealous and bring him to his knees. When she was assigned to his movie set as a Secret Service adviser, she never dreamed that Rod Bishop would be anything but a beautiful cardboard cutout, a tan Adonis made of papier-mâché and styling gel, an egocentric jerk. Instead, he'd turned out to be sort of sweet and smarter than most and always sympathetic. Most of all, though, he was patient and persistent. And he loved her! Or so he said. Repeatedly.

In the past few months, Angela's little fairy-tale fling had somehow turned into the real thing. The prince was more than charming. The glass slipper was a pretty good fit. Shit.

"May I get you something to drink?" The flight attendant sounded ungodly cheerful for half past one in the morning.

"Coffee, please. Black." It would keep her awake, Angela thought, as well as obliterate the lingering taste of Rod's champagne and cheroot kisses.

A moment later the flight attendant was back. "Here you go, Ms. Holland. Coffee. Black. Careful, it's hot." She perched on the armrest of the seat across the aisle. "The manifest says you're a federal agent, flying armed."

"That's right." Angela blew on the steaming coffee. "Is there a problem?" *Please let there be a problem so I don't have to sit here and think anymore.* Well, not a problem with the plane. Not *that* kind of problem. She didn't mean *that.* Jeez. She needed to be a lot more careful what she wished for.

"Not yet. We have a passenger in back who was pretty tanked when he boarded. You may have seen him at the gate."

Angela shook her head. She'd been the last one to board, thanks to Rod and his unwillingness to let her go. She'd actually had to jerk her hands out of his and dodge his amorous lips one last time.

"Well, anyway," the woman said, "we're about to close the bar on this guy in back, and he looks like the type who could get fairly unruly. I hope not, but I thought I'd better touch base with you, just in case."

"I'm glad you did." She tried not to sound too eager or too relieved that a crash wasn't imminent. "Let me know if you need my help."

"Thanks."

The flight attendant rose, squared her shoulders, and headed toward the rear section of the plane. Sipping her coffee, Angela listened for raised voices, almost wishing for a little ruckus to take her mind off Rod. And Bobby. Always Bobby.

The two men in her life couldn't have been more different. Dark night and bright day. Closed and open. Dry and wet.

In the theater this evening, when the violins came up and his character breathed his final, heroic breath on-screen, Rod had surreptitiously offered Angela his handkerchief, but then she'd had to give it back when Rod's wet sniffling threatened to surpass her own. Tears and testosterone. What a guy. What a deadly combination, at least in Angela's book.

She hadn't always felt that way. In fact, she'd grown up feeling quite the opposite, thanks to her big, melodramatic, hand-wringing, breast-beating family. The men, her father and four brothers, cried at the drop of a hankie, just like her mother and four sisters. There was a time when Angela swore she wasn't even a Callifano. She was the only blond in the bunch, after all, but her mother always said that was from the Milanese Fragossis on her father's side of the family. "Blonds, all of them," her mother had said, "and fussbudgets, too, just like you, Miss Prim."

She wasn't. She was simply organized, more restrained, more self-contained. She wept right along with the rest of them, but quietly, without the histrionics and the wet boo-hooing that used to humiliate her in public. That was probably the reason she'd fallen so hard for Bobby. She had taken his emotional reticence for strength. His silences signified the depth of still waters. A single twitch of a smile from Bobby Holland had meant more than all the melodramatics in the world.

But the trait that attracted her in the beginning had repelled her in the end. That emotional reticence of Bobby's was the reason she had walked out on him. And it was also the reason, once she returned to California from Hassock, Illinois, she was going to divorce him and the six-foot-high brick wall he'd built between them.

"Ms. Holland?" The flight attendant was back, looking distinctly harried. "I wonder if you'd come back and give us a hand with this clown?"

Angela gulped the last of her coffee, unbuckled her seat belt, and stood. Good. Hallelujah. She wouldn't have to think anymore about anyone or anything. Not Rod or Bobby or even Crazy Daisy Riordan. Out of habit, she touched the small of her back, but she was still wearing her black jersey dress, so of course her handcuffs weren't there. She picked up her handbag with her weapon and cuffs tucked inside. Maybe she wasn't so good at marriage, but she was damned good at her job.

"I'll follow you," she said.

2

Bobby Holland had been in a bad mood for the past eleven months, two weeks, and four days, but who was counting? Almost everyone in the agency knew it, and they pretty much tiptoed on eggshells around him. But Mike Burris was new, which was why he was currently on the receiving end of an ice cold stare.

"Come on, Bobby. Give the kid a break," Special Agent in Charge Doug Coulter said.

Mike Burris stuck out his hand. "Whatever I said, hell, I'm sorry, man. Bygones, huh?"

"Sure," Bobby said, grasping the kid's hand. "Sorry." He wasn't even all that certain now what the young agent had said. All that had registered was "your wife" and "candy-ass actor" before Bobby's temper had almost gotten away from him.

Doug Coulter clapped him on the shoulder. "Save it for the bad guys, son," he drawled in an avuncular tone that matched his gray brush cut. He'd been in the Secret Service long enough to claim he'd just missed taking a bullet for Lincoln. Right now he was special agent in charge of this hastily put-together operation. In other words, Bobby Holland's boss.

Bobby shrugged as he looked around the hangar at Andrews Air Force Base, where one of the Treasury Department Lear Jets was undergoing some last-minute maintenance before flying him halfway across the country to Springfield, Illinois, where he was scheduled to meet up with his female partner for the thirty-mile drive to Hellhole, otherwise known as Hassenfeld, the birthplace of President William Riordan and current residence of his mother, Crazy Daisy. Hassenfeld—otherwise known as the last place on earth Bobby wanted to go.

Los Angeles. That was where he'd planned to go. Not that he had a clue what he'd do when he got there, aside from hunting down the candy-ass actor who was moving in on his wife and leaving this pretty boy, Rod Bishop, with a face good only for horror movies.

He'd been adamant in his refusal of this Illinois assignment. No way. He had the seniority. He had enough sick days built up to accommodate a hundred bouts of flu. No freaking way! He'd told Doug yesterday.

Then, at ten last night, he'd picked up the phone and known immediately that he was a goner when the operator said, "Mr. Holland? Please hold for the president."

"You know I don't want to do this, Doug," he growled now to the man standing at his side.

"I don't see where that counts for much, Bobby, do you?" the gray-haired man responded quietly before he called out, "You boys got that bird about ready to fly?"

~

Bobby carved out a place for himself in the aft of the Lear Jet, slung out his legs, crossed his arms, and fell asleep listening to a muted debate on the merits of the standard-issue Sig Sauer P229 semiautomatic versus the new and improved Glock, figuring either one would have sufficed at the moment to blow his brains out.

God only knew how long he'd have to be in Illinois. Los Angeles seemed like more than a few thousand miles away right now. The City of Angels—the city of Angela—might just as well have been on the dark side of the moon.

Angela. Jesus. Half the time he wanted to strangle her for walking out on him. Half the time he didn't blame her one bit. Hell, he didn't even like living with himself. Why would she? All he did was make her cry.

She had been crying the day they met. He'd gone to Cavanaugh's with a couple of the guys when their shift was over at the White House. They were sitting at the bar, and somebody—Jack Sears?—hooked a thumb toward the front door and asked, "Hey, did you get a look at the new pussy on the vice president's detail?"

"Who?" Bobby asked.

"She's outside. Go have a look for yourself."

There she was, out in the snow and sleet, sitting at the top of a stairwell and looking like she was in agony. He thought maybe she'd twisted her ankle on the frozen sidewalk in front of the bar, so he squatted beside her to ask if she was okay.

She rolled her wet green eyes, swore like a drill sergeant, and told him to go away.

Fat chance, babe.

"Look, if you're hurt, let me help you," he said.

"I'm not hurt. Just go away."

"Then what's the problem?" He clenched his teeth,

turned the collar of his suit coat up against the cutting wind. "Shit. It's freezing out here."

"That's the problem," she said. "Look."

She eased apart the bunched lapels of her trench coat, and Bobby found himself staring at another pair of big green eyes.

"It's a fucking cat," he said, trained observer that he was.

"It's a freezing cat, you idiot. I can't take him home because they don't allow pets in my apartment, and I won't take him to the pound. I just don't know what to do."

Neither did Bobby, which was unusual, because he always knew what to do. As it turned out, he wound up taking the damned cat back to his place. Angela came to visit it Friday night, then stayed till Monday morning, when—obviously under some sort of wicked feline spell—Bobby had asked her to marry him.

Mr. Whiskers, the ingrate, ran away as soon as the temperatures warmed up. Angela waited a year and a half to do the same.

Somebody nudged his foot. "Bobby."

He opened one eye. Doug had moved to the seat next to his, and was wearing his game face. The new kid, Mike Burris, leaned forward across the aisle.

"I want to go over a couple things before we land in Springfield," Doug said.

"Shoot." Bobby straightened up.

"This is a real weird assignment."

Bobby snorted, earning a flicker of ire from his boss.

"But weird or not, the job's gotta be done and done right." Doug glanced at Mike, who nodded eagerly. "The director seems to consider this threat serious enough to warrant the expense of additional protection. The president, obviously, doesn't want to have anything happen to his mother." He sighed softly before continuing. "The president doesn't want the old lady upset, either."

Bobby wouldn't have called Daisy Riordan an old lady exactly. She didn't look her seventy-some years. Still, he'd never seen the woman in person. That was probably why he had the dubious honor of working undercover in her house.

Out of habit, Doug patted his empty shirt pocket in search of one of the cigarettes he was trying to quit. His game face turned a bit more sour. "Mrs. Riordan has declined our protection ever since her son took office, as I'm sure you know, and our surveillance team, installed at the president's direction, has to keep a respectable distance on her property."

"Otherwise she nails them with her BB gun," Bobby added for Mike's edification. "How long do you think it's going to take her, Doug, to catch on to the fact that I'm no goddamned butler?"

"You're going to *be* a goddamned butler, Bobby, or a goddamned chauffeur or bottle washer or Indian chief or whatever the hell else she wants you to be. This woman is not to know that there are Secret Service agents under her roof. Is that clear? Because if it's not clear—"

"Yeah. Yeah. I've got the picture."

"Who else will be inside, sir?" Mike asked.

"A female agent. She'll be meeting us in Springfield."

Bobby stifled a groan. He hated working with new people, women most of all, especially on protective detail. They distracted him because he always felt responsible for their safety, no matter their level of skill on the job. Angela said he felt that way about working with women because he was a natural-born protector, or—in her words—"one-third German shepherd and one-third mama hen."

"What's the other third?" he'd asked, always the ideal straight man.

"Male chauvinist pig."

As if reading his mind, Doug said, "I guess I don't have to tell you that your ability to get along with this female agent is crucial to the success of this job."

"No, sir."

"You won't be wearing radios or earpieces, for obvious reasons, and your weapons are to be concealed at all times."

"Yes, sir."

"If it turns out that you and your partner don't get along or even hate each other's guts for some reason, you'll keep those personal feelings under wraps, at least while you're in the presence of Mrs. Riordan. She's been informed that her new housekeepers are married."

"Christ," Bobby muttered. "You don't know if anybody told her happily or not, do you, boss?"

"Let's *make* it happily, Agent Holland, shall we? The less we upset the old lady, the easier this duty will be, and the better we'll be able to protect her."

"Yes, sir."

While Doug clarified some routine protective duty ops for Mike, Bobby slumped down in his seat again, wondering if he even remembered what it felt like to be happily married. He and Angela had only had a brief six months of happiness before his brother, Billy, was killed while standing post for the visiting president of Uzbek-istan. The asshole assassin might just as well have fired point-blank into Bobby's marriage because it probably flat-lined then, too, a whole hard year before Angela finally walked out.

Now, nearly a whole hard year after her exit, Bobby was going to get her back. Maybe he'd been paralyzed before. Maybe he'd been too proud to beg her to come back, or too pissed that she'd walked out on him in the first place. But a little over a week ago, when some-body from the L.A. field office had let it slip that Angela was more than casually involved with Mr. Movie Star Candy Ass Pretty Boy Bishop, Bobby had found himself in the men's room ten minutes later, vomiting on his shoes.

The following day he'd made an appointment to see the department shrink, as Angela had begged him to do. Basically, the woman had told him he was a mess, but a redeemable one, provided he made the effort.

Effort? Hell, he'd worked his whole life. He'd raised his little brother single-handedly when their father wouldn't even acknowledge them and their derelict of a mother opted out. He'd fought his way into West Point, then fought his way to fifth in his class, dragging Billy up behind him—one year, one class, always one rank be-hind—until finally they were both special agents on the elite protective detail.

Effort? He was thirty-six years old, and he could still finish a marathon in close to three hours, bench-press al-most twice his weight, and put a neat cluster of holes in a target at 250 yards. He knew all about effort, for chris-sake.

"You need to talk about your brother's death," the shrink had said. "With me, if you'd like, but especially with your wife."

That was what he hadn't been able to do.

But, by God, he was determined to try. And maybe, just maybe, by the time he made it out to L.A.—after four, maybe five weeks in Hellhole, Illinois—he'd figure out how to talk about Billy's death. Sweet Jesus. He had to figure it out.

For now, though, Bobby didn't even want to think about it. He tipped his head back against the seat, closed his eyes, and programmed himself to sleep.

~

Ducking his head, Bobby exited the Lear Jet into a bright midwestern morning. Apparently it was still summer out here in the heartland. Even this early the tarmac shimmered with heat. He put his shades on, along with an expression that said he was here to do a job, but by God he didn't have to like it.

Doug motioned him to join the little knot of agents who'd been awaiting their arrival. "This is Bobby Holland. He'll be on the inside with the female agent. Is she here yet?"

One of the guys gestured toward a nearby hangar. "Got here a few minutes ago. She was about an hour late. Said there was trouble with some drunk on the flight to Chicago, and she had to wait for the locals to take him off her hands at O'Hare."

Oh, good. A hotshot, Bobby thought as he finished the round of handshaking. This deal was getting worse by the minute. The local agents all looked either headed out to pasture or fresh out of college. The older guys seemed miffed that their cupcake duty had turned serious, while the younger ones were making a distinct effort to hide their grins and tamp down on the testosterone.

One of the geezers, an agent by the name of McCray, pointed to a blue Taurus station wagon with a bent antenna and a crimped front fender. "That vehicle is for you and your partner, Holland. We thought it hit the right note."

"Yeah." A young turk snickered. "Dull and domestic."

"We put new steel-belted radials on it," the older agent continued, "and had the engine souped up a little. It should be fine."

"Great. Thanks," Bobby said. "I don't suppose anybody has a sketch of the layout of the house."

All of them, old and young, shook their heads.

"Never been inside," McCray said.

"Crazy Daisy hardly ever goes out," said one of the kids. "Some sort of recluse, I guess you'd say."

Doug intervened with a quiet, "Uh. Let's call her Mrs. Riordan, shall we, fellas?"

There was a general chorus of coughing and throat-clearing as Bobby gazed up at the sun, then glanced at his watch. He wrenched it off and set the time back an hour, hardly appreciative of having an additional sixty minutes tacked on to his day, not to mention his whole miserable stay here.

When he looked up again, a door swung open in the nearby hangar to reveal a shapely backside and long legs clad in crisp black slacks. She, presumably his partner, Agent Hotshot, was wrestling a huge suitcase through the narrow doorway. He had to stifle the urge to walk over and help. They only resented it, these female agents. Everybody just stood there and watched, obviously enjoying the view.

"Here comes our agent now," he said just as she tugged the suitcase through and turned toward them with a pretty swing of her long blond hair.

Holy Mother of—

Doug, beside him, made a kind of gulping sound, swore, then said, "I didn't know, Bobby. I swear to God I didn't know."

3

Angela was so tired she had almost dozed off while she changed clothes in the deserted hangar. The flight from L.A. had been a nightmare in which she and two flight attendants had spent the final half hour of the flight actually having to sit on the drunk and disorderly passenger. Once they'd landed in Chicago, the guy had sobered up sufficiently to charm the stripes off the pants of airport security. Angela, still in the black jersey she'd worn to the premiere, had to flash her badge half a dozen times before anybody would even give her the time of day. Which happened to be dawn. Dammit.

And then the short hop from Chicago to Springfield had been bumpy as hell for some reason, even though the skies were clear and bright. It might have been because the plane was propeller driven and about the size of a giant mosquito. Man, she hated flying. The good news, though, was that she'd gotten her wish. She hadn't had a moment to think about *anything* in the past five or six hours, much less *anyone*.

After she maneuvered her heavy suitcase through the hangar's door, Angela turned, a stoic smile on her face, intending to wave to the waiting agents. Her gaze seemed to gravitate naturally to Doug Coulter's familiar, silvery buzz cut. And then she saw who was standing at Doug's side.

Oh, no. Nuh-uh. No way.

She dropped her suitcase and reached into her handbag for her cell phone. Across the tarmac, she swore she saw Bobby flinch, as if he thought she were going for her gun. Which wasn't such a bad idea, come to think of it. She stabbed in the number for the L.A. office, then glared at the clump of agents, who were shrugging their shoulders and scratching their heads and staring at her stupidly.

All except one. The one she'd last seen when she walked out his door. The one currently wearing the shades and the big, shit-eating grin.

They picked up in L.A. "This is Agent Holland. I need to speak with Bannerman. Now."

She let her focus glaze in order not to see the muscular contours of Bobby's gray suit, the solid length of his legs, the challenge of his stance, or the way his tie wafted over his shoulder in the warm morning breeze. God. She could practically smell him.

"What do you mean, Bannerman's not in? Put me through to him in the field, then. This is an emergency."

Doug Coulter was ambling toward her now, shaking his crew-cut head as if to say, "Well, don't this just beat all?"

Out in L.A., the operator from hell refused to put her through. "When will he be back in the office?" Angela demanded. "What do you mean, he didn't say?"

"Hello there, Angela," Doug drawled. "Looks like you're even more surprised than I am."

She snapped the phone closed. "I'm not staying,

Doug. You're just going to have to find somebody else. Really. Today. Right now. I won't do this."

"Well, now." Doug crossed his arms, sucked in his lower lip, and stared heavenward for a long, probably prayerful moment. "I appreciate the predicament you find yourself in here. I really do. But the fact of the matter is you *have* to do this, Agent Holland. Today. Now. If you want to try and work out some alternative arrangement once we're set up, you be my guest. I doubt it'll happen, but you're sure welcome to try."

It was Angela's turn to stare at the sky, less for divine guidance than a stray lightning bolt to put an immediate, sizzling, blessed end to her distress.

"You know we're separated, Doug."

"Not now, you're not."

"I'm this close to filing for divorce." She measured an inch in the air with her thumb and index finger, then closed the distance to half an inch.

"Nothing says you can't go on and do that," he said calmly, "after you've done your job here."

"This is nuts."

"Probably."

"Bobby's over there grinning like a fool."

"I see that."

"Did he know?"

Doug shook his head. "Nope. Neither did I. I don't know what idiot is responsible for this, Angela. But I do know this." He lowered his voice ominously. "If you walk, you're going to find yourself stationed in Buttfuck, Alaska, for the rest of your career."

Angela knew that, too. Oh, boy, did she know it. The Secret Service wasn't the army, by any means, but the agency didn't cut anyone a lot of slack when it came to refusing assignments. You were either on the team or you were shipped off to a one-room office in a strip mall someplace that was a thousand degrees in the summer and a thousand below in the winter, spending your time attending Career Day at the local high schools and watching your former colleagues on the evening news. Shit.

She hadn't worked as hard as she had all these years only to wind up looking for funny money in Alaska, not to mention that it would put her a thousand miles away from Rod. As if he mattered at the moment. As if anything mattered but her job, the only thing she had now that she didn't have Bobby.

"Okay," she said through clenched teeth, reaching down for her suitcase. "Oh, God. I hate this. I really, *really* hate this."

"I can tell. Want me to give you a hand with that bag?" Doug asked.

"No," she said. "With a free hand right now, I'd be way too tempted to draw my weapon."

Bobby had been ready to dive for cover when Angela whipped out her cell phone, but now he was biting the inside of his cheek to keep from grinning while he watched his wife's magnificent fury a couple hundred yards away. Lord, she looked good. California obviously agreed with her. Or something did.

He wasn't the only one who thought so, judging from the comments of his colleagues, which ranged from McCray's appreciative "Mm-mm" to the more sexually explicit observations of the young turks. Bobby just let it all wash over him. He was too damned happy. And, what the hell, they were right. She was a beautiful woman. And she was his. Oh, yeah.

His heart was pumping so hard that he had to fold his arms to keep it from bursting right out of his chest while he watched her. Angela never did like surprises, did she? Of course, neither did he, but this was different. This was more along the lines of an answered prayer. So, on the off chance that it truly was, Bobby prayed again. Dear God, please don't let me screw this up.

As he had earlier, Doug oversaw the round of introductions, ending with a slant of his head toward Bobby and a murmured, "I think you already know this gentleman."

"Ange," Bobby said softly, when what he really wanted to do was leap on her, wagging his tail and licking her pretty face like a jubilant hound.

"Hello, Bobby." Her voice was neutral enough, although her green eyes were giving off little topaz sparks in the sunlight and she wrenched a hank of hair behind her ear, always a sign of agitation.

"Well, now that everybody's here, let's get this hootenanny on the road," Doug said. "Angela, Bobby, let's get your luggage in the car, and then I want a couple words with you. The rest of you might as well get started. We don't want to look like a goddamn parade coming into town."

"See you later, Bobby," Mike Burris said. "Sorry about what I said before. Well, you know."

"Yeah. I'll see you, kid. Good luck."

Bobby reached for Angela's bag.

"I've got that," she said, snatching the handle and turning to follow Doug to the blue Taurus wagon.

Still wearing his shades, Bobby allowed himself an exaggerated roll of his eyes and a silent sigh before he collected his own gear and followed in her wake, fully appreciating the flare of her hips and the nice nip of her waist. She must be wearing an ankle holster, he decided. She hated those. No wonder she was such a pisser.

After he tossed his stuff in the back of the wagon, Bobby said, "Don't look so worried, Doug. We can handle this."

"Speak for yourself," Angela muttered.

"You better handle it, the both of you, or you'll be working third watch for Eagle Eye Security Service." The special agent in charge glared from one to the other. "You get my meaning?"

"Yes, sir," they answered in unison.

"You're going to have to come up with some kind of story to satisfy the old lady. Mrs. Riordan, I mean. Some bullshit about how you're working as domestics. I don't care what you tell her as long as she believes it. Think you can do that?"

"We'll work it out on the way there," Bobby said, glancing at Angela for affirmation as well as pure pleasure.

"Right," she said.

"You can contact us with your handsets or by regular phone. I'd appreciate a report on developments inside the house every couple of hours. And a map of the interior as soon as you can come up with one, Bobby."

"You got it."

"I'll do that," Angela said. "His handwriting's terrible."

"What do you mean? My handwriting's just fine," Bobby said.

"No, it's not. It's—"

"People!" Doug raised both hands. "We're here to protect the mother of the president of the United States, not to squabble like a bunch of kindergarteners. You got that?"

"Yes, sir."

"All right, then. I believe there's a map in the car showing you just how to get to the house in Hassenfeld. I'll expect you to check in with the surveillance trailer as soon as possible after you're situated. Any questions?"

"No, sir."

"Fine. The keys are in the car. I'll talk to you later." Doug turned to join the agents who were waiting for him beside a big black SUV.

"I'll drive," Bobby said, slamming the hatch.

"I'll drive," she said, opening the driver's door and sliding behind the wheel before he could reply.

~

It took Angela a few miles to settle in behind the wheel, to keep her eyes on the road rather than sneaking peeks to her right. Her husband looked good. He looked great! Tan and fit and none the worse for her absence this past year. She noticed he hadn't taken off his wedding ring. But, then, neither had she.

She'd started to remove the plain gold band once several months ago, thinking it would be a step in the right direction, figuring if she couldn't bring herself to sever their tie legally, at least she could do it symbolically. But when she'd gotten the ring just past her knuckle, the feelings of finality and loss were so painful, so overwhelming, that she almost couldn't breathe. It was like being caught in a riptide, losing her balance, gasping for air. So, back went the ring, and back came her ability to breathe, along with all her confusion about her marriage.

Actually, she thought she was holding it together reasonably well at the moment, considering the circumstances. Her knuckles weren't white anymore, now that she'd relaxed her grip on the wheel. The tension in her neck had eased. Her breathing was still a bit shallow, but that was mostly because of the cross breeze from Bobby's open window, which carried his scent of sandalwood and musk and just pure Bobby across the car to directly assault her senses. Surely Rod smelled that good, if not better, but Angela couldn't for the life of her summon up a memory of the actor's cologne or aftershave.

In the eleven months they'd been apart, Angela hadn't once anticipated the strength of her physical reaction to the sight of her husband. The shape of his mouth was suddenly the object of intense, albeit sidelong, scrutiny as she remembered his kisses. The sprinkling of dark hairs on the back of his hands made her stomach clench at the thought of his touch. The hard contour of his left thigh beneath the gray gabardine of his trousers was making her insane. His physical presence simply clobbered her. She wondered vaguely if she was drooling down the front of her blouse while she was telling herself she really needed to get her mind and all of her highly attuned senses back on business.

"State Route Twenty-nine?" she asked, glancing toward the passenger seat again. "Is that the road we want up ahead?" Bobby was hogging the map, dribbling out directions a half mile at a time.

"Uh-huh."

"Let me see the map, Bobby."

"You're fine. Just take a right at the next intersection."

In all the time they'd been together, they'd never been actual partners on the job, and Angela was thanking her lucky stars for that at the moment as she snapped on the directional signal and maneuvered into the right-hand lane of traffic.

"When did you turn into such a control freak?" she asked.

"I'm glad to see you, too, sweetheart."

She gritted her teeth, braking at the light. The funny thing was, he really did seem glad to see her. Bobby, who was usually as stingy with his smiles as he was with the stupid map, had been grinning like a silly Cheshire cat ever since he'd laid eyes on her this morning. If Doug had been telling the truth, that this shared assignment had been as much a surprise to Bobby as it was to her, he seemed awfully pleasantly surprised.

Taking her hand off the wheel long enough to snag back a hank of hair, she gave him another little sideways glance in the process. Still smiling. Like an idiot. Like some kind of pervert. If that was because he thought he was going to jump her bones tonight or anytime in the near future, he had another think coming.

"You're looking really good, Angela," he said as if on cue.

That *was* it, then. He *was* thinking about sex. The jerk.

He looked really good, too, but that didn't mean she was considering resuming relations. They were separated, for heaven's sake. Well, sort of. Not legally, of course, but they hadn't been this close in nearly a year.

"Don't even think about it, Bobby," she muttered. The light changed, and she turned the wheel to the right, stepped on the gas. "How far south on Twenty-nine now? Does this take us all the way to Hassenfeld?"

"All the way," he said, shifting in the seat so he was looking directly at her. "You just look good, Ange. That's all."

"Thank you. You look good, too. Do you think maybe we should start planning what two good-looking people are doing out in the middle of nowhere, working as domestic help?"

"Okay." He crossed his arms and settled back, one shoulder slanted against the door. "We're here doing research on a book?"

"On what? Scut work in the Midwest? I don't think so."

He shrugged. "It was just an idea. The speed limit's fifty-five along here, Ange."

"I know that." Her gaze dropped to the speedometer, where the needle registered a healthy sixty-seven. She eased her foot off the gas as imperceptibly as possible. "How about saying we got burned out on big-city life and we're doing this as a kind of transition, until we find something else?"

"Sounds good," he said without much enthusiasm.

"We should probably agree on what we did before we opted out of the rat race."

"How about if I was a brain surgeon and you were my nurse?"

She rolled her eyes. He could be such a knee-jerk chauvinist sometimes. "How about if I was a brain surgeon and you were my patient, but the operation was a total disaster? Or I was a brain surgeon, and you were the studly hospital maintenance man who stole my heart in spite of our vast educational and socioeconomic differences?"

"Studly?" He was grinning again.

"Forget it." She sighed. "If Mrs. Riordan even asks, we'll say we used to be in advertising, all right?"

"Fine." He was quiet a moment, fiddling with a button on the sleeve of his jacket, pulling a loose thread on the cuff. "How's your dad, Ange?"

"He's fine." *Pop thinks I'm a coward for running away from my marriage, even though he hasn't said it in so many words. I can hear the disappointment in his voice.*

"And your mom?"

She thinks whatever Pop thinks. They're a team. The way I always thought we'd be. "She's fine, too." Angela answered a bit more crisply this time, hoping he'd drop the personal stuff. But he didn't. He took it up a notch.

"I was thinking about Mr. Whiskers this morning," he said. "Remember him?"

Angela felt the knots tighten in her shoulders and neck. Did she remember? If it hadn't been for Mr. Whiskers, the little ingrate, she and Bobby probably would never have exchanged more than an occasional handshake at meetings and a few professional words in corridors here and there. But then came that horribly cold day, when he volunteered to take that mangy stray back to his place, when he shrugged out of his suit coat to keep the poor thing warm while they trudged five long blocks against an icy wind, through knee-deep snow and driving sleet to the lot where their cars, as it turned out, were parked side by side.

Big, solid, stone-faced Bobby Holland. He seemed bigger than life that afternoon, carrying a balled-up gray jacket while a little marmalade cat face kept poking out through sleeves and bunched lapels. By the time they reached the parking lot, Angela was already half in love with Bobby Holland. Dammit. She was still in love with him. Not half, but wholly. But that wasn't the point, was it?

"Bobby. Please. I'd rather not talk about us. Really. I don't even want to be here. And I don't want to start fighting and have this whole assignment blow up right in our faces. You heard what Doug said."

He was quiet again, then said, "Want to talk about Billy?"

Angela's breath stalled in her throat. That's all she'd ever wanted him to talk about these past eighteen months. His brother. How he loved him. How he missed him. How guilty he felt. How Billy's death had affected him to the core of his being. She'd begged him and begged him to discuss it, and finally she'd left him behind that big brick wall he put up.

He wanted to talk about Billy now? Now, while they were on duty? Now, going fifty-five miles an hour on State Route Twenty-nine between Springfield and Horse-feathers, Illinois? Now, when it was too damned late? My God. Angela bit her lip, but even so, she thought she might just scream. The top of her head felt as if it were going to explode. She swerved onto the shoulder of the road.

~~~~~

After an almost involuntary shout of "What the hell are you doing, Angela?" when his wife unexpectedly veered off the pavement into the weeds at the side of the road, Bobby just sat there. For a man who had the instant reflexes of a mountain cat, he felt strangely dull and unresponsive. He felt stupid, too, not knowing what to say or do while Angela sat white-knuckled at the wheel with her lips compressed and her gaze aimed straight ahead.

What had he done, for chrissake, to upset her so? What had he said? The thing about Billy? Billy was all she ever wanted him to talk about. Now he'd finally volunteered, and Angela was suddenly all bent out of shape.

"Honey," he said, reaching to touch her arm.

"Just leave me alone." She batted away his hand. "I don't want to talk about anyone or anything. Don't you understand?"

No, he didn't understand. Bobby didn't understand at all. "Jesus Christ, Ange." He ripped his fingers through his hair, then clenched his fists to keep from reaching out for her again. He couldn't stand not touching her. "What do you want from me?"

"I don't want anything from you, Bobby. Not anymore." She swiped at a tear that had broken loose from the corner of her eye. "My God, we can't even be together twenty minutes without fighting. Doesn't that tell you something?"

If it did, he couldn't name it, other than his wife's stubborn refusal to give him a chance, to simply listen to him, to even look him in the eye for more than a fleeting second. Why was that?

"Angela," he began, only to be cut off by a brusque wave of her hand.

"We better get back on the road." She reached to turn the key, forgetting she hadn't cut the motor in the first place. When the ignition screeched in protest, Angela jerked back her hand, swore fiercely, then just sat there with her eyes closed.

"Move over." Bobby got out of the car and slammed the door, then stalked around the rear and wrenched open the driver's door. "Come on. I'm driving."

He stood back, giving her just enough room to get out of the car, intentionally menacing her with his height and his weight and the sheer heat he was generating.

"Give me the map," she demanded, holding out her hand while her chin jutted up into his face.

"You don't need it. I know how to get there."

"God damn you, Bobby." Tears started to cascade, leapfrogging each other down her cheeks. "I hate you. I really do."

His arms were already moving around her, pulling her in, never wanting to let go. "I know, babe. I know."

As much as he longed to kiss her, Bobby simply held her. And as much as he yearned to speak, to make right all the things that had gone wrong between them, he kept silent.

Ah, God, it was good to have his wife back in his arms, even if she was crying, even if she truly hated him at the moment. At least she felt something for him. It was a start.

~~~

Twenty minutes later, after Bobby took the wheel and maintained the speed limit along with a blessed silence, they passed through beautiful downtown Hassenfeld, which Angela grudgingly admitted was fairly quaint.

Its wide main street was cobbled and lined with buildings that sported awnings and bore names like Nellie's Notions, Whodunit—A Mystery Bookstore and Magic Shoppe, and Your Grandmother's Attic. There was a little restaurant, Chez Moi, that almost reminded her of New York with its tiny sidewalk cafés where people were actually sitting, sipping from white china mugs and perusing crisp copies of *USA Today*.

In the heart of the charming village sat a shaded square with a Victorian bandstand and a big Civil War monument. Just at the edge of Main Street was a small cinderblock building bearing the sign "Village Constable." An American flag flapped gently over its shingled roof.

"This is nice," she said a bit wistfully, thinking of the leisurely weekends she and Bobby had spent in similar towns while ransacking Maryland and Virginia for antiques, newlyweds happily furnishing their nest. Those weekends seemed like a thousand years ago.

Special Agent Bobby Holland wasn't the world's most enthusiastic shopper. Usually he'd amble along, a pace or two behind her, patient and indulgent, like Prince Philip tagging along after the queen. But there were times when he'd get into the spirit, such as when they discovered their big old brass bed in a back room of an antique shop not too far from Charlottesville.

They'd paid way too much for it, with its massive headboard and footboard, but oh, the lovely times they'd spent in that bed. Sad and lonely times, too. She didn't dare think about them, or she'd lose her hard-won composure again, and Bobby would find another excuse to wrap his arms around her and pretend that everything was okay.

A mile or so beyond the town, Bobby turned the station wagon into a long, tree-lined driveway. "This is it," he said, as if he'd been here a hundred times before.

The drive swung to the right, around an enormous, two-story red-brick house, then ended at a three-car detached garage. There was a freestanding toolshed adjacent to the garage, and not too far from that a wonderful white gazebo banked by rosebushes, a few of them holding forth with mid-September blooms. Through the trees and shrubs at the back of the property, Angela could just make out the Secret Service's surveillance trailer.

She reached for the rearview mirror, adjusting it in order to check her makeup. Just as she had suspected, there were mascara smudges under both her eyes. She licked her finger and attempted to wipe them away, all the while aware of Bobby's presence and his unyielding gaze.

"That didn't mean anything," she said, still concentrating on the mirror. "Earlier, I mean. On the road. I don't want you to get the wrong idea, Bobby. About us."

"Hey." He held up his hands defensively. "No big deal. I'm used to my partners falling apart and needing a little TLC. Just part of the job, Ange."

She shot him a watered-down version of a screw-you look, then dug in her handbag for a tube of lipstick.

"You're still wearing your wedding ring," he said.

"Yeah." She dragged some waxy pink color across her upper lip. "So? You are, too."

"I'm still married."

Angela pressed her lips together, refusing to rise to the bait.

"That's probably why they chose us, you know," Bobby said. "It makes perfect sense. At least when Crazy Daisy catches on to the fact that we're agents, she won't think we were living in sin right under her nose."

"I'm not planning on living in sin," she said, taking a last glance in the mirror before twisting it back. "I'm here to keep some crackpot from hurting the president's mother. And so are you. That's all. We're just doing the job."

"Right. But part of this job is being married."

"Acting like we're married," she corrected. "There's a big difference."

"Oh, yeah. I forgot." His mouth twitched in a grin. "With one, you just fight and go to bed. With the other, you fight and then you get to go to bed and make love."

"That's about the sum of it, pal." She pulled on the door handle. "And the sooner we get started, the sooner this whole silly charade will end. Let's go."

Keep your mind on the job, bubba, Bobby warned himself as they walked up the driveway to the front of the house. He'd already made about seven mistakes this morning while keeping his eye on Angela instead of on the ball. Not professional mistakes, but personal ones, not the least of which was getting an erection the size of Baja California when he was holding Angela close against him, warranting one of her "How dare you, you filthy pig" looks.

As he walked, he slid his holster farther back on his belt to prevent Crazy Daisy from catching so much as a glimpse of it, then he tightened the knot of his tie a bit, befitting a brand-new butler or whatever the hell he was supposed to be. He was already screwing up with Angela. No sense screwing up his job, as well.

The place was expensively and incautiously land-scaped, with thick shrubbery covering the better part of the first-floor windows. He had to assume that the agents in place had been discouraged in any attempt to cut the bushes back. Discouraged with BBs, no doubt. Okay. So he'd play gardener, too. It was a good place to start. And he'd wash the windows, which would give him an opportunity to check out the condition of the locks.

"Those shrubs have to go," Angela murmured beside him.

He glanced sideways at her pretty face with its intense expression, her bright green gaze doing a thorough one-eighty sweep as she walked. Sometimes—okay, often—he forgot she was a well-trained, conscientious Secret Service agent. Sometimes—all the time—he shuddered to think that she was as committed as he to taking a bullet for her protectee. Like Billy. He shunted that thought to the back of his brain as quickly as it occurred.

"That's no good," Angela said.

"Huh?"

She pointed. "Look up there."

No bulb in the yard light. Damn. He should have caught that even before she did. "I'll put it on my list," he said.

"This is weird." She nudged his arm as they meandered up the herringbone-brick front walk. "I've never worked with you before, or undercover, either, for that matter."

Bobby let out a surprised little laugh. "I wouldn't exactly call this undercover, Ange." He hoped he didn't sound too dismissive. His own undercover experience in a Russian mafia counterfeiting ring a few years back had resulted in a pretty tense hostage situation and shoot-out on Long Island. This butler business was a cupcake deal in comparison.

"Still—" She made a little clucking sound with her tongue as they arrived at Mrs. Riordan's doorstep.

Bobby punched the doorbell. "Here we go."

The woman who opened the door was five feet tall and about a hundred and twelve years old. Her face looked like an apple that had fallen off a tree in the Garden of Eden. Her hair was light orange, short, almost viciously spiked. She was wearing white leggings and a big turquoise shirt, draped with half a ton of multicolored beads. The shirt matched her eye shadow.

Bobby actually gulped. "Uh . . . Mrs. Riordan?"

"No, no. I'm Bootsie Rand. I'm the dummy, so I got to answer the door."

Both of them must have given her such blank, befuddled looks that the woman tossed back her head and hooted. "We're playing bridge, children," she said.

"Daisy's right in the middle of a grand slam. Come in. Come in. Are you the new maid and butler?"

"Yes, ma'am." Bobby nudged Angela across the threshold ahead of him. A human shield.

"Good. Good. Well, now." Bootsie's turquoise lids dipped, and she began to take Bobby in, slowly, from the shine on his wing tips to the top of his head. "Oh, you're a good one, you are."

"Thank you, ma'am." He didn't know what else to say, and Angela, behind her grim facade, was biting the hell out of her lips to keep from laughing.

The woman stepped closer to him, lifted on tiptoe to whisper, "If this gig doesn't work out, sonny, you can come over and buttle for me. I live just down the road."

"Yes, ma'am."

"If those are my new people, Muriel," someone called from a nearby room, "show them to the kitchen and tell them I'll be there in a moment."

"Say please," Bootsie yelled over her shoulder.

For a minute it was quiet enough to hear the hall clock tick. Tick. Tick. Bobby felt a trickle of sweat beneath his sleeve.

"Please," the voice finally shouted back.

Bootsie's sudden, victorious grin completely rearranged the wrinkles on her face. "Follow me, children. The kitchen's right this way."

4

Bobby was drumming his fingers on the kitchen table. "What do you think?" he whispered.

"I think we're in the fifth circle of hell, and it's all up-hill from here." Across the table from him, Angela swung one leg over the other, peeked to make certain her ankle holster wasn't visible, and then gazed around the room. "This is really very nice."

Daisy Riordan's kitchen reminded her of Rod's, with its warm cherry wood cabinets, sleek white appliances, and slick gray granite counters. The only thing lacking was a glorious view of the Pacific. Well . . . and Rod, of course. She'd never known a man who enjoyed cooking so much, whether it was a simple pasta or a complicated paella with three kinds of clams, two live lobsters, and a small fortune in saffron.

She'd learned a lot about preparing food from Rod in the past few months. Not that her culinary skills were inadequate before she met him, but as the youngest child in a family with four older sisters and a father who made the world's greatest marinara sauce, Angela hadn't spent much time in the kitchen when she was growing up. The mess drove her crazy.

Her mother was a fabulous, intuitive, even cheerful

cook who wasn't the least bit fazed by car keys and squirt guns and tennis balls on the counter where she worked, magnetized homework flapping on and falling off the refrigerator door, or half a dozen dog and cat bowls underfoot, not to mention the cats and dogs. Rose Callifano could put together lasagna while she fielded questions about world geography and the location of lost objects, while she laughed at knock-knock jokes, kissed away tears, and slapped bandages on skinned appendages. And her lasagna was the best in the world.

It was only while she lived in relative quietude with Bobby that Angela had made a concerted effort to become a good cook. In the beginning, it had been simply to please and impress him, but after Billy died, she had cooked to make Bobby happy. It hadn't worked. Nothing had.

The grin he'd worn earlier this morning had vanished. At the moment, he looked positively glum. Even a bit apprehensive.

"What do you think of Bootsie?" he whispered.

Angela tried not to laugh. Once the bizarre little woman had led them into the kitchen, Bootsie had continued to ogle and drool over Bobby, even reaching up to measure his biceps through his jacket with both of her gnarled little hands. She'd probably pinched his butt, too, while Angela wasn't looking. If the woman had been about fifty years younger, Angela might have been tempted to smack her.

"What do I think of Bootsie?" She couldn't help but grin. "I think you better watch your back, Agent Holland."

"Yeah." He shuddered.

"I told you that you were looking good these days," she said, regretting the comment as soon as it passed her lips. Good? He looked great.

His light brown hair was a tad longer than she was used to seeing it, but still neatly clipped. You could take the man out of West Point, but you couldn't take the Point out of the man. His black wing tips, as always, glistened like patent leather. She guessed his weight was about the same—a solid one-ninety-five on his six-foot frame— thanks in part to his daily six-mile loops around the White House, which also accounted for the burnished bronze of his face. Bobby did those runs with an almost monastic devotion, rain or shine, in sickness and in health, before their marriage and during it, so she had no reason to believe he'd changed his routine in her absence.

The color of his eyes was a dark jade at the moment, given the indirect lighting in Daisy Riordan's kitchen. Angela thought the creases at the corners of those eyes might have deepened in the past year, but she couldn't be certain.

He wasn't handsome. Not in the Hollywood way that Rod was handsome. But he was a damned good-looking man, one who easily turned a woman's head and turned her thoughts to . . .

. . . to things she had no business thinking about under the circumstances, Angela warned herself. She was here for one reason, and one reason alone. To do a job. To protect the mother of the president of the United States while posing as a stupid maid. She'd noticed an assortment of cups and saucers and cocktail glasses by the sink, so she made herself useful, rinsing them and putting them in the dishwasher.

"I want you to know that I'm not establishing any precedent here," she said over her shoulder.

"What do you mean?" Bobby asked.

"I mean I don't want to get stuck in the kitchen all the time we're here, Bobby. I could do the shrubbery out front. I'm pretty good with pruning shears, you know."

He gave an obnoxious little snort. "Are you referring to that Scotch pine you crucified our first Christmas, by any chance?"

"I did not."

"You did, too. You kept saying it wasn't quite balanced, and by the time you were done 'balancing,' that poor tree didn't have enough branches left to hang any ornaments on."

Angela slammed the dishwasher closed. "We didn't *have* any ornaments. You sat on the box. Remember?"

"Who left it on my chair?"

"I most certainly—"

"Well, now." A voice wafted from the doorway. "I've always thought that bickering was a very healthy thing for a marriage. Like a tea kettle, letting off steam a little at a time rather than simply exploding."

The president's mother strode into the kitchen, clutching a worn blue canvas binder. In spite of having seen photos of the woman, Angela was somehow expecting Crazy Daisy to be a somewhat younger version of her friend and bridge partner, Bootsie. She couldn't have been more wrong. Mrs. Riordan was attractive, obviously young for her age, and quite elegant in a gray skirt and pale gray silk blouse with a soft bow at the neck and a subtle string of pearls. Gray hair framed her lovely, nearly unlined face.

"Mrs. Riordan." Bobby stood up. "I'm Bobby Holland, and this is my wife, Angela. We're—"

"How do you do?" she responded briskly. "I'm not particularly interested in your references, young man. The fact that my son recommended you is good enough. Quite frankly, I'm surprised William managed to get you here so quickly. Or at all, for that matter." She put the binder on the table with a thump, pulled out a chair, and sat before Bobby could assist her.

Bobby and Angela traded glances. So much for their bogus advertising credentials. They seemed to share an inaudible sigh of relief.

"I nap at two," Mrs. Riordan said, "so if you'll both sit, I believe we can get through the essentials fairly quickly and painlessly."

"Yes, ma'am." Bobby pulled out a chair for Angela, then settled beside her, folding his hands on the table, perfectly servile and attentive. For such a tough guy, he was pretty good at this.

The president's mother opened her binder, all neatly organized with colored tabs. "Meals ought to be relatively simple," she said. "I have my breakfast on a tray upstairs at eight. Fruit juice, one bran muffin, and black coffee." Her gaze lofted to Angela. "Strong coffee, and none of those silly perfumed varieties."

"Yes, ma'am."

"I have lunch upstairs, as well." She flipped to the next section of the book. "You'll see sample menus here and may use them as a guide. I don't mind a small surprise now and then." The flimsiest of smiles touched her lips, then disappeared as she turned another page.

"My evening meal is also upstairs, on a tray," she continued, her finger drifting along the edge of the binder.

"Not much exercise," Bobby murmured.

Her pale blue eyes snapped up. "I beg your pardon?"

With his hands still respectfully folded, Bobby brushed his thumbs back and forth. Angela found herself staring rather stupidly at the gold band on his left hand while she waited to hear how he was planning to extract his foot from his mouth. He was going to need that foot to walk back to the car when Mrs. Riordan booted them out.

For somebody who found it so difficult to express himself, he'd certainly chosen the wrong time and place to start voicing opinions. Crazy Daisy was regarding him as if he were a worm who'd suddenly appeared in her kitchen. Bobby seemed unfazed.

"I said, that's not much exercise, ma'am. Plenty for us taking trays upstairs and bringing them back down again all day, but not nearly enough for you."

Her blue eyes were icy, her gaze frozen on his face. "Really," she said, her voice like audible frost.

"Yes, ma'am."

Oh, Bobby. God, you are such a jerk. Angela slid down a few inches in her chair, hoping to avoid the coming fireworks.

"How old are you, Mr. Holland? What was your first name?" The woman's lips were so rigid she could barely speak.

"Bobby," he said.

"I don't like diminutives," she snapped. "How old are you, Robert?"

"I'm thirty-six, ma'am."

Angela slid lower. Goddammit. She'd forgotten his birthday last month. How could she have forgotten? Not that she would've done anything about it, but she should have remembered it, at least. Then she could've done nothing on purpose.

"Well, I'm seventy-six," Mrs. Riordan said, "and I'd very much appreciate it if you kept your opinions to yourself."

"Yes, ma'am."

She shifted her shoulders but didn't soften her glare. "If I wanted a trainer, I'd have hired a trainer. Is that clear?"

"Yes, ma'am."

"Fine." Crazy Daisy nearly ripped the next page out of her book. "Shall we continue?"

"Yes, ma'am."

When she had concluded her monologue about meals and food preferences and schedules, casting the occasional black look across the table at "Robert," Mrs. Riordan pointed toward what appeared to be a small mud room just off the kitchen. "Your room is through there. The Itos find it quite comfortable, and I trust you will, as well. Any questions?"

Angela shook her head and was enormously relieved when Bobby did the same.

"Very well. I'll let you get settled in, then. Please have my dinner tray upstairs by six. My room is the last one on the left."

"Yes, ma'am."

They all stood. Crazy Daisy glared one final dagger at Bobby before she left the room.

~~

The minute Mrs. Riordan stomped out of the kitchen—probably the most exercise she'd had all day—Angela lit into Bobby like a string of firecrackers.

"What do you think you're doing, Bobby?" She did a two-handed hair wrench, sliding the fingers of both hands into her hair and hooking it behind both ears. "Dammit to hell. You almost got us fired before we even started. It's none of our business whether the woman gets any exercise or not. We're just here to see that nobody hurts her."

He shrugged. "Lemme have your cell phone, will you, Ange? I need to check in with Doug."

"Use your own," she snarled, thumping shut the thick binder that Mrs. Riordan had left on the table.

"Fine." He walked toward the small room adjacent to the kitchen and began gathering up the luggage they'd stashed by the back door. His. And hers. He got a good grip on the handle just in case Angela tried to wrestle the bag away from him. "Let's go take a look at our room."

She brushed past him without even a glance at her suitcase. Following her, Bobby enjoyed the angry twitch of her backside even as he made a mental note of the broken pane in the back door and reminded himself to keep his eye on the ball rather than his wife's incredible behind.

Angela opened another door, stepped inside, and immediately moaned, "Oh, my God."

It didn't take a brain surgeon or a Philadelphia lawyer to figure out why. The room was big enough, but the bed—the only bed—wasn't much bigger than a postage stamp. Well, now. Well, well, well.

"Where are *you* going to sleep?" she asked tartly, poking her head into what was probably a bathroom.

"Where do you think?" He dropped the luggage on the floor, then knelt to hunt for his cell phone.

By the time he'd found it and located the number of the surveillance trailer, Angela had completed her inspection of the facilities.

"I'm not *sleeping* with you," she said, glaring at the bed. Bobby wasn't exactly a mattress maven, but this one seemed about half the width of their queen-size bed in Washington. There was barely room for the two pillows that were tucked beneath the flowery bedspread.

"I'm not *sleeping* with you, Bobby." She lifted her hands and wiggled her fingers in quotation marks to make sure he got it. She wasn't quote sleeping with him unquote. "Bobby? Did you hear me?"

He pressed his finger to his lips as Doug picked up the call in the trailer. "We're in," Bobby said.

Special Agent in Charge Doug Coulter let go of a resounding "Yee-ha" before he asked, "Any problems?"

"Nothing serious." Bobby had to fight a grin. "Agent Holland, female, would like to register a complaint about the bed, sir."

"What's wrong with it?" Doug asked at the same moment Angela growled, "Give me that phone."

He deflected her grabby hands. "Uh. It's small, sir."

"Well, you tell Agent Holland, female, to sleep on the friggin' floor, then. Have you had a chance to map the interior yet?"

"Negative," he said into the phone, then to Angela whispered, "Doug says you can sleep with him if you want."

"Give me that," she snapped.

"Bobby," Doug said, "I don't want to hear another word about any goddamned bed, you hear me? Now go make me that map." He hung up.

Bobby closed the phone. "He hung up."

"Well, I'll just damn well call him back."

She grabbed for the phone again, but Bobby held it well out of her reach, then, with his free hand, caught her wrist and, with one quick flip of his own wrist, brought her down onto the mattress. She landed on her back with a pronounced *oof*. He tossed away the phone as he twisted up and over, straddling her even as she was trying to buck him off.

His body reacted instantly to the contact, even though it was closer to a rodeo than foreplay. "Don't stop, baby," he teased her. "That feels great."

Naturally, she lay still as a corpse then, glowering up at him. "Get. Off. Me."

Bobby's heart flickered, and an odd feeling of warmth surged in his chest. It was all he could do not to say, "I love you," over and over again. The words churned up inside him, threatening to boil over, about to explode, before he regained a measure of control. Necessary control. The crucial lid on his emotions.

"Is this the part where I tell you you're beautiful when you're mad?" he asked.

"No." She bucked again. "Dammit. This is the part where you let me go and then I ram my knee between your legs. Now get off."

He didn't doubt for a second that she meant it, or that she might just be able to do it if she caught him off guard. "Angela," he said softly. It wasn't to mollify her. His emotions bubbled up again. He just wanted to touch her somehow, even if it was only with his voice. He ached for her, ached for her to want him half as much as he wanted her. But because he had a job to do, he forced those feelings down, tamped them into temporary oblivion.

Still clamping her wrists with his hands, Bobby pinned her with his gaze. "Listen to me, Ange. This is serious. We *are* liable to blow this if we can't come to some kind of truce. Doug's already pretty disgusted."

She blinked. "I know. I'll try not to take everything so personally."

"Me, too. Hey, I'll even sleep on the floor, if you want. Or pitch a tent outside. Whatever."

She nodded. "Okay. We'll see."

Bobby couldn't quite let the moment go. Or her. "It would be nice, just being next to you in bed."

"We'll see," she repeated.

"All right." He started to ease his grip on her, then stopped. "When I let you go, you're not going to wait till I'm not looking and then give me a shot, are you?"

"No."

"You sure?"

"I'm sure." Her scowl smoothed out, and she almost laughed. "I'm going to wait until this is all over, and then I'm going to put a bullet right between your eyes."

"That's fair," he said. "God knows I'll probably even deserve it by then."

He shifted his weight, and Angela immediately scrambled out from beneath him. True to her word, she didn't retaliate, but started unpacking instead. Bobby picked up his garment bag and opened the closet door, only to be greeted by a rackful of clothes and a floor covered with shoes, men's and women's.

He shook his head. "Who worked here before?" He pushed back enough clothes to make room for his bag.

"A Japanese couple, I think," Angela said. "They're taking an unexpected holiday at government expense."

"A well-deserved one, I'm sure," he said without a trace of irony as he stashed his briefcase behind the dresser.

"Mrs. Riordan's a tough cookie, isn't she?" Angela paused on her way across the room, her arms full of pastel silky things. "I liked her, though, didn't you?"

"Yeah. She's okay." The woman was going to be a handful, just as he'd expected. Between Crazy Daisy and Angela, he was going to need a vacation when this was all over. He sat down on the bed, leaning slightly to his left to peer into his wife's open suitcase, not looking for anything exactly, just looking. He wondered if she was still on the pill.

"I'll probably be just as finicky when I'm seventy-six," Angela said.

"You're already that finicky."

"I am not." She whirled around, her eyes flashing and soft, lovely silks dripping from her arms.

"Fine." Bobby stood up, resisting the temptation to pull her back down on the little bed. "You're not finicky. That must've been one of my other wives. I get confused."

"I'm sure." She turned, opened one drawer after another until she found one to her liking, then laid the gowns and undergarments in with exquisite care, all the while muttering that she was no more finicky than the next person. He could have stood there all day just watching her. Yeah, well . . . He had work to do.

"I'm going to case the joint, sweetheart," he said. "Catch up with me, okay?"

"All right. I'll be done with this in a minute."

Casting one last glance at the bed, Bobby walked out, pretty sure it would be closer to half an hour before he saw her again.

Angela was passing through the kitchen on her way to join Bobby when it suddenly occurred to her that she was going to have to come up with dinner for three in a couple of hours. It was nearly two o'clock now, and Mrs. Riordan wanted her tray at six. This wasn't quite what she'd had in mind when she joined the Secret Service.

Actually, she'd wanted to be a CPA. Working with numbers in neat columns suited her. Even as a kid, she far preferred sitting in a quiet corner doing crossword puzzles to roughhousing with her exuberant siblings. But with a cop for a father, three brothers on the force, and a sister with the FBI, she felt a certain obligation to uphold the family tradition. In truth, after she got her degree in business, she'd hoped to fail the Secret Service exam when she took it, but she'd passed with flying colors. After that, to her amazement, she'd been outstanding in the physical training, so instead of being assigned to a quiet little desk somewhere, she'd found herself moving up the ranks with the agents on protective detail.

She had no regrets, though. She was very good at her

job, and she enjoyed the feeling of competence that came after a decade of experience.

Of course, those ten years had culminated in her present assignment as a short-order cook. Angela sighed mightily, opening the refrigerator to check the contents, hoping she could cobble together something in the way of a decent meal.

Eggs. Milk. Orange juice. A tub of light margarine. Mustard and ketchup. The ubiquitous Tabasco. All the usual suspects. Below, the bins were well stocked with standard veggies, broccoli, carrots, and cauliflower—not the exotic flora she always discovered in Rod's refrigerator, fennel and bok choy and Swiss chard. There were a couple of pork chops in the meat keeper. All right. Things were looking up. Then a quick tour of cupboards and cabinets disclosed potatoes, onions, garlic, and a cautious variety of pastas. Piece of cake.

She sat down at the table to consult the blue binder. There was a section entitled Foods to Avoid. No pork chops there, and it seemed the only vegetable Daisy Riordan didn't like was brussels sprouts. Bobby, on the other hand, looked at all vegetables as if they were radioactive and posed him some sort of lethal threat. She'd had a devil of a time getting him to eat right when they were together. A smile tugged at the corners of her mouth. If this whole thing turned into the disaster she was expecting, at least Bobby would be getting proper nutrition for a couple of weeks.

Earlier, while he was accosting her in the bedroom, she'd had a chance to look at him more closely. He probably had dropped some weight. Up close, his face seemed slightly drawn, especially around the mouth, and the creases at the corners of his eyes were definitely more pronounced. She hadn't seen him since the day she'd left D.C., even though he'd been in L.A. twice on presidential visits. Angela had made sure she'd been nowhere to be found during those two visits because she was afraid he'd try to convince her to come back to D.C., back to him.

To try again. To wear her heart down to a nub trying, when he had no intention of trying, himself. He had stunned her this morning, really thrown her for a loop, when he'd said, "Do you want to talk about Billy?" Even that was a huge improvement from his standard refusal to discuss his brother's death. Instead of falling apart the way she had, Angela wished that she had pressed him on the subject.

"Sure. Let's talk about Billy," she should have said, daring him to expose even a micron of his feelings. "You go first."

Ha! Bobby's idea of a talk would have been a brief, tight-lipped acknowledgment, two sentences max, that, yes, his brother was dead, and yes, it hurt like hell, but now let's just get on with life, Ange, okay?

No. It wasn't okay. Not anymore.

Maybe at first, when Bobby's emotional reticence had stood in such stark, strong contrast to her opera-buffoonish clan. Maybe at first, when it seemed so wonderful to be able to depend on Bobby's silent strength to pick her up whenever she fell apart. Maybe, too, when Billy was alive and could "interpret" Bobby's moods for her. Certainly not later, though, after Billy died, and Angela learned the hard truth about rocks. They were impenetrable, immutable, and cold.

Even as she was thinking that, Bobby sauntered into the kitchen, giving a believable impression of a warm human being. "Want to take a look at this map, Ange, and see if you can read it?" He slid a small page of lined notebook paper onto the table in front of her.

The sight of his familiar scrawl made her throat close for a second. He'd written her a love note once—just once—and tucked it in her cosmetic case, where she'd be certain to find it on the road with the First Lady. Where had she been? San Francisco? San Diego? Wherever, it had taken her about an hour to read the little note, what with his terrible penmanship and her eyes flooded with tears.

His map wasn't so bad, she decided, even if his *o*'s and *e*'s were difficult to distinguish and he rarely, if ever, crossed his *t*'s. "It's a big house," she said. "What's this?" She pointed to a square on the second-story diagram. "The scrun perch?"

He growled deep in his throat. "Screen porch. It's over the den on the east side, probably with access to Mrs. Riordan's bedroom. We'll need to take a look at the lock in there as soon as possible."

"If she ever leaves her room," Angela said with a sigh. "How long has her husband been dead?"

"A couple years. Let's see. The president came out here for Senator Riordan's funeral in 'ninety-nine, I think. I remember I stayed in Chicago, doing the advance work for his speech there."

"She must be lonely."

"Yeah," he said. "It's tough being left alone."

Her gaze flashed to his face, where she expected to see cold accusation in every feature. *How dare you walk out on me?* But his expression was neutral for the most part, perhaps slightly hopeful. You left me first, she was tempted to say. You left me emotionally. You froze me out. I lost Billy, too, and you wouldn't say a word to comfort me. Not a single word.

But Angela held her tongue. It wouldn't have done any good. She slid the little diagram across the table. "You better give this to Doug before he chews his way through a case of antacids."

"I guess you're right."

He picked up the map and left her sitting there alone. A rock couldn't even begin to know the meaning of the word.

❧

Daisy Riordan—Margaret, as she habitually thought of herself—parted the venetian blinds with her fingers and watched her new employee, Robert, pick his way through her neglected dahlia bed at the far side of the backyard, then slip into the brush on his way to the surveillance trailer. He was going to get cockleburs on his black wool socks and in the cuffs of his gray gabardine trousers. It would serve him right, the young fool.

She made a small *tsk* sound, ran a finger across one slat to check for dust, then closed the blinds and went back to the high four-poster bed she'd shared with her husband during their fifty-three years of marriage. The mattress creaked comfortingly as she climbed in, drew an afghan over her legs, then settled her head on the pillow and closed her eyes.

Idiots. All of them. Her son included. Especially

William, since he knew her. How could they think for one minute that she'd believe their silly masquerade? Why did people assume, because she was seventy-six years old, that she wasn't as intelligent as she'd been at twenty-six or even at sixteen, for that matter? At sixteen, she'd fallen madly and wisely in love with Charles William Riordan, future senator from the state of Illinois, future father of the president of the United States. She hadn't been a stupid girl, and she wasn't stupid now.

Rolling her head to the right, she looked at Charles's photograph, smiling back at her from its silver frame. "You never thought I was stupid," she muttered.

Charles had never considered her difficult, either, the way most people did. Or even if he had, he stood up to her while relishing her opinions and her sense of independence. She missed that. Oh, how she missed it. There was only Muriel now to take a stand, to talk back to her, to give her a good fight. Otherwise all she ever heard was "Oh, yes, Mrs. Riordan" or "Whatever you say, Mrs. Riordan" or "Yes, ma'am."

She worried about her old friend and nemesis, who'd undergone chemotherapy this spring and whose hair was only now beginning to grow back. And with a vengeance, it seemed. Muriel—she had refused to call her Bootsie half a century ago when her friend was young and somewhat attractive, and she certainly wasn't going to do it now that the woman was a withered old hag.

Daisy considered herself one, as well. She rarely looked in mirrors these days because she was appalled by the face that looked back at her. Her mouth seemed to pull down at the corners more than ever before, making her appear bitter, almost terminally disgusted. Her color always seemed off, and there was no shine in her eyes. They were lackluster and pale as a winter sky.

Closing them again, she listened to the tick of the clock on the nightstand. A lawn mower droned somewhere in the distance. A blue jay screeched in the sycamore just outside her window.

"Not much exercise," indeed! That comment had merely cemented her belief that Robert Holland was a Secret Service agent; only a man wearing a gun would have had the audacity to say something like that to Daisy Riordan. Neither one of the Itos would have dared speak with such insolence. Of course, that's why she couldn't stand the couple. They never talked back. The more she berated them, looking for a good fight, the more they smiled and bowed and scraped. They dulled her wits, those agreeable people. She was glad to see them go.

Daisy thought she might actually enjoy having the Hollands in her house awhile. She had no intention of exposing them for the agents they truly were. Not right away, at least. Let William think he'd pulled the wool over her pale, ancient eyes. It might do him good.

She sighed. It was silly, having all these people on the premises to protect her when she didn't give a hoot whether she lived or died. With Charles gone, life really wasn't all that interesting anymore.

5

When the First Lady was out of town, William Riordan usually ate his dinner at his desk in the Oval Office. If he dined alone in their private quarters, it was always too tempting to turn on the television to listen to what the so-called pundits were saying about him these days, thus guaranteeing not only indigestion but insomnia as well. Unfortunately for him, he hadn't inherited his mother's thick hide.

With a glance toward his paunch, he thought he hadn't inherited her trim figure either. This evening, while he ate one of the low-fat, low-cholesterol, low-taste meals his wife insisted they serve him, and while he attempted to read the first draft of a speech he was due to make next week at the UN, his mind kept drifting west to Hassenfeld.

Now that he was halfway through his second term, he found himself thinking more and more about the eventual destination of his personal papers. The obvious choice was his birthplace, Hassenfeld. Ye gods. He'd heard that name today every hour on the hour. What a backwater. Jimmy Carter, in all his modesty, had established his presidential library in lowly Plains, but William Riordan wondered if perhaps he couldn't work something out with his alma mater, the University of Chicago, instead. He'd much prefer his legacy to be enshrined on the shores of Lake Michigan than at the edge of a field of test corn.

Why his mother insisted on staying in Hassenfeld was a mystery to him. She had never really seemed to like the place. She had never really seemed to like anything or anyone, for that matter, including him, her only child.

Over the years, he'd come to the conclusion that they were simply on different wavelengths, if not different planets. Perhaps if he spent more time with her, they could reach some sort of amiable adult relationship, but the problem was that in his mother's presence, at the mere sound of her voice, his behavior immediately regressed to that of an incompetent and petulant ten-year-old.

"Your mother didn't mean it, William." Now there was a sentence they should have needlepointed on a pillow, as many times as it was spoken.

"I know, but why did she *say* it, Dad?"

He picked at the measly salmon fillet before him, then pushed his plate away. Maybe later he'd call down to the kitchen and see if they couldn't put together a hot fudge sundae with real ice cream and honest-to-God whipped cream. If he was feeling like a foolish and furtive child, then he might just as well go all the way.

What a relief it would be when this whole Secret Service operation was over and he didn't have to hear his mother's name or a reference to Hassenfeld every time he picked up the phone. Henry Materro, almost giddy at the prospect of violence upon a matriarch, had kept the Oval Office updated hourly on the situation in Illinois. Apparently Bobby Holland and his wife had entered the sanctum sanctorum without so much as a scratch. It was a comfort, all things considered, to know his mother was in such capable hands, even though he didn't give much credence to this threat business.

People had been threatening Crazy Daisy for years. The old bat positively thrived on it.

∽

"How are the pork chops?" Angela asked Bobby, who sat across from her at the kitchen table. "Not too dry?"

"They're perfect," he said. "What did you put on the carrots?"

Angela almost choked on the one she was in the process of swallowing. What did she put on the carrots? Bobby never showed the least bit of curiosity about food. It was either edible or not. Usually carrots weren't. He'd scatter them around his plate like a weasely six-year-old, or hide them under a baked potato skin if one was available. Who did he think he was all of a sudden, the Galloping Gourmet?

"Butter, some lemon juice, and a little rosemary," she said. "Plus a teaspoon of lemon zest." Rod had shown her that nifty little trick.

Bobby nodded and forked up another orange disk. "They're great."

"Thank you." I think. What was he trying to do, wear her down with kindness? Compliment her until she yelled, "Okay. Uncle. You win. I'll go to bed with you"?

"What's lemon zest?" he asked.

That did it. "God, Bobby. What do you care?" She

dropped her fork on the plate, then snatched it up, along with her water goblet, and carried them all to the sink. The pork chops *were* dry, dammit. Like shoe leather. She suspected Daisy Riordan would soon let her know it, too, in no uncertain terms.

Angela scraped the remains of her dinner into the trash can, aware that her behavior seemed temperamental and pure PMSy. If Bobby even looked as if he were going to mouth those three initials, she was going to shoot him dead right now, then happily spend the next twenty years in prison, hopefully in California, where Rod would visit her once in a while.

"I'll clean up," Bobby said, suddenly standing behind her.

She drew in a long, deep breath. He was good. Ooh, he was good. He was going to reel her in with a few acts of domestic kindness, a few well-placed tidbits of conversation, and then—Bam!—he'd clam up again, just like always.

"Fine," she said coolly, setting her scraped plate in the sink and edging away from the radiant heat of his body. "I'll go up and get Mrs. Riordan's tray. Maybe I'll have a chance to scope out that screen porch door."

Angela hastened out of the kitchen and up the stairs. It was seven o'clock, still light outside on the western portion of the house, but darkening in the east wing, where Mrs. Riordan's bedroom was located. It was such a lovely house, so comfortable and restrained and quiet. It came close to matching Angela's mental picture of her dream house. If there was an air of clutter here, it was clutter of the nicest sort—framed photographs, fine porcelain pieces, Senate memorabilia, leather-bound books with gilt edges and tasseled bookmarks.

It was nothing like the clutter in the house where she grew up. There, sweatshirts and jackets dangled from every doorknob, piles of magazines were always spilling across floors, golf balls and pretzels and headless Barbie dolls gathered on end tables. On every staircase, clothes baskets and in-line skates and other lethal toys waited to trip the unsuspecting.

In the Riordan house, the upholstery in every room picked up on a theme of muted beiges and soft blues. In the Callifano house, couches and armchairs always wore out on an irregular schedule, so the replacements never matched as stripes battled with florals and an endless variety of plaids. Here an air of elegant quiet pervaded each and every room. Back home, if it was quiet, it meant that somebody was up to something. This was a museum. The Callifano house was a circus.

Maybe she was a changeling, Angela thought. That was the only way she could explain it. The chaos and clamor never bothered anybody else. Her parents were oblivious to the havoc, and her siblings, all eight of them, seemed to thrive on it while Angela couldn't wait to escape.

It was still the same. Maybe even worse, because, with one glaring exception, the children who moved out were soon bringing back children of their own. At last count, Rose and Angelo Callifano had twenty-seven grandkids. It went without saying that they never missed an opportunity to remind her about number twenty-eight.

As she passed down the hallway, she switched on a small porcelain lamp that sat on an antique mahogany cabinet. A few steps more, and she knocked on the bedroom door. "Mrs. Riordan?"

"Come in."

The bedroom was already dim, lit only by the light of a television. Angela glanced at the door she assumed opened from the screen porch, and noted the small brass bolt in the locked position. That would have to do for now, she supposed. With Mrs. Riordan always in here, it would be tough getting in to exchange the bolt for something more secure.

"I've come for your tray, if you're through," she said, surreptitiously eyeing the leftovers. Oh, brother. The president's mother had taken one bite of her pork chop, chewed it a while, half an hour probably, and returned it to her plate.

"Your carrots were delicious," Daisy Riordan said graciously, then added, "Just for future reference, I prefer them julienned."

"Yes, ma'am." Angela hooked some hair back before reaching for the tray. "I'm sorry about the pork chop. I'll do better next time."

Mrs. Riordan gave a small, dismissive wave of her hand. "Speaking of next time," she said, "I've decided to take my evening meal downstairs in the dining room from now on, Angela. Will you set my place at the foot of the table? That would be at the end nearest the kitchen door."

"Yes. Of course."

Angela managed to keep from looking surprised by the woman's request until she was back out in the hallway with the tray, then she shook her head in amazement. The president's mother had sounded so casual, so matter-of-fact, as if dining downstairs had been her own idea, conjured out of nowhere, completely unrelated to Bobby's comment about her lack of exercise. My God. With that one little murmured observation, he had apparently succeeded in blasting Crazy Daisy out of her stubborn sanctuary.

He *was* good. He was positively scary. She reminded herself that this was the same man who had used a lost cat to sweep her off her feet in about ten minutes and who had her saying Yes, she'd marry him, after only knowing him for a little more than forty-eight hours. She was *really* going to have to keep her guard up while they were here.

∾

Bobby sat on the wooden bench that circled the inside of the gazebo, watching the pink and orange tints in the western sky. Sunsets depressed the hell out of him because they reminded him of his mother. How she'd loved her sunsets. Wherever they lived, whether it was a dilapidated shack, a rusted-out trailer park, or some smelly spare room in a relative's house, Treena Holland had to have her sunsets. While she pondered the colors of the sinking sun, she'd sing softly to herself or brush her hair with long, languorous strokes or just quietly rock, if she was lucky enough to be someplace with a rocking chair.

Then, when the sun disappeared and the colors bled out into darkness, Treena switched from beer to the hard stuff. Sooner or later she'd say, "You see Billy gets to bed all right, Bobby, will you? I'll be back in a while." He was probably seven or eight years old before he realized the expression "in a while" wasn't a synonym for "at dawn."

He heard the door of the mud room open and watched Angela's gaze swing across the backyard before it zeroed in on him. She stood there a moment, as if trying to decide whether or not to join him, before she started toward him. Well, hell. He'd spent half the day trying to convince her to listen to him, but now his mood had taken a sunset turn, and talking was the last thing he wanted to do.

Angela had a walk like no other woman he knew. A heads-up, eye-on-the-target, purposeful stride that was accompanied by the most subtle, unaffected, fetching sway of her backside. A train coming straight down the track with a waggling caboose. He loved watching her. God, he loved watching her.

"There you are," she said, stepping into the gazebo, giving it an appreciative glance. "This is lovely, isn't it?"

"Pull up a piece of bench," Bobby said. "I was just watching the sunset."

"You hate sunsets," she said, lowering herself onto the bench several safe feet away from him.

"I hate Texas sunsets," he said. "This is Illinois, where they're kinder and gentler and not half as pretty."

She sighed and stared west. Her hair took on some of the sky's burnished gold. She'd let it grow during their separation. Maybe that was a California thing. Maybe she just hadn't found a good hairdresser. Whatever the reason, his fingers fairly itched to bury themselves in all that rich warmth. He wished she wore it piled high on top of her head so he could pull the pins out, one by one by one.

"Congratulations, by the way," she said.

"For what?"

"Mrs. Riordan just announced her intention to come downstairs for dinner every evening. You should have gone into sales, Bobby, instead of law enforcement."

He wanted to say he wasn't doing such a bang-up job of selling his new and improved self to his estranged wife, but he didn't want her to leave in a huff. Anyway, he probably wasn't as new and improved as he'd imagined. "Good for her," he said instead. "Did you get a look at that door to the porch?"

"It's bolted." She was quiet a moment before stretching her arms out in front of her. "Well, it's been a long day. I thought I might just take a nice warm bath and then turn in."

"Sure. Go ahead."

"I guess we're kind of doing twenty-four/seven while we're here," she said a bit guiltily, "but jeez, we've got to sleep."

"Don't worry about it. They've got at least two men in the trailer on every shift. They'll let us know if somebody shows up on one of the surveillance cameras."

"Yeah. I guess so." Her forehead crimped in a frown. "What about this threat, Bobby? All they told me in California was that a letter had come to the White House. How serious is this?"

He shrugged. "I don't know much more than you do, Ange. Apparently the letter was legit, but just between you and me, it sounds like Materro finally found a good way to suck up to Honcho," he said, using the president's code name. Just about everybody in the agency was aware that, after being appointed director of the Secret Service six months ago, Henry Materro had yet to earn any kudos from the White House. "But that's just my opinion. And they're—"

"—not paying you for your opinions," she finished with a little laugh.

"I guess I've said that before, huh?"

"Once or twice." She stood up. "Well, see you."

"See you."

Angela didn't turn to leave immediately. Something hung in the air between them. A cool mist. A vibrating current. A push-pull magnetic force that said, Get up and kiss her, you fool, while at the same time it cautioned, You're a dead man if you do.

Take her, it said.

No. Let her come to you.

Bobby shifted his gaze to the western tree line, where the colors were beginning to fade. "Night, Ange."

Call her back. The voice in his head was half Billy's, half his own. *Jesus. Call her back.*

And then what? Huh? What if he said everything and said it right, what if he opened his fucking veins, and she just turned and walked away again? What then?

~

It had taken Angela years to learn how to completely relax in a warm tub, to convince herself that the moment she tipped back her head and slid down until she was up to her chin in fragrant bubbles, the second she sighed and closed her eyes, somebody wouldn't pound on the door, wanting in.

She didn't truly relax this evening, either, half expecting an alarm to go off somewhere in the house. In all honesty, it surprised her a little that Bobby hadn't wandered into their room while she was in the tub, that he hadn't rapped softly on the door and made some sort of suggestive comment.

His failure to do that may have surprised her, but it certainly didn't disappoint her. She'd told him to back off, hadn't she? To lay off the sexual innuendoes and the meaningfully waggling eyebrows. She was glad he'd taken her warning seriously.

While she dragged her brush through her hair, she pondered the bodice of her navy silk gown, the one she'd just put on with all the modesty of a preteen behind a locked bathroom door. Right now she almost wished she were the pajama or sleep-shirt type, feeling resentful that she even had to be concerned with what she wore to bed. That was one of the lovely advantages of marriage. It never mattered what she wore because she never wore it long and always wound up sleeping comfortably and quite happily nude.

The hairbrush stalled in midair. Oh, God. Bobby didn't even own a pair of pajamas. He slept naked as a carved-chested, washboard-abbed, hard-legged jaybird. Her mouth went dry at the thought, and her face in the steamed mirror seemed to color considerably. It had been eleven months, two weeks, and four days since they'd made love. Since she had, anyway. God only knew about Bobby. Women had practically wept from coast to coast when he got married. They had no doubt formed a line at her husband's door five minutes after Angela slammed it on her way out.

But she *had* slammed it, and he hadn't done a thing to open it back up, not to her anyway, and she wasn't going to make love tonight or tomorrow night or any night they were here. Why in the name of God was she even thinking about it?

This was work. This was business. She was here to ensure that no harm came to the president's mother. It didn't matter that the threat might be bogus or insignificant, nor did it matter that her boss, Henry Materro, might have jumped the gun in an effort to ingratiate himself with the president. It was still her job.

She slapped the brush down onto the vanity, yanked up the neckline of her silk gown, and unlocked the door. Bobby was stretched out on the bed—fully clothed, thank God—his arms linked behind his head. The only light in the room came from the tiny television on the dresser.

He glanced at her briefly, not even a hint of salaciousness in his expression, then returned his gaze to the small screen. "We're locked down for the night. I'm really beat, Ange. Let's not hassle about the bed, okay?"

"Okay," she said, reacting to his obvious weariness. Suddenly the prospect of actually lying down beside his long, solid body made her stomach quiver and her heart give an extra little tick. Those weren't good signs at all for someone determined to avoid conjugal bliss. "I'm not all that tired, actually. Plus, I've got a few calls to make. I'll just take my phone in the kitchen for a while."

He stifled a yawn, his eyes still directed at the TV. "Sure. Don't worry about waking me up. You know it only takes me a second to get back to sleep."

She knew. His years at West Point and in army intelligence all over the world had trained him to catch sleep where he could, as well as to wake and be up to speed more quickly than the average person could open his sleep-besotted eyes. There had been more than a few occasions during their marriage when he'd had to put a mug of hot coffee in her hand while she blinked and sputtered and groped for semiconsciousness.

Angela pulled her navy robe from a hanger in the closet. Then, cell phone in hand, she wandered into the kitchen. After pouring herself a glass of milk, she sat down at the table. It was her intention to call Rod, but she found herself punching in her parents' number instead, knowing she'd regret it even as she placed the call.

"Callifano." Her father's deep voice resonated across hundreds of miles. She could almost see him, his short-sleeved sport shirt smartly tucked in the waistband of a pair of perfectly pressed chinos, his dark eyes about to mist over just at the sound of her voice.

"Hi, Pop. It's Angela."

"Baby!" His hand covered the mouthpiece, but not well enough to prevent her from hearing him call, "Rose! It's Angela. No. No. On the phone."

It was impossible to call home and have less than a three-way conversation. Usually it was four- or five-way, depending on who was there. Her mother would be bustling toward the kitchen now from wherever she had been, clad in her soft-soled slippers and flowered, snap-down-the-front housecoat.

"How's my little G-man?" Pop asked, a smile evident in his voice as he waited for her habitual response, her playful correction.

"G-woman, Pop. I'm fine. How's your retirement going?"

Six months ago Sergeant Angelo Callifano had taken off his blue uniform, his badge, and his heavy utility belt for the last time. "He cried like a baby," her mother had said, "but he'll be fine."

"Your mother's running me ragged. This is harder than walking a beat. Wait a minute, honey."

Angela heard the muffled sound of the receiver being wedged under his chin and the ensuing conversation with one of her nieces or nephews. "No, you can't wear your slicker and rain boots to bed. I don't know why. Because Mamo said so, and she's the boss."

She wondered whose kids he was talking to. Probably Joey's. He and Beth only lived a block away. Ah, God. For a minute she was swamped by all her old hopes and dreams about the babies she and Bobby would have one day. Their children and grandchildren. How they'd grow old together. And Uncle Billy, too.

"Where are you, honey?" her father asked her, repositioning the phone. "Still in California?"

"I'm in Illinois at the moment, working protective detail with the president's mother."

"Ah," he said to her, and then called out, "She's in Illinois, Rose, watching out for Riordan's mother. What's her name? Crazy something? Daisy?"

"That's it," Rose Callifano called from across the kitchen. "We saw her on *Larry King* a few years ago. You remember."

"So." He was back. "Is it good duty?"

"It's okay," Angela replied, shaking her head at the perpetual circus on the other end of the line whenever she called home. Even though it made her crazy, a part of her just then longed to be surrounded by all that rambunctious, no-holds-barred affection.

"Good. Good." Her father cleared his throat, a portent of what was coming. "So, how's Bobby?"

"He's fine." *He's the same. Granite in the shape of a man.*

"Still in Washington?"

Ah, God. She never could lie to her pop. "Well, no. Actually, he's here in Illinois. With me."

His big hand muffled the phone again. "Bobby's in Illinois, too, Rose. I dunno. She didn't say." Then, to Angela, he said, "Hold on. Your mother wants to talk to you."

No. No way. That would be comparable to being put in a small cinderblock sweat box with a klieg light shining in her eyes. Her mother would want to know how long they'd been back together, was Angela still on the pill, what did the Secret Service offer in the way of maternity leave, and was she taking her vitamins every day because those were so important. "I can't, Pop. I've got to get back on duty. I just called to say I love you. Give Mom a hug for me, okay? Bye."

Angela broke the connection. They'd be staring at each other in their kitchen now, Rose and Angelo, both shaking their heads. Disappointed. Dismayed. Clutching at straws. "He's there with her," her father would say. "That's a good sign," her mother would reply. "Maybe, Rose. I dunno."

It wasn't a good sign. It wasn't even her choice. It was an accident, dammit, and Angela felt like a victim. Suddenly Bobby was sleeping in her bed, not only against her wishes but against her better judgment. Taking up space like a big, hard rock. Like a meteor that had crash-landed in her life.

She dragged in a breath and punched in Rod's number now, wishing she had called him first. "Hi, it's me," she said when his answering machine picked up. He never answered his phone and kept having to change his unlisted number, sometimes once a month, thanks to the crafty investigative work of a few of his die-hard female fans. It never failed to amaze Angela that, with his pick of a sizable portion of the female population, Rod Bishop had chosen her. Why? she continually wondered.

Of course, they had a lot in common. His father was a retired cop, just like hers, and he had a boatload of brothers and sisters, as well. Before he became the proverbial overnight success at the age of thirty-eight, he'd worked hard, supporting his acting ambitions with carpentry, truck driving, even a fair amount of ditch digging. If Angela had met him before she'd met Bobby, maybe . . .

"Hi, sweetheart." Rod's warm baritone made her smile. "I'm going to put you on the speaker phone, if you don't mind. I'm trying to tie my bow tie and not having a lot of success. How's Illinois?"

"Oh, fine." Her voice echoed as if she were calling from a cavern. Funny. That was how she felt. "You've got a party tonight, I guess."

He sighed roughly. "I have to play nice for some studio executives and their wives."

He always complained about the social demands of his business, but Angela was convinced he secretly loved the glitter and the designer clothes, the limos and caviar and champagne. She, on the other hand, detested all that and hardly made a secret of it.

Rod sighed once more. "If you see anything about this in the supermarket checkout line, please know, love, that it's not my idea to have Caitlin Corday draped on my arm all evening."

Angela laughed. The busty little redhead had worked with Rod on his last picture. Apparently no one had ever told Caitlin that she didn't have to sleep her way to the top in business these days, because she certainly made a concerted effort to try. "I'll look forward to reading about it," she said. "How's the tie coming along?"

"Almost there. How's the president's mother?"

"Safe and sound," she said, hoping he wouldn't ask for any more details about her assignment.

But he did. "How's that Neanderthal you're still married to?"

Angela winced. She wished she'd never cried on Rod's all-too-willing shoulder. How Bobby was and how they were together was no one's business but their own. And nobody got to call him a Neanderthal but her!

"Everything's fine," she said.

"Oh, before I forget, Angela, I've got some names and numbers of attorneys for you."

"Attorneys?"

"Why wait until you get back here to get the ball rolling, love? Do you have a pen or pencil?"

Mrs. Riordan's blue binder, with a ballpoint pen clipped to its cover, was right by her elbow. She removed the pen and turned to a blank page in the back. "Okay. I'm ready," she said.

"You don't sound very enthusiastic."

She wasn't. Saying she was going to call a lawyer and actually writing down names and numbers were two entirely different things. "I'm just tired," she lied.

Rod gave her three names. "That last guy is expensive,

they tell me, but he gets the job done with the precision of a surgeon."

Just what she needed, Angela thought, as she scribbled. Somebody with a scalpel to cut Bobby out of her heart.

"Well, the tie is tied, the cuffs are linked, and I have to run, sweetheart. Will you call me tomorrow? I leave for Mexico the day after that, and I probably won't be easy to reach. I wish you'd fly back and come with me."

"Have a good time," Angela told him, a bit surprised that she actually meant it. She shouldn't want him to have a good time without her, should she?

"Not without you, love. Promise me you'll call tomorrow."

"I'll call."

"And call one of those lawyers," Rod insisted.

"I will. I will."

"Good." He made a kissing sound. "Wish me luck with the studio crocodiles. Bye, sweetheart."

"Bye."

"Who was that?" Bobby said behind her.

She nearly jumped out of her skin. "I thought you were asleep." Angela put down the phone as if it were scalding her hand, then closed Mrs. Riordan's notebook before Curious George got a look at the list of lawyers.

He sat, gave her cell phone a black look, and asked again, "Who was that?"

"I called Mom and Pop," she said, feeling quite the model of truthfulness, and then a deceitful bitch when she saw Bobby's shoulders relax and the creases in his brow smooth out. He believed her. "They said to tell you hello," she added.

"Just hello?" He lifted an eyebrow. "If I know Angelo, he said something more like 'Tell that son of a bitch he better start treating you right or he'll be wearing my fist for a nose ring.'"

"He wouldn't say that."

"Ha."

"He doesn't blame you, Bobby. Both of them know I'm the one who walked out. If anything, they blame me." She took a swig from her glass of milk, realizing that, for the forty-seventh time that day, she was discussing the subject she swore she wouldn't discuss. "I don't want to talk about this," she said for the forty-eighth time.

Bobby leaned back in his chair, crossing his arms, shaking his head. "You really take the cake, Ange. Jesus."

"What is that supposed to mean?"

"It means you ragged me for a year and a half about talking. Talking about Billy. About me. About us. Here I am"—he uncrossed his arms, gestured with his hands out, palm up—"here I am, ready to talk, just dying to spill my guts, and you don't want to hear word one."

She stiffened her spine and flattened her mouth, then sounded just like her horrible fourth-grade teacher, Mrs. Quill, when she said, "This isn't the time or the place."

"Well, when would the time be? And where's the freaking place?"

Never. Nowhere. She craved a conversation, not a confrontation. She wanted her husband to open his heart as well as his mouth. Bobby still just didn't get it. It wasn't supposed to be like this. "I don't know."

Bobby swore and shot out of his chair as if it had suddenly caught on fire. She'd seen him react quickly before, moving with the agility of a great cat, but always in a situation that demanded some specific action such as deflecting a weapon or deterring someone bent on violence. Now, though, it was as if there was no specific action to dissipate all the energy and anger coursing through him. He looked like he was about to explode.

After stalking to the sink, he turned the water on full force, then shut it off. With his back to her, he stood there for what seemed like an eternity, breathing deeply, his shoulders rising and falling as he stared into the wet sink. When he finally spoke, his voice was thick, but totally composed.

"Is there somebody else?"

Oh, God. The question was like an arrow through her heart, the bullet that she'd been trying to dodge all day. She wanted to scream "No! How could there ever be anybody else?" when he turned toward her with a look on his face that caused her even more pain. There was no anger in his expression. No sadness. No pain. Not even curiosity. Just that heartless cop stare. The dead look that said nothing could surprise him or shock him or make him lose his balance. The look that said he was invulnerable, to everything, even to her.

Her heart felt desiccated, like a chunk of wood in her chest, and her voice sounded parched when she dropped her gaze and whispered, "Yes."

Angela's breath came hard. Her heart ached, and tears stung her eyes. It wasn't supposed to be this way. She hadn't meant to tell him. Not now. Not here. God, maybe not ever. Her sudden confession had surprised her. Shocked the hell out of her, in fact.

But then Bobby did something that didn't surprise her

at all. Without saying a word, he walked past her, out of the kitchen, out the back door, just out, taking all his feelings with him.

If rocks could feel.

She wasn't sure.

But she was sure they couldn't change.

6

There wasn't much of a moon, just a translucent sliver—like a fingernail paring—on the black sky overhead. Bobby was surprised he could even see it, considering the red haze in his vision, while he made his way to the surveillance trailer to let the guys on duty know he was leaving the house for a while. Mike Burris opened the door for him, and Bobby stepped inside, willing himself not to put a fist through something, anything. Somebody else. There was somebody else. Jesus Christ.

"How's it going on the inside?" Mike asked, resuming his seat in front of a small bank of monitors that displayed the Riordan house from half a dozen vantage points. "Want some coffee?"

"No, thanks."

McCray, the older agent Bobby had met at the airport, emerged from the depths of the trailer, picking cashews out of a bag. "How'd that Taurus drive, Holland? Did it give you any problems?"

"No. It was fine," Bobby said. "Good choice."

"Well, we figured the household staff probably shouldn't show up in a reinforced SUV," the older agent said, popping another nut into his mouth, angling his head toward the house. "How's it going up there?"

Great. Fine. My wife's in love with somebody else. "Piece of cake. I just wanted to let you guys know I'm going out for a while. Just gonna take a walk around the neighborhood and get the lay of the land." Bobby edged back toward the door before he could vomit on his shoes, before somebody started to make conversation to break up the monotony of staring at a console full of monitors where the activity was less than the average tropical fish tank.

But before he could exit, Agent Burris swiveled around in his chair. "Hey, you didn't happen to hear the Red Sox score, did you?"

"Sorry."

Bobby nearly ripped the door from its hinges as he stepped outside. He cut diagonally across the backyard, then walked slowly and deliberately down the drive, in the steady eyes of the surveillance cams, looking to his left and right and straight ahead like a man who actually had his mind on business.

Once out on the road that ran past the Riordan place, he started to jog, and then broke into a run. In his street shoes, the repetitive pace on the hard pavement was punishing to his knees, but he was barely aware of it.

Yes. Angela had said yes. There was somebody else. Who? That actor the guy from the L.A. field office couldn't wait to tell him about? Some celluloid scumbag with caps on his teeth and a perpetual tan. A pretty boy with designer hair. What was his name? Oh, yeah. Rod. Rod Bishop with the velvet voice and soulful eyes and soft hands and a heart worn prominently, no doubt, on his silken sleeve. Pussy.

Did the guy appreciate the finely honed strength beneath Ange's soft exterior? Did he have any inkling of her courage and her skill? How could he possibly know what it was like to stand between a target and a gun?

Jesus. Was he fucking her?

Did Angela's eyes melt when Bishop touched her? Did he know that secret spot just behind her ear where she loved to be kissed? And that sweet, erotic hollow at the base of her spine? Did he know how to make her catch her breath with a well-placed, perfectly timed flick of his tongue? Did he take his time when he loved her, discovering as much pleasure in her rising passion as he did his own? Did she cry out his name again and again when he finally pushed her over the edge?

A movie star, for chrissake. A shallow, candy-ass, cardboard cutout pussy.

If that's what she wanted, fine. Fuck her. Fuck them both.

He ran harder. Faster.

After a mile he pulled up, bending over, breathing hard, his hands braced on his knees while a wave of nausea rolled over him. He fought it, just as he fought everything in him that smacked of weakness, of loss of control. He fought as if his life depended on it. Lifting his head, Bobby forced himself to focus on a cluster of lights far down the road while he took in deep, measured breaths of the cool night air and let them out slowly through pursed lips.

Yes. She'd said yes. There was somebody else.

God damn her.

She's the best thing that ever happened to you, bro. All of a sudden Billy's voice sounded as clearly as if he were standing by the side of the road. His image flashed in

Bobby's brain, first as a skinny kid with a milk mustache, then as a nervous, newly shorn plebe, and finally smiling at the wedding as he lifted his champagne glass in a toast, unaware that he only had six months before a bullet would rip the life out of his body.

Bobby swallowed, forcing the bile back down his throat. The lights in the distance wavered and blurred, and for a moment he couldn't breathe at all. He was sick, coming apart at the seams, hearing his dead brother's voice telling him what he already knew. What he'd always known. Angela *was* the best thing that had ever happened to him. The best thing that ever *would* happen to him.

But he wasn't the best thing that had ever happened to her. Or to Billy, either. They were *his* best things. His brother and his wife. But somehow he couldn't keep them. All his strength and intelligence, all his determination and skill, every fiber of his will, they were useless when it came to the people he loved. Billy. Ange. He couldn't keep them.

No more than his mother had been able to keep the sun from sliding past the horizon, taking all the daylight with it.

He cursed his brother one more time for stepping in front of that maniac's gun.

"You think you could do it, Bobby?" Billy used to ask him after he'd had a few too many beers, leaning close, wearing the goofy half grin that exposed the crooked incisors the poor kid never had braces for. "I mean," he'd whisper, "if you saw it coming, that bullet with your protectee's name on it, if you saw it coming almost in slow motion, like in a movie, do you think you could do it?"

Bobby's answer was always the same—a shrug and a curt "Hey, it's the job."

"Yeah, but do you think—?"

"Let it go, Billy, goddammit. We do our fucking job. That's all."

"Yeah," he'd say, leaning back. "Still, you gotta wonder."

No, he didn't. Bobby wasn't one to wonder, to let doubts and questions wreak havoc in his head. Not then. Not now. Not ever.

He straightened up, hauling in another long breath of the crisp early autumn air, looking for the moon and finding it hanging over a cornfield like a pale question mark.

Jesus. What the hell was he supposed to do? Let her go? Quit? Just fucking quit? He didn't know how. He'd never quit anything in his life. And, by God, he wasn't going to start now.

Maybe he never would be able to figure out the right things to say. Maybe he never would be able to expose his feelings the way she seemed to need. Maybe he couldn't keep Angela, but he could sure make it hard—damn near impossible—for her to go.

He felt a little better, back in control, but not yet enough in control to face his wife in a bed the size of a large bath towel, so he headed down the road toward the distant lights.

⁓

Angela tossed and turned, tussled with her pillow, and tangled the quilt and sheets. She got up and opened the window for fresh air, then got up again and closed it five minutes later because the crickets sounded like banshees out in the nearby cornfields. She knew it was five minutes later because she looked at the clock on the nightstand every five minutes, wondering when Bobby would return.

Before getting into bed, she had called the trailer, ostensibly checking in, and Agent McCray told her that Bobby had gone out for a walk to get a feel for the neighborhood. But that had been over two hours ago. It wasn't that big a neighborhood, for chrissake!

She never should have told him about Rod. It was just that he'd looked at her with his damned cop face, and everything in her had rebelled at the sight. His expression had almost dared her to say yes, there was somebody else, even if she wasn't so sure of that herself. That sticks-and-stones look of his always made her want to lash out, to cut him to the quick, to hurt him and those galvanized, invisible feelings of his, to bring tears to his eyes. Tears that, God help her, she could then kiss away.

Angela flopped over on her side, jamming the pillow under her cheek. It wasn't that she was mean or vicious. She wasn't. All she wanted was for her husband to share his heart with her as generously as he shared his body. Was that too much to ask?

According to Billy, yes, it was.

It had been Bobby's quiet stoicism that had attracted her, yet only days after their wedding, she was already bugging her new brother-in-law, pumping him for clues to her husband's emotional reticence, already seeking advice on how to get him to open up. "Good luck," Billy used to say.

"I asked him about your father," she'd said. "He told

me what the man looked like, but that wasn't what I meant. How did you *feel* about him, Bobby? He just looked at me as if he couldn't even comprehend the question." She'd laughed then and added only partly in jest, "I'm almost beginning to think he's a robot, Billy. Every time he cuts himself shaving, I look to make sure he bleeds."

Her brother-in-law faked a look of horror. "He does, right?"

"Be serious, Billy. Your brother just won't open up at all."

She went on to tell him what had happened when their cat, Mr. Whiskers, disappeared. How cool and distant Bobby had seemed even as she was sobbing her heart out. How Bobby had said, "It's just a cat, Ange." How Bobby had then slipped out of their bed that night and hadn't come home till dawn, denying he'd done anything but go out for a little fresh air. How their neighbors had reported seeing him trudging through alleys and shining a flashlight in every dark nook and cranny, while softly calling Mr. Whiskers's name.

"He loved that cat," Angela had wailed to Billy. "He was devastated, but damned if he'd admit it."

"You've just got to cut him a little slack, Ange," he told her. "He's always been like that. Stoic. Self-possessed. It goes way back. Bobby's got feelings. He just can't afford to let them show."

"You show *your* feelings," she'd answered irritably, "and you go just about as far back as Bobby does."

They were barely ten months apart, those two, the sons of Treena Holland and the married-but-not-to-mama chief of police of Wishbone, Texas. Bobby was apparently a dead ringer for their father, suffering the small-town slings and arrows of that resemblance as a consequence. Billy was built on a smaller scale, his features much softer, and his disposition sweeter by far. If Bobby was a rock, hard and immutable granite, then his younger brother was water, warm and yielding. And everywhere Bobby carved out a place for him, Billy just naturally flowed.

Bobby bashed his way into West Point, pulling his brother inevitably along behind him. After that, there was the army and then the Secret Service. First Bobby, then Billy on his heels. It hadn't seemed to matter that Billy was mathematically inclined and a talented painter to boot. Bobby got his brother out of Wishbone, Texas, and then on to the only place he truly knew how to get, to the pinnacle of an agency where Bobby Holland's protective instincts made him the best of the best.

To all appearances, it was the younger Holland who depended on the older one. The funny thing was, when she'd pointed out to Billy that maybe it was Bobby who desperately needed *him*, he'd given her one of those blank, unfathomable looks so like his brother.

Angela opened her eyes now to look at the clock again. Past midnight. Part of her was furious that Bobby had left her here alone, on duty in Daisy Riordan's house. The part that wasn't furious was worried sick that she'd hurt him deeply and he was out there, somewhere, alone. If there was such a thing as angels, she dearly hoped that Billy was watching over his big brother right now the way Bobby had always watched out for him.

As far as she could tell, Bobby had watched out for his younger brother from the start. She used to look forward to the times when Billy would drop by after work and she would prime him with a couple cold beers and then listen to his soft-spoken drawl as he told her stories, the ones in which he always cast his big brother as the hero.

Once, according to Billy, their mother had given six-year-old Bobby a couple dollars and, with Billy in perpetual tow, had sent him off to Sledge's, the neighborhood gas station and convenience store, to pick up a package for her.

"When he was just six years old?" Angela had exclaimed. "That's criminal."

Billy had just laughed at her outrage, and his hazel eyes crinkled deeply at the corners, the way Bobby's would if he'd practiced smiling more. "Well, you've got to understand, Angela, that Bobby was about forty when he was born, so that would have made him forty-six. Anyway, we got to Sledge's, and Bobby handed over the cash in exchange for a paper bag, which, as it turned out, had a six-pack of beer inside.

"I don't think either one of us had had anything more than a couple crackers to eat that day, so Bobby put the bag back up on the counter, then picked a box of corn flakes off a shelf and got a half gallon of milk out of the cooler, then told old man Sledge, 'We'll take these instead.' Man, I can still see the look on that old guy's face."

Angela imagined she could, too. "What happened when you got home?"

"Bobby sneaked me in the kitchen and fixed me a big bowl of cereal, then told me to eat quick while he went to tell our mama what he'd done." Billy shook his head and sighed. "Needless to say, Treena took her belt to him. You know that pearly little scar on his shoulder, kind of looks like a comma?" Angela nodded, and Billy continued, his eyes distinctly moist. "That's a souvenir of that day. She opened him up like a fucking can of tuna."

Of course, when she'd gently touched that scar in their big brass bed that night and asked Bobby how he'd gotten it, he said he couldn't remember.

It was ludicrous for Angela to ever have thought that, because they were so close in age, the Holland brothers had grown up similarly. As Billy himself had put it, "I had Bobby. He . . . well, hell, he didn't have anybody."

Now Angela curled tighter in the little bed, drawing up her knees along with the tangled bed linens, and sinking her head deeper into the pillow, thinking that her husband still didn't have anybody. His father had never acknowledged him. His mother had traded her sons for alcohol decades ago. His brother was dead. His wife had left him, and tonight had pretty much told him she wasn't coming back.

God damn you, Bobby Holland. You made me do it. You made me hurt you just to see if you would cry or bleed. If that's what you're doing now, crying out in the dark someplace, I'll never know it, will I? You'll never let me see. You'll never, not for a second, wear that tough-guy granite heart of yours on your sleeve.

She bit her lip to keep from weeping. Dear God, she needed her husband's arms around her, yearned for his comfort more than anything in the world. She was so afraid, so terribly afraid that, when all was said and done, now that Billy was gone, Bobby had nothing left to give.

Bobby was feeling better, sitting on a barstool at a honky-tonk called the Wayward Wind, the source of the lights on which he'd focused so hard earlier. Right now he was perusing the pattern of wet circles on the bar top in front of him, but damned if he could figure out if this was his third or fourth beer. Fourth, probably, judging from the pleasant buzz in his veins and the increasing attractiveness of the women around him. It was funny how, in a dive like this with sawdust and peanut shells on the floor and country music wailing on the jukebox, Wishbone, Texas, just naturally crept back into his speech.

The hell with the job for a few hours tonight. He was taking a time-out from the hard-nosed hero business. Time out from his marriage, too. The hell with Ange and what's-his-name, the actor.

"What did you say your name was?" The stick-thin blonde on his right nudged his arm with her bony elbow.

"I don't think I said, darlin'." He took another pull from his third or fourth beer, contemplating her appearance indirectly, in the bottle-lined mirror behind the bar. It was probably a good thing her platinum bangs disguised nearly a third of her face. On the other hand, her glossy mouth was generous and, unless he was just fantasizing, very suggestive.

"So, what is it?" she asked between dainty but distinctly audible sips from her own long-neck bottle. "Your name?"

"Bobby."

"Hi, Bobby. I'm Cyn. That's short for Cynthia and long on sin." She laughed as if it were the first time she'd said it. "You're not from around here, are you?"

He shook his head, already weary of the boy-meets-girl banter that had only just begun. He used to be pretty good at this. Good? Hell, he used to be a legend when he worked the advance teams in thirty states during Riordan's first campaign. Right now that seemed about a million years ago, not to mention an incredible waste of time and energy.

"So, where are you from?" Cyn, having edged her barstool closer, now nudged his knee with hers.

"Washington."

"No kidding? Are you one of those guys in town for Crazy Daisy? Like a Secret Service guy or something?"

Ah, Bobby. A million years ago this was your cue to reach for the old badge and in the process give the young lady a glimpse of your gun. Hadn't he come here in the first place with the intention of nursing his wounded ego, and in the process maybe starting a little liaison to make Angela sit up and take notice? The gander on the make for what the goose already had with Pretty Boy Floyd. Sure it was petty and immature, but what else was he supposed to do? Only now he didn't seem to be able to rise to the occasion. Literally. Where's your manly pride, son? What did you do, leave your balls at home on the nightstand right next to the remote?

"Are you?" Cyn asked again. "Like one of those Secret Service guys?"

"Not really," he said. "I'm more like the electrician who tags along and fixes all their fancy gadgets."

"That's cool," she said, obviously disappointed, even though her face, at least the visible lower two-thirds, registered nothing except a sudden distaste for her gum, which she disposed of in a cocktail napkin. "So, you wanna dance, Bobby?"

"Absolutely." He levered off his barstool and held out his hand.

The music was slow and achingly sad—one of those long-gone, she-done-me-wrong songs, a perfect fit for Bobby's mood—but the woman in his arms was all wrong. She was all bones and sharp edges instead of his wife's supple flesh and sleek curves. Her voice was a rasp compared to Angela's smooth tones.

When the music stopped, Cyn didn't let go of his hand. She turned it, blearily contemplating the gold band on his finger. "You married?" she asked.

"Not very," Bobby said, pulling her thin body against him as a new, even sadder song started to play.

~

It was nearly two o'clock when Angela heard a car door slam and then the hushed conversation of agents outside. Bobby's voice, indignant, irritable, rose above the rest. A moment later the back door opened, then quietly closed again. She hadn't slept a single wink, but she closed her eyes now and breathed a silent sigh of relief as Bobby came into the bedroom.

In the unfamiliar dark, he took the change from his pocket, deposited it on the dresser, and swore softly when some of it jingled to the floor. Angela heard the leather slap of his holster on the dresser, then the muted unthreading of a belt and the unlacing of shoes. It had been a long time since she'd listened to him undressing in the dark, trying not to wake her when their schedules didn't mesh. Usually what came next was his naked body radiating warmth beside her in their bed, then a foot reaching out to find hers or a hand seeking her breast, and then, at last, the long, deep, comforting sigh as he surrendered to sleep.

It was different now. After fumbling with the buttons of his shirt and lobbing it into the corner where he'd tossed his slacks, Bobby didn't take off his briefs. He eased down onto his side of the bed without drawing back the covers, then muttered another curse as his head met the pillow. He smelled like beer and sweat and cheap perfume. Chantilly, as a matter of fact. Now *that* was really desperate.

Angela flopped on her side, facing away, wrenching the pillow under her chin and digging a hip into the mattress. No one knew better than she that Bobby Holland needed sex the way flowers needed sunlight. That had seemed obvious even from that first night they were together, when they'd had to keep nudging Mr. Whiskers off the bed. The poor cat had fallen into an exhausted sleep long before his new owners.

When she'd really thought about it, rather than purely reaping the benefits of their frequent lovemaking, Angela had concluded that her husband's intense sexual drive had something to do with his locked-down emotions, that for Bobby orgasm was just as much an emotional release as it was a physical one. After Billy died, she was even more convinced of her theory, because Bobby's need seemed to increase in direct proportion to his inability to grieve. For Angela, though, fucking one's brains out was not an acceptable alternative to tears. Sometimes, after they made love and Bobby fell asleep, she'd lie beside him feeling not satiated or complete, but used, as if he'd taken from her and given nothing in return.

She listened to his breathing now. Even and boozy and thoroughly sated, the rough catch in his throat threatening to blossom into a full-fledged snore.

All during their separation, she hadn't really questioned his fidelity because, according to the grapevine, her estranged husband had become a teeth-gnashing, curse-hurling, nearly impossible son of a bitch. That seemed a pretty good indicator to her that Bobby wasn't getting any. But now it was pretty obvious that wasn't the case anymore.

Angela tugged up the covers none too gently, not caring if she disturbed his postcoital relaxation, actually hoping she woke him up. God damn him.

When his even breathing didn't alter one little bit, she lashed a foot out in his direction. How dare he sleep with some cheap, Chantilly-drenched bimbo and then return to their shared bed?

Finally, furious, she jerked upright, grabbed her pillow, and smacked him as hard as she could.

His reflexes only slightly diminished by the recent tryst, Bobby jackknifed up. "Jesus, Angela. What do you think you're doing?"

"Get out of my bed."

"What?"

"Get out of my bed, you son of a bitch." She reached out a hand to turn on the lamp. She wanted to see his guilty face.

"Ange—" He blinked in the sudden, unexpected light.

"How dare you come back here, back to this bed, after you slept with somebody else?"

"After—?" He rubbed his eyes. "After I *what?*"

"After you slept with . . . How should I know who?"

She heard her own, normally well-modulated tones climb somewhere in the vicinity of a screech. "Some law enforcement groupie wearing a thong and dime-store perfume."

"Jesus," he muttered. "Is that what you think?"

"What am I supposed to think, Bobby? It's two o'clock in the morning and you sneak in here smelling like a—" She threw up her hands. "I don't know. Like a brewery with a French whorehouse next door."

"Give me a break, will you?" he said angrily, then got up and stalked to the bathroom, slamming the door.

By the time he came out a few minutes later, Angela had snapped off the light and practically barricaded herself on her side of the bed. She felt the mattress cant when he lay down again on his side.

"I didn't sleep with anybody, Ange," he said quietly. "I haven't slept with anybody since you left. Are you listening to me?"

"Yes." And she believed him. Bobby was a lot of things, but a liar wasn't one of them.

"Do you believe me?"

"Yes," she whispered.

"I'm not saying I wasn't thinking about it tonight." He tacked on a soft curse at the end of the confession. "But when the time came to close the deal, it wasn't what I wanted. I wanted you."

On her side of the bed, Angela made herself stay absolutely still, even though her innate response to Bobby's words was to throw her arms around him and weep that she wanted him, too. She ached for him, but what good was being satisfied physically when he couldn't or wouldn't even try to satisfy her emotional needs? She didn't think he'd changed a bit in that respect. Making love might be a comfort to him and an emotional as well as physical release, but it had turned into torment for her, being so close and so alone.

With her eyes tightly closed, she whispered, "I appreciate your honesty. We should probably get some sleep now."

If he was disappointed—if she'd just dashed his hope for a sexual reunion and put an end to his every dream of reconciliation—he didn't let it show. This was Bobby, after all. The rock. The night she'd told him she was leaving him, taking the job in L.A. to think things over for a while, all he'd said was, "All right. If that's what you want."

"Yeah," he told her now. "I guess we should. G'night, Ange."

7

Daisy Riordan scowled at the battery-operated clock on the table beside her chair, not trusting it completely. She much preferred winding a clock herself, but mechanical timepieces were difficult to find in this dreadful, digital, electronic day and age.

Assuming the clock was correct, the time was ten after eight. She'd been bathed and dressed since seven-fifteen, and she was decidedly hungry. The fact that she could have gone downstairs for her muffin and juice and coffee was beside the point. When she informed the Hollands that she wanted her breakfast tray at eight o'clock, that was by God what she meant. As much as the Itos had annoyed her, at least they had been punctual.

She didn't like starting her day on a sour note like this. It was difficult, once she committed herself to a mood, to talk herself out of it. She was liable to be cranky the rest of the day, she feared.

That was another reason she detested growing old. Along with hardening of the arteries, there seemed to come a certain hardening of the personality. She could see it in herself. Her levels of tolerance had never been high, but they'd declined dramatically, especially since

Charles's death. Her ability to suffer fools was now practically nil.

She could see the same petrification in her friend, Muriel, who'd aged from a silly young twit into a silly old fool. One would have thought her recent cancer scare would have matured her somehow, but it hadn't.

Daisy sighed as a soft knock sounded on her door.

"Come in," she muttered, then watched the knob turn, the door swing in, and a grim-looking Robert step into her room. Well, she hadn't really expected the young man to be all sunshine and smiles this morning. She didn't sleep much these days, and she'd been looking out the window at two this morning when he had extracted himself from a little vehicle in the driveway—a little blonde-propelled vehicle—then done a rather poor imitation of a sober person making his way toward the back door. At the moment he looked as if he had the headache he deserved.

"The clocks downstairs are all in working order, I presume," she said as he put down the tray on the table beside her.

He gave her a look that more than confirmed the dull ache behind his finely shaped eyebrows, then said, "If you mean your breakfast is ten minutes late, Mrs. Riordan, you're absolutely right. There was a small dispute about the designation of duties, but it's been resolved."

Daisy returned the look, minus the headache. "I see. What you're saying then is that Mrs. Holland didn't appreciate your condition last night or the hour you got in."

Robert's frank, but forlorn, hazel eyes stayed fastened on her face as he quietly replied, "You could put it that way, ma'am."

"So you lost the battle of the bran muffin and the tray, I take it."

A woeful little smile touched his lips. "Something like that, ma'am."

Daisy offered him a smug smile in return. "All right, then. That will be all, Robert."

She liked him. He struck her as forthright and honest . . . well, as honest as he could be considering the damned subterfuge that William had instigated. She liked this young man quite well, as a matter of fact. As she felt her own sour mood sweeten a bit, she thought it a shame that Robert seemed so unhappy.

He was almost out the door when she summoned him back. "I'd like you to drive me into town at ten o'clock. I've agreed, against my better judgment, to host my bridge group again tomorrow, so I'll be needing refreshments. We'll take the Cadillac. I believe the keys are on a hook somewhere in the kitchen."

"Yes, ma'am."

"If Angela would like to come along to do some shopping, that's perfectly fine with me. I'll be down at ten. Sharp."

After she had prepared Mrs. Riordan's breakfast, which basically had amounted to pouring orange juice and coffee, then plopping a big bran muffin on a plate, and after she battled with Bobby over who would take it upstairs, Angela went outside, as much to get a breath of fresh air as to check out the rear exterior of the residence. She noticed that most of the yellow roses around the gazebo had dropped their petals overnight. Well, seemed like everybody had had a bad night.

She wondered how Rod's party with the studio execs had gone, and then decided she really didn't care. Sometimes his occupation struck her as frivolous beyond belief. Yes, she knew people yearned to be entertained, to take time off from the grind of daily business, to get their minds off their troubles, but still . . . She was probably prejudiced, but her admiration was reserved for the law enforcement people who made it possible for everybody else to safely play.

"Well, I'm off to keep the forces of evil at bay." That's what Sergeant Angelo Callifano had said with a big smile every morning when he left for the station house. Bobby, on the other hand, was more succinct about his career in law enforcement. "Fucking up the bad guys" was the way he put it. Same difference.

She bent to pick up some of the fallen yellow rose petals, sniffed their lovely fragrance, then let them drift through her fingers.

"Mornin', Mrs. Holland," Doug Coulter called to her on his way to the trailer. "Everything all right this morning?"

She gave him a thumbs-up and a bright smile, behind which she was thinking, Everything's just peachy, Special Agent Coulter. Maybe you'd like trying to do the job while lashed to Mrs. Coulter's apron strings.

"By the way, that truck coming up the driveway has been cleared," he called. "Same milkman who's been delivering for the past fifteen years."

"Great," she replied, turning toward the drive to see the big white step van with the black-and-white cow painted on its side and the word *Smoooooooth* in a cartoon bubble above the cow's head. She should probably double up on Mrs. Riordan's regular order, she thought, walking to greet the man who jumped down from the driver's seat.

"Good morning," she said in what she thought was the perfect maid-to-milkman tone. "I'm Angela, Mrs. Riordan's new housekeeper."

She knew immediately that there was going to be trouble, judging from the grin on the guy's face. It was lascivious. Lurid. Like he'd been in lockdown at a federal penitentiary for the past fifteen years, and hers was the first female face he'd seen since getting out. Except he wasn't looking at her face. The creep.

He was in his early thirties, probably close to her own age, with a face only a mother ferret could love. He wore white pants held up by a skinny Elvis belt, a white shirt, and a black bow tie that Angela could have sworn was plastic. His Adam's apple poked out above it.

"I'm Eugene," he said, accenting his name on the first syllable so it sounded like You-gene. "What happened to that little Jap couple?"

Oh, brother. Now she *really* didn't like him. "They quit," she told him.

He didn't look surprised. "Hey, I would too if I had to work for Crazy Daisy. What a bitch. That old lady busts my chops every couple of months. Like it's my fault if the milk's no good. What am I? A cow?"

No, a jerk, Angela thought. The guy was still looking at her chest as if he considered that eye contact.

"So, you're new here, huh?"

She nodded.

"When's your day off, Angel? Maybe we could see a movie or go bowling or something. You like to bowl?"

"Not especially," she said

Eugene looked disappointed, but undeterred. He moved a few steps closer, and she noticed he smelled like a sour dishrag. "You don't bowl, huh? Well, what do you like to do on dates, Angel?" He made a little guttural sound, somewhere between a growl and a grunt. "I'm up for anything."

I'll just bet you are, bucko. Being in the Secret Service not only did wonders for a woman's self-esteem, it also gave her the confidence—the unmitigated balls, really— to take on bozos like Eugene. She could've had him spread-eagled on the ground in two seconds flat, but it was a lot more fun to bring him down verbally.

"What'll it be, baby?" he whispered, assaulting her with his terrible breath.

"Handcuffs," she said.

"Excuse me?"

"Handcuffs. I like to fool around with handcuffs." She could almost see the illicit little thrill blaze down the guy's spine, so she smiled and said, "For starters, anyway."

He blinked. "For . . . for starters?"

She winked. "No pain, no gain. I don't suppose there are any leather shops in town."

"Leather? What? You mean like gloves?"

"I mean like whips."

"Uh. Not that I know of."

"Oh, well." Angela shrugged, gratified to see that Eugene was staring in her eyes now rather than at her chest. He was starting to hyperventilate, too. "It doesn't matter.

I've got plenty of paraphernalia. So which are you, Eugene? S or M?"

"I dunno," he croaked.

"No problem. I can go either way."

His Adam's apple did a triple Salkow above his stupid tie, and his face was rapidly draining of color. "Where are you from, anyway?"

"New York," she said, then added, "Hell's Kitchen," while trying not to cackle.

Eugene took a step back, so Angela held her breath—God, he smelled bad—and advanced on him.

"Did you ever do it with handcuffs, Eugene? Wearing leather?" she asked.

He shook his head and stepped back again.

"Do you like whips? Stun guns?"

He shook his head harder. Another step, and his shoulders made contact with Bossy on the side of the truck.

"Cattle prods?"

Eugene made a little strangling sound just before he bolted. The next thing Angela knew, he was shoving two wet quarts of milk at her; then he leapt into the driver's seat and gunned the vehicle backward down the driveway.

She laughed out loud, and was still laughing when Bobby called to her from the back door.

"Ange, grocery shopping at ten. Sharp."

Oh, good. Action.

⌒

Mrs. Riordan came downstairs on the stroke of ten, as she had threatened, and by ten-oh-two they were in the ancient Caddy, headed toward beautiful downtown Hassenfeld. Bobby was at the wheel, Angela in the passenger seat, while the president's mother sat in back, unaware that behind *her,* at a discreet distance, were Doug and another agent in a reinforced SUV.

After her little interlude with Eugene, having to come up with instant menu plans for the unscheduled shopping trip didn't do much for Angela's mood, and it only worsened when she noticed Bobby's jaw tighten along with his grip on the wheel as they drove past a seedy roadhouse called the Wayward Wind. So that was where he'd picked up the bimbo.

Staring daggers at him was not an option with Mrs. Riordan in the back seat, so she merely cleared her throat knowingly and readjusted her seat belt to relieve some of the pressure on her heart. Okay. So he hadn't slept with the little tart. What did he want? A medal for gallant restraint? Angela hadn't slept with Rod either, and he wasn't just some pickup. The man was practically begging her to marry him, for heaven's sake, and still she wouldn't go to bed with him. She wouldn't do that. Not while she was Bobby's wife.

Outside the Caddy's window the cornfields and scattered farmhouses were gradually giving way to homes with neat little yards as they approached the town. They bounced over some train tracks and blew past a big blue Kiwanis billboard that welcomed them to Hassenfeld.

"Turn left on Madison," Mrs. Riordan commanded from the back. "Save Mart is halfway down the block."

To his credit, Bobby didn't even clench a muscle in his cheek when he had to brake hard to make the turn on such short notice. To his discredit and eternal damnation, he looked amazingly sexy today in a pair of faded jeans that hugged his muscular legs and perfect butt, along with a white polo shirt that looked molded to his chest. Even the president's mother hadn't expressed the slightest disapproval of her new employee's rather casual uniform.

The other new employee, however, was having an exceptionally bad hair day and probably looked like a dog after only a few restless hours of sleep, all of them spent turned on her unaccustomed side, away from her bedmate. She was already tired of wearing slacks to conceal an ankle holster that was making a permanent crease on her leg, and the very last thing she wanted to do this morning, next to going bowling with Eugene, was push a cart around a supermarket to buy food that she would then be obliged to cook.

Like most things in her life, she couldn't take the cooking part of this assignment halfheartedly, without caring how the meals turned out. Another agent might've fed Mrs. Riordan peanut butter and jelly sandwiches and Kentucky Fried Chicken for the duration, but it just wasn't in Angela not to give her best effort. She wasn't a quitter or a shirker, in spite of what *some people* thought after she'd walked out on her marriage.

Bobby dropped them off at the door. Angela followed Mrs. Riordan inside the supermarket, giving the place a quick once-over and finding nothing at all suspicious, just average Hassenfelders going about their daily business. The president's mother wouldn't allow her to assist her with a cart.

"I'm quite capable of doing this myself," she said, wrenching a metal cart from its snug mooring among others, then flowing ahead toward produce, leaving Angela standing stupidly for a moment before tugging out her own cart and following in Crazy Daisy's wake. Where that nickname came from, she had no idea. The woman was difficult, no doubt about it, but Angela only hoped she would be this independent when she reached the age of seventy-six. At the rate she was going, she thought, that just might be next week.

While Mrs. Riordan was hefting cantaloupes, sniffing and inspecting each one from stem to stern, Angela snatched a plastic bag from a rack and began to fill it with the Golden Delicious apples she intended to use for a tuna Waldorf salad. The recipe was one of her mother's greatest culinary tricks, adding apples and onions and raisins and walnuts and mayo to canned tuna, instantly waldorfing the bland fish into a delicious meal. The president's mother had said she didn't mind a few surprises now and then, and the tuna salad would make an excellent lunch for her, especially with a slice of cantaloupe, and because Bobby hated tuna, that gave it even more appeal.

Smiling almost wickedly, she picked up some Boston lettuce to serve as a lovely bed for the salad, then wheeled her cart toward the onion bins to choose a few of those. While she was debating between the yellow and the white varieties—one was milder, as she recalled, but which?— she felt a distinct warmth at her back, an aura of heat punctuated by the fragrant scent of familiar aftershave.

"We have to stop meeting like this," Bobby whispered close to her ear, his warm breath sending a succession of little shivers across her neck and along her spine. The temptation to turn, to melt in his arms, was nearly overpowering.

"Fine with me." Angela moved a few safe inches away and reached for a big white onion. "Why don't you make yourself useful, Bobby, and find me a box of raisins? Not the generic kind. The good ones in the red box."

"Aye, aye, Captain." He snapped a crisp salute. "Where's Mrs. Riordan?"

"Right over—" Angela looked toward the display of cantaloupes where she'd last seen the woman. "Oh, God. She was right over there by the melons."

The playfulness drained from Bobby's expression. Without another word, he took off like a broken field runner, pushing shopping carts and shoppers out of his way.

They'd screwed up. Oh, boy, had they screwed up. And they had absolutely no excuse. The fact that nobody seemed to be taking this threat all that seriously, other than their politically motivated director, didn't mean she and Bobby shouldn't be doing the job they'd been sent here to do. If they kept allowing their personal problems to interfere with their duty, they weren't just risking their careers, they could be risking Mrs. Riordan's life as well.

Bobby, of all people, should have realized that from day one. He should never have let anything come between him and his protectee. For her part, she needed to remember she was Mrs. Riordan's protector first and her cook a distant second, so she didn't become distracted by apples and onions and Boston lettuce, not to mention Bobby's aftershave.

She cursed again, wishing Doug had allowed them to use the radios and receivers that kept agents instantly in touch with one another. She could have worn her hair over her earpiece, and Bobby could have pretended to be almost deaf as long as he was pretending to be almost human. Just as she was about to sprint toward the front of the store, she saw Bobby give a thumbs-up signal from the end of the aisle. He'd found her. Thank God. Angela let out an audible sigh of relief.

~

When Bobby found her, Mrs. Riordan's shopping cart was blocking the liquor aisle, where she had abandoned it while she stood yards away, pondering the bottles on a shelf, oblivious to the bottleneck she was causing. He moved the cart and offered an apologetic shrug to the inconvenienced customers.

"You don't happen to know anything about sherry, do you, Robert?" she asked, as if he'd been standing right there beside her all along.

"Not a thing, ma'am. I'm pretty much a beer and pretzels man, myself."

"So I gather." She gave a knowing little cluck of her tongue, then followed it with a sigh. "Well, I'm at a loss here. My husband was the one who had the expertise in wines. I might just as well throw a dart. Do you have any suggestions at all?"

Bobby eyed the bottle-laden shelf. "This would be for your bridge group?" he asked.

"That's correct."

"Well—" He reached for an import. "This might give your friend, Bootsie, a proper little jolt."

She started to laugh, but quickly suppressed it. "Put it in the cart, will you? Now I need to find some interesting cookies or crackers. Come along."

He moseyed behind her, pushing the cart. She was a

trim woman, despite her lack of exercise. Today she was wearing tailored beige slacks and a matching sweater with a scarf draped around her neck. A stiff-sided handbag swung from her crooked elbow, bumping every customer she passed, but nobody seemed to mind. She was the president's mother, after all. Crazy Daisy. Crazy like a fox, Bobby thought.

As they rounded an end cap, he caught sight of Angela, deep in conversation with a butcher. She was hooking her blond hair back, left and right, so the guy must've been giving her an argument about something. God, she was pretty. Bobby could've stood there all day and watched her.

He didn't envy the poor butcher. Who argued about meat, for God's sake? Only Angela, or Miss Prim, as she was known in her family. Once she got an idea in her head, there was nothing anybody could do to dislodge it. Her opinion of him was a prime example. She thought if he didn't howl like a lone coyote over Billy's death or break down and blubber the way her father and brothers did, he wasn't properly grieving. She thought . . .

"Robert!" Mrs. Riordan called out from the adjacent aisle.

Christ, he'd lost her again.

"Yes, ma'am," he muttered, casting a final glance at his wife and the poor bedeviled slob behind the meat counter. Hell, it looked as if Angela wanted him to cry, too.

Angela prowled the dairy department, cooling off. Stupid butcher. Everybody in Washington and Los Angeles and every other place she'd ever lived did a custom grind for chili—every butcher! everywhere!—but this bozo didn't even want to hear about it. She heaved a wet gallon of milk into her cart, cursing Eugene for good measure, then tossed in half a dozen yogurts, feeling as if her confrontation at the meat counter had just depleted her calcium levels drastically, not to mention what it had done to her blood pressure and her mood.

Okay. She was crabby. But who wouldn't be when their exciting career in law enforcement had suddenly become a drab, domestic hell? Maybe being a cook was secondary in this assignment, but she still had to come up with some decent meals, for heaven's sake. How could she do that when she couldn't find the proper ingredients?

She was crabby, and she was once again neglecting her primary duty, mere moments after she'd vowed not to do it again. It was just so hard, being with Bobby like this. She kept thinking about Button Brothers, the little corner grocery in Georgetown. When they were first married and were lucky enough to have a weekend off together, which wasn't often, she and Bobby would stroll down O Street arm in arm just as the sun was setting.

Sunsets usually made him blue, so Angela would knock herself out trying to cheer him. She'd gotten better at it, too, turning his frowns into smiles and sometimes into outright, genuine, sidesplitting laughter. He didn't laugh often, though. But when he did . . .

One evening, when they'd stopped in Button Brothers to pick up something for their dinner, Angela was in the dairy section when she heard Bobby's rare and wonderful laughter ring out. She rushed back to the other side of the store just in time to see her husband and brother-in-law, both of them still in their serious Secret Service suits and ties with their sidearms barely concealed, in the middle of their boyhood juggling act.

Oranges and cucumbers, three of each, arced high between them and fell into their hands with glorious, colorful precision, around and around and around, while shoppers and checkers and stock boys stood watching, their mouths open and their hands clapping in absolute delight.

Angela picked up a zucchini to use as a microphone. "Ladies and gentlemen, out of Wishbone, Texas, by a strange, circuitous route, and now appearing in your neighborhood supermarket, the one, the only, the Amazing Holland Brothers."

The show went on a full ten minutes, Bobby laughing all the while, his head thrown back in sheer joy and his eyes sparkling, making it look so easy, simply effortless, keeping all that produce in orbit. He even managed at some point to throw Angela a happy look that somehow said "You're a part of this act, too." That look of love and inclusion, along with Bobby's laughter, had zapped her heart more effectively than any stun gun.

It was Billy who seemed to be struggling. It was Billy who started to blink and to sweat and to lurch a bit until finally their perfect timing deteriorated, the flying oranges and cukes thunked one by one to the floor, and the Amazing Holland Brothers collapsed in each other's arms, laughing, to wild applause—none of it wilder or happier than Angela's.

Dear God. She hadn't thought about that incident in a long, long time. Little wonder. Just a week after that amazing moment, Billy was dead, and the world itself seemed to deteriorate, to tumble down around her.

"You're part of this act, too," Bobby had said with his shining eyes and his warm smile, and then he'd shut her out.

Glaring down now at the shopping list she'd scribbled, Angela realized she'd forgotten the celery for her Waldorf tuna salad. She maneuvered her cart around and headed back to the produce department, against the flow of traffic, looking for Mrs. Riordan as she went, but not seeing either her or Bobby. Great. It was a safe bet they weren't juggling somewhere. They were probably already through the checkout lane, cooling their heels at the front of the store, waiting for her.

After she grabbed a bag of celery, she aimed her cart toward the checkout lanes, where she discovered Bobby paging through a copy of the *National Enquirer*.

"I'm ready," she said. "Where's Mrs. Riordan?"

"Right there." He angled his head toward the checkout line on his right, apparently far too intrigued by the baby who was born whistling "The Star-Spangled Banner" to break his concentration.

"Where?" Angela demanded.

"Right there. In line."

"No, she's not."

Bobby looked, then snapped the tabloid closed and shoved it back into the rack. "She was standing right here," he said, moving toward the unattended cart that was being pushed along in line. "This is her stuff in here. Sherry. Crackers."

"Jesus, Bobby," Angela breathed.

"Okay." The brief confusion disappeared from his face, replaced by grim determination. "She probably went back for something she forgot. You take the front, Ange. I'll sweep the aisles from the back. She's got to be someplace in between."

"Right," she replied, far too professional to point out that their protectee had probably just been snatched from under his nose while that nose was buried in the scandal of the week.

Angela wove through carts, scanning each aisle as she passed, seeing Bobby on the other end, doing the same. They repeated the procedure. There was no Mrs. Riordan in between.

While Angela spoke with the store manager, Bobby trotted outside. "She's not in the car," he said when he came back.

"She's not in the store, either. The manager checked."

Angela could almost see the color drain from Bobby's face. She forgave him for reeking of beer and Chantilly last night. He was in a sea of trouble now. And so, dear God, was she.

8

"Let's get Doug," Angela said.

"Not yet," he snapped.

"Bobby, we have to. Mrs. Riordan's gone."

He didn't think so. There was no way in hell that woman would have gone quietly with an abductor, even at knife- or gunpoint, and no way anyone could have bagged her or drugged her without being seen by at least a score of snoopy midwestern housewives or retirees. In fact, now that the initial adrenaline rush was releasing its grip on his brain, Bobby was beginning to feel pretty foolish, like the victim of a really slick con.

While they stood in the checkout line, Crazy Daisy had plucked a tabloid out of a rack, opened it, and after an indignant sniff had handed the magazine to Bobby.

"Read this, Robert."

"Uh. No, thank you, ma'am."

"Read it."

The woman would've made a hell of a drill sergeant, Bobby thought, and he reminded himself that on this assignment the Secret Service was tasked with keeping their protectee not only safe but happy, as well. They weren't supposed to upset the president's mother in any way, shape, or form. In light of that, he gritted his teeth, took the tabloid from her clenched fist, and focused on some cockamamie story about Martians and a high-level coverup in the Cincinnati police department.

That was it, of course. The diversion. The con.

"Where are the rest rooms?" he asked the manager, who'd been hovering around them, wringing his hands and quietly moaning, for the past few minutes.

"Over there." The man pointed. "Just to the left of the courtesy counter."

"Thanks." Bobby turned his attention to Angela, who was looking a little pale and panicky herself.

"We lost her," she said, as if she couldn't quite believe it.

"No, we didn't. Stay here, Ange. I'll be right back. Don't alert Doug."

"But regulations—"

"Not one word. You hear me?" He was throwing away the rule book on this one, and he hoped to God he was right.

"But—"

"Just don't, Ange," he growled. "Not yet. Give me two minutes."

～

Daisy's knees were stiffening up from sitting cross-legged on the commode. She had briefly considered standing on the white plastic seat, but it had looked slippery, and she was afraid of falling in. Now that would be a headline! President's mother drowns in public toilet!

She was glad she had had the foresight to choose the rather spacious handicapped stall, because by now she would have been quite claustrophobic in one of the smaller ones. As it was, the pernicious odor of faux pine was nearly making her swoon.

Cloistering herself in the ladies' room to elude her armed guards hadn't been her intention originally. She'd sincerely wanted to come to the store for sherry and treats for tomorrow's bridge game. On the drive into town, however, and then in the store itself, she had sensed the hostility between the two young people. Well, hostility on the part of the young woman, at least. Poor Robert seemed less hostile than enshrouded in gloom. Naturally he deserved to pay for his actions of the previous night, but Daisy felt sorry for him nevertheless. He reminded her of her husband, Charles, in some strange way, and Daisy devoutly wished she could take back every dagger she'd ever glared at him and every frosty word she'd ever spoken.

It wouldn't hurt to shake her two protectors up a bit, she'd decided, and make them work together instead of at cross-purposes, so when Robert obediently began reading a copy of that abhorrent newspaper, Daisy had slipped off to the ladies' room, locked the stall door, sat and pulled her feet from view as she'd seen somebody do in some silly movie recently, and stifled her laughter when they came looking for her.

Now, though, she was suffering the consequences of her shenanigan. Her knees ached like the very devil as she stretched out her legs and stood. Hearing the outer rest room door open and footsteps coming in, Daisy flushed the toilet even though she hadn't used it. It seemed the proper thing to do before she pulled back the bolt on the stall door and stepped out.

"Real cute," Robert said. He had a hip cocked on one of the washbowls, and his arms were crossed.

Daisy's surprise immediately turned to defensive indignation. "I beg your pardon," she said, striding on her stiff knees toward the other sink. "This is the ladies' room, in case you hadn't noticed." She gave the handles a jerk and proceeded to wash her hands.

"I won't even ask why you did it, Mrs. Riordan," he said calmly, "but I sincerely hope you won't do it again. We were worried about you, ma'am."

"That's very comforting," she said, flicking water off her fingers before she punched on the electric dryer.

The door opened again.

"You found her," Angela said a bit breathlessly.

"You both found me," Daisy snapped. "Good work. Now, shall we go?"

~

"She doesn't know," Angela insisted while she chopped celery. "How could she possibly know?"

Bobby, sitting at the kitchen table, shrugged. "She's not a stupid woman."

"Well, neither am I, Bobby, and I don't think I've done anything to give us away." Her hair swung fetchingly as she looked over her shoulder and pointed her knife, not so fetchingly, in his direction. "Which, of course, leaves you."

He shook his head. "I think she's just having a good old time playing cat and mouse with us. That's fine. As long as she doesn't boot us out of the house."

"What did she say when you found her in the bathroom?"

"Mostly she just bristled up like a cat." He chuckled. "Kind of like the way you do when you've been caught doing something stupid."

Angela didn't say anything, but the squaring of her shoulders and the little twitch of her butt pretty effectively told him to go to hell. She was frustrated with this assignment. He was, too. As Secret Service agents, they were used to working with people who wanted their protection, who were even grateful for it.

In her frustration, she was attacking the celery so viciously it was a miracle her knife didn't go right through the chopping block. Bobby wondered why he'd never spent more time watching her cook, when she put on such an enjoyable show. If he had it to do over again—*when* he had it to do over again—he'd study her articulate body language in addition to her incredible body. Hell, maybe he'd even put on an apron and cook with her. One of those denim deals.

While she scraped the little pieces of celery into a bowl, she said, "Do you really think she suspects that we're agents?"

"Probably. She's just twitting us a little."

"Why, for heaven's sake?"

"I dunno, Ange. Probably because she resents being misled, even if it is for her own protection. Probably because she's lonely and a little bored being cooped up in this house most of the time."

"That makes sense." She nodded solemnly while she reached into one of the shopping bags they'd brought home from the store and came up with an onion the size of a baseball, then tossed it from hand to hand as she leaned a hip against the counter. "The manager of the store told me he hasn't seen Mrs. Riordan in there in months. He seemed to be genuinely concerned. You know, we should probably offer to take her out, Bobby, as long as we're cooped up here, too."

"Sure. Let's ask her."

She stopped tossing the onion back and forth to level an accusing glare at him. "Unless that conflicts with any future engagements you might have down at the local honky-tonk."

Lousy as he felt about the night before, Bobby had to admit some degree of satisfaction, if not outright pleasure, in the fact that Ange appeared jealous. Pressing a hand over his heart, he offered his wife a look of such sweet, undiluted innocence it would have made an angel weep. "Who, me?"

"Right." She made one of those annoying *tsk*ing noises, then pitched the onion at him. "Here, Romeo. Chop this. I'm going to go check in with Doug."

~

Bobby was standing by the sink ten minutes later when Angela came back to the kitchen. His head was bent forward, and every inch of his posture signaled sadness, like a mourner standing over a grave. The second she heard him draw in a wavering, wet breath, Angela rushed to him, curling her arms around him from behind, pressing her cheek to his warm back.

"Oh, sweetheart," she whispered.

He sniffled again. She could hear his voice clog in his

throat, so she held him tighter. "Bobby, please let me help you. Tell me. What's wrong? What is it?"

He dragged in another wet breath and let it out. "God-damned onion."

"Excuse me?"

"I'm dying from these fumes."

First Angela clenched her teeth in order not to take a bite out of his shoulder blade, next she willed her hopeless heart to change from pudding to concrete, then she loosened her arms and stepped back. "Move," she told him. "Give me the stupid knife. Get out of my way."

Bobby handed her the knife, then dragged his forearm across his wet eyes. "That was brutal. You did that on purpose, didn't you?"

Angela gave him a shove with her hip, then took his place at the cutting board and hacked at the onion as if it were his flesh. She should be so lucky.

He reached into a cabinet for a glass, filled it with water from the tap, and drained it in a couple big gulps before he asked, "Did you get hold of Doug?"

Her lips were compressed so tightly she could hardly speak. She squinted in the onion fumes. "Yes," she finally said, drawing out the s in a hiss.

"And?"

Ignoring him, she transferred handfuls of the diced onion to the bowl with the celery, then rinsed her hands in the sink. No one could make her as angry as Bobby did. Damn him. And no one else could turn her heart to instant pudding, either. Not even Rod. She hated the emotional bind her husband had her in. Why couldn't she be free of the useless anger as well as the hopeless love?

"And?" Bobby asked again.

She drew in a long breath. God. She'd already broken her vow not to let personal issues get in the way of the job. After what the special agent in charge had just told her, the job seemed to be heating up. "Doug said they received another threat in D.C. A letter similar to the one the other day. They're faxing him a copy."

Bobby swore. "I was really hoping there wouldn't be a follow-up. Where was this one postmarked? Did he say?"

"Florida. Same as the first. The forensics people can't come up with anything much other than 'generic.' "

"Great," he muttered, raking his fingers through his hair. "Well, I'm going to hunt up some pruning shears and have a go at those generic bushes out in front so our generic stalker can't take cover in them. What time is lunch?"

"Mrs. Riordan's is at twelve-thirty," she said with only a slight dash of acid in her voice. "Yours is whenever you want. It'll be in a bowl in the refrigerator. Just slap it on a plate, and please rinse your dishes and put them in the dishwasher when you're done."

He stared at her a moment, apparently trying to figure out her mood and failing in his effort. "Look, I know you're not wild about this kitchen duty. If you want to go out and hack at the shrubbery, Ange, be my guest. I'll fix her lunch and take her tray upstairs. It really doesn't make any difference to me."

I thought you were crying, she ached to say. *I thought you were finally going to let me comfort you, and that maybe you'd comfort me, but it was just the stupid onion.*

Her throat tightened painfully. "No, you go on outside. I really just want to be alone for a while."

After he was gone, Angela washed her hands for the gazillionth time that morning, then peeled and chopped apples and put together her Waldorf tuna salad, all the while trying not to think about how desolate Bobby had looked when she'd come into the kitchen or how all her best intentions had been foiled by onion fumes.

She almost wished the threat to the president's mother would materialize today so they could put the bastard in cuffs and leg irons and be done with this.

⌒

Daisy thought her female bodyguard was looking decidedly pale and shaky when Angela placed the lunch tray on the table by her chair. She hoped she hadn't gotten the two young people in trouble with their superiors with her disappearing act this morning, when her intention had been for it to bring them together.

This assignment—having to cook and clean for a fussy old woman—had to be a far cry from what Angela expected when she joined the Secret Service. Certainly Robert hadn't signed on to trim shrubbery, as he was doing at the moment below her window. Perhaps the tension she kept witnessing between them was merely professional displeasure in being relegated to this duty, which must have been the equivalent of keeping watch over William's ancient Labrador retriever.

Daisy sighed softly and looked down at her plate. Good God. "What an interesting way to prepare tuna," she said. "Are those raisins?"

"Yes, ma'am. It's my mother's recipe. Part tuna salad, part Waldorf salad."

It looked a bit heavy on the mayonnaise, but she held her tongue. Angela seemed distressed enough already, and Daisy assumed it was her fault. "I enjoyed getting out this morning," she said, intending to work her way up to a vague, veiled apology for her behavior in the supermarket.

"I'm so glad," Angela said. "We'd be happy to take you anywhere you'd like to go, Mrs. Riordan. Day or evening. A concert. The theater. Anything. Tonight, if you'd like."

"That's very kind of you. Perhaps next week. With my bridge club coming tomorrow for the second time this week, I'm afraid that will be the extent of my socializing for the time being." She didn't add that the impending card game would also put a strain on her ability to tolerate fools.

When Muriel had insisted, and rather vehemently too, on the second get-together, Daisy had agreed just to shut the woman up. Merely contemplating another few hours with Muriel was enough to give her a headache, and the other two, Norma and Adele, were no picnic either.

"Any time," Angela said. "Just let us know." She moved toward the door. "Don't forget that I'll be setting your place in the dining room tonight, Mrs. Riordan."

"No. I haven't forgotten."

"Good. Enjoy your lunch."

"Thank you."

When Angela closed the door, Daisy cast a baleful glance at the tray, telling herself she needed to remember, once the Hollands were gone, to amend the section in her binder that listed Foods to Avoid. Tuna salad was going to go at the top of the revised list.

How kind and truly good-hearted of them, though, to want to take an irritable old crone out on the town. It had been several years since she'd attended a concert or the theater or even a movie. A movie! Now that was an inspired idea. Not for her, but for the Hollands. Daisy smiled. She could already imagine the two of them, Robert and Angela, holding hands in a darkened theater, while a love scene played across the screen.

⁓

Bobby half expected Crazy Daisy to drop a flowerpot or a water balloon on his head while he lopped off the scraggly tops of the shrubs at the front of the house. He was convinced that she knew he and Angela were special agents. It had been pretty boneheaded for their superiors in the agency to think otherwise. The president's mother was a bright woman, for chrissake, and she knew the difference between domestic help and federal agents.

For a moment Bobby considered just telling her the truth about their protective assignment. If the woman was apprised of the threat against her life, maybe she wouldn't pull any more stunts like the one this morning. The fact that she wasn't nabbed in the supermarket didn't necessarily mean there wasn't somebody out there waiting for the opportunity to do it, and he and Angela were working hobbled without radio communications. That new threatening letter was not good news.

Still, if he told her the truth, then, being the stubborn woman that she was, Daisy Riordan would probably feel compelled to insist on her right to privacy and have both him and Angela duly removed from the premises.

That was what he didn't want to screw up. Even more than his assignment, maybe even more than his career right now, Bobby didn't want to screw up his proximity to Angela. The longer he could be here with his wife, the better. Whether she hated him or not, the mere fact that Angela was here in Illinois with him meant she wasn't in California with Harry Hollywood, the frigging movie star, the "somebody else."

He'd watched her through the kitchen window this morning while she deftly, almost surgically castrated the amorous milkman. What a woman. He was so in love with her he almost couldn't see straight. There had to be a way to make her know that.

"Talk to your wife," the department shrink had told him. "Share your feelings with her." But the shrink hadn't told him how, and Bobby hadn't asked. Feelings? My God. He was sharing his *life* with Angela. That was how he felt. What was there to share beyond that? How did you put that in words?

He whacked at the greenery with a vengeance. The pruning shears he'd dug out of a bin in the toolshed probably hadn't been sharpened since the first Reagan administration, so by the time he had the bushes the way he wanted them—low enough so they wouldn't conceal an intruder—Bobby had worked up a fairly good appetite, not to mention a shirt-soaking sweat. He was standing, hands braced on his waist, stretching the kinks out of his back, when a little pickup truck—turquoise with pink feathering on the front fenders and doors—wheeled into Mrs. Riordan's driveway.

Cyn. As in sin. Judas Priest.

Bobby trotted down the brick sidewalk toward the

truck, and reached it just in time to see Doug and young Mike Burris hustling up the driveway from the backyard, their hands just itching to go for their weapons. Maybe he should let them, he thought morosely. Maybe they'd miss the blonde, hit him instead, and put him out of his misery.

Coward that he was, he waved them off and shouted, "I've got it, Doug."

Special Agent in Charge Doug Coulter, a tad out of breath from his sprint from the trailer, appeared to be mentally consulting agency rules and regulations for any excuse to put a bullet in his colleague. Instead he shot Bobby a look that said, "You got it, and you best get rid of it, too, son. Pronto."

Bobby braced his hands on the pickup's roof and bent down to speak with Cyn through the open window. She hadn't been all that attractive in the muted neon illumination of the bar, and daylight didn't improve her looks one little bit. Her overbleached hair was the color and texture of straw. The lips that seemed so lush and glossy last night looked chapped and pale today. Her perfume smelled vaguely familiar and thoroughly rank in the warm afternoon sunshine.

"Remember me?" she asked. Her breath smelled like bubble gum today instead of peanuts and beer.

"Sure I do, darlin'. Did I thank you for the ride home last night?"

"Well enough." She squinted through the windshield, down the driveway where Mike and Doug still stood, staring at her truck. "Those are Secret Service agents, huh?"

"The older one with the beer gut is," he said, angling

his head toward Doug, biting down on a grin. "The younger guy's an electrician just like me."

"Oh." Cyn sighed. It clearly wasn't easy for a little girl from Hassenfeld to find her fair share of excitement these days. She turned her hopeful gaze back on him. "Oh, well. So I was wondering if I'd be seeing you at the Wayward Wind tonight?"

He shook his head, managing to look somber and deeply regretful even as he was thinking, Sorry, darlin'. My wife won't let me go. "Gotta work," he said. "I probably won't be getting off duty much anymore."

"Lemme give you my number, just in case, okay?" She rummaged through the glove compartment, pulled out a crumpled receipt, and scribbled on it.

Bobby straightened up and stashed the little paper deep in the back pocket of his jeans, then gave the pickup's roof a tap. "Guess you better go. You're making these government boys a little nervous. See you around, Cyn."

"Yeah. Okay. See you." She threw the little truck into reverse and stepped on the gas, maneuvering the turquoise vehicle back the way it had come.

It was a comfort to know he hadn't lost his touch with women, but Bobby was relieved as hell to see her go, especially before Angela came outside to see what was going on in the driveway. Making her jealous had been a dumb idea. All it did was make him appreciate her more in comparison.

"Bobby." Doug had come up behind him. He was wearing his take-no-prisoners look while his gaze roved from Bobby to the shrubs at the front of the house.

"Everything going okay inside?" he asked. "They're updating the president every few hours."

"Everything's fine. No problems."

The older agent angled his head toward the street where Cyn had just shifted into drive and pressed the accelerator to the floor, laying a little rubber to punctuate her exit. "See that it stays that way," he said, "because if I have to pull you from this duty, I can't for the life of me imagine why William Riordan would want you back at the White House. You know what I mean?"

Bobby nodded. He knew exactly what his supervisor meant. He just wasn't all that sure he cared anymore.

⁓

Dinner hadn't been too bad, Angela thought, while she cleaned up in the kitchen. True to her word, Mrs. Riordan had come downstairs to the dining room, where Angela had set her place with an ecru linen place mat and matching napkin, plus the good silver and Wedgwood china she'd carefully taken from the breakfront. A sautéed chicken breast and rice and broccoli might not have been considered a gourmet meal, but the strategically placed parsley and lemon wedges had helped make it look decent enough.

"Did she say anything?" Angela asked when Bobby pushed through the door from the dining room, carrying a plate and an empty water goblet.

"No, but she left you a handsome tip."

For a second she believed him, until his face cracked in one of those killer grins she so rarely witnessed. "Very funny," she said, taking the plate from him, trying not to trip over her own heartstrings.

"I didn't even see her," he said. "She had already made a beeline back upstairs. She must've liked the chicken, though, since she ate every bit."

"It wasn't bad," she said, carefully holding the delicate Wedgwood dinner plate under running water. Angela had taken her own dinner to the bedroom, as much to watch the six o'clock news as not to watch Bobby across the kitchen table from her during their meal. All afternoon she kept thinking about the way he'd looked when he was chopping that damn onion and how she'd rushed to comfort him and what a jerk she'd been. Again.

She'd looked out the kitchen window when she saw Doug and the other agent running down the driveway, and then she'd raced into the dining room to see what was happening out in front, half expecting to have to rush outside herself to assist in the subduing of an armed intruder. Not quite. The intruder turned out to be a bleached blonde driving a Barbie truck, no doubt the bimbo responsible for making Bobby reek of cheap perfume the night before.

"Did you ask her if she'd like us to take her out somewhere?"

His voice came from so close behind her that it startled Angela, and for a split second she thought he was referring to the bimbo before it dawned on her that he meant Mrs. Riordan. The plate she was washing was squeaky clean now, but she kept washing it anyway so as not to have to turn and face him.

"I asked," she said, "and she seemed to think it would be nice. Maybe next week. It sounds as if her bridge club tomorrow is enough socializing for the time being." She aimed a wicked little smile into the sink as she added, "You'll get to see your friend Bootsie again, big guy."

"I can't wait."

He had moved even closer, and Angela could feel the heat of his body seeping into the muscles of her back, threatening to melt her spine. Between that sensual heat and the warm water running over her hands, she felt literally caught between the devil and the deep blue sea. Bobby lifted her hair and pressed his lips to her neck so softly it made her want to weep.

"Don't," she said.

"God, baby, I—" His voice was rough with need.

"Stop it." She wrenched the water off, hand by hand, in order not to drop the plate, then moved away.

"Angela—"

"No." Snatching a dish towel from the counter, she wiped the wet plate with a vengeance, nearly rubbing off the blue and platinum bands along its rim. "No." She said it again, a refusal directed as much at herself as it was at Bobby. It would have taken so very little to change her mind. A glistening in his eyes. A catch in his voice. The slightest trembling of one of those hard-carved lips.

But he simply stared at her, eyes dry and fierce, his mouth battened down against any betrayal of weakness or wanting. And when he spoke, there was only anger in his tone.

"Screw it," he said. "If you want a divorce, go ahead. Call a lawyer. I won't give you any trouble. I'm done with this."

After he slammed out of the kitchen, Angela almost

couldn't breathe. It felt as if all the air had rushed out with him.

~

He slammed out the back door, then just stood in Crazy Daisy's backyard for a bleak moment, wanting to howl, needing to ram his fist into something or someone, wishing lightning would strike him dead. He didn't mean it, what he'd just said about divorce. He meant exactly the opposite, and yet the words had come ripping from his mouth as if somebody else had been speaking.

It was her *no* that had blinded him with anger, that had turned all the passion he was feeling to misspoken rage. No. It was so goddamned cold and final. Not spoken like a wife who merely wasn't in the mood, but like a stranger who considered his touch way out of line, inappropriate, and yeah, even insulting. On a par with the milkman. It made Bobby realize—hit him like a ton of cinder blocks, in fact—that Angela wasn't coming back. Their marriage was dead. Done. Over. Maybe it had been over since the day she walked out, and he'd been too stupid, too full of his own confidence—Angela probably would have said arrogance—to know it.

He sat on the hard bench in Daisy's gazebo for a long time, trying to come to grips with this revelation. The sky was blessedly overcast, so there was no sunset, thank God, to drag his mood down further. For a man who had a talent for picking up women, he sure didn't know how to keep them. How to keep *her*. There had never been anybody else he'd wanted to keep.

She's a keeper, bro. Wasn't that what Billy had said

when he'd met Angela that first weekend she came to visit her cat? And said it with such a warm and wistful expression on his face that Bobby was truly able to believe in his own feelings. He was in love with her! That fast! Billy knew it before he did.

Hell, Angela knew it before he did. He remembered they were sitting at the breakfast table in his apartment that first Monday morning after an entire weekend in bed—blissfully wrung out, sleep-deprived, hung over from touch and taste and all the trials and errors of two bodies coming together—when he'd become intensely depressed for no reason he could even begin to comprehend.

It didn't make any sense for a man who'd just had the most incredible sex of his entire life with a woman who was unimpressed with his badge because she wore one of her own, a woman who was responding to him as a man rather than a Superman or a Secret Service dick, a drop-dead gorgeous woman who was the emotional equivalent of an open book that he wanted to read again and again until he had her memorized.

"Bobby, don't look so sad," she had said, laughing as she spooned up another bite of cereal from her bowl. "It's only Monday morning, not the end of the world."

That's what it felt like, the end of the world, but he couldn't say it. There just weren't any words for utter desolation born of sheer happiness.

While she looked at him, Angela's expression had turned from delicious mirth to sweet sobriety. The most beautiful woman in the world was sitting across the table from him, wearing one of his shirts, and the pink abrasions from his weekend growth of beard glowing on her cheeks and chin, reaching out to him, taking his hand, and saying, "It's not the end of anything, sweetheart. It's just the beginning. For us, I mean. At least, if you want it to be."

All he could think then was that he wanted her forever and he needed a ring, so he reached into his bowl of cereal, came up with a soggy Cheerio, and asked her to be his wife. The fact that she said yes still amazed him nearly three years later.

Except she'd just said no.

The word kept echoing in his head like the report from a rifle, kept ricocheting in his gut, ripping him apart.

~

It was dark when Bobby eased himself out on the half foot of vacant space on his side of the little bed. On her side, Angela was burrowed in the covers, still as a corpse, but her vital warmth and sweet fragrance pervaded the sheets and the quilt and the pillows. He lay there quietly a moment, then drew in a breath so deep it sent a tremor through the mattress.

He wanted to tell her. Ah, God. More than tell her, he wanted to touch her, to do whatever the hell it was he'd done that first weekend that ended with her saying yes. He put out his hand, resting it lightly on the familiar curve of his wife's covered flank. She wanted a man who wore his heart on his sleeve. Bobby just didn't know how.

When she sighed softly in her sleep and seemed to relax more deeply under the warmth of his palm, he wondered if somehow she sensed his love, his need, all the things he couldn't communicate to her when she was awake.

"I need you, Ange. I feel like I'm dying without you." He wasn't even sure if he whispered the words aloud or merely thought them, but he knew he felt them. They were breaking his heart.

9

For a few minutes the next morning, Angela forgot she was on the brink of divorce. The alarm on her watch tweaked her into consciousness, she opened her eyes on her husband's sleeping face, and her heart blossomed inside her like an American Beauty rose.

Asleep, Bobby always seemed so vulnerable. All the hard angles softened. All the intensity turned to sensuousness. His eyelashes seemed infinitely long against the delicate skin beneath his closed eyes, and his mouth appeared gentle and sweet rather than the grim line it held during his wakefulness. He was relaxed. Unplugged. Off duty. Accessible in every way.

When he was sleeping, he reminded her of the little boy in the photograph that Billy had given her shortly after they were married. Bobby was about three years old in the faded Polaroid, playing with a pail and shovel in a sandbox, smiling like a frail-shouldered, shaggy-haired urchin at whoever held the camera. "This is just to prove that he was a kid once," Billy had told her, adding with a wink and a wistful smile, "For about five minutes, anyway."

That one faded print was the only picture of her husband when he was a child. There wasn't a single picture of Billy. In the Callifano house, the failure to take pictures of babies, toddlers, and teens on every conceivable occasion would have been considered child abuse. Her mother had a steamer trunk of photographs just of Angela alone, which she'd dragged out during one of their visits home.

"This is our Angela on her first day in kindergarten. Oh, and here she is on Halloween dressed as a gypsy princess. Such a cutie! This is Christmas morning, when little Miss Snoop tried to act surprised at the new bike Santa brought her."

"Enough already, Mom. Bobby really doesn't want to see six million pictures of me before I even had boobs." Angela had reached out to pull the album away, but Bobby wouldn't let her take it. He held on tight.

"What's this one, Rose?" he asked, apparently savoring every image and pose, maybe even considering them the outright manifestations of a parental love that he and Billy never had. Typical of Bobby, he never told her in so many words, but he did buy a camera, tons of film, and half a dozen photo albums as soon as they returned to D.C. But after Billy was killed, the camera went into a drawer and the empty albums gathered dust on a shelf.

It was all Angela could do not to edge closer to Bobby while he slept, to meld her warmth into his, to defend him from bad dreams and worse memories and all the things he wouldn't speak of. Instead, she carefully slid out from under the covers on her side of the bed, deciding to let Bobby sleep in. Lord knew he could use an extra hour or two after tossing and turning most of the night. It nearly broke her heart when she'd slipped the bedspread over him and he sleepily murmured her name.

By seven-thirty, she had brewed a pot of strong coffee and made a quart of orange juice. She put the last of Mrs. Ito's heavyweight, homemade bran muffins on a plate, then sat sipping her own coffee until it was time to take Mrs. Riordan's tray upstairs. She glanced at the blue binder, still in its place on the table, then idly thumbed through it until she came to the back page, where she'd written the three California attorneys' names and numbers.

Rod! She'd completely forgotten to call him last night. How could she have forgotten? A glance at her watch told Angela what she already knew. It was before six on the West Coast now, way too early to roust him out of bed. She knew, unless he had a studio call, Rod never awoke before ten or eleven. Her knowledge wasn't firsthand, of course, since she'd never spent the night with him, but he'd laughed once and claimed the reason there was a crack in dawn was because he'd put it there with a hammer when he worked so many early-morning jobs as a carpenter. Then he'd laughed at his own joke, which tended to annoy her when she didn't think it was all that funny. Come to think of it, none of Rod's jokes were all that funny. She wondered bleakly if Bobby's rare but brilliant wit hadn't spoiled her forever.

When did Rod say he was leaving for Mexico? Was it today? No, tomorrow, she was sure. Sort of. What was wrong with her, for heaven's sake, that she hadn't paid attention to her almost fiancé's schedule?

Nothing, she thought, answering her own question. Nothing was wrong with her. She'd just been distracted, that was all. Distracted and a little overwhelmed by her persistent sexual feelings for Bobby, by the memories they shared, and even by her useless, knee-jerk jealousy of a tacky blonde in a turquoise truck.

All of that had nothing whatsoever to do with her feelings for Rod Bishop. She was crazy about him. She adored his openness, his willingness to admit fear and pain and passion. Rod, if anybody, should have been the one to inspire rampant jealousy in her with his studio-imposed dates with beautiful, busty starlets and his legions of drooling, devoted fans. She should've been jealous of all that, shouldn't she? God. Why wasn't she? Instead, here she was being a green-eyed monster because Bobby was getting it on with some honky-tonk hussy in Horseblanket, Illinois.

At five till eight, rather than drive herself crazy with recrimination, Angela took Mrs. Riordan's tray upstairs. As on the previous day, the president's mother was already dressed, this time in a pink-and-gray tweed skirt and jacket that reminded Angela of a Chanel, probably the only designer whose name she knew or whose clothes she could identify. She was more familiar with designers of bullet-proof vests and holsters than she was with those of haute couture. Of course, that was bound to change in her future life with Rod.

"I trust you and your husband are comfortable in your quarters," Mrs. Riordan said, pulling a chair up to the table where Angela had placed the tray. "The bed is rather small, I realize."

"It's fine," Angela said, feeling her heart shift slightly in her chest as she pictured Bobby still asleep there, trying hard to ignore her reaction. "That's the last bran muffin, Mrs. Riordan. Mrs. Ito left her recipe. Shall I make more, or would you like a change?"

The woman looked at her as if Angela had just accused her of a capital crime rather than merely suggesting she alter her diet or change her routine. "I see no reason to change," she answered stiffly.

"Well, I'll bake some more, then. I don't suppose you'll want your regular lunch with your bridge group coming at eleven-thirty, will you?"

"No. If you'll prepare several trays of the crackers and cookies I bought yesterday, that ought to suffice. And the sherry, of course." A smile flirted with her lips. "Those old bags enjoy their afternoon tippling."

Angela laughed. "My mother plays canasta with a group of ladies who use it as an excuse to drink Manhattans and whiskey sours."

"Is your father still alive?"

When Angela responded yes, Mrs. Riordan nodded somberly and said, "Well, at least your mother has that. I do hope she appreciates it."

"She does, although since Pop retired, I think it's taking her a while to get used to having him underfoot all day long."

She nodded again, took a sip of her coffee, then returned the cup to its saucer. Her voice was level and stern when she said, "Underfoot, my dear Mrs. Holland, is far better than six feet under, and you may quote me on that."

"Yes, ma'am." Angela felt her cheeks flush. What an insensitive thing to say to a woman who so obviously missed her late husband. "I'm so sorry. I didn't mean—"

Mrs. Riordan dismissed her apology with a brusque wave of her hand. "Never mind about that. Speaking of husbands, is yours intending to hide from my friend Muriel this afternoon?"

"Muriel?"

"Muriel Rand," she said. "The old crone who let you in when you arrived the other day. Oh, wait. She probably introduced herself as Bootsie, didn't she? The silly fool."

Angela could hardly suppress a laugh. "She did appear to take quite a shine to Bobby. But I'm sure he can handle it." What's one more? she was tempted to add. For all she knew, Bootsie Rand was the great-grandmother of the blond bimbo. Tackiness no doubt ran in the family.

"Muriel tends to make a fool of herself in the company of men," Mrs. Riordan said as she broke off a bit of muffin and began to butter it. "Even when she was a girl. She was infatuated with my husband, you know, before he began courting me. I don't know that she's ever truly forgiven me for taking Charles away from her all those years ago."

"I think the senator made the right choice," Angela said.

"Yes, well, if he'd married Muriel, it would have altered the course of history, wouldn't it? There wouldn't be a President William Riordan in the White House now." She rolled her eyes. "Muriel's son is some sort of underworld figure in Florida these days. A bail bondsman or bounty hunter or some such thing. Of course, she does see him fairly regularly, especially since her cancer diagnosis. I wish I could say the same for my own son."

Bootsie had cancer! That probably explained her short, punk hair. She tucked that little kernel of information away in the back of her brain. As for the rest of Mrs. Riordan's statement, Angela merely nodded in agreement, not wanting to appear too knowledgeable about the president or his busy schedule. Bobby may have thought that Mrs. Riordan knew they were agents, but Angela wasn't so sure.

"I suppose you and Robert intend to have children one of these days," Mrs. Riordan said. "Or are you one of those modern, professional couples who only feel disdain for family life?"

"Oh, no, ma'am. Just the opposite." Her answer was as sudden as it was sincere until she reminded herself that the modern, professional couple in question would probably be visiting a divorce court rather than a maternity ward.

"That's good to hear," the president's mother said. "Well, that will be all, Angela."

"Yes, ma'am."

~

Bobby stood at the kitchen sink, sipping coffee, thinking it was a hell of a thing to feel like he had a hangover when he hadn't drunk so much as a drop the night before. This business with Angela was killing him.

Speak of the devil, she came into the kitchen from the dining room, looking happy to see him at first before she put on her "I hate you, Bobby" face.

"I was going to let you sleep in," she said.

"Gotta get ready for the big bridge game, babe."

"She wants the card table set up in the living room."

"Got it," he said.

"And one of us has to go to the grocery store for bran and molasses for muffins."

"I can do that."

"Fine."

She started pulling bowls from cabinets and utensils from drawers, while Bobby stood there wondering if they were speaking in code, where *card table* and *bran* and *molasses* stood for things that truly mattered, like *love* and *loyalty* and *desire*.

"I just learned something interesting about your pal Bootsie," Angela said, her head in the refrigerator while she searched for God only knows what.

"I can't wait to hear it."

She'd been searching for eggs, which she put on the counter alongside her other ingredients and equipment. "Well, two things, actually. She's being treated for cancer, and she was Senator Riordan's girlfriend before Daisy came along. What do you think of that?"

Bobby was about to reply when there was a knock on the back door. A second later, Doug Coulter whispered from the little mud room adjacent to the kitchen, "Is the coast clear?"

"All clear," Angela said. "Want some coffee, Doug?"

"No, thanks." He stared at Bobby for a moment while Bobby returned the stare over the rim of his cup. "How's it going?" Doug asked cautiously, as if he expected a bomb to go off in one of the cabinets at any second.

"Great," Bobby said. "Dandy." I'm sharing a bed with a woman who hates my guts and wants me out of her life so she can marry some goddamned fairy actor. I don't have the proper equipment to do my job adequately. How the hell do you think it's going?

"Good. Glad to hear it."

"How about some orange juice, Doug?" Angela asked.

"No, thanks. I just wanted to let you have a look at the

latest letter. They faxed it this morning." He stepped forward to hand the paper to Bobby, then continued, "And I wanted to let you know about some personnel changes. Seems there's been a death in Mike Burris's family, so he's out of here this morning, and his replacement's coming down from Chicago, due to arrive later this afternoon. It's nothing that'll affect the two of you."

The special agent in charge looked from Bobby to Angela. "So, what's on tap for the old lady . . . er, Mrs. Riordan today?"

"Bridge," Angela said, and as she elaborated Bobby studied the cutout words and images on the threatening letter.

Instead of using the word *Daisy,* the threatener had cut out a picture of the actual flower and pasted it before her last name. It struck him as playful, kind of like a rebus, one of those picture-and-word stories for kids. The guys in forensics claimed it was a professional job—no prints and no salient details in the paper—but it still seemed amateurish to Bobby, intended more to annoy than to harm. He was wondering if Mrs. Riordan might recognize some of the phrasing, such as "see you in hellfire" or "consider yourself warned," when Doug took the paper back.

"I'll file this in the trailer," he said. "No sense getting the president's mother all het up about something that's out of her control."

"Whatever you think," Bobby said. "Personally, I don't think she'd bat an eye at the news, and she might even appreciate knowing what's going on."

Doug gave him one of his "I need an antacid and I need it now" looks. "Well, that's already been decided in

Washington, hasn't it, Agent Holland? And in the Oval Office, I might add. The woman is not to know a thing about this. She's not to be disturbed."

Bobby held up a defensive hand. "Hey. No problem." He closed an imaginary zipper across his lips before giving his boss a little irritating grin. "That's why they call us secret agents, right?"

"You best remember it, too."

Doug Coulter shambled out the way he had come, muttering to himself. Then it took just about a second for Angela to explode.

"You really are trying to get us fired, aren't you? God, Bobby." She picked up a mixing bowl and thumped it on the counter for emphasis. "It might not hurt your career because of your seniority and the agency's whole macho good ol' boy thing, but my career's likely to disappear with a big, giant flush."

He poured another couple inches of coffee into his cup, then leaned back against the counter. "I wouldn't worry about it, darlin'."

"Don't you 'darlin'' me, you son of a bitch. I'm not one of your honky-tonk floozies, Bobby Holland. I'm your—" Her mouth snapped closed.

"My wife," Bobby said softly, not taking his eyes off her angry face, feeling his heart kick in an extra few beats, wondering if she'd slug him if he told her she was beautiful when she was mad, wondering if she loved him anymore, way too afraid to ask. "You're my wife."

Her eyes flashed. "I was going to say your partner, dammit. We're in this together, and that means that if you screw up by disobeying a direct order, you take me down with you."

He watched her rake her hair back with enough ferocity that the gesture nearly amputated her ears. A sudden lump formed in his throat that even a swig of coffee couldn't dislodge. His face felt strange, numb and almost out of his control, and he couldn't quite breathe right. If he lost Ange, his life wouldn't be worth living, job or no job. If only there were a way of making her know that. If only the words would come. The right words.

He swallowed hard and cleared his throat.

"Well?" Angela demanded.

His words and feelings weren't going to match. Bobby knew that as soon as he opened his mouth. "Will you quit worrying about this, for God's sake. You know Doug. Hell. He just feels obliged to growl every once in a while to show he's still in charge."

"But he *is* in charge, Bobby, so don't you dare say a word to Mrs. Riordan. Not one word. Even though you think she already knows. You promise me."

He lifted a hand with two fingers raised. "Scout's honor."

"Okay, then."

With another little crisis averted, she drew in a slow, calming breath, then chewed on her lower lip as she studied her bowls and cooking paraphernalia. It was too late now, Bobby realized, for whatever it was he'd wanted to say about loving her and dying if he lost her. Another moment of truth and reckoning had come and gone. Another opportunity to slap his goddamned heart on his goddamned sleeve had eluded him.

"How soon before you're ready to leave for the store?" she asked.

He drained his coffee. "How 'bout right now?"

It was a beautiful September morning with a clear, crystalline sky and just a little bite in the air. Bobby opened all the windows in the Taurus wagon and pressed his foot to the floor, sampling McCray's souped-up engine. It wasn't often that he missed Texas, but every so often, on mornings like this, he craved a road straight as a ruler and nothing in the distance but distance.

He remembered the morning when he was sixteen and his old man had pulled him over on the blacktop between Wishbone and Hectorville. Tom Jessup had punched on his lights and siren and floored his big Crown Victoria until he just about drove up the tailpipe of Bobby's rusted-out Datsun.

"Goin' a little fast, aren't you, boy?" His father had bent and braced his meaty, tattooed forearms on the driver's window, squinting in at Bobby. "It's too early to have a hot date, ain't it?"

"Yes, sir." He'd stared straight ahead, refusing to meet the eyes identical to his own, once again limiting his speech to "Yes, sir" and "No, sir" because if he ever said what he felt, he'd wind up killing the son of a bitch and spending the rest of his life in Huntsville, and then where would Billy be?

He blew by cornfields now, only easing off the gas when he reached the train tracks, the big blue Kiwanis billboard, and another one that cheerfully proclaimed, "Hassenfeld, Home of the Valkyries, Welcomes You." Well, it was nice to feel welcome someplace.

It took him half an hour in the Save Mart because Angela's list had multiplied from a single box of bran to an entire page of highly specific items. After all, a woman who always ordered a steak "medium rare but more medium than rare" and a salad with dressing on the side couldn't be expected to write a simple dozen eggs on her list. It had to be a dozen extra-large eggs, and the milk had to be 2 percent, and the salt iodized, and the pound cake Sara Lee. Christ. Maybe that was why he loved her so much. After living with Treena Holland, the queen of indifference, maybe he was hard-wired for loving finicky women.

He put the groceries on his credit card, kept the receipt for his expense record, then crammed the paper bags into the back of the Taurus and slammed down the hatch. He wasn't quite ready to go back to the Riordan place and take up his role as emotionally stunted bodyguard, so he parked on Main Street, got a cup of coffee at the little café, and sat in the town square awhile, pondering the granite memorial and communing with the long-dead veterans of various wars.

Maybe he should have stayed in the army, he thought, happily ensconced in one BOQ after another. He'd probably be a colonel by now, which would make Billy a major. It would have been something, going back to Wishbone for Tom Jessup's funeral in their dress uniforms, all that brass blazing in the Texas sunshine. As it turned out, Bobby had been in the Netherlands with the president, and Billy had been knee-deep in training in Georgia when their father died, and they'd missed his funeral completely. Not that they would have been welcome, anyway.

For the very first time, he found himself wondering what their old man would have thought about Billy's death if he had lived to see it. Would he have been secretly pleased that his offspring showed courage and devotion to duty and was buried with full military honors at Arlington? Or would he have been relieved that one bastard boy was down, with only one to go?

Angela had asked him once if he didn't want to go home just one more time to at least make sure his mother's grave was the way it ought to be. Grave sites were big in the Callifano family. Angelo and Rose already had their side-by-side plots picked out. They bugged the groundskeeper regularly about the health of the maple tree that would eventually shade them, and the kids all had to promise that they would make sure the stones stayed clean.

"No way," he'd told her. He didn't much care whether his mother's grave was up to snuff or not. He'd done his filial duty by making sure they got the wrong date on her marker. Treena had always lied about her age, so Bobby had made sure the stone was inscribed 1949 instead of 1947, the actual year of her birth.

"She's lucky I didn't have a six-pack bronzed in her memory," he had added.

"That's pretty heartless, Bobby," Angela had said.

Maybe so. Hell, maybe he didn't even have a heart, he thought now. Or if he had, maybe it broke eleven months, three weeks, ago and he was just surviving on the remnants. Any way he looked at it, this whole thing just struck him as a losing proposition. Ange just wanted more than he was capable of giving. He could no more wear his heart on his sleeve than he could wear a goddamned dress.

He crumpled his empty cup in his fist and tossed it in

a trash can on the way back to the car. Then, just as he was sticking the key into the door, something caught his eye across the street. Wedged in between Boechler's Pharmacy and Hagemann's Real Estate was a little place called the Tattoo Parlor, and in its window hung a big red paper heart just above a sign that said "Come In. We're Open. "

Son of a gun.

~

Daisy Riordan came downstairs at eleven, determined not to find fault with whatever Angela had done with the refreshments, even if it meant biting her tongue until she drew blood. The young woman wasn't a trained domestic, after all, and she seemed to be sincerely attempting to do her best. Anyone who peppered a tuna salad with raisins was certainly making a genuine effort at being creative, if nothing else.

Actually, the trays she'd laid out on the kitchen counter didn't look too bad. The heavily embossed silver wasn't what Daisy would have chosen for the little Italian cookies, but that was all right. The Quimper serving plate was fine for the macaroons. Lord knew Muriel and Norma and Adele weren't coming to be impressed. Norma and Adele were coming to play cutthroat cards, and Muriel was coming in order not to swill sherry alone, and to irritate her ancient friends in the process.

Daisy did a little rearranging of crackers around a cut-glass bowl of dip, then licked a dab of it from her finger. It needed more Tabasco. Young people failed to appreciate the inevitable decline of taste buds after a certain age. She wasn't sure when she had passed that invisible barrier, exactly. The day after Charles's funeral, she had awakened a crotchety old woman. She'd always been crotchety, though she preferred to consider it discriminating, but she'd never been old—really, really old—until that morning. Dear God. She'd taken one look in a mirror that morning, then climbed back into bed, and hadn't left it for the next two weeks.

People seemed to think her abnormal for staying home as much as she did. Little did they know what a temptation it was to stay in bed with the covers pulled over her head, day after day. When she awoke, if she didn't immediately bathe and dress, there was always the danger of just not getting up at all. Suicide by bedsores. How cowardly was that?

"I didn't hear you come in the kitchen, Mrs. Riordan." Angela appeared from around the corner, looking young and lovely, with hair freshly brushed and lipstick newly applied.

"Everything appears in order," Daisy said, gesturing to the trays on the counter. "The sherry glasses are in the breakfront. I wonder if you'd—"

"I've already washed them and put them on the liquor cart in the living room," she said. "I was just getting ready to set up your card table in there."

"It's rather heavy. Perhaps you should have your husband see to it."

"Bobby's not back from town yet." Creases of annoyance dug in between the young woman's eyes and at the corners of her mouth. "I'm sure I can handle it. Maybe you could just show me where you'd like it set up?"

"Yes, of course."

Daisy made her way toward the living room, wondering if Robert was actually being derelict in his official Secret Service duties or if his being in town had something to do with her own protection. She refused to even contemplate that he was having some lurid assignation with the little tramp in the turquoise truck who'd come sniffing around the day before.

"The card table is in the hall closet, Angela, and I'd like it right over there." She pointed to the open space behind her blue-and-beige floral sofa. "I always use the chair from the cherry secretary over there. Dining room chairs will do for the others. I wouldn't want them to get so comfortable that they overstayed their welcome."

The doorbell rang, then rang again immediately. Muriel. God in heaven, the woman couldn't do anything simply. Daisy looked at her watch and scowled to see that the silly old bag was ten minutes early. If she said, "The more, the sherrier" as she crossed the threshold, cancer or not, Daisy was going to throttle her.

"I'll get that," Angela said.

"That isn't necessary."

Despite a forty-some-year disparity in their ages, Daisy and Angela arrived at the front door simultaneously, and their hands collided reaching for the knob. Angela, intelligent young woman that she was, drew back, and Daisy opened the door.

"Surprise!" Muriel exclaimed.

She might as well have said "Trick or treat!" for the fright mask of wrinkles on her face and the spiked orange hair that reminded Daisy of an electrocution in progress.

"You're early," Daisy snapped, stepping back to let her old friend and nemesis in.

"Yes, I know I'm early, but I didn't think you'd mind, considering what I've brought with me. Norma called me this morning. She's down with a sinus infection, poor baby, so I invited someone very special to join us."

"Who?" After all these years, Muriel knew damn well that Daisy didn't like surprises, particularly when they were human.

Muriel reached behind her, pulling at somebody's sleeve. "Come, come. Daisy won't bite, in spite of what you might have heard. Or if she does, I assure you, Gerald, she's had her shots."

From the look on the gentleman's face as he stepped forward, Daisy couldn't tell if he was inherently shy or merely horrified to find himself in the presence of, indeed the grasp of, Muriel "Bootsie" Rand. He was tall, with a fine head of silver hair framing a quite handsome face that time had chiseled rather than ravaged like her own. His eyes were the deep blue of a much younger man. And one of those eyes winked at her, not like a lascivious old man, but like a young and hopeful suitor. Daisy's heart blipped oddly, enough for her to imagine for a second that she was suffering sudden angina.

"Daisy Riordan," Muriel cooed, "I'd like you to meet Professor Gerald DuMaurier Gerrard."

Daisy grudgingly extended her hand in greeting. "What an unexpected pleasure."

"Well, let the poor man in, Daisy," Muriel said. "He's already been checked over by your goons, dear. Head to toe. He's perfectly safe." She angled her spiked head toward two young men on the sidewalk. "I offered to let them frisk me, but they declined. I must have an honest face."

"Either that, or they didn't want to touch you without latex gloves, Muriel," Daisy said. "Won't you come in, Professor?"

10

It was a little after noon when Bobby pulled into the driveway and saw Angela with her hands on her hips, standing in front of the garage, looking like a human auger just waiting—dying!—to take a bite out of him.

Okay. The tattoo had probably been a bad idea. He wasn't the kind of person who made rash decisions or did things on the spur of the moment. Other than his proposal of marriage, this was probably the only other impulsive thing he'd ever done in his life. When he'd blithely walked into the tattoo parlor, he didn't have a clue what was involved or how long the process would take.

Tiny, the sole proprietor and tattoo artist in residence, who looked like a guy who'd quit his day job as a linebacker for the Chicago Bears and currently moonlighted as a Hell's Angel, told Bobby that the fully shaded red heart job that he'd described shouldn't take more than twenty minutes.

"Hardly any line work," Tiny had said. "It's your dragons and your gargoyles that take time. A red heart? Hell. Piece of cake. Get in the chair."

That was where it started going downhill faster than a kid on a tin tray. The chair Tiny pointed to was one of those dentist deals, and Bobby broke out in a cold sweat as soon as he slung himself out in the damned thing.

"First I'm gonna shave your arm," Tiny said. "Right or left?"

For a moment Bobby couldn't remember which side his real heart was on, but then he felt it pounding in the left side of his chest. "Left."

Judging from the way the linebacker wrenched up the sleeve of his polo shirt, Bobby fully expected the disposable razor to cut his biceps to shreds, but big Tiny's touch was surprisingly deft, even gentle, so much so that Bobby began to worry about more than the dentist chair or the ghoulish array of tools on a nearby counter. Those particular worries only increased when the man began to massage a floral-scented ointment into his arm.

But before Bobby was able to clear his throat and say something macho like "How 'bout those Cubs?" Tiny had pushed away his stool and turned to his counter full of instruments. "Relax," he said. "It'll take me just a sec to prepare the design transfer."

"Sure." The word came out an octave below Bobby's normal range. He hardly recognized his own voice.

"New in town?" Tiny asked over his massive shoulder.

"Yeah." He thought that might be the right time to offer his résumé. West Point. Army intelligence. The Secret Fucking Service. Then, just in case he wimped out, he could claim it was for national security reasons.

With the same gentle touch, Tiny applied a small paper to his arm and after a minute pulled it away. "That's how she'll look," he said. "Okay?"

Bobby glanced down at the purplish-blue outline of a

heart, small as a baby's fist on his biceps. "This is permanent," he said. "Right?"

"Right."

What the hell. It was probably the closest he'd ever get to wearing his heart on his sleeve, he figured. "Go for it."

"All riiight! One more sec while I fix my inks."

The funny thing was, Bobby thought now as he continued down the drive toward his wife's ferocious glare, he had started to relax in the chair while Tiny putzed around with bottles and a harmless-looking little machine no bigger than a staple gun. Even when the man swiveled his stool around and swerved toward him with the implement, Bobby hadn't batted an eye.

"Ever had a tetanus shot?" Tiny asked, pressing the cold metal to his arm.

"Yeah."

"Well, this doesn't bite any worse than that. Except it keeps biting, if you know what I mean. You'll get used to it after a minute, man."

Jesus. Bobby had never passed out in his life, but the next thing he knew Tiny was waving an ammonia capsule under his nose and looking blurred and worried and pretty goddamned amused all at the same time.

"You wanna do this some other time, man?" Tiny asked.

"No. Finish it."

So now, of course, he was going to have to explain the bandage on his left arm to the woman who looked like she'd just as soon sink her teeth into his right one.

"Where have you been?" Angela practically spit the words at Bobby as he climbed out of the car. Her tone softened a little when she asked, "What's wrong with your arm?"

"I snagged it on a . . . uh . . . thing at the supermarket."

"What kind of *thing*?"

He babbled something about side doors and faulty copper weather stripping and suing the hell out of Save Mart. She didn't believe him for a second. Bobby was a rotten liar, probably because he was such an innately honest man.

"Let me see it," she said, reaching to peel the square bandage back. "You should probably get a tetanus booster, Bobby. Did you need stitches?"

"Don't worry about it, Ange." He jerked his arm out of her grasp. "It's just a scratch. It took a while to stop the bleeding, is all. Just leave it the hell alone." He slapped away her insistent hand, then stalked to the back of the little station wagon and opened the hatch.

It irked her no end that he seemed perturbed with her when it was she who had every legitimate reason to be pissed at him for abandoning her so long.

"Well, I wish you had called me. I really could have used a little backup with this bridge club deal."

"What do you mean?"

She dragged back a hank of hair. "I mean Mrs. Riordan's guests aren't the three harmless little old ladies we were expecting. Your friend Bootsie showed up with a man."

"What do you mean, a man?"

"Jesus, Bobby." He could be so dense sometimes for such a smart guy. "I mean a man. One of those tall people who wear pants and carry their change in their pockets. A man!"

The cop look claimed his face. "Did you pat him down?"

Angela's hands flailed helplessly. "Pat him down? Are you kidding me? What was I supposed to say? 'Excuse me, sir. I'm the maid, and I'd like to check your clothes and body cavities for dirty rags or unauthorized cleaning products'? Anyway, I'm pretty sure Doug and Mike gave him a once-over before he came inside."

"Pretty sure?" He swore with such ferocity that she actually took a step back. "Where is this guy right now?" he demanded.

"In the living room playing cards. I've been keeping an eye on him, Bobby, for heaven's sake. But when I saw the car turn into the driveway, I wanted to give you a heads-up."

She hadn't screwed up *that* royally. Angela knew procedure inside and out, and she also knew that following it under these circumstances would blow her cover. She had allowed a stranger into the Riordan house without double-checking for weapons after Doug's initial check, but what else could she have done? She'd then left her protectee alone with him. Well, for all intents and purposes alone. What good would Bootsie and the other old lady be if Professor Gerald Gerrard pulled a knife or a gun?

"I'm sorry," she said to Bobby's back because he was already sprinting toward the rear door of the house. "Shit," she muttered then, hurrying in his wake.

When she caught up with him in the hallway just beyond the kitchen door, Bobby had already removed his gun from his ankle holster and had it shoved in his belt at the small of his back. He motioned her close and whispered, "You go on in. Ask if they want cookies or drinks or something. Be sure to see how this guy reacts, and yell if anything seems hinky."

"You don't actually think—"

He cut her off. "Just do it, Ange."

Angela knew the difference between a direct order and a suggestion, and since Bobby was the senior agent here, she did exactly as she was told.

Only Bootsie wanted a refill on the sherry. The professor wasn't drinking anything and seemed not the least bit unsettled by Angela's presence, even though he did put his cards down several times in order to wipe his spectacles. Adele was comfortable enough. Mrs. Riordan, actually, was the only one who struck Angela as uncomfortable. There was an air of urgency in the way she raked in the cards, as if she were playing in a burning building and couldn't leave until the game was done.

"He seemed okay," she told Bobby in the hallway. "Mrs. Riordan seems on edge, but I'm guessing it's just because she doesn't like surprises, and—trust me—the professor was a big one."

"I'll wait here until it breaks up," he said. "Maybe you want to bring the groceries in from the car."

Maybe she wanted to be on a beach in Mexico, Angela thought churlishly, except Rod wasn't on the coast, but inland in Chihuahua or wherever it was that they filmed all those westerns.

"Call me if you need me," she said. "I'll be in the kitchen baking bran muffins and cleaning my gun."

Daisy didn't slam the door exactly, but she closed it with authority on her departing guests before peering out the sidelight to watch that fool Muriel link her arm through the professor's and dangle from his sleeve like a wretched Kewpie doll the man had just won at a fair. She might have muttered an oath if it hadn't been for the wraithlike presence of Robert, looming in the hallway behind her. Even as she ignored him, she wondered how he was enjoying his job of keeping her safe from idiots and fools.

It was three-thirty. She'd missed her nap, and it was too late now to even think about closing her eyes, because that would guarantee her wakefulness throughout the night. If there was any good news, it was that she wouldn't have to play bridge again for an entire week. Norma's sinus difficulties would surely be cured by then, so she'd never have to see Gerald Gerrard again.

As Daisy turned toward the staircase, Robert's shadow edged back into the hallway. She was half tempted to ask to borrow his gun. Whether she wanted to use it on Muriel or herself, she hadn't quite decided yet.

Hauling a man into her house! Plopping him down right under her very nose! Muriel must have lost the only marble she had left.

With ten minutes remaining before she had to take her muffins out of the oven, Angela sat at the kitchen table, paging through one of Mrs. Riordan's cookbooks, sinking deeper into a slough of domestic depression. What she wanted to do was run out to a KFC and bring back dinner in a couple of buckets, but somehow she didn't think the president's mother would be terribly pleased with extra-crispy chicken, coleslaw, and a pool of gravy in a crater of mashed potatoes.

After the card players left and Mrs. Riordan went upstairs, Bobby had gone out to the surveillance trailer to begin the process of checking out Gerald DuMaurier Gerrard. Angela was sure the man would come out squeaky clean. If he'd wanted to kill Crazy Daisy badly enough, he probably wouldn't have hesitated at taking out Adele and Bootsie with her. He'd had the opportunity, after all.

She wondered if Bobby would report her for dereliction of duty. He'd done it before with colleagues who'd messed up. Let him. In fact, if Doug canned her within the next half hour, she wouldn't have to cook dinner. That alone would be a paltry price to pay for a ticket back to L.A.

She returned to her uninspired perusal of the cookbook, waiting for Bobby's return. When he walked into the kitchen, he didn't look like a man who'd just ratted on his partner.

"Did you find out anything?" she asked.

He shook his head. "Seems our professor is just what he claims to be. I talked to the dean at the college. They hired him away from Harvard with a nice salary and the title of professor emeritus, which basically means that Gerrard gets to give one or two lectures a semester while lending his name to boost the image of their faculty. He's the real deal."

Thank God. Angela wanted to moan with relief in light

of her screwup. "That's good," she said, avoiding Bobby's gaze so he couldn't read her concern. The man might not be able to express his own emotions, but he could be pretty astute when it came to others.

"Hey," he said softly, settling into the chair across from hers. "I didn't say anything to Doug, if that's what you're thinking. You did the best you could under the circumstances, Ange. Undercover's different from a regular detail. Don't worry about it, okay?"

"Okay." She sighed. Undercover, in her case, was just another name for scut work. "So, what do you want for dinner?"

He smiled. "What was that dish you used to make with hamburger and tomatoes and those little green things?"

"What little green things?"

"I don't remember what they're called. They looked like little green rabbit droppings."

"I never in my life cooked anything that remotely resembled rabbit droppings."

"Yes, you did. They came in a little jar—"

"Capers," she exclaimed, suddenly realizing what he meant.

"That's it."

"They don't look like rabbit droppings."

"Yes, they do." He laughed. "Little perfect pellets from little green bunnies."

"I thought you liked my cooking," she said a bit indignantly, rising from her chair and stalking toward the refrigerator while Bobby kind of chortled behind her.

"I do like your cooking, babe. That dish was one of my favorites. What was it called?"

"Rabbit-poop stew," she said, her voice muffled

slightly because her head was halfway inside the refrigerator. "I'm so glad you liked it."

"Seriously, Ange. What was it?"

"Picadillo," she said through clenched teeth.

"Yeah. That was it. Make that."

"I can't." Angela tossed a bunch of broccoli onto the counter, then put her head back into the fridge. "I don't have any ground beef. Or capers. Or rabbit turds, as you so clearly and fondly remember."

"Ange."

She didn't hear him get up or cross the room, but suddenly he was right behind her, one hand on each of her hips. She could almost feel a hot blue ribbon of electricity arcing through her pelvis. When she righted herself, his hands came away, but Bobby didn't step back. Angela could feel the warmth of his belt buckle on her spine and his breath on her neck.

"Angela," he said softly.

It was one of the first things about him that she'd loved, the sound of her name just brushed with the remnants of his Texas accent. She'd never really liked her name until Bobby spoke it almost three years ago. She stared straight ahead into the brightly lit shelving, reading the expiration date on the carton of eggs rather than allow herself to entertain the notion suddenly sizzling in her brain.

Bobby Holland had the world's best hands. Such competent hands that knew instinctively where to go and what to do, and just exactly when. He was her husband. She was his wife. What would be so wrong if—

Now he was gathering back the hair at the nape of her neck, his touch so gentle it was comparable to a breeze.

"Why don't you just sit, Ange, and let me do the cooking tonight?"

That brought her back to her senses as well as any splash of ice cold water could have. "I don't think Mrs. Riordan mentions baloney sandwiches and potato chips anywhere in her little blue book." She reached into the meat keeper for the steaks she'd bought the day before and tossed them onto the counter next to the broccoli.

"I'll do it, Ange. How hard can it be to cook broccoli?"

"Too hard for somebody who was eating Cheerios for dinner until I came along," she said, nudging her hip into his to throw him off balance just enough for her to elude him on her way to the sink, where she turned on the cold water and let it flow over her wrists just to make sure her temperature didn't shoot up again.

"Let me help you, then," he said. "Just tell me what to do."

Stop being such a devastating combination of sexy and sweet. Quit trying to reel me in with those warm, wonderful hands, only to make me regret it when you turn back into a cold brick wall. Leave me alone!

"How about going upstairs and asking Mrs. Riordan if she wants to have her dinner in the dining room again tonight?"

"Easy enough," he said, already on his way to the door. "Be right back."

"Take your time," Angela answered with a sigh. Take an hour. A couple years.

He had only been gone a few minutes when there was a knock on the back door. Angela put down the stalk of broccoli she was rinsing and called, "Come in," fully expecting to see Doug's gray brush cut and glum face in the doorway. To her surprise, however, the face that appeared there was framed by soft chestnut hair and was very familiar, not to mention quite pretty.

"Hi, Angela. Remember me?"

Oh, yeah. She hadn't seen Tricia Yates since they'd gone through nine arduous weeks of training together at the federal facility in Georgia. Maybe "together" was the wrong word. They'd been fierce competitors from day one, and Tricia, with her almost boyish, lithely muscled, long-legged body, had bested Angela in every category but one. Firearms. Angela used to pretend she was firing her weapon right between the agile brunette's big gooey brown eyes.

"Tricia," she said now with what she considered the proper amount of good cheer as she reached for a towel to dry her dishpan hands. "I thought you were working in Miami." Angela extended her hand, then watched the agent grimace slightly as she shook her still-damp fingers.

"I was in Miami, but I've wanted protective duty for a long time, so they pulled me in on this," she said. "How's it going?"

"Fine. We haven't had any problems on the inside."

Tricia cocked her head, exposing a little diamond stud in her ear. Suddenly Angela remembered that the woman's navel sported a small gold ring, and she remembered Tricia's nickname during training—the Man-Eater. Back then she'd been the Secret Service equivalent of a hungry Hollywood starlet.

"No, I meant how's it going with you?" Tricia said. "With you and Bobby Holland. I heard you were separated."

"Not at the moment," Angela replied, almost sweetly.

"Yeah. That's what he told me when he came out to the trailer. Oh. That reminds me." She reached into the pocket of the navy blazer that matched her short, tight little navy skirt. "Bobby wanted a copy of Gerald Gerrard's dossier as soon as it came through on the fax. This is all we've got so far." She handed a single sheet of paper to Angela.

"Thanks. I'll see that he gets it." When Angela noticed the way Tricia was scoping out the door that led to the hallway where Bobby had disappeared, she added, "You probably shouldn't stay here much longer, just in case Mrs. Riordan comes in."

"Right." The agent's eyes snapped back to Angela's face. "Well, it's good seeing you again, Angela. Maybe we can do a run together or something while we're here. You do still run, don't you?"

"Oh, sure." The last time they'd run had been in a 5K toward the end of their training. Tricia had beaten her by a solid ten seconds. But only because her legs were about a mile longer than Angela's. "That would be fun," she said. Almost as much as swimming in a vat of boiling oil.

"Great. See you later, then."

"See you."

Angela didn't miss the quick little sneer her colleague aimed at the broccoli on the countertop before she turned to leave.

~

The president's mother had a bee of indiscernible origin up her behind. Bobby, at any rate, didn't have a clue why the woman was in such a foul mood, insisting that not only was she not going downstairs for dinner, but that she might never set foot outside of her bedroom ever again.

When he took her dinner up at six o'clock, she had the venetian blinds battened down so tight that he could hardly see where to put her tray.

"How 'bout a little light on the subject?" he asked, quite affably, he thought, and Crazy Daisy nearly bit his head off with her abrupt "Get out."

"Yes, ma'am." He was at the door, leaving, when he heard a vehicle pull into the drive.

"Now who the devil is that?" she snapped. "Robert, take a look out the window and tell me who it is."

"Yes, ma'am." Bobby lifted a slat and peered out in time to see two of his colleagues descend upon the unwitting young driver of a floral delivery truck. One of those colleagues, Tricia Yates, he couldn't help but notice, was wearing a very short skirt that added about half a mile to each of her shapely legs.

"Well? Who is it?" Mrs. Riordan demanded.

"Flowers."

"Flowers! What fool would send me flowers at this time of night?"

Bobby kept looking out the window at Agent Yates's legs. "Well, first off, Mrs. Riordan, it's not exactly night," he drawled, "and how do you know they're for you?"

She gave a nasty little cluck with her tongue. "I suppose the poor delivery person is being put through the third degree by a squad of Secret Service people."

"Looks like it." He was thinking there was some history between Angela and this Tricia Yates. Whatever it was, he couldn't recall, but he knew his wife always snorted whenever the woman's name came up. Those legs, and the agent's willingness to show them off, undoubtedly had a lot to do with it, he decided.

"Well, you might as well go down and get them," Mrs. Riordan said, her irritability obviously giving way to curiosity.

By the time Bobby trotted down the stairs, the delivery boy was pressing on the doorbell. Bobby handed the kid two bucks, made a mental note to enter it in his expense book, and carried the big paper-wrapped package up to Mrs. Riordan's room. It didn't escape his notice that she had switched on a few lamps, the better to see the flowers she wasn't at all interested in.

It suddenly occurred to him that they just might not be for Mrs. Riordan. Christ. What if they were for Angela from Harry Hollywood? He was ripping off the little envelope stapled to the paper wrapper just as Mrs. Riordan said, "Well, go ahead. Read it. What fool are they from?"

Bobby pulled out the card and breathed a sigh of relief. They weren't from Rod Bishop. "It says, 'Thank you for a lovely afternoon, Margaret,' and it's signed G. G."

"Oh."

He didn't think he'd ever heard surprise, annoyance, and pleasure all combined in such a short little word before. He nearly laughed while he tore off the paper cone to reveal the huge bouquet. Man, if Angela thought he had a problem expressing his finer emotions, it didn't hold a candle to Crazy Daisy's reticence.

"Any place in particular you want me to put these?" he asked her.

"Yes," she said. "Downstairs."

"You sure?" he asked.

"Quite."

⁓

"Your dinner's keeping warm in the oven," Angela said when he came back into the kitchen. "Who was at the front door?"

"Not who," he said, putting the huge bouquet on the table in front of her. "What." He watched her face light up.

"Oh, aren't they beautiful?" She leaned forward over her plate, burying her nose in the blooms. "Let me guess. They're from Gerald Gerrard."

"Yep."

"Doesn't Mrs. Riordan want them in her room?"

"Nope. At least not tonight." He folded a dish towel to take his plate out of the oven, then took a seat at the table across from Angela, pushing the pretty flowers aside so he could see her even prettier face.

"That was sweet of the professor," she said as a touch of mist glistened in her eyes.

Bobby picked up his knife and began to cut his steak. "You think so? That surprises me, Ange. I never knew you cared all that much for extravagant but meaningless gestures."

He meant it as a joke really, but Angela didn't laugh. Her expression turned wistful, almost sad.

"Well, then, I guess you don't know me as well as you thought you did, Bobby. Besides—" She gestured toward the bouquet. "This isn't meaningless. It says he cares about her."

"I guess." He chewed on the leathery steak a while, wondering how somebody so precise about ordering steak in a restaurant could get it so wrong at home. Then he forked up some broccoli and refrained from his usual anti-vegetable remarks. All he wanted to do was please her, to make her happy. If eating broccoli would accomplish that, then so be it. He swallowed the nasty stuff like a good soldier.

"You never gave me flowers," she said, her voice soft and sad but still accusing as her gaze floated past his shoulder.

His gut instinct was to blow up, to crash his fist on the table and say that he guessed ol' Rod probably sent her a dozen goddamned roses a day. To shout that if he'd known she'd wanted flowers, he'd have given her a fucking field full on a daily basis. To roar that when it came to pleasing women, he seemed to do just fine except when it came to his wife.

But Bobby didn't blow up. He just sat there for a long moment, suddenly drained of energy and hope, no longer sure he had enough breath left to speak, much less yell. He pushed his plate away and stood.

"No, I never did give you flowers, Ange. Hell, baby, I gave you me. I always thought that was enough."

Before she could say anything in response, Bobby walked out of the room.

11

Bobby knocked on the door of the surveillance trailer, then stepped inside to find that the guys who should've gone off duty, back to their budget motel rooms and pay-per-view movies and a couple relaxing beers, hadn't. The reason they were still hanging around was obvious. Agent Tricia Yates.

The brunette was currently ensconced in front of the bank of monitors, scanning their screens, while every other eye in the room was scanning her. There was a time when the sight of such long lithe legs would have had Bobby immediately thinking about them being wrapped in a pretty bow around his neck. Not at the moment, though.

"Is Doug around?" he asked, on the off chance anybody was paying attention to him.

"In the back office," one of the young turks replied, jerking a thumb toward the rear of the trailer.

He knocked on the door, then opened it to discover his supervisor leaning back in his chair with his boots up on the desk. "Got a minute, Doug?" he asked.

"Hell, I've got all night, son. If you're gonna ask about reassignment, though, I've got to tell you that your wife just beat you to it." He aimed a dark scowl at the phone on the desktop. "I just this minute hung up."

Bobby slumped in the chair on the opposite side of the desk and shook his head. Never in his life had he had a problem he hadn't been able to solve, whether it meant using his head or his fists. But this . . . It was like being in the middle of the ocean, trying to latch on to twigs. Drowning.

"I'll tell you just what I told Angela. I don't like playing baby-sitter to a couple of kindergartners. And I don't like supervising agents who can't put their own personal difficulties aside for as long as it takes to do a job." Special Agent in Charge Coulter let a growl rumble through his throat. "You hear what I'm saying here?"

Bobby nodded.

"I also told Angela that as soon as we arrived here, I anticipated these difficulties, and I put in a request to have the two of you replaced asap. The wheels in Washington are still grinding on that, I'm sorry to say."

"Okay."

Doug growled again. "I just hope the two of you don't screw this up in the meantime, and wind up sending your résumés to police departments in cities with populations of less than five thousand because nobody else would be crazy enough to touch you, if you catch my drift."

The older agent reached into the breast pocket of his shirt for a cigarette, glared at it, then lobbed it into a trash can. With a weary sigh, he angled back farther in his chair. "Look, Bobby, just between you and me, I think Materro jumped the gun on this threat deal. Personally, I don't think it's all that serious. But the director's new, he wants to look good to the president, and what better way than to protect and preserve the man's elderly mother's life."

It was Bobby's turn to sigh. "So, I'm here suffering the tortures of the damned for the sake of somebody's political agenda?"

"I'd put money on it."

Bobby swore.

"That's not to say I won't put your ass in a sling if you don't stick to proper procedures, however. You and Angela both." He dug another cigarette out of his pocket, and this time reached for a lighter. "Should've had more goddamn sense than to marry another agent, the both of you. I hope that's not a mistake either one of you will make a second time."

Bobby left the office just as Special Agent Coulter snapped his lighter and succumbed to his need for nicotine.

Only one young turk remained in the outer office, where he sat staring glumly at the monitors while Agent Yates poured herself a cup of coffee.

"Want some?" She gestured toward Bobby with the glass pot in her hand. "Some nights are longer and tougher than others."

Wasn't that the truth? "No, thanks," he said.

"I asked Angela to join me if she wants a running partner," the woman said. "The same goes for you, Bobby." She cocked her head and let her lips slide into a grin. "I'd give you a pretty good workout."

"I bet you would, darlin'," he said, pushing out the door.

Angela was just hanging up the wall phone in the kitchen when Bobby came back in. For the second time in half an hour, she had tried politely to convey Daisy Riordan's less than polite refusal to speak with Professor Gerald Gerrard. The least she could have done, in Angela's opinion, was to thank the poor man for the flowers.

"Poor old guy," she muttered, hooking the receiver onto its cradle.

"Who's that?" Bobby asked.

"The professor." She gave a little sigh of disgust. "Mrs. Riordan won't speak to him, and the word *no* doesn't seem to be in his vocabulary. He's a persistent old codger."

Bobby pulled a chair out from the table, turned it, and straddled it with his arms braced on the back. He looked tired, she thought. The lines in his face ran deeper than usual, and his mouth seemed weighed down at the corners. Her husband never wore exactly what she'd call a cheerful countenance, but right now he looked seriously depressed.

"Doug's doing his best to find replacements for us," he said quietly.

"I know. I talked to him right after you left." Rather than just stand there looking at his woebegone face, she began clearing off the tray she had brought back downstairs. Mrs. Riordan had hardly touched her steak. Neither had Bobby. Good thing this wasn't a real job, she thought dismally as she scraped a plate. She wouldn't last a day.

"Do you want a divorce, Ange?"

She kept scraping the plate, even though there was no longer any food on it. Her insides wound themselves into a series of hard knots, and her throat tightened.

"Angela?"

"I . . . I don't want to talk about it now." She fit the plate into the bottom rack of the dishwasher, then turned to face him. "This isn't a good time."

"There's never going to be a *good* time," he said, rising, then shoving his chair back under the table.

For a minute he stood there with his fists clenched and his lips pressed tightly together while Angela prepared herself for another explosion. If he were half as good at expressing grief or sadness as he was at expressing rage, they wouldn't be where they were—on the brink of divorce.

Then his hands relaxed just enough to drag his fingers through his hair. "You don't have an aspirin or something, do you?" he asked. "I've got a real beaut of a headache here."

"Aw, Bobby." She grabbed a towel to dry her hands before she went to him, then eased her arms around his waist and tucked her head into his shoulder. "I'm the one who's giving you the headache. I'm so sorry, sweetheart."

She led him to the bedroom, where she insisted he lie down while she retrieved a couple Tylenol from her cosmetic case in the bathroom. While he took those, she soaked a washcloth in cold water.

In all the years she'd known him, Bobby Holland had never admitted to even a headache. She'd watched him go to work during bouts of flu and colds. Only once did he ever take to bed, and that was when a fever of a hundred and four had him shivering so badly he could hardly speak.

"Ah. That feels good," he said now when she placed the cold compress on his forehead and over his closed eyes.

"I'll let you sleep."

"Stay." He caught her hand before she could turn to leave. "Stay with me, Ange."

She lay down on her side of the little bed, closing her eyes, battling a minor headache of her own. At the center of that headache was a dark and nagging doubt. What kind of woman walked out on her husband when he needed her most, while he was suffering under a huge burden of grief? Whether he'd been able to express it or not, grief had colored each of his actions after Billy died, and rather than stay and help him endure it in his own silent way, Angela had taken a powder.

Granted, she'd had her reasons, not the least of which was her own psychological survival, but that didn't alter the fact that she'd walked out on him when he was in pain.

The fact that he'd shut her out hadn't meant he wasn't suffering. The fact that he'd shut her out only meant he was totally alone.

She reached for his hand, adoring its warmth and inherent strength, so grateful that he didn't pull away but gently gathered her fingers in his as if he'd just been waiting for the opportunity. Oh, how she'd missed this. Him. What kind of woman let go when all she wanted was to hold on tight?

When she'd packed her bags those eleven months

ago, Angela had been so sure, so absolutely certain, that what she was doing was right. Even the department shrink had agreed. Not only was she fleeing for her own sanity—it had been such a long, lonely time on her side of Bobby's brick wall—but she was fleeing in the hope that her husband would finally, painfully, see the light. Her exit hadn't been heartless. It had been hopeful, instead.

Still, the fact remained that Bobby hadn't walked out on her.

What if she'd done irreparable damage by leaving?

She moved closer, and Bobby's arm curved naturally to let her in, to bring her against his side. It was where she belonged, after all. And that brick wall didn't strike her as quite so daunting at the moment. He'd just admitted to a headache, after all. Maybe, just maybe, he would admit to heartache now.

Easy now.

With his headache diminished to a dull, dark throb at his temples, Bobby felt the rest of him coiling tighter, first at the touch of Angela's hand, and then when she moved so hesitantly against him. Through sheer will, he kept his breathing slow and even and didn't move a muscle except to provide his arm as a pillow for her head.

He pictured himself in a corral—maybe at the Westons' place just south of Wishbone—ignoring the sharp bite of a horsefly, hardly breathing so as not to spook a skittish dun mare.

Easy.

He imagined himself sitting in a garden, absolutely still, not breathing at all now while he waited for a butterfly, a painted lady, to light upon his wrist.

He tried to slow his heartbeat, to keep the blood from roaring through his veins, to keep his body gentle, tame, and willing to wait forever for his wife to close the distance between them. Little by little, she did just that, draping her arm across his chest and snugging her leg against his. They used to fall asleep this way, but this wasn't about falling asleep.

Her hand moved softly over the contour of his shoulder, then rested at his neck, where his pulse pounded. When she sighed, he turned his head a fraction to press his lips to her warm hair, willing her to lift her face and offer him her mouth.

She did.

He held back as best he could, just brushing her lips with his, just sampling with his tongue, until she invited him in. And even then he kept it sweet and warm and undemanding. Whatever she wanted, that's what he'd give. No more. No less.

"Bobby," she whispered. "I love you so much."

It was no surprise that her eyes were wet, and this time the brine of her tears was sweet as honey. Ah, God. Angela's tears, whether happy or sad, never failed to express just what he was feeling.

"I love you, too, baby."

Needing to touch her, all of her, he shifted his arm from beneath her head, and in his awkward hurry, slammed the bandaged tattoo against the solid headboard, sending a jolt of pain clear through him. His breath whistled in and came out in a curse.

Angela jerked upright. "What? What's wrong?"

"Nothing," he said through clenched teeth. "I banged my arm, that's all." He reached to pull her against him again, but the tension in her body told him the prelude was all, and it was over.

Except for the shouting.

"I want to see your arm," she said, snapping on the light on her side of the bed. "You've probably got an infection."

"No, I don't. It's just a little tender." Tiny, in fact, had told him, "That'll hurt like a son of a bitch for a day or so, then it'll scab over. But in a week, it'll be just fine."

"Bobby."

Her arms were crossed, and her green eyes looked like emerald fire. The flush of love on her cheeks had turned to ire, and her chin was pointing like a bayonet. Everything was coming apart again. As it always did. Angela would demand. He'd defer. Hell. They'd be right back where they started. No. Right back where they ended.

Unless . . .

Unless he changed. Unless he talked. Unless he told the truth.

"I got a tattoo."

Her narrowed eyes blinked wide, and Bobby wasn't sure which surprised her more—the fact that he'd done something stupid or the fact that he'd actually, willingly, confessed to it.

"You got a what?" she exclaimed, her breath coming out in a shocked little laugh.

"I got a tattoo."

"On your arm?" Her gaze zeroed in on the limb in question. "A tattoo?"

"Yes."

She sat there, apparently pondering his revelation or his candor or his sheer stupidity; then she asked, "Of what?"

No. He wasn't ready yet. Getting a heart tattooed on your sleeve was still a far cry from wearing the real thing there. "I'll show you when it's all healed and pretty," he said.

"Bobby," she said sternly.

"Nope. Sorry. You're just going to have to wait, Ange. It's—"

Before he could say it was a secret, an alarm screeched from the surveillance trailer and running feet pounded on the driveway.

～

Bobby blew out the back door. Angela raced through the house and flew out the front door just in time to see somebody being taken down by Agents Coulter and Yates. Tricia rammed a knee in the man's back while she deftly cuffed him.

At the same moment that Bobby skidded to a halt on the sidewalk, Daisy Riordan leaned out her second-story bedroom window.

"What, in the name of the Almighty, do you people think you're doing?" she screamed. "Let that man go immediately."

It was only then that Angela focused on the white hair

of the man now spread-eagled on Mrs. Riordan's lawn. Professor Emeritus Gerald DuMaurier Gerrard. "Oh, brother," she muttered.

"No kidding," Bobby said, brushing past her. "What's going on here?" he demanded in the perfectly protective tone of a loyal butler.

"This man was throwing rocks at Mrs. Riordan's window," Doug said rather sheepishly, looking suddenly bemused and perturbed at the same time.

"He was trying to get my attention, you infernal idiot," the president's mother called down, pounding her fist on the sill. "Now unhand him this moment."

Tricia Yates appeared extremely reluctant to remove her knee from the professor's back. A collar like this would've looked so good on her record. The Man-Eater scowled at her hapless victim, then angled her head up to Doug, seeking advice, no doubt hoping her supervisor would direct her to terminate the man. With prejudice.

"Take the cuffs off," he growled, his voice trailing off in a few well-chosen curses before he called up to the window, "My apologies, ma'am. We were just being cautious."

"Cautious, my derriere. Rest assured my son will hear about this. Tell me your name and your rank or title or whatever it is you people go by, young man."

Doug blinked, probably at being called a young man, and then sputtered, "Special Agent in Charge Douglas Coulter, ma'am."

Above him, Daisy snorted in a most undignified fashion. "You'll be special agent in charge of my son's Labrador retriever if I have anything to say about it."

"Yes, ma'am."

"And who is that Amazon with the handcuffs?"

Angela almost burst out laughing. It looked as if Bobby was also having a hard time keeping a straight face while Crazy Daisy was kicking ass and taking names.

"She's Special Agent Tricia Yates, Mrs. Riordan," Doug said. "Again, ma'am, we were merely being cautious."

"Well, tell her she's not that special. And go be cautious somewhere else," she snapped. "Robert, assist that poor man onto his feet, and tell him I'll be right down."

"Yes, ma'am," Bobby said, trying to sound serious as he took the professor's arm and helped him up.

"My apologies, sir," Doug grumbled to Gerald Gerrard, then he latched on to Tricia's elbow and escorted her briskly down the sidewalk and out of sight.

The front of the professor's light gray seersucker suit was drenched with dew and spotted with grass stains. His tie was askew, and his Phi Beta Kappa key dangled precariously from a ripped vest pocket. Bobby, playing the helpful valet, assisted him in brushing off assorted twigs and clippings. The poor man appeared stunned for a moment, then he chuckled.

"Well, that ought to teach an old dog not to behave like a pup, eh?" He winked in Angela's direction while he produced a large white handkerchief from his pocket and proceeded to wipe his eyeglasses.

"They were just doing their job, I guess," Angela said, quietly thanking God for averting yet another civilian lawsuit against the agency.

"Quite ferociously," the professor said, fitting his glasses to the bridge of his nose, then rotating his shoulders rather stiffly. "Well, nothing seems to be broken that I'm aware of, although I must say my dignity took a pummeling."

"It seems pretty intact to me," she said.

"Thank you, my dear." His eyes twinkled in the light from the porch. Then he folded his hands prayerfully and lofted that twinkling gaze heavenward. "Give us grace and strength to forbear and to persevere. . . . Give us courage and gaiety and the quiet mind, spare to us our friends, soften to us our enemies."

"That was lovely." Angela smiled. "Shakespeare?"

He shook his white head, and the answer was just at his lips when Bobby answered, "Robert Louis Stevenson."

While Angela stared at her husband in astonishment, the professor clapped his hands together and exclaimed, "Exactly so, young man. Let me guess. You attended Andover or Choate."

Bobby laughed. "No, sir. Wishbone-Hernandez Consolidated High. But that was a favorite prayer of the chaplain at West Point."

"Excellent," the professor murmured. "Excellent."

Just then the front door opened, and the president's mother, despite her small size, loomed within its frame. "Bring him in," she commanded. "I suppose we're obliged to see that the old fool is all in one piece before we send him on his way."

Instead of taking offense, Gerald Gerrard merely smiled. His face fairly glowed as he started for the door. Well, why not? The man had accomplished what he'd come for whether because of or in spite of the United States Secret Service. He was *in*.

Angela and Bobby followed.

"Robert Louis Stevenson," she muttered.

"So?"

"Oh, nothing. It's just that I'm not used to you surprising me twice in one night, *Robert*."

Bobby laughed and looped an arm around her shoulders.

"Well?" Angela asked.

"Well what?"

"Are you going to tell me what it is?" she grumbled.

"What what is?"

"The tattoo, Bobby."

"Oh. That."

"Oh. That," Angela echoed. "So, are you going to tell me?"

"Nope."

She could hear her own teeth gnashing as he propelled her through the door in the professor's wake.

⁓

Ill-tempered as she may have seemed, Daisy Riordan hadn't had so much fun in years. It hadn't been easy stifling her laughter when the agents pounced on the nattily attired Gerald Gerrard and pinned him to the ground like a butterfly in a three-piece suit. Silly man.

Still, she was flattered by his attention. He was quite good-looking for a man who wouldn't see seventy again. His white hair was thick and healthy. His eyebrows were relatively tame and didn't straggle all over his forehead.

His nose was nicely chiseled, his chin was firm, and his earlobes didn't hang down to his shoulders, as happened with so many old coots.

Better yet, the man didn't squirm at all beneath her intentional withering gaze and didn't shrivel when she made the occasional . . . well, perhaps frequent . . . caustic remark. In many ways, he reminded her of her late husband, and that similarity unsettled Daisy as well as intrigued her. Romance? At her age? How absurd. How utterly ridiculous.

How . . . interesting.

Of course, his charm may have had a great deal to do with the fact that he was aware, as was Daisy herself, of Robert's nearby and constant presence in the hallway just beyond the living room. He coughed on occasion to make that presence known. No doubt the professor thought it natural for a bodyguard to remain at hand to protect the president's mother. For her part, Daisy considered it a hellacious waste of talent, not to mention taxpayers' money, as well as a good indication of the agents' boredom and desperation if Gerald Gerrard qualified as a suspect.

"Would you care for another glass of sherry, Gerald?"

His smile was quite fetching, actually, and his teeth appeared to be his own as far as she could tell. "I'm really more of a brandy man, Margaret."

"Ah." She was unable to suppress a wistful sigh. "So was the senator, my late husband."

Gerald set his empty glass on the table beside his chair, then took off his glasses to polish the lenses with his handkerchief. A nervous habit, Daisy supposed, or an academic quirk. He'd done it several times over the course of the evening.

"I've enjoyed our conversation, Margaret," he said, "but I really suppose I ought to be going."

Amazingly, Daisy felt a little pang of regret in the vicinity of her breastbone. She so hoped her face didn't reflect it.

"I'm not familiar with the local restaurants yet, I'm afraid," he said, "but I would love for you to join me for dinner tomorrow evening."

"One or two are acceptable," she said as the pang gave way to a distinct flutter. She remembered, with a little rush of guilt, how it felt when she was falling in love with Charles a half-century before. This wasn't right. She was being a foolish old woman. Worse than Muriel.

She stiffened her shoulders. "Unfortunately, I have plans for tomorrow evening. My young housekeeping couple are taking me to a movie."

The man's smile remained steadfast. Undaunted. Undeterred. Damn him. "Perhaps I could join you?" he murmured.

"Well—"

The phrase "It's a free country" poised on the sharp tip of her tongue. She swallowed. "Yes. Well, why not? That would be lovely, Gerald."

It was nearly midnight when Angela heard the front door close on the departing professor. She still couldn't believe Mrs. Riordan had let him stay so long, but then she'd been shocked that the woman had invited him in to begin with. Crazy Daisy. Go figure.

Actually, she couldn't figure Bobby out either. What was this business with the tattoo? And earlier, the Man of Steel had even confessed to a headache, and then had seemed so uncharacteristically accessible when she'd cuddled against him. Even now, the memory made her stomach do an erotic little flip. My God. Had she ever wanted him more than she had tonight before all hell broke loose in the front yard?

She looked up from the cookbook she'd been absently paging through just in time to see Bobby come into the kitchen after standing mind-numbing post in the hallway for the past few hours. Well, on second thought, it probably wasn't any more mind-numbing than attempting to read "The Year of the Chicken—365 Recipes to Delight Your Family."

"What's up?" she asked, feeling her stomach perform another one of those incredible swan dives at the sight of him.

"We have a movie date tomorrow night."

"We?"

"You, me, Daisy and the professor."

Angela laughed. "Wow. He works fast."

"No kidding." He stalked across the room and began opening drawers, staring at their contents, then closing them again.

"What are you doing, Bobby?"

"I need a clean dish towel or rag and some kind of bag." He jerked open another drawer and then slammed it closed.

"Mind telling me why?"

"I want to get Gerrard's empty sherry glass and have Doug send it out for prints. I just don't trust that guy."

"I thought they already checked him out," she said, getting up and going to the linen drawer near the sink, where she pulled out a towel.

"I want him rechecked," he said adamantly.

From another drawer, Angela extracted a little plastic baggie. "Don't you think you're being just a little paranoid? Jeez. The professor seemed like a perfectly charming, very romantic guy to me. Mrs. Riordan obviously agrees. What in the world did he do to make you so suspicious?"

Bobby shrugged.

"Well, he must've done something," she insisted.

His face hardened to stone, and there wasn't a trace of humor in his voice or a twinkle in his eye when he replied, "I don't know, Ange. Maybe I'm just naturally suspicious of perfectly charming guys who send flowers to lonely old women and toss pebbles at their windows."

Angela's stomach stopped pirouetting and took a sickening turn. This was the real Bobby. The hard-ass, take-no-prisoners, feel-no-feelings cop. The one earlier, the vulnerable one, the one she'd ached for, was probably just a fragile figment of her imagination.

"Here." She handed him the towel and the plastic bag. "Well, I guess you would be suspicious, then," she said, almost hissing, "since you're not a flower-sending, pebble-tossing, meaningless-romantic-gesture kind of guy."

If that cut him the way she intended, he didn't let it show. Not her Bobby. There wasn't so much as a flicker in his eye or a twitch in his hard-carved cheek. His voice was cold as ice when he said, "Hey, I'm just doing my job here, Ange."

"How's your headache, Bobby?"

He just stood there, staring at her as if she had suddenly gone berserk. "What headache?" he snarled.

"Never mind." She turned away before he could see the deep disappointment on her face. "That must've been somebody else."

12

At seven-thirty the next morning, the president's mother came downstairs. As if her appearance in the kitchen at that hour weren't surprising enough, Crazy Daisy was also wearing an electric blue jogging outfit and a pair of Nike cross-trainers. And, unbelievably, a smile.

"Good morning," she said with uncharacteristic cheer while Angela struggled up from her chair and blinked her bleary, nearly sleepless eyes.

"Good morning, Mrs. Riordan. I haven't even started to fix your tray yet. If you—"

"Oh, don't bother. I was wondering if Robert would like to accompany me on a walk this morning."

"A walk?" Angela, no doubt, sounded as dumbstruck as she felt. This woman, the one who had barely left her bedroom in the past three years, wanted to go for a walk? At seven-thirty in the morning?

"Yes. It's such a lovely morning, and I feel like a bit of exercise, except I'm not sure these old tendons and bones are entirely trustworthy, so I was hoping for a companion."

"Bobby's still—"

"I'm here."

Angela turned to the doorway and the sound of her husband's voice. He was there, all right. Why was it, she wondered, that the more disillusioned she grew with him, the handsomer he became? With his shower-wet hair slicked back, the strong bones of his face jutted out in stark relief. His blue oxford cloth shirt had damp patches that molded to his chest. His jeans—Ah, God—looked as soft as velvet and faded to a robin's egg blue and clung to his long, muscular legs like a second skin.

Even the president's mother seemed to breathe a deep sigh of appreciation before she chirped, "Good morning, Robert. Would you care to accompany me on a walk?"

He glanced at Angela, who could only respond with a subtle lifting of her shoulders that translated as, "I have no idea what's going on."

"Sure," he said. "Let me put some shoes on, and I'll be right with you."

Bobby yanked his shoelaces tight. Crazy Daisy wanted to go for a walk. After years of sitting in her room, she wanted to go for a walk. Fine. Great. He'd encouraged her, hadn't he? Where was the surprise in that?

"Women," he muttered. The only one he'd ever known who was at all predictable was his mother. If it was sunset, Treena Holland had a drink in her hand and distance on her mind. If you crossed her, she smacked you. It was all pretty simple, really.

It was his wife who held the world record in the surprise department, nestling up to him in bed one minute and the next minute cutting him off at the knees or, more precisely, chopping off his head about some damned headache he did or didn't have. Dogging him half the night about the damned tattoo, and then, after he'd taken the professor's glass down to the trailer and left instructions for prints, when he'd finally fallen into bed and said wearily, "Okay, Ange. You win, baby. I'll tell you about the tattoo," she'd flopped on her side—away from him—and practically hissed, "I could care less."

Christ. And the tattoo, when he'd taken off the bandage this morning, was nothing but a huge bruise that was beginning to scab over. He was already debating whether to demand his fifty bucks back from Tiny, or take the guy out in the alley behind his shop and give him a huge full-body bruise he'd never forget.

By the time Bobby got his holster firmly settled against his leg and went out the back door, Mrs. Riordan was pacing back and forth across the driveway.

"There you are," she said as if he'd kept her waiting for an hour.

"Here I am." He gestured down the drive. "After you, ma'am."

The woman took off like a jackrabbit, a pace likely to bring on a coronary if he didn't slow her down, so he trotted up beside her and suggested they take it a little slower since he'd only just rolled out of bed. She glared at him, but seemed content enough to reduce her speed.

At the end of the driveway, she halted, looking left and right along the blacktop. "Well? Any suggestions?"

"Not really," he said. "It's corn to the east and more corn to the west. Take your pick."

She picked east, toward town, so Bobby took her elbow and guided her across the road where he could keep an eye on oncoming traffic, then ambled along beside her with Mrs. Riordan on his left, close to the shoulder, just in case he needed to shove her unexpectedly into the ditch.

It was a beautiful morning, with just the right bite in the air and dew glistening on the roadside weeds. The sky was almost azure, unmarred by even the hint of a cloud. High overhead, he could see the shine of a jet heading west at thirty-five thousand feet. Sooner or later, that's what Angela would be doing. Flying west. The thought turned his stomach sour and heightened the ache in his arm.

"This is very nice," Mrs. Riordan said.

"Yes, ma'am."

"I'm curious, Robert. How long have you and Angela been married?"

"A few years," he said.

"The senator and I were married for over fifty years."

"Yes, ma'am."

"That must sound like an eternity to a young man like you."

"It sounds good, Mrs. Riordan," he said in all sincerity.

"Yes," she murmured. "It was. It was very good. Mind you, I didn't say easy. Just good."

They walked the next quarter mile in silence with his fellow agents well behind them, inching along in the big black SUV. The only vehicle that passed them was an empty yellow school bus, and the driver was careful to swing toward the center line when he blew by. Not too long after that, the president's mother stopped abruptly, planting her feet in the gravel and crossing her arms.

"Well?" She lifted her chin to his face. "Did he check out?"

"Excuse me?"

"You know very well whom. Professor Gerrard. Did he check out? Did the poor man pass whatever tests you people use?"

"He . . . uh . . . I . . . "

"Oh, for heaven's sake, Robert." Her soft blue eyes flared. "Surely you're aware that I know about this ridiculous charade my son has arranged. I'm not a stupid woman."

"No, ma'am."

He knew she knew all along. But what Bobby didn't know at the moment was why this had taken the wind out of him so completely. He was standing there, shuffling from one foot to the other, looking like a blue-ribbon fool. Women. Old ones. Young ones. Smart ones. Dim ones. Christ. They were all way out of his league.

"Well?" she demanded.

Bobby sighed. "Our initial investigation didn't turn up anything worrisome, Mrs. Riordan. The professor checked out fine." He decided not to tell her that the investigation was still in progress at his request.

"That's good. I'm pleased to hear it." She lifted a hand to shade her eyes while she continued to look up at him. "Are you surprised, Robert? Or should I call you Agent Holland?"

He had to chuckle. "No, ma'am. I'm not surprised. Like you said, you're not a stupid woman. And anybody who'd take my wife for a cook would have to be a few points shy in the IQ department."

"She's doing her best," she said, tamping down on a

small chuckle of her own as she slipped her arm through Bobby's. "Shall we head back to the house?"

"Sure. We've got to cross to the other side, though, so I can watch the traffic, ma'am."

"Oh. Of course."

They crossed, and Bobby once again positioned himself on the side closest to the road.

"What would be the plan here, Agent Holland?" she asked in a playful tone. "I mean, if a speeding car comes directly for me."

"I'd shove you in the ditch," he said.

"You'd break my hip, young man."

"Well, I'd try not to, ma'am."

They both laughed. Bobby thought it was probably something Daisy Riordan hadn't done for a long, long time. Neither had he, for that matter.

"Tell me," she said, "have you people given me one of those cute little names?"

"A code name, you mean?"

"Yes. Do I have one?"

"Actually, you don't, ma'am. Do you want one?"

"I'll take it under consideration." She sighed, partly, it seemed, from relief, but mostly from the effect of the unaccustomed exercise. "Frankly, Robert, I'm just relieved to know that I'm not being referred to as Crazy Daisy. I'd hate that. I truly would."

"Yes, ma'am," he said softly, thinking Daisy Riordan was probably the least crazy person he'd ever known. And maybe one of the toughest, too.

Not that Angela was into drudgery, exactly, but while Mrs. Riordan was out on her walk it seemed the perfect time to strip her bed and make it up with fresh linens. Besides, if she didn't do it, it was a sure bet nobody else was going to.

While she was wrestling the fitted bottom sheet off the mattress, the phone on the nightstand rang. The professor, no doubt, still in hot pursuit. Angela picked it up, politely announced "Riordan residence," and then heard, "This is the White House calling. Please hold for the president."

Good God. She nearly slammed the receiver down in her panic. She'd never spoken to the president before. Not even during her stint on the First Lady's protective detail. Her mouth went dry, and when she tried to swallow, it sounded like a cartoon gulp.

To distract herself while she waited, Angela gazed at the photograph of Senator Charles Riordan beside the phone. He reminded her a little of Harry Truman, whom she'd always thought of as handsome in a kind of nerdy way. The sort of man who might take off his stodgy spectacles to disclose a pair of eyes as deep and blue as the Pacific Ocean. Or unbutton his geeky short-sleeved shirt with its pocket protector to reveal a dynamite chest. Raw sex appeal in a plain brown wrapper. A bit like Bobby in one of his subtle glen plaid, blend-into-the-woodwork suits.

"Mother? How are you?" the familiar State-of-the-Union, my-fellow-Americans, most powerful voice in the world inquired.

Angela gulped again. "I'm sorry, Mr. President. Your mother is out for a walk at the moment. This is Special Agent Angela Holland, sir."

There was dead silence at the other end of the line. For a second she thought they'd been disconnected.

"Mr. President, sir?"

"Did I hear you right, young lady? My mother is out for a walk?" William Riordan sounded amused and confused all at once.

"Yes, sir." In spite of her nerves, she nearly laughed, tempted to say, "If you think that's so surprising, wait'll I tell you about her date tonight."

"Well, that's good news. I'm glad to hear it," he said. "Everything going all right there, Agent Holland?"

"Just fine, sir."

"Good. Good. Then she's not giving you any problems, I gather."

"No, sir. None at all."

"Well, that's fine. If you'll tell my mother I called, I'd appreciate it."

"I will, sir."

"Fine. And tell her I'll try to get back to her as soon as I can."

"Yes, sir."

"All right. Thank you very much. Oh, and tell that husband of yours that the White House is a much brighter place without his grim visage in it." He laughed softly. "You tell him I'm glad my mother is in good hands. I'm grateful to you both."

"Thank you, sir. I'll tell him."

After she hung up, Angela went back to stripping the bed, trying not to think too much about either the grim visage or the good hands. Especially the good hands. She made up the bed with fresh sheets and pillowcases, then took the used ones downstairs to the little laundry room off the kitchen, where she got them going in the washer.

She checked the little window again, knowing it was secure but needing to do something, anything, to feel like a Secret Service agent instead of a cook and laundress. Undercover work really wasn't her forte, she decided. Maybe she was just too good at it because she was actually beginning to feel like a servant, and a rather incompetent one at that.

When the phone rang, Angela rushed to answer it in the kitchen just in case it was the president trying to reach his mother again, but it turned out to be Norma, yesterday's missing bridge player.

The woman seemed slightly confused about exactly who she was talking to, forcing Angela to finally say, "The maid." Once that was established, she seemed taken aback when Angela told her Mrs. Riordan was out for a walk.

"Oh. A walk? Do you mean outside?"

"Yes, ma'am."

"Oh. My goodness. Well, I'm glad to hear that. I was concerned when Bootsie said Daisy was under the weather yesterday. I suppose it was just a twenty-four-hour bug. Was that what it was?"

Angela murmured noncommittally, all the while trying to remember the name of the bridge player who had canceled the day before. It was Norma, wasn't it? At any rate, she was certainly confused.

"Now who is this I'm speaking to?" she asked again.

Angela rolled her eyes. "I'm the new maid."

"Oh, yes. Well, if you'll please tell Bootsie I called, I'd be ever so grateful."

"You mean Mrs. Riordan."

"Yes, dear. That's what I said. Good-bye now."

Angela hung up, feeling a renewed appreciation of Daisy Riordan's mental faculties.

With nothing else to do just then—no bad guys to wrestle, no counterfeit bills to survey, not even a jerk like Eugene to put down—she went into the bedroom and gathered up her own dirty clothes and towels. Bobby, as she well knew, tended to pile his dirty stuff in the closet until the door would hardly close. She opened it now and stared at the shirts and jeans and briefs and socks, along with the Itos' shoes.

Let him do his own damned laundry, she was thinking even as she bent to pick up a white polo shirt. And then, helpless to resist the urge, she buried her face in the soft cotton fabric and breathed in Bobby. Musky aftershave. The sweetish, sticky scent of his deodorant. A residue of masculine sweat. She could have wept.

"Ange?"

"What?" She flung the shirt down onto the pile and turned to see Bobby standing in the doorway.

He cocked his head. "What are you doing in the closet?"

"Nothing," she snapped. "You should probably do some wash one of these days, or you're going to run out of clothes." She pushed the door closed, even as his wonderful scent lingered in her senses. "How was your walk?"

"Nice and uneventful. Mrs. Riordan worked up a pretty good appetite, so I said I'd scramble her some eggs. Want some?"

That sounded so good. Bobby made the world's greatest scrambled eggs, probably because he'd fixed so many breakfasts for himself and Billy when they were kids. "No, thanks," she said, feeling crabby all of a sudden and utterly perverse for sniffing her husband's dirty shirt. Worse, feeling utterly lost because she wanted to do it again if she couldn't have the real thing.

"You go ahead," she said. "Oh, and tell Mrs. Riordan the president called and will try to get back to her later."

"Okay." A devilish grin touched his lips. "Does he miss me?"

She rolled her eyes dramatically. "He didn't say."

"I'll bet he does."

"Well, next time I'll ask him, all right?"

He leaned against the door frame, crossing his arms, lifting his eyebrows, looking as confident and cocksure as the sole rooster in an over-crowded chicken coop. "I'll bet you miss me, too, Ange, only you're just too damned proud to admit it."

Miss him? *Miss him?* Burying her nose in his dirty laundry only meant she was a pervert. It had nothing to do with missing. By God, the next time she left L.A., she was going to pack some of Rod's dirty clothes just to take a hit every now and then.

"Miss you?" she screeched, losing control of her voice just as she had obviously lost control of her senses. "How can I possibly miss you when you've been in my face for the past four days?"

"You miss me." He shoved off the door frame and turned to leave. "Sure you don't want some eggs?" he asked over his shoulder.

"No," she shouted. "And don't mess up my kitchen, either."

〜

Bobby didn't mess up the kitchen. In fact, he left it cleaner than he found it before he spent the rest of the afternoon in the surveillance trailer, logged onto the Internet in search of anything he could find about Gerald DuMaurier Gerrard.

The guy had a résumé to make the average academic weep. Actual degrees in both literature and economics from Harvard, Yale, and MIT. Honorary ones from a score of prestigious schools. A list of publications, in literary rags and economic journals, long enough to pave an interstate. Testimonials out the wazoo, not to mention much speculation about Nobels and Pulitzers.

Bobby was impressed. And he was still suspicious as hell, although he couldn't exactly say why. The guy was just so goddamned persistent. Not that Daisy Riordan wasn't an attractive woman for her age, or excellent company when she chose to be. In fact, Bobby really liked her, even to the extent that he now felt intensely protective toward her on a personal level rather than merely a professional one.

It was that realization that made Bobby question his own competence. Maybe he was reacting to Gerald Gerrard and his romantic attentions more like an overly protective son than a coolly rational Secret Service agent. Maybe it was this business with Angela—being with her, sleeping with her, *not* sleeping with her—that was getting to him. He wasn't sure.

"Hey, Bobby. How's it going?" Tricia Yates, just coming on duty, passed behind his chair and riffled her fingers through the back of his hair where it met his collar.

It was far from an innocent gesture on her part, but she was probably unaware that it was comparable to lighting a match in a forest where not a single drop of rain had fallen in nearly a year. His entire body snapped to attention.

"Hey, Tricia," he said, sounding if not feeling like Agent Cool.

She slid into the chair next to his. Today's attire, he couldn't help but notice, included a black skirt with a slit up the side that was just a miracle to behold when she crossed one long leg over the other.

"Still scoping out the professor, I see," she said, peering at the monitor in front of him. "Come up with anything interesting?"

"Nope. But I haven't visited the card-carrying wacko site yet. There might be something there."

"Doug thinks it's a waste of time," she said, her voice low as she leaned closer in order to aim all of her choicest, nearly irresistible pheromones right at him. "Just FYI."

"Doug thinks a lot of things are a waste of time," he said, keeping his eyes on the screen, "including tying his shoelaces and changing his underwear more than once a week."

She laughed. If Bobby turned his head even slightly to the left, their noses would have collided. He wondered vaguely if she was one of those women who only came on to married guys, wondered if that was her chosen sport, wondered if he should even consider himself married anymore.

The phone gave a sharp little ring. Tricia answered it before the second ring, then handed the receiver to him.

"Your wife," she said, somehow managing to make it sound almost as pleasant as "Your dentist."

Bobby lodged the receiver against his ear at the same time he turned away from Agent Yates. "Hey, babe," he said softly.

"Change in plans, Bobby. Mrs. Riordan and the professor want to go to dinner before the movie. You've got about twenty minutes to change."

"Okay. Be right there."

She didn't hang up on cue. Instead, Bobby could hear the steam fairly hissing out of every one of her pores. God bless her Italian temperament. Go ahead, Ange, he dared her silently. Go ahead. Say it. I'm an immature, jealous asshole. You might as well be one, too, babe.

"How's Tricia?" she finally asked.

"Fine," he said, trying his best not to laugh, loving her and the green-eyed monster she rode in on.

But he didn't laugh. He felt like crying instead as he hung up.

～

The restaurant, midway between Hassenfeld and Springfield, was called Via Veneto and sported the clichéd red-and-white-checkered tablecloths, candles flickering in little red fairy lamps, and murals of the Grand Canal complete with gondoliers. The odors of garlic and oregano blended with wine and beer fumes. Her parents would have adored the place, Angela thought.

Bobby, however, looked as if he wished he were anyplace else. Mrs. Riordan had suggested separate tables at the last moment, and there had been nothing Bobby could do except politely accede to her wishes, then sit with Angela, where he could keep one eye on the front door and one eye on the happy couple in the nearby booth.

"I wonder how their cannelloni is?" Angela mused, surveying the menu.

Bobby shifted his chair slightly so the kitchen door was also within his general purview. "I wonder if anybody would blame me if I ordered a double martini," he said glumly.

"Relax. She's fine." Angela tilted her head toward the booth. "Look how happy she is. I think it's been so long since she's been out like this that she's just relishing every second."

He muttered something unintelligible under his breath while his gaze accomplished another thorough one-eighty.

Angela closed her menu, having decided to take a chance on the cannelloni, after all. "So, did you find out anything more about Gerrard this afternoon?"

Bobby shook his head. "My instincts are usually right on, but this time I think they just might be wrong."

She laughed. "That would be a first. What was it Billy used to call you? Mister I-think-therefore-I'm-right?"

"That's *Major* I-think-therefore-I'm-right."

A wistful little smile edged across his mouth, and he appeared to relax just a bit, which pleased Angela. In the past two years, she'd seen him wound so tight it seemed he couldn't possibly do anything but explode. She reminded herself that it was the explosion that she wanted so desperately to see. But not tonight. Not now.

"Remember that little place near Arlington? What was

it called? The place with the grape arbor and Chinese paper lanterns."

He settled into his chair, relaxing even more. His jaw loosened a little and his eyes lost some of their wariness. "Il Biscotta di Fortuna," he said with a halfway decent Italian accent.

"Right. That was it. The Fortune Cookie." She sighed and sipped from her water glass. "That was where we kept ordering bottles of Chianti to toast our *buona fortuna*. I always thought you could hold your liquor until that night. In fact, that was the night I realized you were a real puss when it came to red wine."

"Well, unlike you, Ms. Callifano, I didn't have it pulsing through my veins practically from birth."

"We took a cab home, didn't we?"

He nodded, leaning back and crossing his arms, a little glint in his eyes. "Yes, we did. And if memory serves, one of us puked in the back seat."

"I did not," she said indignantly, even as she was remembering her complete humiliation and Bobby's sweet, if somewhat wobbling, concern when he carried her upstairs to their apartment. She remembered the next morning, too—oh, boy, did she remember—when they'd awakened absolutely ravenous for each other in spite of their hangovers. If Bobby was remembering that as well, his expression didn't give him away.

"May I take your order?" The waiter was a lanky young man with his long hair pulled back by a rubber band.

"Is the cannelloni made with a white sauce?" Angela asked.

"I don't know. I can go in the kitchen and ask, if you want."

"Well, if you—"

"She'll have the cannelloni," Bobby said, cutting her off. "And I'll have the spaghetti and house dressing on my salad."

"Yes, sir." The waiter looked back at Angela. "House dressing for you, too, ma'am?"

"Is it Italian?"

He nodded, his pen poised over his order book.

"Creamy or vinaigrette?" Angela asked.

"She'll have the house dressing," Bobby said.

"Yes, sir."

Then, before she could say it, Bobby told the waiter, "On the side."

They'd done this dance a hundred times before, but this time it amused her more than it annoyed her. Bobby, too, seemed to find it pretty funny as opposed to his usual teeth-gnashing, eye-rolling irritation.

"I guess I haven't changed," she said, a bit sheepishly, meeting his gaze across the table.

"I never wanted you to, Miss Prim," he said softly. Then, before he could say anything else, something or someone caught his attention across the room. "Stay here and keep an eye on the professor, Ange. I'll be right back."

She watched him weave quickly and gracefully through tables and chairs until he disappeared out the restaurant's front door. Five minutes later, she was drizzling creamy Italian dressing on her salad when he resumed his seat across from her.

"That was Doug," he said.

His tone was so somber and his face so grim that Angela immediately set down the little cup of dressing and leaned forward attentively. "What's up?"

"Another threat arrived in Washington."

"Oh, brother." She instinctively glanced at Mrs. Riordan's booth to make sure nothing was amiss. "Just like all the others?" she asked.

"Yeah," he said. "Except for one little detail."

"What?"

"This one was postmarked Hassenfeld."

13

Daisy sensed that something was wrong when Robert returned to his table looking rather like a pallbearer and then barely touched his dinner because he spent the whole time glaring at waiters and busboys and arriving diners. She suspected that it was bad news that had altered his behavior, and she was sure that bad news, whatever it was, was somehow related to her. She was doing her best to forget it, though.

Earlier in the day, while enjoying a plate of his delicious scrambled eggs, she and Robert had agreed to maintain the Secret Service's secret and to go along with this charade.

"So, are you going to blow my cover?" he'd asked her.

"I think not," she'd replied. She could have added that part of the reason was that she enjoyed his company, that she got so terribly tired of people always deferring to her, bowing, scraping, never talking back.

Let the old lady have whatever she wants.

In truth, she hadn't wanted anything—even to live—until these past few days. But now . . .

What a grand time she was having. In her crusade as matchmaker, she'd insisted on separate tables so the Hollands could be alone, but it had turned out to benefit her, as well. She was thoroughly enjoying every moment of sharing this rather dim and quite intimate booth with Gerald, sipping a glass of the excellent Bordeaux he had chosen, looking at his handsome face, and listening as he regaled her with anecdotes of his students and colleagues, many of whom Daisy was acquainted with herself from their tenure in the capital. Normally a stickler when it came to details, she found it didn't really bother her that now and then Gerald got his facts and dates a bit mixed up. Like Charles, Gerald was a busy man, brimming with ideas, and far more concerned with the overall picture than with each petty and insignificant detail.

He called her Margaret. That alone raised him high in her esteem. The white carnation against his tweed lapel was another factor in his favor. A boutonniere was quietly masculine, to Daisy's way of thinking. Dapper. Natty. Extinct words and bygone traits of charmers like Cary Grant or Fred Astaire. Her Charles had always worn a red carnation. The florists between Saint Louis and Chicago had run out of them three years ago during his memorial services, she'd been told.

Above the snow-white flower on his shoulder, Gerald's hair shone silver in the candlelight. His nails were clean and clipped and beautifully buffed. His eyes were a perfect blue. If he just wouldn't keep removing his glasses and going at them so laboriously with his handkerchief.

Well, no one was perfect, but she was perfectly happy to sit across from him this evening and to savor the masculine companionship she didn't even realize she had missed. She really ought to thank Muriel for the introduction. Well, perhaps that was going a bit far. If Daisy ever expressed gratitude, Muriel might just have a stroke or something.

"Would you care for dessert, Margaret?" he asked.

She was tempted to say yes, to linger here in the candlelight over melting vanilla ice cream and cup after cup of coffee, listening intently, gazing across the table, simply appreciating this man and his surprising presence in her life. But then she reminded herself that the movie was for the Hollands' benefit, so the tense young couple could hold hands in a darkened theater, and that her life was comprised of a sensible seventy-six years and she had no business whatsoever behaving like a flighty, moonstruck girl. Cary Grant and Fred Astaire, indeed.

"I think not, Gerald." She peered at her watch. "If we don't leave very soon, we'll miss the beginning of the movie, and then there wouldn't be much point in seeing it, would there?"

"You're absolutely right." He signaled the waiter for the check, then plucked off his glasses once more, pulled out his handkerchief, and had himself another good and thorough polish.

"Must you?" Daisy heard herself say testily.

Gerald fixed her with his deep blue, currently unadorned eyes. "Yes, Margaret. I must. The better to see you, my dear."

She felt something comparable to a blush steal across her cheeks as she clucked her tongue softly. *The silly old fool.*

Bobby swung the Caddy into a No Parking space directly in front of the ticket booth and then killed the engine, knowing Doug would see to it that the local cops turned a blind eye to the violation.

"You can't park here, Robert," Mrs. Riordan announced from the back seat.

"I just did, ma'am."

Beside him, he could hear a tiny hitch in Angela's breath.

Behind him, there was ice in Mrs. Riordan's voice when she said, "I'd like to speak to you in private, young man." Then her voice defrosted a bit when she added, "I'll only be a moment, Gerald." No sooner had she spoken than she was out of the car, marching a bit stiffly— the unaccustomed exercise this morning had probably taken a toll on her—several yards down the sidewalk while she motioned Bobby to follow her.

"The professor and I will get out here, and then I'd like you to park the car elsewhere," she said.

"Parking close to the door is best for security reasons, Mrs. Riordan."

"I understand that, Robert. However, I'd still like you to park elsewhere."

"Ma'am . . . "

"Don't argue with me."

"Ma'am . . . "

She snagged the lapel of his suit coat, pulling him closer with suprising strength. "I feel foolish enough on this so-called date, Robert, being chaperoned by a parade of armed guards. I'd rather not advertise it to the population of three counties. Is that clear? Now move the goddamn car."

Doug sauntered up. "Is there a problem here, Mrs. Riordan?" he asked, looking from the president's mother to Bobby and then back again at Crazy Daisy's irate face and the hand clenching Bobby's lapel.

Just as Bobby was shaking his head, Mrs. Riordan snarled at the special agent in charge, "My butler and I are having a slight disagreement about parking. I'd like him to move my car out into the lot. Now."

In his inimitable, unflappable, down-home Texas fashion, Doug rubbed his jaw a moment and stared at his boot tips before he said, "Sounds reasonable to me. If you and your gentleman friend would like to get out here, ma'am, we'll see that the car gets safely parked out on the lot."

Without blowing his cover, there wasn't much Bobby could do except roll his eyes and refrain from swearing. Doug's orders from Washington were clear. Don't upset the old lady. Fine. Great. We'll just get her killed instead.

"Thank you, Agent . . . um . . ."

"Coulter, ma'am. Special Agent in Charge Douglas Coulter."

"Yes. Well, thank you." Mrs. Riordan eased her grip on Bobby's lapel, smoothed the gray fabric, then gave him a conqueror's smile. "We'll meet you in the lobby, Robert, after you park the car."

Fine. Great. He couldn't do much but follow orders, could he? If Doug thought making her happy was more important than securing her car, what could Bobby the Butler do? Earlier, after hearing about the origin of the latest threat, he'd done his damnedest to get Mrs. Riordan to give up this movie idea, escorting her out of the restaurant and practically telling her flat-out that he had serious concerns for her security. She'd clucked her tongue at him, though, and promptly traded his arm for the professor's.

After he locked Daisy's big Caddy, he dodged through parked cars toward the multiplex cinema, idly reading the names of the current attractions. He stopped dead in his tracks when he read, "Rod Bishop in *Deadly Dilemma*." Then he muttered a choice expletive before continuing toward the building, where he located Daisy and company in the crowded lobby, not too far from where Doug sat on a bench, eating popcorn and pretending to read a newspaper.

Angela handed him a ticket. He couldn't figure out the expression on her face until Mrs. Riordan announced cheerfully, "We've chosen to see *Deadly Dilemma*, Robert." Ah. The expression was guilt, then, and plenty of it.

"Great," he said, trying to sound enthusiastic rather than suicidal.

"Popcorn, anyone?" Gerrard asked. "Anyone care for a beverage?"

Bobby nearly asked for a large hemlock. Then, when no one took the professor up on his offer, Gerrard gestured toward the guy who was tearing tickets. "Shall we go?"

"I'm sorry about this, Bobby," Angela whispered as they followed behind Mrs. Riordan and the professor. "I know how you hate these kind of movies."

His teeth were clenched so tight he could hardly speak. "No problem."

Bobby didn't even last ten minutes.

While the opening credits rolled, he busied himself picking imaginary lint from his pant legs and sleeves. In the dark, for heaven's sake! Then he fidgeted with his shoulder holster underneath his jacket and loosened his tie. The rest of the time was spent hunkering down in his aisle seat, crossing his arms, crossing his legs, uncrossing everything, and continually shoving Angela's arm off their shared armrest.

She knew this would happen, dammit, but what could she do? The president's mother had insisted on seeing the film starring "that attractive young man." Angela knew how Bobby hated movies like these, where the principal characters were cops who handled semiautomatic weapons with blithe indifference to life and limb, where the word "perp" was used ad nauseam, and where procedural lapses were frequent and dire enough to make any law enforcement professional shudder.

Her father, bless his heart, adored action movies like these and always quietly chuckled his way through the stupid jargon and gross inaccuracies.

Not Bobby. He glowered at the screen as if everything that appeared on it was a personal affront aimed directly at him. Tonight he was particularly obnoxious, making crude comments, barely under his breath, that drew glares of disapproval from people in seats nearby, and that finally forced Mrs. Riordan to whip her head around and fiercely shush him.

Bobby stewed another thirty seconds, gnawing on a cuticle, then leaned toward Angela and growled, "I'm outta here."

Good riddance.

At last she was able to focus on the screen, on Rod's face with its lovely ice blue eyes and the sexy stubble on his jawline. This was the same movie that had premiered in L.A. just a few days ago, but it seemed entirely different now. Perhaps because her arm wasn't linked through Rod's, or her hand warmly clasped in his and their shoulders touching while they whispered back and forth, then finally sobbed in silly unison.

Doug slipped silently into the seat beside her, taking Bobby's post. "Any good?" he whispered.

"It's okay," she said, unable to take her eyes off the screen. Several rows away, a woman sighed audibly as the camera dollied up and paused lovingly on Rod's face. Funny, it looked rather plastic to her now, Angela thought, and far too pretty. Expressive as it was, compared to Bobby's face, Rod's didn't have much character. She'd noticed that a few times during the past few months, but she'd chosen to ignore it.

"Popcorn?" Doug angled his big paper bucket her way.

"No, thanks."

She was thinking that when she'd met Rod, she hadn't seen Bobby in seven or eight months, so perhaps his features had blurred a bit in her memory. But that couldn't be. She'd never forget a thing about her husband. Not a single scar or a swirl of hair or all the varied textures of his skin. It was Rod who seemed the blur at the moment, even though she was staring right at him on the screen.

Now, instead of paying attention to the twists and turns of the movie, she started thinking about the patterns of Bobby's scars, beginning with the pale crescent on his shoulder where his mother's belt had taken a bite out of him. There was the nasty one on his shin from a losing battle with barbed wire when he was a kid. His knuckles had a history all their own of the numerous times he'd had to defend his mother's honor, his brother's hide, or his own illicit parentage.

All Rod had was a smashed thumb, a souvenir of his years in carpentry, that his studio had hired a plastic surgeon to repair.

Suddenly it seemed as if she were looking at a complete stranger on the screen. A complete stranger whom she was seriously considering marrying. My God. Was she nuts?

"I'll be right back," she whispered to Doug, who grunted his acknowledgment, turned his legs sideways, and protected his bucket of popcorn as Angela slipped past him into the aisle.

She emerged from the darkened theater blinking, fully expecting to find Bobby sitting on one of the solitary benches in the lobby, still wearing a look of supreme disgust while he fumed inwardly about the liberties Hollywood took with details of law enforcement. Bobby. How she loved him. Another moment, she thought, and she'd be kissing away all that righteous, macho indignation. Maybe this was her fate—to be wildly and permanently in love with a man whose only way of showing pain was through the scars on his body.

He wasn't sitting on one of the benches, though, or standing post by the theater's main door. And when she finally saw him on the far side of the lobby, he wasn't alone. Judging from the sleazy smile on Tricia Yates's face as she gazed up at him, he wasn't planning to be alone later, either.

～

The moment Bobby realized what an unbelievable asshole he was being was when Agent Tricia Yates smiled
and whispered, "I bet the old lady's Cadillac has a really
big back seat."

Up until that moment, he'd been just a depressed guy
walking around a theater lobby, trying to be vigilant. He
didn't even know what he'd said to the brunette to make
her think he was coming on to her. Whatever it was,
though, he regretted it. Big-time.

He stepped back from her hot, buff little body and
raked his fingers through his hair. "That was way out of
line, Tricia. Let's just forget it, okay? We've got a job to
do here."

"Maybe later," she said, readjusting her come-hither
smile and her shoulder holster at the same time. "Maybe
sometime when we're both not trying to keep one eye out
for shooters."

Not to mention keeping an eye out for his wife, he
thought. "I'm going to step outside for a little fresh air.
You want to take over here for a couple minutes?"

"Sure. No problem."

Bobby blasted out a side door and walked around the
parking lot for a while, checking out the Cadillac, trying
to get his head back in the job. What had he always told
Billy? "The job comes first, bro, and don't you ever forget that."

Billy had grinned. "What's second?"

"Nothing."

He'd meant that. He'd *lived* that until this past year.
Jesus. Billy was probably looking down on him now and

shaking his head as he watched his brother floundering around a parking lot while his wife was ogling Harry Hollywood on the silver screen and another agent was lying in wait for him in the lobby.

What a mess. Billy had probably laughed his heavenly ass off at the tattoo, too. Bobby looked up at the star-sprinkled autumn sky, feeling his throat clog as he located the three-starred belt of Orion, the Hunter, figuring that if Billy was up there, that's the vantage point he'd choose.

"I'm screwing up here, kid," he whispered roughly before he turned to go back inside the theater, where he stood in the back, in the dark, on post, only occasionally letting his gaze idle on his wife as she watched her lover on the screen.

When the movie was over, Bobby preceded them into the lobby. Mrs. Riordan emerged, clinging to Gerald Gerrard's arm, while Doug ambled along behind them, looking for a place to stash his empty popcorn bucket.

Then, last but hardly least, came Angela of the red, swollen eyes and the wet, spiky lashes. Crying over Harry Hollywood, no doubt.

"I'll go get the car," he told Doug, turning and walking out before he had to see her tearstained face up close.

～

The Caddy was splattered with eggs from its shattered headlights to its busted taillights.

Bobby sprinted back to the theater and told Doug, who coopted the manager's office with a flash of his badge, then propelled Daisy Riordan into it over her vehement objections. Tricia followed Doug, and that left an irritated Bobby, a tearstained Angela, and a rather befuddled professor standing in the lobby, which was quickly filling for the last showings of the night.

"Oh, dear," Gerald Gerrard said, taking a swipe at his glasses. "What seems to be the problem?"

"Somebody vandalized Mrs. Riordan's car," Bobby said.

"Any other cars on the lot get the same treatment?" Angela asked.

Bobby shook his head.

Doug signaled him from the office doorway. "Agent Yates and I are going to see Mrs. Riordan and Dr. Gerrard home," he said. "I've already called in a report to the local police. They'll be here to take a look at the vehicle any minute. You and Angela talk to them, and then figure out how to get the woman's car back to her clean and in working order, will you?"

"Who's going to stay with Mrs. Riordan in the house?"

"I'm keeping her in the trailer until I can get some clarification from Washington. The president needs to know about this incident and decide just how he wants us to proceed."

"Good luck," Bobby said with a distinct snort. Crazy Daisy would probably take out the trailer like an F5 tornado.

Special Agent in Charge Doug Coulter replied with a beleaguered sigh. "All I know is if she were my mother, I'd have her on a plane to Washington tonight. If he doesn't want to play it that way, then so be it. Anyway, at least this way we won't blow your cover for being on the inside."

Bobby didn't bother to tell him that Daisy Riordan already knew. The evening was bad enough without having his supervisor all over his ass about that. Goddammit. Now he was going to have to spend the next hour or so with the local cops, then get on the phone, trying to find a garage or a dealership that was open at this hour and able to make the repairs. And he was going to have to spend all that time in the company of his wife, the president of the Rod Bishop fan club. The only thing worse would have been if Doug had decided to leave Agent Yates behind.

"I'm sorry the evening turned out this way," Angela was saying to the professor as Bobby rejoined them.

The guy looked pretty disconcerted, but then who wouldn't when his transportation had just been vandalized and his date hustled away by federal agents?

"Not to worry, my dear," Gerrard replied. "I suppose incidents such as these are customary when a woman has as high a profile as Margaret. I'm just heartened to see that she's receiving adequate security. I really wasn't aware that we were being—what's the proper expression?—shadowed by anyone this evening."

"They keep their distance," Bobby said. "And they'll take you home now, Professor. They're waiting just over there." He pointed toward the office door, where Mrs. Riordan was just emerging, looking none too happy.

"Oh. Very good. Thank you very much." He'd been wiping his glasses, but now he put them on, stowed his handkerchief in a pocket, and reached out his hand to Bobby. "Well, good night, Agent Holland."

"Thanks for the promotion, Professor," Bobby said, "but I'm not on the government payroll. My wife and I just take care of things around the house for Mrs. Riordan."

"Sorry," he said. "I had assumed otherwise."

"They're waiting for you, sir." Angela gestured across the lobby.

"Oh, yes. Well, good night."

"Good night," both Bobby and Angela said in unison.

"Agent Holland my ass," Bobby muttered when the man was out of hearing distance. "What's he trying to pull?"

"It was a logical mistake," Angela said.

He glared at her. "In your opinion."

"Fine." She returned the glare with gusto. "In my opinion it was a logical mistake. Look. I didn't trash the car, Bobby, and I didn't choose the stupid movie, so give me a break, okay?" Her voice dwindled to a rough little growl. "We've got work to do here, and I'd really like to get home before dawn. Do you want me to go out and wait for the locals, or should I get on the phone and try to find a garage?"

"Whatever you want."

"Okay. Then I'll go outside and take care of the police report. I could use some fresh air." She stuck her hand out, palm up. "The keys, please."

He slapped them in her hand. It wasn't his anger about the vandalism or his suspicions about the professor that were eating at him just then, but rather his wife's red-rimmed eyes.

"You better check your mascara, Agent Holland," he said coldly, "before you try to hold your own with the local police."

She stiffened. "Thanks. I'll do that."

Far too angry to go back inside and ask Bobby where he'd parked the stupid car, Angela roamed around the parking lot, muttering to herself, until she finally found it. What a mess. There must've been five or six dozen eggs splatted on it, their slimy yellow ooze relieved every few feet by what looked like rotten tomatoes. In addition to the headlights and taillights, the rear right window was broken. Bobby hadn't mentioned that.

No. He'd mentioned her mascara. The jerk. She dug a mirror out of her handbag and angled it toward the light overhead to check out the condition of her makeup. It wasn't so bad. From what Bobby had said, you'd have thought she looked like a raccoon, for heaven's sake. Anyway, how was she supposed to look after seeing her husband reveling in the attentions of the Man-Eater?

He should have had more sense than to make such a spectacle of his libido when he was on duty. By the same token, Angela should have had more sense than to rush back to her seat and do a real number on herself with Rod up on the screen and Bobby in her heart. Rod with his emotions on display for her and the entire world to see. Bobby with his brick wall and Terrible Tricia trying her best to breach it. All Angela could think was, Thank God the movie had a sad ending, so her smudged mascara didn't look altogether inappropriate.

There was no time for repairs now, though, when she saw the police cruiser with its flashing lights turn into the parking lot. Angela swore, dropped her mirror back into her bag, and waved her arms to attract the officers' attention. They weren't even looking, apparently. The cruiser pulled up to the front door of the theater, and one of the cops went inside, only to emerge a minute later with Bobby close behind him. The two of them jumped into the black-and-white, and then it headed in Angela's direction.

What? He didn't think she could handle this? That she couldn't find her way around the local constabulary?

When the cruiser stopped a few yards away, Bobby was the first one out. "This is my wife," he said. "We work for Mrs. Riordan."

Oh, so that was it. He thought she was going to blow their cover with these guys. It was a comfort to know he had so much confidence in her. And naturally, now that Bobby was here, the cops would just give the little lady a tip of their caps while they gave their undiluted attention to her supposedly better half.

The two uniformed officers got out of the car and did indeed nudge the brims of their caps in her direction. "Evening, ma'am," the one with the sergeant stripes said.

She was furious with Bobby, even though he did do a pretty subtle job for a supposed civilian in directing the local guys to take adequate photographs and notes of the scene. They finished up in about half an hour, radioed a truck to tow the Caddy to the local dealership, then got back in their cruiser and pulled away.

Angela leaned a hip against the only dry spot on the right rear fender. "How long do you think it'll be before the tow truck gets here?"

Bobby glanced at his watch. "Five, maybe ten minutes."

"You still think the professor had something to do with this?" she asked.

"Maybe."

"So he sneaked out of the theater, made egg salad of the car, and then sneaked back in? Is that your theory?" Angela tried not to curl her lip, but didn't quite succeed.

"I don't know, Ange. You were sitting right behind him, so you tell me. Did he sneak out? Or were you so overcome by the sight of your boyfriend, Harry Hollywood, that you didn't even notice?"

Angela's mouth opened, closed, then opened again just enough for her to stammer, "You know? About . . . about . . . ?"

"You and Bishop?" he shot back. "Yeah. I know."

"How?" The word came out as a startled little gulp.

"Some big mouth in the L.A. field office who just couldn't wait to pass along the happy tidings."

"Oh, Bobby." Oh, God. "I didn't think anybody knew." Not you. "At least nobody in Washington. Hardly anybody in L.A." She was babbling all of a sudden, not knowing what to say, not knowing how to stop saying it. Feeling guilty as hell, too, but damned if she'd apologize. Not after she'd just seen him with Tricia the Tart.

"I just . . . I just didn't realize you knew," she said finally, lamely.

"Yeah. Well." His mouth thinned with anger. Even in the erratic illumination of the parking lot, she could see the hurt in his eyes, but damned if his voice betrayed it when he said, "A year's a long time, I guess."

Eleven months, three weeks, and three days, she was tempted to say. Every one of them long. Every one of them full of longing.

"Bobby, I didn't—"

His sad eyes sparked ominously. "Let's not talk about

it, Ange." He glared at his watch, turned away from her, and looked toward the entrance to the parking lot. "Where the hell is that truck? It ought to be here by now."

"We have to talk about this," she said.

If he heard her, he ignored her, so she said it again, slowly and distinctly. "Bobby, we have to talk about this."

He turned. There was pure murder in his eyes and a chilling calm in his voice when he said, "Angela, you talk about it all you want. You can sit out here and talk about it to every single person who walks across the lot. Be my guest."

He stabbed a finger at the sky. "Talk to the stars, for all I care. But if you think for one minute that I'm going to stand here and listen to my wife telling me she is or is not fucking some candy-ass movie star, you better think again." He swore for punctuation before he added, "I'm going back inside and call those bastards with the tow truck."

Angela didn't have to think again. What was the point in saying anything to someone who didn't listen?

～

"How is she?" Bobby asked when he entered the surveillance trailer, where both Doug and Tricia sat gazing at monitors.

"Madder than a wet hen," Doug said. "Where the hell have you been?"

"Goddamned police department tow truck," he said, summing up the nightmare of missed communications and mixed signals that had taken a good two hours.

After they finally arrived at the Cadillac dealership, the general manager, a Mr. Seymour, who'd apparently been rousted from his bed by a couple of overeager young cops and who still had his striped pajama top tucked into a pair of gray gabardine slacks, was hesitant about supplying a decent loaner for Mrs. Riordan based solely on the request of "her damn houseboy."

It was well after midnight, the damn houseboy was beat, and he wasn't looking forward to sharing a bed with the president of Rod Bishop's fan club. "Where's Mrs. Riordan now?" he asked.

Doug jerked a thumb toward the rear of the trailer. "Stewing in my office. The president called her about an hour ago and told her she was supposed to take orders from me for the duration, and she didn't like that one little bit."

"Where's Angela?" Tricia asked, smiling at Bobby as if she were hoping his reply would be either "California" or "dead."

"She's checking out the house before we bring Mrs. Riordan back in. She'll call down with an all-clear."

No sooner had he said that than the phone rang. Tricia picked it up, said hello, and then good-bye. "All clear," she announced.

"I'll take Mrs. Riordan on up," Bobby said, heading for Doug's office, donning his invisible armor in preparation for a few quick lashes of Crazy Daisy's tongue. He knocked softly on the closed door, then opened it when there was no reply.

The president's mother was fast asleep, sitting nearly straight up in Doug's swivel chair, her hands folded primly and properly atop the handbag on her lap, her head bowed, and her chin resting not so elegantly on her chest. Her even breathing was verging on a snore. She'd had a long day, Bobby thought, and a lousy end to her date. If Gerald Gerrard turned out to be anything less than he claimed to be, if he hurt this woman in any way, Bobby was going to personally kill the guy.

He walked quietly around the desk, bent his knees, and gathered Daisy Riordan up in his arms.

She stirred a little as he settled her against his chest. "You're a good boy, Robert," she murmured sleepily.

"Thank you, ma'am. I'm sure glad somebody thinks so."

14

The next morning, after the debacle of her date, Mrs. Riordan refused to leave her room.

"She's pissed at the president," Bobby said when he brought her breakfast tray down.

Angela, just back from a run and in the process of stretching her calf muscles, merely sniffed and replied, "So are a couple million Democrats."

That turned out to be the longest sentence his wife spoke to him all that day. It was just as well, though, that she confined her speech to the bare essentials—yes, no, maybe, and I don't know—because Bobby didn't want to hear what Angela had seemed so eager to discuss the night before. Namely, ol' Rod and whether or not they were making it with each other.

He was thankful for her silence. All that day and the one that followed. But while Angela wasn't talking, the president's mother *was*. The woman was not only accepting calls from Gerald Gerrard but, as near as Bobby could figure, making calls to him as well. Every time he knocked on her door with a tray, he could hear her say, "Just a moment," into the phone. Every time he picked up the phone in the kitchen to call the trailer, Mrs. Riordan would curtly announce, "This line is occupied."

All in all, things were pretty quiet during the two days following the big date. No more threats arrived. The local police failed to turn up a single witness or a partial print that might lead them to the parking lot vandals. Tricia Yates behaved herself, and Bobby walked around more or less mute, more rather than less turned on by the proximity of his wife.

In those two days his tattoo had progressed from an ugly bruise to something resembling an actual heart. As for his own heart, it was nowhere near his sleeve as yet.

On the third day, however, things picked up considerably, beginning when Bobby was shaving after his morning shower. Someone rapped on the bathroom door.

"Bobby, are you decent?" Angela asked. "I need my eye drops."

Two whole sentences, he thought. Practically a speech compared to her recent silence. Was he decent? He studied his lathered face in the mirror for a second, then glanced down at the towel fastened around his hips. Decent enough, he figured. "Come on in."

She stepped into the little room tentatively, almost shyly. "Sorry to bother you," she said.

"No problem." He angled his chin and dragged his razor just beneath his jawline, trying to pretend he wasn't affected by her presence or fazed by the floral scent that always clung to her or the least bit aroused by the sleek satin curves of her dark blue nightgown. In the mirror, he concentrated on his wife's face rather than his own.

"Ouch. Shit." The unwatched blade took a little bite out of his chin.

"Here." She handed him a tissue, then nudged him

aside with her hip. "Move, Bobby, so I can get in the medicine cabinet."

"What do you need drops for?" he asked while he stuck a piece of tissue to his wound. "What's wrong? Are they prescription?"

"No. Nothing's wrong. It's just that my eyes get dry sometimes."

He had to laugh. "I don't think I've ever seen you with dry eyes, Ange. I always thought it was some sort of tear-duct defect that ran in the Callifano family."

"Very funny."

While she perused the contents of the cabinet, Bobby took a few more strokes with the razor, then rinsed it in the sink and reached for a towel to wipe the remnants of shaving cream from his face. He was remembering other mornings when they'd had to fight for the mirror in their bathroom after they'd postponed getting out of bed to make love just once more, then had to scramble in order to report for work on time. Those were the best mornings of his life. Man, how he wanted them back. The mornings, the nights, and everything in between.

"There they are," Angela said irritably. "They were behind your deodorant. You know, if you'd just put things back in the same place where you got them, Bobby, you wouldn't have to spend so much time looking around for them."

"Hey. You're the one who lost something. Not me." He reached in front of her for his aftershave. "This is nice, Ange. Remember when we—"

She was staring in the mirror with a weird look on her face.

"What's the matter?" he asked. But as soon as he said

the words, Bobby knew the answer. The tattoo. Shit. He'd completely forgotten about it.

"Is that a heart?" She stared at it a moment longer in the mirror before she dropped her gaze to his arm. "You had a heart tattooed on your arm?"

"Well. Yeah." He felt like the biggest jerk in the world.

Now there was the hint of a smile on her face. "I thought, when you said you got a tattoo, that it would be more along the lines of a coiled snake or a dragon. A dagger, maybe. I dunno." Her smile widened to an outright grin. "But a heart?"

The more she grinned, the more he battened down his lips and clenched his jaw. All that stuff he was going to tell her about wearing his heart on his sleeve suddenly sounded dopey, like something a fifteen-year-old kid would say. Angela was trying to turn his arm now to get a better look at it. Bobby pulled away.

"Don't you have to put those eyedrops in?" he asked.

"Not till I get a better look at this." She went for his arm again.

He jerked away. "Cut it out, Ange."

"Bobby, let me see."

He swore roughly, and then he stood still, allowing her to closely inspect his upper arm.

"Did it hurt?" she asked.

"Nah."

That was a lie, of course, and he reminded himself that the whole point of the heart was to expose his feelings, but he wasn't about to confess that he'd passed out when Tiny was poking those needles in his arm.

"I think it's sweet," she said, then added with a chuckle, "Maybe even more macho than a coiled snake."

"Yeah?"

"Yeah."

Her voice was as soft as the touch of her fingers on his arm. It sent a wave of longing through Bobby that threatened to buckle his knees, a longing that went far beyond sexual desire. It was like nothing he had ever felt before. He reached to tip her chin up and realized his hand wasn't all that steady.

Talk to her. Find the words. Tell her how you feel.

"It was a pretty goofy thing to do, I guess," he said, fixing his gaze intensely on hers, "but I thought maybe it was a step in the right direction. And dammit, Ange, I couldn't figure out any other way to wear my heart on my sleeve the way you want me to."

She looked away for a second, long enough for his heart to cringe, but then she looked back at him as her green eyes moistened. "Oh, Bobby."

"I'm really trying here, Ange," he said, working around the rough catch in his throat. The urge to clam up was powerful. His need to shut down battled with his need to reclaim his wife. "I'm honest to God trying as hard as I know how. It just isn't easy for me to talk about how I feel, to let it all hang out."

"I know." She sighed. "It's not fair for me to ask you to be something that you're not. To want you to feel things that maybe you don't even feel."

His thumb gently stroked her cheek while he replied. Slowly. Measuring his breath, forcing the words. Holding tight, tighter, so he didn't explode. "I want to be what you want. Angela, I *have* to be what you want. Jesus. I can't lose you."

She uttered a painful little cry, then threw her arms

around his neck and kissed him with the same kind of desperation that he was feeling. It felt like two people trying to consume the exact same breath of air, two people dying of thirst and trying to drink the same drop of water. Her face was wet with tears now, and to Bobby she tasted like heaven. No. Not heaven. She tasted like home.

He cradled her face in his hands, kissing her mouth and her nose and her eyes, almost afraid that if he stopped, she might vanish. Afraid that this was just the hallucination of a lonely, starving man.

Starving for the taste of her, he lowered his head to her breast, and the moan of pleasure he wrung from her only increased his appetite for the firm curves of her flesh and the sweet, varied textures of her skin. He splayed his hands across her backside, pulling her hard against him, needing more of her, needing to be inside her, to lose himself, to find himself, to crash and burn and be reborn in her dark heat.

"Now, baby," he whispered as he picked her up in his arms. "I've got to have you now."

~

When Bobby's head sank into the crook of her neck and all of his warm weight upon her slackened, when her heart resumed something close to a normal rhythm and her sanity returned, it was a little bit late for any regrets or recriminations, Angela decided. Even so, she had to fight back her tears. Sex, after all, had never been their problem. It was the life between the lovemaking that tore them apart.

For a man who found it nearly impossible to express

his emotions in words, her husband didn't have the slightest difficulty using his body to express his desires or to awaken the same in her. My God. This time they both had climbed so high so fast that the spin of the fall had left her almost dizzy. It didn't have anything to do with the fact that she'd been celibate for nearly a year. It was Bobby. It was both of them together. They just went up in flames.

Now, she thought, she deserved to be lying here feeling burnt to a crisp. She should have been smarter. Stronger. More sensible. She should have told him no, instead of yes, yes, yes. And now, after nearly setting the little bed on fire with their passion, how in the world was she going to tell him they couldn't make love again? That this had been the only time, the last time? That great sex just wasn't enough to sustain a marriage?

Tilting her head, she could see the clock on the nightstand. Seven-thirty-five. They still had a few minutes before kitchen duty called, and Angela wanted to just lie here, holding Bobby, savoring every second of those remaining minutes, savoring *him*.

His hair was damp, and she couldn't help but smile at the scent of her own shampoo blended with his sweetish-smelling shaving cream and the bit of healthy perspiration he'd worked up while they made love. Nobody ever smelled as good to her as Bobby did, and she wondered if he wasn't her perfect mate based on scent alone. How could two people so right keep getting it so damned wrong? she wondered.

She wished Billy were here. He always had a way of making her more comfortable with Bobby's reticence, more able to accept it. He'd tell her about some incident in Wishbone years ago that had an effect in forming her husband's personality. He'd describe Treena and her sunsets and wastebaskets full of empty beer cans, or their father's constant presence on the streets of town coupled with his cool indifference.

He used to tell her how Bobby quietly stood up to anyone who didn't treat them right, which meant confrontation on just about a daily basis with neighbors, classmates, just about everyone in town. He told her how Bobby never lost his temper. He would simply stand there like a wall, absorbing all the ill will and the taunts and the cruel condescension. He'd fight if he had to, but never, ever threw the first punch. Angela could almost hear Billy's sweet, slow drawl right now.

Honey, I suspect Bobby's just scared that if he lost his temper, he might not ever find it again. Hell, Angela, look what happened when he lost his heart to you. I mean, that sucker's just plain gone. No way he'll ever get it back.

Her fingers drifted across the powerful muscles of Bobby's back and shoulders, thoroughly appreciating the slight cushion of warm flesh over the solid iron just underneath. Not so surprisingly, in spite of all her sadness and regrets, she wanted him again. Fiercely. Deep inside her again. She literally ached for him. Mere seconds after acknowledging that this had been so wrong, it was all she could do not to start writhing sensuously beneath him. Thank God his breathing had the slow and even cadence of wrung-out sleep, because if he awoke and started kissing her again, touching her again, she wouldn't be able to resist.

And she had to resist! She wasn't going to be able to

make a rational decision about their marriage—whether to end it or resume it—if sex kept getting in the way.

As she stroked him, her hand came to rest on his solid upper arm. The tattoo! She'd almost forgotten Bobby had a heart tattooed on his sleeve! What an incredibly sweet thing to do. Only a coldhearted bitch would fail to appreciate what that highly visible and permanent gesture meant. It proclaimed his need for her and his willingness to try to work things out. He had said as much.

But, dear God, that wasn't enough. Unless he changed, a square inch of red ink wasn't going to take the place of expressing his deepest feelings, of sharing those feelings with her, of listening and responding to *her* feelings rather than leaving her out in the cold. Did Bobby actually believe his gesture was enough and would make her change her mind?

She couldn't. She wouldn't.

And what about Rod, who seemed to be everything Bobby wasn't emotionally? If that's what she truly wanted in a mate, why was she having such an impossible time telling him yes?

On the nightstand beside the bed, her cell phone gave a soft little bleep. Bobby breathed a warm curse into her neck before he rolled over onto his side. Angela answered the phone, listened to Doug's gruff voice a moment, then hung up.

"Who was that?" Bobby asked.

"Doug. He said the report just came in from forensics on the professor's sherry glass."

Bobby levered up on an elbow. "And?"

"No prints," she said.

"None?"

Angela shook her head. "Not a single one. Not the professor's. Not even mine, and I served him the sherry that night."

"He wiped it clean." Bobby sat up, looking no longer like a languorous lover but like his normal, grimly professional and highly suspicious self. "The son of a bitch wiped it clean."

～

While he carried Mrs. Riordan's breakfast tray upstairs, Bobby tried to confine his thoughts to the job, but the memory of making love to his wife kept intruding. Little wonder, when his body was still ringing like a damn bell. The word *gangbusters* kept knocking around in his head. That's how they'd come together this morning—like gangbusters. It was probably a good thing that during their estrangement he'd pretty much forgotten or suppressed the memory of just how good they were in bed together. If he had clearly remembered, he'd have gone insane about eleven months ago.

All of a sudden, Bobby had hope again, now that he knew Angela still wanted him. Sweet Jesus, how she'd wanted him a while ago. He couldn't help but grin as he climbed the stairs. If the tattoo did nothing more to bring them together or solve their problems, at least he had it to thank for what happened this morning. He wasn't kidding himself. He knew the little red heart was just a gesture, a symbol of the emotional work he had yet to do. But it was a damn good start.

He felt like whistling. He felt like jumping up and clacking his heels together in midair. Like a Secret Service Fred Astaire. Like a cartoon lover wearing a goofy grin while his heart was *sproing*ing out of his chest. He felt like a man who had just made love to the woman he loved and who couldn't wait to do it again. And again.

He felt like a man who better get his mind back on business, which in this case meant the surprising lack of latents on the professor's sherry glass. Angela was right. The lab should have picked up a couple of her partials, if nothing else. She was probably right, too, when she'd said, "The way that man is constantly whipping out his handkerchief to wipe his glasses, I'd bet next month's salary that he just got carried away and wiped the sherry glass, too."

Yeah. Bobby would be willing to bet his salary, too, that the old guy had wiped it clean, but not because he'd gotten carried away. Gerald Gerrard might have lulled everybody else's suspicions with his mild manners and academic credentials, and he might have swept Mrs. Riordan off her feet with his charm, but Bobby wasn't lulled or charmed. He was still pretty damned suspicious.

The president's mother was on the phone again when he entered her room, but instead of scowling at him and postponing her conversation with a hand covering the receiver, this morning she hung up as soon as Bobby crossed the threshold, and then she offered him a fairly decent imitation of a smile.

"Those clocks downstairs must all be off again," she said by way of greeting, informing him that he was several minutes late.

He grinned as he put the tray down on the table, more immune than usual to her sarcasm. Well, hell. He'd just made love to his wife. He was immune to everything this morning. "Yes, ma'am."

"I'd like to go for another walk today, Robert," she told him, lowering herself into the chair while he held it for her.

"Good," he said, trying not to sound surprised. He was glad to see her coming out of her funk.

"I'd like to go at ten o'clock."

"No problem. The sun'll be well up by then to take some of the chill out of the air."

"I suppose you're required to inform all of the thugs out back in the trailer of my plans." She scowled up at him. "What do they have, a little chart or something on which they write my every move? Do they use different-colored markers for different days of the week?"

"No. Nothing like that. They're just seeing to your safety, Mrs. Riordan. The same as Angela and me."

"At least the two of you are pleasant company," she said with a little snort. "I'll be furious if there is anyone following us this morning in a car that they think I can't see, or sneaking from tree to tree or trying to make themselves invisible among the cornstalks. I won't have it, Robert. Not this morning. Is that understood?"

He nodded, certain that Doug would comply, since the order of the day seemed to be, Whatever Daisy wants, Daisy gets. "Just you and me," he said. "We can do that."

"All right, then." She shook out her napkin and draped it over her lap. "I'll be down at ten."

"Yes, ma'am." He turned toward the door.

"Oh, and Robert?"

"Yes, ma'am?"

"Have I thanked you for what you did the other night

when the car was vandalized and afterward, when I fell asleep in that horrible trailer?"

"Not yet," he drawled, suppressing another grin. Gratitude wasn't Daisy Riordan's longest suit, especially gratitude to a Secret Service agent, but he wasn't going to make this any easier for her. Hell, she wouldn't want him to. It was one of the reasons Bobby liked her so much. He thought he had a fairly good take on the president's mother. She didn't really *want* to walk all over people. She wanted them to stand up to her. The woman just enjoyed a good fight.

"Well . . . " She took a sip of orange juice before she added a pretty stiff and grudging, "Thank you, Robert."

"You're welcome."

"And see that you're ready at ten," she said. "Sharp."

Bobby trotted down the stairs, glancing at his watch, wondering if there was time to nudge Angela back into the bedroom for a quickie. This morning hadn't been nearly enough, not after waiting over eleven months, and tonight was a long way away. He turned into the kitchen from the hallway with another goofy grin on his face that he just couldn't remove. Hell, he didn't want to remove it. Let her see how damned in love with her he was.

Only it turned out to be Doug, sitting at the kitchen table, who witnessed the lovestruck expression.

"Kinda getting into this houseboy stuff, aren't you, Bobby?" his supervisor asked, not bothering to hide his own grin, one that came dangerously close to a smirk.

"Where's Ange?"

Doug aimed a thumb toward the bedroom. "In there. Packing."

"Packing?"

"Yep. I just gave her the good news. Washington called. Your replacements are coming in late this afternoon."

"Replacements." It wasn't a question. It didn't even qualify as a statement. Bobby just found himself repeating the word. And then again. "Replacements."

Doug glanced at his watch and then at the clock on the oven. "One's flying up from Atlanta. The other, the woman I believe, is driving over from Indianapolis. Turned out the agency did have another married couple on the payroll, after all."

"Who?" Bobby asked with a hint of belligerence in his voice.

"Demmler. Daimler." Doug shrugged. "Something like that. The paperwork hasn't come through yet."

"Never heard of them."

"Maybe that's because they've never done protective duty before. Hell of a time to start, with a woman under a death threat. But nobody asked me for my opinion."

Bobby's brain was clicking at warp speed, trying to process this information, but mostly getting stuck on one image. Angela was packing. Packing to leave. Him. A kind of panic was building in his chest.

"Do you think that's fair to Mrs. Riordan, Doug?" he asked.

"Excuse me?"

Bobby pulled out a chair, sat, and leaned his forearms on the table. "I mean, the lady's just getting used to having us here in her house. Then suddenly we're out, and she has to start all over again with two new people."

Doug's stare was inscrutable—part astonishment, part annoyance. His tone was wholly annoyed. "Who was the one begging me to get him off this detail? Was that you in my office, Agent Holland, practically down on your knees, or was I just hallucinating, just making it all up?"

The panic made Bobby's heart feel too large for his chest. Not a good fit anymore. It was hitting his ribs, moving up in his throat and choking him. How he could wave his hand and smile so cavalierly was a mystery to him, but he did and then said, "Hey, Doug. We're here. We're settled in. The old lady's accustomed to us. It's no big deal."

Doug's eyes narrowed to fine, gray slits. "You're telling me you want to stay?"

"Yeah." Bobby swallowed. "That's what I'm telling you. I want to stay."

"Well, your wife doesn't, mister," he snapped. "She lit up like a two-hundred-watt bulb a few minutes ago when I gave her the news, then she rushed off to pack so fast she just about laid rubber on this shiny tile floor."

"Oh." He couldn't think of anything else to say. He couldn't think of anything except Angela packing, Angela walking out on him again. He didn't even know how many minutes passed before his supervisor spoke again.

"What the hell's that on your arm?" Doug asked.

"Tattoo."

"I never noticed that before. You had it long?"

Bobby sighed. "Years," he said. "I had it done when I was at the Point."

"That long, huh? Well, I'll be damned. I usually notice things like that."

"Yeah, well, I guess you're losing your touch, Doug."

The older agent shook his head. "Could be, son. This job has a way of wearing you down every once in a while.

You look like you could use a little vacation yourself, Bobby. Cheer up. Go fishing or something. They don't expect you back in Washington before next Monday."

"Both of us?" Bobby's heart leapt up for a second.

"No. Just you. Angela's going back to California."

15

The moment she saw Bobby walk into the bedroom, Angela knew that Doug had given him the news, and that for her husband, it wasn't good news at all. He looked as if he were trying to hold himself together with spit and a couple lengths of frayed string. He looked as if Doug had punched him in the gut instead of informing him he could bid a fond farewell to Has Been, Illinois, today.

She, on the other hand, had been thrilled with the news, not only because she wanted to go home, but also because she didn't know how she was going to be able to continue sleeping in the same bed with Bobby and keep her vow of "never again." After this morning, her willpower was about two-ply, maybe less. There was no bed big enough to prevent her from saying yes. But three thousand miles, an entire continent, the Appalachians and the Great Plains and the Rocky Mountains, between them ought to do the trick.

"Hi," she said softly while she turned in the sleeves of a silk blouse, then folded the whole garment over a piece of tissue paper and put it in her suitcase.

"Doug came through for us," he said, then chuckled almost mournfully as he added, "Who knew he had so much clout in Washington, huh?"

"Yeah. Who knew?"

He sat on the edge of the bed, watching her fold another blouse. "Do you know anything about these new agents?"

Angela shook her head. "When Doug talked to me, he wasn't even all that sure what their name was. One's from the Atlanta field office, I think."

Bobby scowled. He swore under his breath. "Kind of a rotten thing to pull on the president's mother, don't you think? I mean, now that she's used to us, even *likes* us, for chrissake."

What was he saying? Angela wondered. Certainly not what he meant. If he didn't want to leave, if he didn't want to be separated from her, why couldn't he just come right out and say it, instead of all this bullshit about Mrs. Riordan? God, he was making her crazy with all this read-between-the-lines business. She was folding her blouse all wrong now, and had to start again. Right sleeve over. Left sleeve over.

Why didn't he do what Rod did? Let his eyes get misty, fall to his knees, and tell her. *I love you. Don't leave. Be with me always.* If Bobby loved her so goddamned much, why didn't he just say so?

"Ange?"

"What?" she snapped.

"It's probably not too late for Doug to change their assignment. These new agents. Then Mrs. Riordan wouldn't get all uptight, and we—"

"It's too late, Bobby." She slammed the blouse into the suitcase, undoing all her perfect folding. "We're through here." Boy, are we through!

"I guess you're right. Doug would never go for it." He gave a long sigh. "So, you're going back to California?"

"Yes." Angela scooped up an entire drawerful of underthings and dumped them in her case. "I'm going back to California. I've already booked my flight."

Bobby reached into the suitcase, idly fingering the thin strap of one of her nightgowns, gazing at it rather than at Angela when he spoke. "I don't have to be back at the White House until Monday morning, you know. I could fly out there with you. We could have a day or two on the beach, then maybe drive up the—"

"No."

His grip on the silk gown tightened. She could see his lips compress and little white crescents of anger appear at each corner of his mouth. Every tendon in his body seemed to grow taut, and every nerve seemed to sizzle. Dear God, where did he keep all that fierce emotion inside him? she wondered. What kind of toll must it be taking on his body, let alone his psyche? When his gaze flicked up to meet hers, his eyes hardly betrayed him, and neither did his voice.

"Just no?" he asked, sounding more perturbed than furious, more disappointed than devastated. "That's it? Just a flat-out no? How about a 'maybe,' Ange, or an 'I'll think about it' or—"

Angela loved her husband more than anyone in the world, but for a split second just then she hated him, truly despised him, for shutting her out so completely from his emotions. The more he did it, the more she wanted to hurt him, to bring him to the point where his carefully tended, closely guarded emotions just exploded. And damn the fallout. She just couldn't help it.

"No," she said, slamming another handful of clothes in her case. "There's nothing to think about. Besides, I won't be staying in California more than a few hours. As soon as I land in L.A., I'm going to book myself on the next flight leaving for Mexico."

It wasn't a lie, exactly. Angela meant to do just that as soon as she could get a call through to the wilds of Chihuahua, talk to Rod, and find out just where she was supposed to go to join him on the movie set. She could already imagine his face glowing with pleasure when he greeted her. She could picture the tears shining in his eyes, hear the lovely words of love pouring from his lips. *I love you. Don't leave me. Be with me always.*

"Mexico," Bobby muttered. Then he reached out and caught her hand. "So, what was that all about this morning, then?"

"When we made love, you mean?" She put a lilt of indifference in her voice and hoped he didn't notice how fake it sounded. When she tried to pull her hand away, Bobby wouldn't let go.

"Yeah," he said. "I mean when we made love."

"That, my dear, was just great sex."

He flinched a bit, and his grip tightened on her fingers. "That's all you wanted from me? Just a goddamned quickie?"

"Bobby, leave it alone," she wailed. "Don't you understand? You can't give me what I want."

"I'm trying, Ange. God knows." He let her go in order to turn sideways, then raked up the short sleeve of his shirt, fully exposing the little red heart. "What do you think this is all about?"

"It's a tattoo," she said, staring at his arm. "It's a dye

job. Red ink injected into your skin. It's not real, Bobby. It's not your heart."

"Jesus, Ange. I know that." His voice grew more desperate. The veins in his neck distended. "But I had to start someplace, didn't I? I had to do something, make some kind of gesture to show you how I feel."

"It's not . . . It's not enough," she whispered.

"Not enough!" he howled. "Not fucking enough! What do you want me to do, cut my chest open and rip out the real thing and put it in your hands?"

"You just don't get it, Bobby." She shook her head and stared at her hands in her lap because she couldn't bear to look at him. "I don't think you ever will."

"Then make me get it, baby. Tell me what you want me to do. Tell me what would *be* enough. Just tell me and I'll do it."

"Bobby, I . . . It's not that easy."

"Do you want me to go to a marriage counselor with you? If that's what you want, I'll do it. Or I'll go by myself to a shrink. I can do that, too. Just tell me."

He was so scared. Not that he'd ever say it, but she could hear it in his tone, could tell from the urgency of his speech, the desperate way the words spilled out of him. He was as scared and confused as she was. How could she tell him what to do when she didn't have a clue?

A strand of hair fell against her cheek, and just as she was lifting her hand to shove the errant lock behind her ear, Bobby did it for her. Without a word. So gently. Just right. Dear God, how could he be so perfectly in tune with her physically and still so emotionally distant? It almost broke her heart.

"Ange," he whispered. "Tell me what you want me to do."

For a minute she couldn't even speak. She sat there, her arm just brushing his where the little red heart peeked from the edge of his sleeve. Tell him what to do? She was finally and utterly convinced that there wasn't enough counseling or headshrinking in the world to make Bobby Holland do what she needed him to do. Words like *sharing* and *emotional accessibility* and *intimacy* simply didn't compute with him. She didn't know how to make him understand, and she was suddenly bone-tired of trying.

If she told him to open his heart to her, he wouldn't have a clue what she meant. If she said she needed him to let her in, he wouldn't know what to do or how to even begin to let down his defenses. How could she tell him what she needed in a way he'd comprehend?

"Tell me," he said again. "What do you want me to do?"

Nothing. Everything. *I love you. Don't leave me. Be with me always.* How could she make him understand?

"I want you to cry, Bobby," she said at last as her own tears began to fall. "That's all. I just want you to cry."

A brusque knock sounded on the bedroom door. "It's ten o'clock, Robert. I'll be waiting for you in the driveway."

Bobby's voice was a little bit hoarse but steady as always when he replied, "Yes, ma'am. I'll be right there."

Daisy Riordan wrenched the zipper of her jacket up as far as it would go beneath her chin. It was chilly this morning, which she should have anticipated, since September was now closer to October than it was to August. She rocked from foot to foot, anxious to get moving out on the road for fear her thin, ancient blood would freeze in her veins if she stood here in the driveway too long.

The notion of her antique bloodstream brought a quick and unbidden little smile to her face. For such an old crone, she was doing rather well. Rather well, indeed, if she did say so herself. There was no sense grinning like a total fool, though. It probably made her look even sillier than Muriel. Now, where the devil was Robert?

He came out the back door just then, looking as desolate as he had sounded a moment ago when she'd knocked on the servants' bedroom door. She hadn't been eavesdropping, exactly, but she couldn't help but overhear the discussion going on inside. Poor Robert. Daisy knew that she'd been right in her assessment of him. He played his cards so close to the vest that there was no getting near his heart. He was so much like her, she thought, that he probably should have been her son. Well, considering his age, her grandson perhaps.

She'd given up wishing for one of those a long time ago. Perhaps that was part of Robert's appeal. Perhaps she saw in the handsome Secret Service agent the grandson she'd never have. At the very least, she recognized her own close-to-the-vest temperament in him, and understood only too well that he probably didn't make the perfect mate. Far from it.

In fact, her heart went out to Angela, whose fondest wish, it seemed, was to see her husband cry. Ha! Don't hold your breath, my dear. Daisy couldn't remember the last time she, herself, had cried. Sometime during World War II, she believed. And there had been no witnesses. If people deemed her cold for not weeping at Charles's funeral, so be it.

"It's chilly," she said when Robert reached her side. "You need a jacket."

"I'm fine."

Daisy narrowed her gaze. "I'll wait."

"Let's go." He clasped his hand firmly around her elbow and started down the driveway.

"I don't want to be forced to turn back just because you're too proud or stubborn to dress properly for the weather," she said stiffly, keeping pace with his long strides. And she didn't want him to catch cold, either. He seemed miserable enough.

He let out a sigh. "It's not pride, ma'am. You can count on that."

Daisy recalled his offer to Angela to do whatever she wanted him to do to save their marriage. Certainly his pride had taken a drubbing with that.

"Well, you're stubborn, then," she told him. "It can be a very irritating quality, Robert."

"Yes, ma'am." A hint of a grin passed over his lips, and he pitched her a sidelong glance that seemed to say, It takes one to know one.

She gave a little snort. "Of course, it can also be a sign of strong character," she said, "and a resolute nature."

"Yes, ma'am." He halted at the end of the driveway. "Which way today? East or west?"

"West," she said.

"West it is."

"With no one following us," she added.

"That's the plan."

"Very well, then."

Once again, Robert positioned himself between her and the oncoming traffic, letting her set the pace. Daisy glanced at her watch. Good. They were right on time. It wouldn't be long now, and Robert would have a little something to distract him from his marital woes.

~

Bobby reached down to snag a weed in passing, then clamped it between his teeth. He was fighting another headache, thanks to Angela. Every furrow in his forehead felt as if it were slicing across his skull.

She wanted him to cry! What the hell kind of way was that to fix a marriage? She might as well have asked him to stand on his head and recite the Pledge of Allegiance backward. Or flap his arms and fly.

Her father cried, for God's sake. And her brothers, too. All the Callifano men turned into wet, blubbering mountains of saltwater and snot at funerals, weddings, christenings, graduations, saying hello at airports, saying good-bye anytime, any place. At the drop of a freaking hat. Angela hated that. It was embarrassing. Humiliating. At least, that's what she'd always said.

Now Bobby was supposed to do it. He didn't think he'd ever cried in his entire life. Well, maybe when he was a baby, put to bed in a pulled-out, blanket-insulated drawer, but he doubted it. What good would it have done, except maybe earn him a shouted "Knock it off!" or a stinging swat on the behind? Hell, what good was wearing your heart on your sleeve when even that wasn't enough? He let a rough curse pass through his clenched teeth.

"You see," the president's mother said with barely concealed triumph. "I told you that you'd be chilly, that you ought to wear a jacket."

Bobby pulled the weed from his mouth and drawled, "That you did."

She made a small harrumphing sound, then said, "I'd be willing to wager that you never minded your mother, Robert. That you were one of those children who always thought he knew best." She glanced up at him. "Am I correct?"

"Well, in my particular case, ma'am, it just happened that I did know best."

"Oh? Why is that?"

Bobby drew in a long breath, then let it out slowly. Other than Angela and Billy, he'd never really talked about his childhood to anyone. Hell. Nobody except Angela had ever asked, and she said it was like pulling hen's teeth to get a response out of him. "My father wasn't married to my mother," he said now, "and she preferred her six-packs and Seagram's 7 over her two boys. Somebody had to know best, I guess, so it turned out to be me."

With her gaze pinned on the distance ahead, she nodded solemnly, then seemed to get lost in her thoughts for a few minutes before she spoke again.

"I was that sort of child, myself. Right here in Hassenfeld." She gestured toward the high corn at the side of the road, and a wistfulness crept into her voice. "Mind you, that was well over half a century ago, but things haven't changed all that much. I don't suppose *I've* changed all that much."

He laughed softly. "I'll bet you were a real little heller, Mrs. Riordan."

"I was. And I'll bet you think my family was among the town's upper crust, don't you, Robert? That would be the logical assumption, wouldn't it? I mean, I'm the mother of the president of the United States, after all, and the widow of a senator. I'm sure you must think that my pedigree is impeccable. I'll bet you assume that my father was a banker or an attorney or a prosperous farmer who owned most of this land." She waved an arm over the cornfield again. "Or maybe you think he was the mayor and that my mother was a very refined, well-educated woman who entertained the local matrons at afternoon teas and who raised me, her only daughter, in her image."

She halted, crossed her arms, and jutted her chin up toward his face. "Well? Tell me. Is that what you think?"

Bobby really hadn't thought about it at all, but he supposed if he had, his impression of Daisy Riordan's background would have been similar to the one she'd just described. "It's pretty close," he said.

"Ha!" She hooked her arm through his and began walking again. "That's what most people think. Why, even here where I grew up, everyone seems to have conveniently forgotten that I, in fact, had no father and that my mother supported us as best she could by cleaning houses and taking in wash, not to mention the occasional sailor or traveling salesman, if you know what I mean."

"I wouldn't have guessed that," Bobby said. Never in a million years.

"I'm sure you wouldn't have. It's not something my son is especially thrilled for me to reveal."

Bobby chuckled. "Kinda sullies that midwestern landed-gentry, Sunday-school image of his, I guess."

"William's biographers have managed to gloss over that part of his heritage to date. One of them described his grandmother as a flapper. Another referred to her as a woman of limited ambitions."

"Beats calling her the town tramp," Bobby murmured, "like they called my mother."

"Indeed." She smiled up at him. "I'm very fond of you, Robert. We have quite a lot in common, you and I."

"Apparently so, ma'am."

He would've smiled back, but he wasn't altogether certain where Crazy Daisy was headed with this two-peas-in-a-pod routine. Nowhere, he hoped. It was making him nervous. If she was anything at all like him, she had a lot more on her mind than she was disclosing at the moment.

"I don't cry, either," she said. "Not even when Charles passed away. It simply isn't in me."

So that's what was on her mind. She'd overheard Angela's ultimatum back at the house. Bobby was hoping the woman would just let the subject drop when she added, "That doesn't mean I don't have tender feelings, however, or that I fail to experience grief or other deep emotions. I just don't cry. Never did. And I probably never will, not at this late date. I'm sure it must have something to do with my upbringing, but I've never wanted to explore it in any great depth."

"Yes, ma'am," he answered noncommittally. Neither did he, as a matter of fact. Not her upbringing or his own.

Let it rest, he thought. Let sleeping dogs lie. And what was that expression about crying over spilt milk? In both their cases, it seemed to apply perfectly.

"I'm sure, if you try, there's a way to communicate your emotions to Angela without weeping. Perhaps you haven't spent enough time alone together. Perhaps the two of you should take some time off from your rigorous duties and take a second honeymoon. Europe's lovely this time of year. I'd be more than happy to put in a word with William, if you'd like."

"I really don't think so, ma'am. Thanks all the same."

"Well—" She looked at her watch. "Oh, my goodness. It's later than I imagined. We'll keep going until we reach Muriel's place up ahead, shall we? Then we can turn around for the trek back home."

"Fine with me."

The big white farmhouse up ahead sat well back from the road on the crest of what passed for a hill in this part of the state. It reminded Bobby of a wedding cake with fancy Victorian frosting decorating every overhang and eave. There were spindles and spools and more weird carpentry than he'd ever seen in one place.

"That's quite a house," he said.

"Looks as if it should be the birthplace of a president, doesn't it? I'm sure Muriel wishes it were."

"Bootsie, right?"

She nodded. "Yes, the infamous, often intolerable, always conspicuous, and obviously memorable Bootsie."

"The two of you have tangled for a long time, I'd guess."

"A very long time," she said. "Ever since the daughter of the town tramp took the most eligible young man in town away from the Belle of Hassenfeld. Muriel's never forgiven me for it, either."

They were directly in front of the big Victorian house now. Mrs. Riordan came to a stop, turned, and lifted a hand to shade her eyes as she gazed at the length of road they'd just traveled. Sunlight glinted off the windshield of an approaching vehicle. Bobby hoped to hell it wasn't Doug in the SUV.

"I'm ready to go back now," Mrs. Riordan said.

"Let's cross to the other side."

He took her elbow and ushered her across the road while he kept one eye on the oncoming traffic. It was close enough now for him to discern the color and make. Thank God it wasn't an agency SUV, but a black Mercedes sedan. Not too many of those around Hassenfeld. So it didn't surprise him all that much when the vehicle slowed as it approached them, or when Daisy Riordan exclaimed, "Oh, look. It's Gerald."

The Mercedes stopped and the window on the passenger side slid down, revealing the driver's beaming face. "Well, this is a pleasant surprise," the professor said. "Out for your morning constitutional, are you, Margaret?"

Bobby thought neither one of them sounded all that surprised as he stood there cooling his heels a discreet distance away from the car while the president's mother and Gerald Gerrard chatted through the open window. After a few minutes, she unzipped the collar of her jacket, as if she were warm, then untied a silk scarf from around her neck. No sooner did she have it off than the breeze snatched the silk square from her fingers and carried it into the ditch, where it caught on a clump of weeds.

"Oh, my goodness. Would you be a dear and retrieve that for me, Robert? It's one of my favorite scarves, and I'd hate to lose it."

"Sure."

The damned thing had blown far enough into the ditch that Bobby had to maneuver carefully down its steeply angled side. Just as he bent to pluck the scarf from the bramble, he heard a car door open behind him. He whirled around just in time to see Daisy Riordan's right leg lift off the pavement to join the rest of her inside the car.

Bobby was out of the ditch in a second, reaching for the door handle just as the president's mother pulled it closed and the professor stepped on the gas. The big Mercedes fishtailed violently, its heavy rear end hitting Bobby hard in the ribs and throwing him perilously off balance. It was all he could do to keep his feet out of the way of the spinning back tire just before the treads bit into the blacktop and the vehicle sped away.

Bobby punched Bootsie Rand's doorbell, waited a couple seconds, then hit it again. The Mercedes had clipped him pretty good, and his side hurt enough to prevent him from sprinting the half mile back to the Riordan house to report the incident.

Incident, his ass. The two of them, Crazy Daisy and the professor, had it all planned out. The flyaway scarf was a nice touch, he had to admit. And he'd fallen for it like a dumb ton of bricks. The same way he'd fallen for her insistence that no other agents accompany them on their walk. Goddammit.

He hit the bell a third time, then pounded on the door with the heel of his hand, yelling, "Mrs. Rand, are you in there?" then muttering, "Come on, dammit. Come on." If Bootsie didn't answer the door, he was going to have to decide whether to break in to access her phone or do a slow, side-aching jog back to Mrs. Riordan's house, losing a precious fifteen or twenty minutes in the process.

Shit. Bobby was just about to reach into his pocket for a credit card to jig the lock when the door opened.

"Well, look who's come down the road to see me," Bootsie said, her turquoise-lidded eyes opening and closing with surprise while her neon pink lips pursed as if to blow a kiss across the threshold. "What happened? Did Crazy Daisy toss you out?"

"May I use your phone, ma'am?"

"My phone? Why, of course you may, young man. Come in. Come in."

She stepped back to let him in, but not so far back that Bobby wasn't forced to graze her wiry little body as he passed. He swore he heard a muted sigh issue from her lips.

"You look like you could benefit from a tall glass of iced tea, Bobby," she said. "It is Bobby, isn't it?"

"Yes, ma'am."

The former belle of Hassenfeld took a step toward him. "I'm so flattered that you finally came to call."

Shrugging helplessly, he took two steps back. Bootsie's hair seemed inhumanly orange and impossibly spiked with gel. She was eighty if she was a day, and he guessed she was trying to look twenty, but in her skinny

yellow jumpsuit and gold sandals and with a circular dab
of rouge on each of her cheeks, Bootsie Rand just looked
like a cockatiel. A little shiver rippled between his shoulder blades when she winked at him.

"The phone?" he reminded her.

"Oh, the telephone. Of course. There's one right in
there." She gestured toward a room just off the hallway
where they stood. "While you make your call, I'll go see
to that nice cool glass of tea. Then we can chat. Or—"
She giggled behind her hand. "Whatever."

Great.

Bobby strode into what appeared to be a sunroom full
of tall potted plants and oversize wicker furniture. A
white rotary phone sat on a little white wicker desk. He
picked up the receiver and dialed the number of the surveillance trailer.

"I lost her," he said when Doug answered.

During the predictable explosion on the other end of
the line, Bobby let his gaze wander over the objects on
Bootsie's little desk. A white plastic tape dispenser with
floral decals. A stack of magazines. A roll of stamps. A
small porcelain vase filled with ballpoint pens, pencils,
and a pair of scissors.

He inspected a photograph in a small gilt frame out of
which Senator Charles Riordan smiled back at him. He
could have been wrong, but Bobby thought it was the
same photograph that sat on the nightstand beside Mrs.
Riordan's bed. The man who got away, he thought, re-
calling her story. Poor ol' Bootsie.

After Doug was through exploding, Bobby explained
that, suspicious as he was of the professor, he didn't consider this an abduction. "More like a well-planned elope-

ment," he said disgustedly. "That old lady played me like a goddamned violin."

"That's just dandy," Doug said, "and maybe they are just out for a little joy ride, but we still have to go on full alert, and I've gotta notify the local and the state police, not to mention the president, if we don't get her back in the next couple of hours."

Even as the special agent in charge spoke to Bobby, he was barking orders to whoever was in the trailer with him.

"Stay on the line, Bobby," he said. "I want you to give the make of that car and the license to Captain Severs in Springfield."

"Sure," Bobby said. "You want to send somebody over here to pick me up, Doug?"

"That's pretty much at the bottom of my to-do list at the moment, Agent Holland," his supervisor growled.

While he hung on the line, Bobby idly paged through a couple of the magazines stacked on the desktop. Bootsie's major interests seemed to tend toward gardening and gourmet cooking and home décor, with a kinky minor in men's action rags like *Soldier of Fortune* and *Mercenary*. His eyes began to glaze over at articles entitled "Parsley, Sage, Rosemary, and Time to Grow Them," "Tomatoes Galore," and "Survival: Twelve Days in the Desert on Two Days of K Rations." He sighed, pulled another magazine from the stack, and flipped it open. All of a sudden his eyes weren't glazed anymore.

The page he was staring at looked like a piece of Swiss cheese. It was full of holes. Square holes. Rectangular holes. Neat, clean holes where words should have been. He flipped the pages, only to find more empty spaces where somebody had meticulously cut out separate words.

Then he checked a second magazine and discovered the same thing. Holes. Empty spaces. And a third, then a fourth and fifth, all of them virtual workbooks for a person sending a crank, anonymous letter.

He looked at the scissors in the porcelain cup that sat beside the photo of the senator. Still holding the phone, he reached down his right hand to pull the drawer out a few inches and saw a little bottle of glue, some sheets of plain typewriter paper, and a stack of plain white envelopes. Generic, all of it. He saw a pair of thin latex gloves. And strewn like confetti all over the interior of the drawer, he saw words.

Go. And. The. Harm. I. You. Hurt.

His heart suddenly felt like a fist, and his blood started pounding in his ears.

Kill. Crazy. Daisy. Daisy. Daisy.

Jesus H. Christ.

"Doug," Bobby said quietly into the phone. "You need to get a technician over here right now."

16

After Bobby left to take Mrs. Riordan for her walk, Angela sat for a long time beside her suitcase and let the tears just roll down her cheeks, drip from her chin, and plop on the hands she kept folded in her lap. She was so tired of crying. It seemed that was all she'd been doing lately. Crying. It felt like her damned day job.

Maybe this time, she thought, if she didn't try to stifle her sobs or attempt to stem the flood in any way, if she literally cried her eyes out, then maybe she'd be done with the stupid tears. Forever. So she sat and cried and cried until she was practically dehydrated. Then she picked up the phone, intending to take another stab at locating Rod in Mexico, but wound up calling her parents instead.

It wasn't until her father asked, "How's my little G-man?" that Angela realized how truly unhappy she was. She didn't want to go to Mexico. She didn't even want to return to L.A.

"Daddy, can I come home?"

His reply was immediate, although he had to speak around an obvious lump in his throat. "The sooner, the better, honey." Then he called out, "Rose! Rose! Angela's coming home."

In the distance, she heard her mother ask, "Is Bobby coming, too?"

But before her father could relay the question, Angela quickly said, "No. Just me, Daddy. I'll call you from the airport when I get in. I have to go now. See you later."

After she hung up, Angela sighed and zipped her suitcase. There was time to prepare a last lunch for the president's mother, and maybe even fix up a plate for her dinner. It wouldn't take long to sauté a chicken breast with a side of pasta and a salad. Poor woman. No sense letting her starve just because the help couldn't get their marital act together.

She was headed toward the kitchen when the cell phone she'd put in her pocket started beeping. For a moment, she was sorely tempted to ignore it, convinced that it was Rose Callifano, the Grand Inquisitor, calling back to give her the third degree about Bobby, literally refusing to let her daughter off the hook. Angela muttered a few well-chosen oaths, then finally answered on the seventh ring.

When she hung up a few minutes later, she was sincerely wishing it *had* been her mother on the other end of the line instead of Doug, informing her that just about all hell had broken loose in Hassenfeld in the past half hour. Mrs. Riordan was missing. Bobby was at Bootsie Rand's, injured somehow, quite possibly in the head, to quote Doug, because Bobby was apparently convinced that the ancient, orange-haired woman was their prime suspect.

"Drive on up there, Angela, and see what's going on," Doug had ordered her.

Good God.

She grabbed the station wagon keys from their hook in

the kitchen, then went flying out the back door. The president's mother had mentioned that her friend Muriel lived about half a mile away, but Angela couldn't recall if she'd said east or west. Since she hadn't pointed the place out on their drives east toward town, Angela guessed the Rand house was west as she turned out of the driveway onto the blacktop and stepped on the gas.

The big Victorian farmhouse didn't quite strike her as Bootsie's style, but it sat at the half-mile point, so she pulled in and trotted up to the front door. Worst case, she'd get directions to the correct address. While she stood on the porch and waited for somebody to answer the door, Angela realized how fast her heart was racing, and that the only thing on her mind was Bobby.

The fact that Mrs. Riordan had disappeared barely fazed her at the moment. Bobby was hurt, Doug had said, but it wasn't serious. Hurt but not too serious. What was that? A sprain, a strained muscle, bruises, cuts and abrasions? His injury could have been much worse, she knew, because this was Bobby Holland they were talking about, after all. Super Agent. Iron Man. The man who would undoubtedly say he was fine even if he had multiple fractures of multiple limbs.

Oh, God. And the very last words she had spoken to him were about wanting him to cry. What if he was? she thought all of a sudden. Crying. In horrible, horrible pain.

No. She wasn't even going to imagine that. If that were the case, somebody surely would have called for emergency medical help. But there were no sirens wailing in the distance. The only sounds Angela heard were crows cawing in a nearby cornfield, a dog barking somewhere in back of the house, and then—finally!—through the closed front door, the sound of clacking heels as they approached.

Bootsie Rand opened the inside door and glared at Angela through the screen as if she were greeting a vacuum cleaner salesman.

"Yes?" she inquired icily.

"It's Angela Holland, Mrs. Rand. Remember me? I'm Mrs. Riordan's housekeeper and cook. I'm looking for my husband, Bobby. Is he here by any chance?" While she spoke, Angela lifted on tiptoe and was straining to see over the wild orange spikes on the little woman's head.

Still looking decidedly annoyed, the elderly woman said, "No, he's not here. Why don't you—"

From somewhere inside the house, Angela heard Bobby's voice call out, "Is that my wife?"

Bootsie's scowl immediately tipped up into a smile, and all the wrinkles on her face reversed, as did her mood. "Oh, that Angela!" she exclaimed. "Bobby's wife! Of course. How silly of me. I should have recognized you, dearie. Do come in." Suddenly the soul of hospitality, the bizarre little woman pushed open the screen door so quickly that Angela had to jump back. "Come in. Come in. May I offer you some iced tea?"

"No, thank you."

Once inside, Angela gazed rather frantically around the vestibule, half expecting to discover a trail of blood across the polished oak floor.

"Your Bobby is in there." Bootsie gestured toward a doorway. "In the sunroom. We were just sipping tea and chatting. Such a pleasant young man." She closed one turquoise-lidded eye in the approximation of a wink. "What is it you young people say? Such a hunk!"

"Ange?" Bobby suddenly appeared in the doorway where Bootsie had pointed. Angela's immediate impression was that he was intact. No blood. No apparent broken bones. No bruises that she could see. Thank God. She lofted a little sigh of gratitude heavenward.

He motioned her to come closer just as Bootsie chirped, "I'll be back with more tea in two shakes of a lamb's tail," then clacked off in her gold sandals.

Now that her heart was no longer racing, Angela's relief turned to irritation. She'd just about had a coronary, worrying about her husband, and here he was, the hunk, blithely sipping iced tea with an eighty-year-old punk rocker. "What the hell is going on?" she asked, approaching him. "What happened with Mrs. Riordan and the professor? Doug said—"

"Ssh." He put a finger to his lips. "Come here. I want to show you something."

Bobby reached out to take her hand and lead her across the sunlit room. His grasp was so warm and strong. She didn't want him to ever let go. What the hell had possessed her, wanting to see his tears? God. She didn't want his tears. All she wanted were his so-hard-to-come-by smiles. When he let go of her hand to open a drawer, she felt lost for a second.

"Take a look in there," he said, barely above a whisper.

Angela looked—at the plain paper and envelopes and glue and latex gloves and the little snippets of words strewn all over the drawer. She made a tiny gulping sound. "Bootsie?" she asked. "You've got to be kidding. Bootsie's the one who's been sending the threats?"

"Ssh," he cautioned her. "It makes sense. Mrs. Riordan

stole the senator out from under Bootsie's nose half a century ago, and the woman has harbored a grudge ever since. Don't forget that the last letter was postmarked right here in Hassenfeld."

"I don't know, Bobby." Angela shook her head, still staring at the bizarre contents of the drawer. "She doesn't strike me as that underhanded. You know? Devious, maybe, but confrontational. I could more easily imagine her starting a catfight with Mrs. Riordan than going to all this trouble to—"

Footsteps sounded in the hallway, and Bobby closed the drawer, then moved Angela away from the desk.

"Don't say anything," he told her. "Just drink your tea, fast, and then let's get out of here."

"Are you all right? Doug said you'd been hurt."

"I'm fine. Ssh."

He wasn't fine. Bobby gritted his teeth as he angled himself behind the wheel of the Taurus, wishing that instead of drinking his iced tea, he had applied the cold glass to his ribs. His side was screaming. He reached down gingerly for the lever to move the seat back from Angela's jockeylike position, which put his nose right up against the windshield, then slowly eased out his legs.

On the other side of the car, Angela called a final good-bye to Bootsie, then climbed in and slammed the door.

The first words out of her mouth were, "I still don't buy it, Bobby, but maybe we should have taken her into custody. Just in case."

"Where's she going to go, Ange?" He twisted the key in the ignition. "And if she does take off, how hard do you think she'll be to find?"

She laughed. "Good point." Her voice became serious then when she asked, "Are you okay? Really?"

"Sure. Fine." The gravel on the driveway crunched under the wheels as he turned the car east, back to Mrs. Riordan's place. "I don't suppose there's any word from Crazy Daisy and the professor, huh?"

"Nothing," she said. "What happened?"

"You mean, how did I screw up?" The words came out a bit more belligerently than he'd intended.

"That's not what I said, Bobby."

He slapped the steering wheel with his open palm. "I did screw up, Ange. The two of them must've had it all worked out. That's probably what all those whispered phone conversations were about. Dammit. She didn't want anybody along this morning other than me. I didn't think it was any big deal. Then Gerrard drove up, Mrs. Riordan let her scarf fly away in the wind, and I went for it, just like a goddamned rookie." He beat the steering wheel and swore again.

"So, you don't think he abducted her, then?"

He shook his head. "She was in on it," he said. "They drove off giggling like a couple of randy teenagers."

"Oh, brother. You don't think they went to a motel or something like that, do you?"

Bobby groaned. "I don't even want to think about it."

"So, Bootsie's our letter writer," she said, "and Gerald Gerrard is exactly what he seemed all along—a septuagenarian on the make."

"I guess."

He didn't like being wrong, and he especially didn't like questioning his instincts, which were dead-on most of the time. Hell, if his instincts hadn't been good, he'd still be in Wishbone, Texas, pumping gas or painting houses. Now, in the space of a few days, he'd been duped by Crazy Daisy, dismayed by the infamous Bootsie, way off base about the professor, and—last but hardly least—hung out to dry by Angela.

Down the road, Bobby could see the snarl of official vehicles at the Riordan house and dozens of people milling about on the driveway and the lawn. Jesus. The full alert. The whole frigging magilla.

He pulled over onto the shoulder of the road and cut the engine, then drew in a deep breath to test his ribs. They flunked. He just wasn't ready to face it all yet. Not Doug and his steely eyes and stony expression, or the richly deserved dressing-down the man was going to be forced to render because he was the special agent in charge. Not the self-satisfied smirks on the faces of Mrs. Riordan and the professor when they inevitably returned. And especially not the coming afternoon when Angela was going to disappear, to walk out on him for what would probably be the very last time.

If he were a crybaby, this would be the perfect time to do it.

"Why are you stopping?" Angela asked.

For a second he couldn't even speak. His throat ached, as if all the muscles there were suddenly in spasm.

"Bobby?" Angela put her hand on his leg. "Honey, are you okay?"

No. He wasn't. Christ. He didn't think he'd ever be okay again.

"Bobby?"

"Yeah. Hey, I'm fine." He was. He had to be fine, dammit, even if it hurt to breathe. He'd always had to be fine. Fine. Smart. Brave. That's what he was all about.

If I'm not back by morning, Bobby, see that Billy gets dressed for school.

Bobby, go see if that nasty Mrs. Corbin needs her windows washed or something, and don't let her give you anything less than ten bucks, you hear? And take your brother with you.

Bobby, I'm cold. Here, take my jacket.

I'm hungry, Bobby. Here, eat my half of the sandwich.

Bobby, I'm scared. Aw, there's nothing to be scared of, Billy.

Bobby, I'm dying. Jesus. No.

He rolled his shoulders now to ease the knots, swallowed hard, then said, "I just needed a couple minutes to get my head on straight before we join that circus up there."

Angela's mouth compressed slightly, and she looked disappointed somehow. Still, she lifted her hand and began to knead his shoulder. "It's not your fault, you know. She would have ditched anybody. I'm sure Doug will understand that. If she knew you were an agent, she probably would have tried it a lot sooner."

"She knows, Ange."

Her hand stilled on his neck. "She told you?"

"She's known all along. She told me the morning after she met Gerrard, when we went for that first walk." He sighed. "She wanted to know if he checked out."

His wife was quiet a moment, apparently letting this new information sink in. "And you told her that he did?"

"I said we hadn't finished our investigation yet, but that it didn't look like we were going to find anything criminal or improper."

"Well, we haven't," she said.

"I know. But I still keep thinking that one of the reasons she trusts him so much is because I kind of gave her my blessing. I should've handled it better somehow. Different. I should've—"

"Oh, Bobby. Don't beat yourself up about this." Her deft hand began working his shoulder once more. "Mrs. Riordan trusts Gerrard because he's a nice guy. That's all. It's not because of anything you said or didn't say. Anyway, I'm sure if you'd told her to back off, she would've done just the opposite. The woman's got a mind of her own, you know. Or haven't you noticed?"

"Do you know what she told me this morning while we were walking? That she was the daughter of the town tramp." He cocked his head toward her and lifted an eyebrow. "Remind you of anybody you know?"

She gave him one of her sweet I-love-you-Bobby smiles. "Yes, it does," she said softly. "Why did she tell you?"

"We bonded," he said, only half kidding. "She also told me that her pal, Bootsie, was pretty much Miss Hassenfeld 1920 or whenever, and thought she had a lock on young Charles Riordan until Daisy lured him away."

"So, that would explain the hate mail, I guess. But, jeez, that's a long time to hold a grudge. Fifty-some years."

"Yeah. Well." He chuckled a bit mournfully. "You women can be tough." Then he reached out to skim the backs of his fingers down his wife's soft cheek.

Angela closed her eyes for a moment, seemingly enjoying his touch. Words surged up in his throat. *I love you. Don't leave. Be with me always.*

"Ange," he whispered.

Those green eyes popped open, dry as a desert, hard as jade. "Don't start, Bobby. Just don't say anything more."

He would have, except just then Doug yelled from the end of the Riordan driveway, "Get the hell back here, Agent Holland. Now."

Bobby started the engine, figuring whatever it was he wanted to say would have come out all wrong anyway. Or, if it had come out right, Angela would have misunderstood. What was the use?

Angela didn't like the way Bobby seemed to favor his left side when he got out of the car and proceeded up the driveway to join the other agents gathered there. It shouldn't have surprised her that most of the younger guys avoided making eye contact with him. He'd lost his protectee, after all. He'd screwed up. God forbid his failure might rub off on them. Even McCray, the older agent, seemed standoffish, contemplating the shine on his shoes rather than stepping forward to shake his colleague's hand.

What really burnt her cookies, though, was the way Tricia Yates was looking at Bobby now. Gone was all the gooey-eyed yearning, along with the hip-slanting, lip-licking, bitch-in-heat, take-me-I'm-yours gestures. Instead, the female agent stood as far away as possible, and when she looked at Bobby at all, it was with a cold dead-man-walking stare. If Angela had wanted to slap the woman earlier for the way she came on to her husband, right now she was sorely tempted to put a bullet dead center in the Man-Eater's callous heart.

It wasn't his fault, she wanted to scream. It could have happened to any of us.

That was exactly what Doug was saying to Bobby when she caught up with them farther along the driveway.

"That's what I told him, Doug," she said, resisting the urge to wrap an arm around Bobby's waist. "It wasn't his fault. Once Mrs. Riordan made up her mind to take off, nobody could have stopped her."

"It'll all be duly noted in my report, Angela," Doug said, then looked back at Bobby. "But you're still gonna have to get your ass down to the training facility for a couple weeks before they'll let you back in the White House. There's nothing I can do about that."

Bobby asked grimly, "Have you informed the president yet?"

"I put in a call. I'm waiting for him to return it right now." He ran his fingers across his jawline, then let out a rough sigh. "I'm not looking forward to giving him the news, I can tell you. I'd rather be run over by a truck."

A few yards away, Agent McCray covered the mouthpiece of his cell phone and called out, "They got her, Doug! The state police are bringing her in."

"Thank you, Jesus," the special agent in charge breathed. "Where'd they find her?"

McCray ended his conversation, then walked over, shaking his head. "They were on a picnic," he said. "Had a big basket, a blanket, fried chicken, the whole damned deal. Can you believe that?"

Beside her, Bobby growled deep in his throat, then muttered, "I'm going to kill her."

McCray's phone bleeped softly, and his face paled just a bit when he answered, then he promptly held out the handset to Doug. "It's the president," he said. "He doesn't sound any too happy."

⌒

From her vantage point in the passenger seat of the Mercedes, Daisy couldn't see much ahead of her or to the rear because the idiotic and overeager state troopers had kept poor Gerald's car hemmed in with their vehicles, before and aft, ever since they'd all left the little park by the river.

"We'll escort you back now, ma'am," the granite-jawed sergeant had decreed, which amounted to a polite way of saying, "Get in the car, lady, and behave yourself."

She was fit to be tied, but Gerald—bless his heart!— was being a very good sport about the entire misadventure. Glancing to her left, she saw his handsome profile and his strong, capable hands on the steering wheel. A beau with liver spots! Daisy almost laughed out loud.

It had been years since she'd felt this alive or this optimistic. When Charles had taken ill five years ago, her own decline had begun in concert with his, despite the fact that she was in amazingly good health. Now, suddenly, she felt ten years younger. Twenty years younger. Whether or not she was in love, she couldn't say. It seemed such a ridiculous concept at her age—falling in love—when the notion of falling at all brought broken bones to mind. But Gerald was in love with her. The old fool. He'd barely brought the fried chicken out of the hamper this morning before he'd confessed his ardor. Then he'd kissed her cheek and whispered, "Come live with me and be my love."

Of course, he hadn't said, "Come *marry* me and be my love," and Daisy hadn't had time to clarify his intentions before the agents of the local Gestapo descended upon them. At the moment, the time didn't seem to be quite right for pursuing the topic, considering that they were boxed in by police cars and about to encounter a dozen disgruntled Secret Service agents. Poor Robert. She hoped she hadn't gotten him into too much hot water with her disappearance.

This was all happening so fast it very nearly took her breath away. When she'd confessed as much to Gerald, he'd just laughed, and his blue eyes had twinkled when he said, "At our age, Margaret, my dear, if it doesn't happen fast, it might very well not happen at all."

Wasn't that the truth? And wasn't Muriel going to simply explode when she learned that the daughter of the town tramp had stolen yet another eligible bachelor right out from under her pert little nose?

"That's quite a welcoming committee, Margaret," Gerald said as they neared her house.

Good God. There must have been several dozen people, in and out of uniform, on her lawn, trampling her ivy not to mention her privacy. Fortunately, as far as she could see, they all appeared to be far more relieved at her reappearance than angry at her disappearance.

With one exception. And he was stalking toward the Mercedes right now as if he meant to tear the bumper off with his bare hands.

Bobby wrenched open the passenger door of the Mercedes and held out his hand for the president's mother. For the twentieth time, he told himself this was professional. It wasn't personal.

Like hell.

"How was your picnic?" he snarled.

"Short," she snapped. "How was your walk?"

"Interrupted."

On the other side of the car, McCray was leaning in the driver's window, having a gruff tête-à-tête with the professor. Bobby leaned down, closer to Mrs. Riordan's ear, and said, "I need to talk to you in private. Now."

"Very well. Let me say good-bye to Gerald first." She angled her head back into the car. "Thank you for a lovely time, Gerald. I'll call you later. Oh, and don't let that thug intimidate you." She shook her finger at McCray.

"Let's go." Bobby grasped her arm and began leading her toward the front door.

"This is ridiculous," she said. "All these people, these paratroopers or whatever they are, called out just because I went for a little drive. I'm sure the taxpayers would have a conniption fit if—"

"Bobby, hold up a minute," Doug called, striding toward them with his phone in hand. "I've got the president on the line, Mrs. Riordan, ma'am. He wants to speak with you."

"Not now," she snapped.

The look on Doug's face slipped from respectful determination to spluttering panic as he stood there with the phone in his outstretched hand and the most powerful man in the world cooling his heels on the other end of the line. Bobby almost laughed. Almost.

"Take it," he told Daisy Riordan.

"I'd rather not," she said.

"Take it."

She rolled her eyes. "Oh, very well." Then she snapped her fingers at Doug. "Give me that, Agent whoever-you-are."

"Yes, ma'am." Doug handed her the phone.

"William?" she said. "Yes, I'm fine. I don't understand all this fuss, however, and I hardly approve—"

When she stopped abruptly and stood there blinking, Bobby figured the president must've shouted something to cut his mother off. That was probably a first. While she listened to whatever it was he was saying, a rosy flush of anger appeared on her cheeks, her free hand tightened to a fist, and her light blue eyes narrowed ominously.

"Yes, William, I hear you," she said finally through tightly clenched teeth. "Now I want you to hear me. I'm getting married in a few days. You're cordially invited to the wedding. You can give me away, dear. Good-bye."

She broke the connection and gave the phone back to Doug, then looked at Bobby and said, "Let's go in the house for that private chat now, Robert. "

17

Rather than add to all the confusion in the front yard, Angela had come in through the back door to get a pot of coffee going, which she figured they could all use right about now. Down the hallway, she heard the front door slam closed and Mrs. Riordan's exaggerated moan of relief.

"Thank heavens."

Barely a second after that, Angela heard her husband bellow, "Are you nuts?"

Oh, jeez. Was *he* nuts? And if he hadn't had a broken rib before, he probably had one now after Crazy Daisy rammed him with her handbag or butted her head into his torso. Angela didn't even want to know what they were arguing about. She was leaving in a couple hours, and she wasn't going to look back. Ever.

Their escaped protectee was back, seemingly unscathed. The mystery of the hate mail had apparently been solved. Their replacements were on the way, if not canceled. Why didn't Bobby just let it go, before he wound up losing his job?

She slumped in a chair at the kitchen table, and while the coffee maker burped and burbled, she stared at Mrs. Riordan's blue binder. Good riddance. Good-bye scut work. Adios ankle holster and preparing three meals a day and sleeping in a too-small bed with a too-big man who had a perfect red heart tattooed on his arm because the one inside his chest was probably defective, chiseled out of granite just like all the rest of him, if it was even there at all.

She remembered then that she had intended to fix lunch and dinner for the president's mother. It was early, a bit before noon, and there was still plenty of time to prepare something before she had to leave. Egg salad sounded good. There were half a dozen hard-boiled eggs just calling to her from the fridge.

Wondering if Mrs. Riordan had written any definitive opinion on the subject of egg salad, Angela reached out to flip open the tattered canvas book. Suddenly the lawyers' names and numbers that Rod had given her swam up before her eyes. She closed the book and sighed out loud, not knowing if she wanted to pull a Scarlett O'Hara and think about that tomorrow, or do a Rhett Butler and frankly not give a damn.

Before Angela could decide whether to be callous Rhett or procrastinating Scarlett, Bobby came muttering and cursing into the kitchen. He was wound so tight that all his muscles were clenched, making the heart on his left biceps appear to be actually pumping. And he was still favoring his left side.

"Ange, do you have a copy of one of those hate letters?" he asked.

She shook her head. "I pitched mine because I didn't want to take the chance that Mrs. Riordan might see it. Why?"

"Well, I want her to see one now. Guess I'll run out to

the trailer and see if they have some spares." He sniffed, then glanced at the brewing coffee machine. "Good. She wants coffee. I'll take it up after I get a copy of a letter."

"I'll go," Angela said, hoping to spare him the long walk across the yard, not to mention save him from a possibly unpleasant encounter with Doug and whatever agents were hanging around after this morning's alert. Bobby certainly wasn't on anybody's dance card this afternoon. "I've got nothing else to do until it's time to leave for Springfield to catch my plane to Chicago."

He just gazed at her without saying a word. Those warm and lovely hazel eyes of his were taking her in as if he were trying to memorize her, Angela thought. As if he hadn't already done that years ago. Just as she had memorized him.

As if he were about to say, "Don't leave me."

As if she'd change her mind if he did.

But he didn't.

"Thanks," he finally said, "but I need to talk to Doug, anyway." He winced just a little as he turned and started toward the back door.

"Bobby?"

"Yeah?"

"What you really need to do is have your side checked out," she said. "Sweetie, I worry—"

"Don't," he told her.

And then he was gone.

Doug was leaning against the side of the trailer, scowling, smoking a cigarette with all the apparent pleasure of a blindfolded man before a firing squad.

"Busy morning," Bobby said.

"You could put it that way." The older agent picked a fleck of tobacco off his lower lip. "I'm standing out here now thinking how I love my job, especially getting reamed by the director a few minutes ago who'd just been reamed by the president, and how I'm looking forward to interrogating an eighty-year-old female this afternoon about some little snippets of paper, latex gloves, and a goddamned bottle of Elmer's glue."

"Can you hold off on that until I've run it past Mrs. Riordan, Doug? I want to show her a couple copies of the threatening letters so she'll start taking this situation a little more seriously."

"Help yourself. They're on my desk." He turned his head away from Bobby and blew out a hard stream of smoke. "Is she serious about this marriage business, Bobby? The minute she hung up on the president, he was on the horn to Henry Materro, wanting to know just what we've dug up about Gerrard."

Bobby shrugged. As far as he could tell, Daisy Riordan had made her announcement about the wedding based more on supreme annoyance than any serious intention. Still, she'd announced it, and he thought he knew her well enough to know that once her pride was involved, there might not be any going back.

Or, hell, maybe she was just damned tired of living alone. It could get pretty brutal, as well he knew. Or maybe she really loved the professor. People did a lot of crazy things for love. Some people even got tattoos.

"Just wait a little while," Bobby had urged her a while ago when they'd come inside the house.

"Wait a little while? For what?" she snapped. "Next spring? June? For Gerald to drop dead of a heart attack? Or me? What would you like me to wait for, Robert?"

"Let me do some more checking."

"I didn't need you people to check out my first husband," she said. "And I don't need you now to check out number two."

"I think she's going to do whatever she wants," Bobby said now, "whenever she damn well wants to do it."

Doug took a last drag from his cigarette, dropped it, and ground it under the heel of his boot. "I get the impression that you like old Crazy Daisy in spite of the fact that she's doing her level best to ruin your career, son."

"Yeah." Bobby almost laughed. "Must be some kind of death wish, my attraction to difficult women."

"You and Angela get things worked out?"

"No."

"Not much time. Your replacements are due to arrive in a couple hours, and you're due for a little reassessment at the facility in Georgia starting Monday morning. After that—" Doug lifted his thick shoulders in a shrug, patted his pocket for cigarettes, then cursed softly as he apparently changed his mind. "I'll recommend they put you back on the White House detail, Bobby," he said, "but I can't make you any promises."

"I appreciate that, Doug."

"Okay. Well, let's get you some copies of those letters, then." Doug opened the door for him. "I've got everybody scrambling now, trying to find out more about this goddamned professor."

Inside the trailer, several conversations stopped cold when Bobby walked in. Everybody turned back to phones or files or monitors, including long-legged Tricia Yates. Obviously, whatever the woman had found so appealing, so irresistible, about him earlier was now tainted by the foul odor of his screwup this morning. A couple of years ago the rejection might have bothered him, but now it was only Angela's rejection that hurt.

He followed Doug back to his office for the letters.

"You let me know what Mrs. Riordan says about these," Doug told him as he handed the copies across his desk. "Maybe she can give me a handle on how to approach the Rand woman. Believe me, the last thing I want to do is scare that poor little old lady to death."

Somehow Bobby didn't think that would be a problem. Bootsie, the poor little old lady in question, would probably have the special agent in charge back on a two-pack-a-day habit before the interrogation was halfway over.

In Mrs. Riordan's room, Bobby put down the tray with the coffee and the egg salad sandwich that Angela had made.

"What's that?" Mrs. Riordan asked.

"Lunch, I guess."

"No," she said, "I mean the papers in your hand. Are those the crank letters that are supposed to convince me I'm in mortal danger?"

He held the chair for her and watched while she lifted a corner of one of Angela's crustless, triangular creations, then clucked her tongue and pushed the plate to the far side of the tray in favor of a sip of coffee.

Bobby put the letters on the table in front of her. "I found a stack of cut-up magazines on Mrs. Rand's desk this morning, and hundreds of cutout words stashed in the drawer. Glue. Latex gloves. Paper and envelopes that I'm sure our forensics people can match to the ones received in Washington."

"So?" She took another sip of coffee, pointedly ignoring the letters, practically ignoring Bobby as well.

"So," he grumbled, "it would help no end if you'd take this seriously. These letters are the reason they sent us here in the first place, Mrs. Riordan. The president was concerned for your safety. He still is. We all are."

She gave him a flat stare, her mouth tightly crimped and her eyes narrowed to slits. "Do me a favor, Robert." She pointed across the room. "Open my closet door. On the shelf, there's a white shoebox. It's on the right side, as I recall. Well, right or left, you'll see it. Take it down and bring it to me."

"This is no time to be trying on shoes," he growled.

"I realize that," she said, pointing to the closet again and raising her voice to the level of a drill sergeant. "Now get me the confounded box."

Bobby did as she directed, cursing when he stretched his injured side to reach for the upper shelf.

"What's the matter, Robert?" She sounded less like a drill sergeant now and more like Nurse Ratchett.

"Nothing."

"Something is the matter. I can tell. I'd feel horrible if my little shenanigan this morning were to blame for an injury of some sort."

Shenanigan. Bobby gritted his teeth. "I twisted my ankle walking back to the house. That's all. It'll be fine. Is this the box you want?"

"Yes. Should you see a doctor? I could call—"

"No."

"Very well."

He gave her the box, then watched as she carefully pried off the lid and began riffling through the many envelopes inside. She extracted one, pulled a folded paper from it, fanned it open in the air, and handed it to him.

"Here," she said almost casually. "I imagine the letters you want me to look at are quite similar, if not identical, to this one."

Damned if they weren't. Bobby wasn't a forensics expert, but the size and set of the words looked the same to him. He lifted his gaze to the president's mother, not too surprised to find a pretty smug, self-satisfied look on her face.

"They're from Muriel," she said, answering his unspoken question. "She's been sending them to me for years. Which, I might add, is precisely how long I've been ignoring them."

"Wait a minute." Bobby's brain suddenly felt like a chunk of concrete. "She's been doing this for years?"

"Yes. At least ten years. Possibly twelve. The letters started arriving after Muriel's arthritis made it much too difficult for her to vandalize my car or pull up tomato plants in my garden or soap my windows or put nasty things in my mailbox. It's her—what do you law enforcement people call it?—her modus operandi. Almost a family tradition. I don't know what the fuss is about all of a sudden."

"You said she used to vandalize your car?" Bobby wasn't sure he'd heard her right.

"Yes. Oh, I'm quite sure that was Muriel's handiwork the other evening at the theater." She clucked her tongue in disgust. "Her arthritis must've gone into remission, or else she employed some local hooligans the way she often does."

"Have you filed police reports?" he asked.

Mrs. Riordan looked sincerely shocked. "No, of course not. Why would I want to do that?"

Bobby could think of about a dozen reasons, not the least of which was that threats of violence tend to lead to acts of violence. The agency had the statistics to prove it.

But before he could begin to enumerate the reasons, the president's mother said, "I've never filed a complaint because, perverse as it may seem, I've rather enjoyed being a burr under Muriel's saddle all these years, watching her go through three husbands in the hope of finding one who was half as good as Charles."

Her gaze strayed to the photo of her husband beside her bed and lingered there a moment before she said, "On our fiftieth wedding anniversary, Muriel had somebody set fire to our gazebo. The one out there now is the replacement."

Bobby felt like ripping his hair out. Or hers. "Is the president aware of this?"

"I doubt it," she snapped. "It's none of his business, is it?"

She paused for another sip of coffee, inspected the yellow-and-green egg salad once more, and made a soft *tsk*. "Have you had lunch yet, Robert? Would you care for my sandwich? I've never been fond of pickle relish in egg salad."

"No, ma'am." Bobby threaded his fingers through his hair. He was going to get her to take this situation seriously if it killed him. "What I'd care for is to know why you've allowed yourself to be victimized all this time?"

"Victimized!" Her pale blue eyes opened wide. "I'd be a victim if I acknowledged any of Muriel's little stunts." She waved her hand in a gesture of indifference. "I simply ignore them. I always have. I'm sure it galls her even more. Besides, I always wonder what the old fool will come up with next."

Bobby pointed to the letters on the table. "I guess sending threats to the White House instead of directly to you was a pretty good way of escalating things."

She nodded in agreement. "To be quite honest, I'm relieved that her bout with cancer hasn't slowed her down. Heaven only knows how she must be thrilling to all the disruption and commotion here of late."

"Yeah, well, I wonder just how much she's going to be thrilled when she's interrogated by my supervisor this afternoon," Bobby said.

"He'll do no such thing."

"Pardon me?"

She banged her fist on the table. "I said he'll do no such thing. I won't have anyone bothering Muriel about this. I don't want anyone to say a word to her. Not one word. Is that clear?"

"Well, it's clear," Bobby answered, "but it's also out of the question. She threatened you, and we're obliged to investigate."

"She threatened *me*," Mrs. Riordan said. "She didn't

threaten the president, so you Secret Service people aren't obliged to do anything as far as I can see. I'm a private citizen, Robert, and I have absolutely no intention of pressing charges against my friend."

"She's not your friend," Bobby said.

"Well, she's a damned fine enemy, then, and I don't want to lose her. Is that understood?"

"I'll mention it to my supervisor, ma'am," he said, gritting his teeth, taking a step toward the door.

"You do that. And while you're mentioning it to him, I'll mention it to my son, the president." She gripped the arms of her chair, pushed herself up, then brushed past him on her way to the phone. "I'm serious, Robert. I want you people to stay away from Muriel."

"You're making a mistake," he said. Then, with his hand on the door knob, he added gruffly, "And, goddammit, I won't be here to help you when you finally find that out."

If she heard him, she didn't reply. She had turned her back on him and was already punching a series of numbers into the phone.

～

Angela was licking the last of the egg salad off her fingers when Bobby stalked past her toward their bedroom. She gathered things hadn't gone so well upstairs. After she rinsed the dishes and wiped off the counter, she followed him.

He had pushed her suitcase to the far side of the bed to make room for his open garment bag, into which he was jamming suits, shirts, ties. She groaned inwardly. No wonder he was on a first-name basis with the dry-cleaning people in every hotel in the country. While she watched from the doorway, Angela couldn't help but notice that he used his left arm as little as possible, for the most part keeping it pinned closely to his side. His heart side, she thought. Assuming he had one.

"Do you want a ride into Springfield?" he asked when he saw her.

"Sure."

"Okay. Get your suitcase."

"Now?" She blinked. They couldn't leave yet, could they? "Don't we need to wait for our replacements to arrive?"

He zipped the garment bag closed, nearly ripping off the little metal tab. "I'm leaving now. If you want to wait, fine. You can tell Crazy Daisy good-bye for me." He grabbed his empty shaving kit and went into the bathroom to collect his things.

"Why are you taking this so personally?" she asked, standing in the bathroom doorway now.

"You mean you and me?" He tossed his wet toothbrush and crumpled tube of toothpaste into the canvas kit.

"No, I don't mean you and me. I mean Mrs. Riordan. You've really let that woman get under your skin."

"Did you do something with my deodorant?" he asked, ignoring her comment. "And my razor? Where the hell's my razor, Ange? You're always moving my goddamned stuff."

She sighed. "Look in the medicine cabinet. If you'd just put things back in the same place where you got them, Bobby, you'd—"

Doug's voice interrupted her from behind. "Holy mother of Floyd! Are you two going at it again?"

"No!" they both shouted in unison.

"Well, you could have fooled me. I just came up to let you know there's been a change in plans."

Angela whirled around to face their supervisor. "What now?"

"The president's coming."

"Here?" Her voice rose half an octave.

"Here," Doug said. "Today. He's flying out and back on a military transport. The press hasn't been notified." He glanced down, squinting at a small notebook curved in the palm of his meaty hand. "He'll touch down in Springfield at seventeen hundred, then he'll helicopter here, have a quiet little dinner with his mother and her intended, and be back in Springfield by twenty hundred for the flight back to D.C."

From behind her, Bobby let out a blistering string of curses while Angela simply stood there staring at Doug, almost afraid to ask the first, the obvious, the only horrible question that popped into her head. She swallowed before she opened her mouth.

"Who's going to fix this quiet little dinner?"

Doug didn't even have to answer. His stern, unwavering, your-leave-is-canceled look said it all. She was. She was cooking dinner for the president of the United States on a few hours' notice.

Angela nearly threw up right then and there.

"I'm staying," Bobby said, stalking Doug across the backyard.

"No, you're not."

"Jesus, Doug. At least let me stay to help Ange. She can't—"

Special Agent in Charge Doug Coulter stopped so abruptly that Bobby almost ran over him. The man turned and glared. "What part of no do you not understand, Agent Holland?"

"Doug," Bobby pleaded, "you're going to need all the help you can get with Riordan coming in a couple hours."

"Yes, I am. But you're no longer eligible for protective detail, and I have a hard time picturing you working the phones here in the trailer or putting up a road block so his chopper can land out there on the road." He fumbled for a cigarette, lit it, then said, "Besides, there's another reason you can't stay."

"What's that?"

"The president's mother wants you out. She told the president. He told Materro. And now I'm telling you."

"She doesn't mean it," Bobby said. "Hell, she's just pissed about this deal with her pal, Bootsie. She wants the whole hate mail thing to be dropped."

"We're dropping it," Doug said.

Bobby could actually feel his temperature shoot up a couple degrees. "You're what? Dropping it! What the hell are you talking about?"

"Do I have to spell it out for you again? She told the president. He told Materro. And now I'm—"

"Materro can't just agree to drop an investigation on somebody's whim," Bobby insisted.

"Well, why don't you just call the director and tell him

that, son. You know, maybe he hasn't read the rule book yet. Or just maybe he's willing to bend the rules to get on the president's sunny side. You might want to ask about that, too, while you're at it." Doug took in a deep drag, exhaled, then dashed the cigarette to the ground and swore harshly. "It's out of my hands, Bobby."

"What if I stick around anyway? On my own time?" Bobby asked.

"You best think twice about that, son," Doug said. "You're good at this job. You'll be right back in the White House after you put in the required time in Georgia. But if Mrs. Riordan sees you around here tonight, I can pretty much guarantee you you'll be served up as sweetbreads for this little dinner of hers."

~

Angela was in the kitchen, looking more like a deer in headlights than any actual deer in headlights Daisy Riordan had ever seen. It occurred to Daisy that, in her obstinacy, she'd set some rather large events in motion, not the least of which was the unscheduled trip to Hassenfeld by the president of the United States. Somewhere in her irate conversation with William, she also thought she might have implied that she wanted Robert fired. She hadn't meant it, of course, and she had every intention of rectifying the situation as soon as she could decently swallow her pride.

In the meantime, Bobby's wife appeared on the verge of a nervous breakdown.

"This dinner needn't be complicated," Daisy said, hoping to reassure her.

The young woman just stared at her bleakly. "In all honesty, Mrs. Riordan, and no disrespect intended, but I'd almost rather take a bullet for the president than have to prepare his dinner."

Given the child's culinary skills, Daisy could well understand that. "As I said, it needn't be complicated. I'd suggest the chicken breasts sautéed in olive oil. You do those quite well, Angela. A simple buttered rice, perhaps, and a vegetable. Anything but broccoli or brussels sprouts. Since William's time here will be limited, dessert won't be necessary. We'll have drinks in the living room before our meal, and coffee there afterward."

"I think I can manage that," Angela said, her face brightening considerably.

"I'm sure you can."

"You must really be looking forward to this evening, Mrs. Riordan," she said. "Is Professor Gerrard nervous about meeting the president?"

"I spoke with him a moment ago. He seems to be taking it all in stride. It's rather ridiculous, really, a man of Gerald's stature having to pass my son's inspection." Daisy gave a little sniff as she peered toward the hallway that led to the servants' quarters. "Is Robert still here?"

She'd come downstairs not to assist Angela with the menu or to discuss Gerald but rather to apologize to Robert for her fit of pique over Muriel and for any inadvertent damage she might have done to his career. She meant to make the proper reparations, beginning with saying she was sorry.

"He's back at the surveillance trailer," Angela said. "Would you like me to call down there for you?"

"That won't be necessary. When he returns, please tell him I'd like to have a few words with him."

"He probably won't have time, Mrs. Riordan. Bobby's been ordered to leave."

"Well, we'll just see about that," Daisy said with a touch of indignation, despite the fact that she was the one no doubt responsible for his dismissal. It wouldn't do much for her matchmaking efforts if these two young people were officially ordered apart.

A sheen of moisture appeared in Angela's eyes. "His things are all packed, and—" Her lips compressed in silence, and she reached up to swipe at an escaped tear. First one and then another.

Oh, dear. Oh, damn. Daisy never knew quite what to do when someone cried. It was one of the reasons she avoided funerals. Not being one to weep herself, she was never quite sure how to properly console a person. She wasn't one to hug people or to murmur a soft "There, there." Usually she waited quietly, uncomfortably, until the waterworks subsided, then sought out the nearest exit and sent the weeper a warm and thoughtful note the very next day.

It occurred to her all of a sudden that it was probably one of the reasons she prized her longtime association with Muriel. The silly fool never cried. She simply got even. Daisy knew how to handle behavior like that. But this?

"I'm sorry," Angela said, sniffing, snuffling, nearly scouring her cheeks with her hands now. "This just happens sometimes. It's genetic."

"Oh, my goodness. Well, I—"

Robert came through the back door like an answered prayer.

"She's crying," Daisy said helplessly. "Do something."

Such a wonderful smile broke out on his face that Daisy's ancient heart performed a slow but decisive little flip. The way he strode across the kitchen reminded her how dearly she missed the inelegant thud of male footsteps in her house. The way he curled his arms around his soggy wife, embraced her so protectively, and pressed his lips into the curve of her neck made Daisy suddenly decide that, yes, she really would marry Gerald. How surprising! How absolutely astonishing! Up until this very moment she'd really only been toying with the notion.

Robert lifted his eyes to hers. "I'm leaving now, Mrs. Riordan. It's been a pleasure, ma'am."

18

Less than an hour later Bobby sat, cooling his heels, in a curtained-off cubicle in the emergency room of the Hassenfeld Community Care Center, taking shallow breaths while he glared at the big round clock on the hospital green wall. He didn't have time for this.

He'd walked into the ER, flashed his badge across the admitting desk at Charge Nurse Vera Kuhlmann, then told her he had a broken rib and needed a scrip for painkillers ASAP.

Vera Kuhlmann had pulled her glasses down her nose, skewered him with her Raisinette eyes, then asked him if he had a medical degree in addition to his badge. When he said no, she promptly informed him that *she'd* tell him whether or not he had a broken rib *after* he was x-rayed.

Bobby hurt too much to argue. He took off his clothes, donned the dinky faded blue gown Nurse Kuhlmann gave him, and tried not to yell obscenities when the technician jammed his injured side against the X-ray screen.

Hospitals weren't so different from the army. Hurry up and wait. Hell. He looked at his gray suit coat now as it dangled from a hook on the cinderblock wall. He'd taken it out of his garment bag and put it on before he left the Riordan house, thinking that "the uniform"—drab suit, a muted tie, the shiny brogans, the dark shades—would help cut a swath through whatever small-town red tape might lie in his way.

The uniform hadn't done much for Vera Kuhlmann. And all the hard-edged federal agent look had done for Angela, after she stopped crying, was make it easier for her to say good-bye. Or maybe her coolness was just a reaction to his. After all, he knew he wasn't really leaving. Not yet, anyway.

"Call me from Mexico," he'd told her. "Just so I know you're all right."

"I'm not going," she said. "I thought I'd spend a couple days with Mom and Dad instead."

He'd been heartened by that. Heartened, hell. He'd wanted to whoop for joy. His wife wasn't winging south to meet ol' Rod after all. She was going home to Angelo and Rose. That had to be a good sign. A hopeful sign. But then she'd averted her gaze and added, "Why don't you call me there from Georgia? We can't just keep postponing the inevitable, Bobby."

The inevitable, of course, was the D word. Divorce. It might as well have been Death. "Yeah," he told her. "Okay. I'll call." Thank God he'd been in too much of a hurry to even think about it then.

As opposed to now, with his forward progress temporarily halted by the brick wall and hatchet face of Nurse Kuhlmann. He looked at the clock again, checked it against his watch. The president would be here in a little under two hours. That didn't give him much more time to come up with something hard on either Bootsie or the professor, and about all he had right now was a bad feeling in his gut and something—what?—gnawing at the back of his brain.

He'd tried to work the phone while he waited for the X-ray results, but it was almost impossible getting correct numbers with the reception cutting in and out every time he leaned an inch in any direction. Besides, he wasn't convinced he'd learn anything over the phone that his colleagues hadn't already found out. The professor kept coming up clean as the proverbial whistle.

"Well, you were right, Agent Holland." Nurse Kuhlmann raked back the vinyl curtain and glided into the cubicle on her quiet white shoes. "That sucker is fractured. Showed up perfectly on the film."

"Told you," Bobby said, edging off the table and reaching for his jacket and shoulder holster. "Where's my prescription?"

She ignored him. "Doctor says you're to rest for at least a week. No strenuous exercise. No heavy lifting. No—"

Bobby shrugged into his holster and jacket while the woman went through her litany of instructions, none of which he was going to be able to follow. All he wanted was a pill to take the edge off the pain and not dull his senses too much in the process.

"The scrip?" he reminded her.

"Follow me out to the desk," she said.

While he waited for her to fill out the paperwork for the precious controlled substance, Bobby asked, "You wouldn't happen to know the Rand woman who lives out on Route Four, would you?"

Nurse Kuhlmann's little brown eyes got bigger. "Bootsie?"

"Yes," Bobby said.

"Sure I know her. I'm related to her. Some kind of cousin. My grandmother was her father's second cousin, or something like that. I always forget. Anyway—" She rolled her eyes. "Mine's not the side of the family with the people chained in attics. What's Bootsie done now?"

"Nothing," he said casually. "What's she done in the past?"

The woman actually cracked a smile. "Cripes. What hasn't she done? Just for starters, I can tell you—"

The phone near her elbow gave a sharp ring, and Bobby was tempted to tell her not to answer it. While she listened to whoever was on the other end of the line, he drummed his fingers, and she scratched a few more notations on his paperwork.

"Sorry," she said, hanging up, then handing him his prescription. "There's been a pileup on Highway Ninety. They're bringing some of the injured here."

"If I could just ask you a couple more questions," he said.

"Sorry." She was already out of her chair and headed away. "Listen, if you want the lowdown on Bootsie Rand, ask Tiny at the Tattoo Parlor. He's her nephew. He'll give you an earful."

"Thanks."

The Tattoo Parlor. Bobby shuddered just thinking about it.

~

"Smells good," Tricia Yates said as she walked into the kitchen.

"Thanks," Angela replied at the same time she thought, Bobby's gone. What the hell could you possibly want from me?

Tricia leaned against the counter where Angela was chopping parsley. The Man-Eater gazed at the dark green leaves with utter disdain. "Doug sent me up to see if you needed any help."

"No," she answered coolly. "Everything's under control."

The agent's sigh of relief was almost audible. No doubt she didn't want the blot of "scullery maid" anywhere on her résumé, the disloyal slut. Angela was still angry that the woman had turned her back on Bobby the minute he was in trouble. Not that it hadn't occurred to her that she had essentially done the same thing, but it was more satisfying at the moment to direct her anger at Tricia than at herself.

"Well, I'll go back to the trailer, then," Tricia said.

"Any new information about the professor?" Angela asked, attempting to sound like an agent despite her appearance as a cook.

"Zip. We're not finding out anything that we didn't already know."

"I guess that's good news," Angela said. "I'm sure the president will be glad to get a clean report. What time are the guys going to do the sweep of the house?"

"They're not."

It was standard practice, whenever possible, to bring in bomb-sniffing dogs and X-ray machines to secure any rooms where the president planned to be. Angela was astonished that it wasn't the case this afternoon.

"Who made that decision?" she asked, her knife now poised in the air above the cutting board.

"Not Doug," Tricia said. "As far as I can tell, it was the director. Sounds like he's on a let's-please-the-president-by-not-upsetting-his-mother kick. Anyway, Doug said they'd based the decision not to do the sweep on the fact that there had been two agents inside the house for a week."

"Makes sense, I guess." Did it? She and Bobby hadn't exactly swept the house, but they were certainly familiar with its every nook and cranny. The place was hardly open to the public, either. Nobody had been here this past week, actually inside, except the old geezers in the bridge club.

"Well, since you don't need me," Tricia said, "I'm outta here."

As fast as her long legs could carry her, too, Angela couldn't help but notice. The fickle bitch was probably afraid Angela was going to change her mind and find some work for her to do.

She transferred the chopped parsley to a bowl, covered it with plastic wrap, and stowed it in the refrigerator until it was time to put it on the rice. She'd already decided to make a huge portion of that on the off chance that, if she burned the bottom, there would still be plenty of edible grains on top. Hey, if she wasn't a great cook, at least she was a clever one.

A busy one, too, which was good. There just wasn't time to think about Bobby right now. Don't even start, she warned herself. She'd already looked like a jerk, crying the way she had this afternoon. No wonder he was so eager to get away from her.

With her chicken already happily marinating in lemon juice and olive oil, she was ready to scrape and julienne the carrots just the way Mrs. Riordan liked them when the president's mother called to her.

"Angela, I'm having a devil of a time trying to decide what to wear this evening. I could use a second opinion. Would you come up here for a moment?"

⁓

Before he visited the Tattoo Parlor, Bobby took his prescription into Boechler's Pharmacy next door, where a bronzed plaque on the wall proclaimed the gratitude of the Hassenfeld Chamber of Commerce for serving their community for over half a century. Some of the stock on the dusty shelves looked as if it had sat there at least that long.

"This will take just a few minutes," the white-jacketed man behind the counter told him. "Any other shopping you have to do?"

Bobby dragged his shades down his nose, then flipped open his badge and ID. "No, no shopping. But I'll take one of those pills right now, okay?"

The pharmacist's eyes widened, and his Adam's apple did a jumping jack above the knot of his tie. "I'm sorry. We usually don't—"

"This isn't usual," Bobby snapped.

The man looked at the prescription slip once more, then reached behind him for a jar and shook out a single tablet, which he slid almost furtively across the countertop. "There's a drinking fountain just over there."

"Thanks." Bobby swallowed the pill. "I'd really ap-

preciate it if I could use your phone. Is there a private office in back?"

"Yes, sir. Right back there." He pointed. "Help yourself."

"Thanks."

Then Bobby sat for a few minutes in the little win-
dowless back room, staring at the phone, wondering who
he could call whom his colleagues hadn't already called,
no doubt repeatedly, with reference to the professor. He
wondered, too, how long before the pill would begin to
dull the pain in his side, and just how much time he had
before all he felt like doing was putting his head down on
any flat surface and zoning out for the next twenty-four
hours.

Think, he told himself. From the various reports he'd
seen this week, he knew that agents had been in touch
with the police in Cambridge, Massachusetts, Gerald
Gerrard's previous residence, and had turned up zero
problems. No traffic offenses. No disturbing the peace.
Not even littering. Sometimes, though, as Bobby well
knew, all a person had to do was ask a different question
to get a different answer.

He punched in his credit card number, got the number
of the Cambridge police from Information, and when his
call went through, he asked for the Homicide desk instead of Records. After the captain on the other end of the
line made a few calls of his own and was satisfied with
his caller's credentials, Bobby asked him, not about Gerald Gerrard, but about any John Does in their morgue in
recent weeks.

"Not here," the captain said, "but Boston's got a real
lulu. No head. No hands. This John Doe will still be on

the books when my baby grandson graduates from the police academy."

Bobby took notes on where the body of the white male was discovered—snagged in fishing line under a boat in the Charles River—and when—two weeks ago. The captain didn't know if the medical examiner's report had come in yet, but he said he'd have someone at the Boston P.D. get back to Bobby with more details about the corpse.

"Great," Bobby said. "Tell them it's top priority, will you?" Then he gave him Angela's cell phone number, since he couldn't depend on having a decent conversation on his own.

After he hung up, he stared at the oversize wall calendar with its sunny blue skies and fields of bright flowers touting instant allergy relief. He wished he had more time. Even a few hours. He wished his head were clearer. If anything happened to Daisy Riordan, it was going to be his fault.

The office door opened a crack. "Your prescription is ready, Mr. Holland," the pharmacist said. "No rush, though. Feel free to—"

"Thanks," Bobby said, standing up and pocketing his notes. "I'm all through here."

~

Mrs. Riordan had called Angela upstairs to help her decide between a rather severe pale pink cocktail suit and a softer, full-skirted dress of navy blue silk. As Angela might have expected, when she suggested the navy, Daisy

Riordan chose the pink. The woman could be as irritating as . . . as . . . Bobby!

"If that's all," Angela said, "I'll go back downstairs and finish the carrots."

"One more thing." The president's mother laid the pink satin jacket on her bed and smoothed a wrinkle with the flat of her hand. "You may think I'm just a meddling old woman, Angela, and that's probably true, but I've become quite fond of you and your husband. It grieves me that the two of you can't seem to find some common emotional ground."

Angela didn't know what to say. An offended "It's none of your damned business" came instantly to mind, even as a part of her was deeply touched by the woman's obvious concern. My God. Was her marriage such a blatant mess that everybody could see it? Before she could conjure up a response, though, Mrs. Riordan continued.

"Some people simply don't cry, my dear. But that doesn't mean they don't have feelings. Quite often, the most intense of feelings."

"I understand that," Angela said. Please don't say anything more, she wanted to scream. Just let me go fix the freaking carrots. My husband, the one who doesn't cry, just left me in such a dry-eyed hurry that he didn't even kiss me good-bye. He couldn't wait to get away from me. He'll call me about the divorce, he said. If the president weren't coming, if I didn't have to hold myself together for a few more hours, I'd be in bed with the covers pulled over my head right now and just maybe—no, probably— definitely—never get up again.

Mrs. Riordan turned, ignoring the wrinkles in her

jacket to fix her gaze almost fiercely on Angela. "I don't cry, myself," she said.

Just as fiercely, Angela looked back at her. God help her, she was about to commit professional suicide by telling the president's mother that maybe she *should* cry, that maybe it would do her good, when the cell phone in her apron pocket started its insistent ring.

⁓

The big red paper heart wasn't hanging in the window of the Tattoo Parlor anymore, Bobby noticed as he walked in, making him wonder if it had only been a figment of his imagination the week before.

"Hey. Look who's back," enormous Tiny said, looking up from his magazine. "You're not having any problems, I hope."

"Not with the tattoo," Bobby said.

"So, did your lady like it?"

Not enough, Bobby almost said. "Yeah. She's crazy about it."

"Great." Tiny closed his magazine and leaned forward across his counter. "So, what can I do for you? You ready to work your way up to a dragon? I can give you a repeat customer discount."

Bobby did his best to work up a good-ol'-boy chuckle. "Maybe next time. Hey, Tiny, I wanted to ask—"

It was the way that Tiny cocked his head that warned Bobby to go slow. A good interrogator was a patient one. First he won his suspect's confidence, then he asked the easy questions before the tough ones. Bobby was hardly a good interrogator. When it came to playing good cop/bad cop, he was always nominated for the bad guy. But he couldn't afford to screw this up. And he was pretty certain he wasn't going to be able to intimidate big Tiny into telling him what he wanted to know.

He fell back on his Wishbone drawl. "Well, hell. You know, I just might do it after all. That dragon. I've got another arm, right? Got any pictures I can look at?"

Tiny's grin was about the size of a slice of watermelon as he reached down behind his counter and came up with one book, then another. "I'll go on back and check my equipment. You just yell out when you see something you like. Twenty percent off, man. Can't beat that."

"Can't beat that," Bobby murmured, opening the first book to a skull with ivy twining through its empty eye sockets. Then he glanced over and saw the name of the magazine Tiny had been reading while he waited for his next victim to come through the door. *Mercenary*. The same rag Bobby had seen at the bottom of the pile on Bootsie's desk.

Okay. Slow was fine when you had nothing but time. But it was time to quit dancing around now. The orchestra was already playing "Goodnight, Ladies."

"Hey, Tiny," he called. "I could use your advice out here."

The big man lumbered from the back room and settled on his stool behind the counter again. "What's up?"

Bobby started to point to a dagger swagged with orange flames, then drew back his hand. "Hey, I nearly forgot. I've been meaning to ask you. Didn't somebody tell me you're related to Muriel Rand?"

"Aunt Bootsie?" He grinned. "Hey, I tattooed her a couple years ago. You'd never believe where."

Bobby didn't want to know where and prayed that Tiny wasn't going to volunteer that particular information.

"What's the old bat done now?" Tiny chuckled. "Excuse me, I mean Aunt Bootsie."

"She's been threatening the president's mother," Bobby said, trying hard not to sound threatening himself.

"Daisy Riordan?" The man didn't look surprised. "That's nothing to get bent out of shape about. Those two have been going at each other for decades. For as long as I can remember."

If he looked bent out of shape, Bobby thought, that's because he was. One rib, at least. The Percocet, if it was kicking in at all, was just making him drowsy. "You know anything about vandalizing Cadillacs or some local kids who might be available for a little arson?"

The big man's mouth twitched tellingly, and his gaze slid sideways for a second. "Hey, man. She goes over the top once in a while, okay, but essentially she's harmless. Hell, she's about a hundred and twenty years old. What kind of trouble can the old bat make?"

"Enough." Bobby took his creds from his pocket, making sure his jacket flared open just enough for Tiny to get a glimpse of his gun. "I've got just a few more questions."

With his gaze lingering on Bobby's badge, Tiny swallowed hard, then muttered, "I hate like hell to get on that old lady's bad side."

"Afraid of getting cut out of her will?"

"What will? Aunt Bootsie gave most of her money to the college this summer."

"What do you mean?"

"You know Hassenfeld College? Just south of town?"

Bobby nodded patiently. *Come on. Come on. Spit it out*. He glanced at his watch. The president would be landing in Springfield in half an hour. It would take him all of ten minutes to chopper here.

"Aunt Bootsie, she sold off a couple thousand acres of prime real estate this summer in order to set up that whatchamacallit. That endowed chair." Tiny gave a snort. "Man, I've seen that professor, the one whose ass is in that chair, and he doesn't look like he's worth any half a million dollars to me."

"Gerald Gerrard?"

"Yeah. Gerald Gerrard." He rolled his eyes and bent one wrist. "He sounds like a real stand-up guy to me."

Bootsie brought the professor to town! Bobby didn't know what he'd just heard, but it felt like somebody had just struck a match across his brain.

"Are you going to be around here for a while in case I have any more questions?" he asked, already heading for the door.

"Yeah. Sure," Tiny answered almost sadly. "So, you didn't really come in because you wanted another tattoo, huh?"

Bobby waved his hand. Shit. He didn't even want the first one anymore.

~

When the doorbell rang, Daisy was sitting at her dressing table, debating whether to wear her freshwater pearls or the lovely strand of cultured pearls Charles had given her for their silver wedding anniversary. If that was Gerald at the door downstairs, he was early. She didn't know whether that annoyed or pleased her. But when she looked into the mirror and saw the bright, almost girlish glint in her eyes and the hint of color on her cheeks, she dared to say that it pleased her enormously that her beau had come a-courting early.

His strong, clear baritone wafted up the staircase when Angela let him in, making Daisy's heart perform an extra beat or two. A week ago she might have suspected an incipient coronary, but now she recognized the irregular beats for what they were—the inner somersault of joy, the delightful drumming of anticipation, the cadence of falling in love.

She put on her anniversary pearls, settling them against the bodice of her jacket, knowing that Charles would approve and be glad for her newfound, wholly unexpected happiness.

"I'll be right down, Gerald," she called.

Now, if William behaved properly and if she could somehow straighten things out between Robert and Angela, her day would be complete.

⁓

Outside the Tattoo Parlor, Bobby angled a hip onto the hood of the Taurus while he punched in Angela's cell phone number. With a little luck and the lack of trees or wires overhead, they'd have a decent connection.

Bootsie had brought the professor to town. She'd spent a fortune to do it. Bobby kept turning that little nugget of information over in his brain while he waited for his wife to pick up.

"Hey, babe," he said when she finally did.

"Bobby! Where are you?"

"In beautiful downtown Hassenfeld," he said.

"But I thought you—"

"Never mind," he said. "Tell me about the day the professor first came to Mrs. Riordan's house, Ange." He recalled it was the day he'd gotten his tattoo. He remembered that Angela had failed to follow procedure and had left the president's mother alone with a stranger. What he couldn't remember, if he'd ever known, was just how Gerrard had shown up in the first place.

She was silent for a moment. "This really isn't a good time, Bobby. I've got chicken and—"

The reception went blank. Bobby leaned to his left. "Ange?"

"—lemon seeds in the stupid carrots."

"Ange, tell me how the professor arrived for the bridge game that day. How did that shake out? Was he—"

"Oh, wait, Bobby," she said suddenly, cutting him off. "Somebody called you a while ago from the Boston P.D. A Lieutenant Cargill. Something like that. He said you wanted details from a medical examiner's report on a headless corpse. I thought he had the wrong number."

"Please don't tell me you hung up on the guy," Bobby said.

"No. I wrote down exactly what he told me. Now wait. Just a minute. I put—"

He was suddenly listening to white noise until he leaned back to his right. Christ. Trying to find a clear connection was worse than a needle in a haystack.

"—other pocket of my apron."

"What did he say about the corpse, Ange?"

"Okay. Here. The medical examiner estimated its height to be about six feet and the weight approximately a hundred-seventy-five. Cargill said the age was a tougher call because of the condition—"

Shit.

"—so long, maybe two, three weeks in the water, but the ME put the age at sixty years, plus or minus ten. Why in the world are you making inquiries about a headless corpse in Boston, Bobby?"

"I'll tell you later. Now tell me about the professor." Who, he thought, was also and maybe not so coincidentally six feet tall, about a hundred-seventy-five pounds, and sixty plus ten years.

"The day of the bridge game?" She made a strangling sound. "Wait a minute. These damned lemon seeds—"

"Angela," he shouted. "Listen to me. Did Bootsie bring him? Did Bootsie bring the professor?"

"Yes. I thought you knew that, Bobby. She practically shoved him in Mrs. Riordan's face."

Dammit. That's what he thought. This wasn't good.

"Bootsie claimed he was substituting for one of the other women, who had taken ill unexpectedly," she said, "but, you know, now that I think about it . . . "

Her voice drifted off.

"What, Ange?"

"Well, the woman who canceled . . . Norma. She called the other day to see how Mrs. Riordan was. It was confusing, but apparently, according to her anyway, Bootsie had told her that the bridge game was canceled because Mrs. Riordan was ill."

Jesus. Bobby didn't know what that meant, but he damn well knew it meant something. He couldn't keep the urgency out of his voice. "What time is he due this evening? Gerrard, I mean. What time is he supposed to show up?"

"He's here now. He came with a huge bouquet and—"

The phone went blank and Bobby cursed. He looked toward the pharmacy and considered commandeering that phone again, but there wasn't time. There was hardly time to think.

And why hadn't he thought about it before? Why the hell would Bootsie, who'd spent the better part of her life stalking Daisy Riordan for taking one man away from her, suddenly arrange to shove a second man right in her enemy's face? And not just any man, but one she'd gone to great expense to bring to Hassenfeld, presumably for herself?

Bobby's brain felt like an engine whose spark plugs kept misfiring. Things just didn't connect, didn't make sense. It was all too bizarre. Even unbelievable.

Maybe the professor just didn't find Bootsie attractive once he'd arrived in town. Maybe he'd threatened to leave, so she'd introduced him to somebody he did find attractive. Maybe the pill Bobby'd swallowed a little while ago was sending him on a wild, psychedelic goose chase.

Hell, even if he assumed the worst, that the headless corpse in Boston was the real Gerald Gerrard, and Bootsie had somehow hired a guy—maybe through that *Mercenary* magazine of hers—to kill both the real Gerrard and Daisy, why the hell hadn't the guy done it? Why hadn't he popped her yet? He'd had all the time and opportunity in the world.

"Ange? Ange?" Bobby shook the phone.

"Yes. Can you hear me, Bobby? This is a horrible connection."

"I hear you. Stay on the line, Ange. Who's standing post outside? Did they frisk the professor before he came in?"

"I don't know. I was here in the kitchen. But if I had to guess, I'd say probably not. Nobody's supposed to do anything that might upset Mrs. Riordan. They didn't even do a—"

"Do a what, Ange?" He wanted to slam the cell phone down on the pavement. "What didn't they do, Angela?"

"Bobby?"

"What did you say? They didn't do something?"

"Right. The usual sweep. They didn't do it. No dogs. No metal detectors. Nothing. It was decided that since we'd been inside the house for a week that—"

While he waited for the connection to cut back in, Bobby tilted his head back, grappling with a headache, the drug-induced confusion, and all the things that just didn't make sense to him. He gazed at the cloudless blue sky, wishing his head were half that clear. Maybe a cup of coffee would counteract the painkiller that was keeping him from putting this all together. Because it fit. It fit like a damned warped puzzle. He knew it did. He just couldn't . . .

The faint whirr of chopper blades droned overhead, a little to the northwest. Bobby blinked and checked his watch. He was early. The president was at least twenty minutes early.

And then it hit him. Like a bolt of lightning from the same sky where the chopper appeared like a dark green speck that grew larger and larger as he watched. The warped pieces suddenly smoothed out and moved perfectly into place. Everything fit.

It wasn't Daisy Riordan. The professor or whoever the hell he was could have taken her out any time, but the reason he didn't was because she was never the target at all.

It was the president, who was about to walk into a meagerly secured house that hadn't been swept.

Jesus. And Bobby was pretty sure he knew just where the assassination weapon was.

"Angela," he shouted into the phone, barely able to hear his own voice for the noise of the chopper's blades directly over his head right now.

"Bobby, I've got to go. I think I hear the helicopter. The president's almost here."

"Angela!" he screamed again.

She hung up.

19

Angela looked out the front door just in time to see the dark green military chopper descend to its final few feet, then land with two small bounces on the street, where all traffic had been stopped for the past half hour. While the huge rotors slowly came to a halt, people stood by their cars and gawked at the unexpected sight.

Wait'll they get a look at the guy who exits the chopper, Angela thought. She was even a little excited herself. Unlike so many of her fellow agents, she wasn't the least bit jaded about the pomp and circumstance of the presidency.

Mrs. Riordan and Professor Gerrard walked arm in arm from the living room, where they'd been sipping Manhattans and quietly chatting in anticipation of the president's arrival. Daisy Riordan looked so happy. She very nearly glowed, and the pink suit that had seemed so severe on the hanger fit her beautifully. She'd made the perfect choice, too, in wearing the single strand of creamy pearls. The woman looked fantastic, nearly twenty years younger than she had a mere half an hour ago. Angela wished Bobby could see her.

The thought sent a sharp pang straight to her heart. She always believed, when she was Daisy Riordan's age, that she'd be walking hand in hand with Bobby, and that they'd eventually be buried side by side, just like Rose and Angelo were planning their interment under their well-tended maple tree. That wasn't going to happen now, and for a moment Angela felt so completely abandoned and bereft that she was ready to lie down in that grave, wherever it was, and pull a thick carpet of sod over her head.

Outside, the four agents who'd accompanied the president from Washington trotted down the helicopter's short flight of stairs. Familiar faces, all of them, behind dark glasses. Cavanaugh, Sweet, McDermott, and Schuetz. Now that Mrs. Riordan knew she was an agent, Angela was wearing her radio clipped to her belt, and through her earpiece she could hear agents checking in from the trailer and various points around the property, giving the all-clear for Honcho, as the president was called, to exit. Then a muted cheer went up from all the surprised bystanders, when William Riordan appeared in the doorway of the chopper.

Beside her, Mrs. Riordan said, "William looks well."

"He looks well surrounded," the professor said rather glumly. Then he sighed as he brought Daisy's hand to his lips for a soft kiss. "Must we share our special moment with a gang of gun-toting strangers, Margaret?"

"No. Of course not," the president's mother replied. "Angela will be the only one inside the house. I've made myself quite clear about that." She turned to Angela as she spoke. "You will see to that, won't you?"

"Yes, ma'am."

Gun-toting strangers, Angela thought. Give me a break. She thought about Bobby's urgent tone on the phone earlier and his recurring suspicions about the professor despite the fact that the guy kept checking out fine. She wondered if her husband's personal feelings about Daisy Riordan hadn't somehow skewed his professional judgment.

She glanced at Gerald Gerrard's face now, and his expression struck her as genuine and utterly sincere. The man's blue eyes shone with such warmth and affection that Angela found it almost impossible to believe he was anything but an aged suitor or that he had any motive other than wanting to preserve the intimacy of this special evening as best he could.

Angela lifted her arm and spoke in her wrist mike. "Doug, Mrs. Riordan only wants Honcho to come in. Nobody else. Do you copy?"

There followed a rumbling of disagreement, a ripple of oaths and objections from assorted agents, before Doug's disembodied voice spoke firmly and quite clearly in her ear. "Roger that, Agent Holland. You've got the inside post. What's for dinner?"

Her rice!

Suddenly Angela went from being a highly professional Secret Service agent to an amateur cook who was desperately afraid she'd ruin Mrs. Riordan's evening with burnt rice and lemon seeds in the carrots and chicken that wasn't cooked through. Good God. Salmonella. *E coli.* Could you get trichinosis from chicken, or was it only pork? She didn't even want to think about the infinite possibilities of poisoning the president of the United States.

There wasn't usually that much traffic on the blacktop heading out of town, but then the president didn't usually drop out of the sky above Hassenfeld. Bobby assumed they had set the chopper down on the road in front of the Riordan house, and were currently diverting the cars of the curious townspeople around the big vehicle a few at a time in each direction.

He pulled the Taurus onto the shoulder and tried his cell phone again. Angela wasn't answering, dammit, and when they picked up in the surveillance trailer, there was so much static it nearly blew out his eardrum.

At this point his options were slim, slimmer, and none. He could try to cram the Taurus, at fifty miles an hour, between the stopped cars and the deep roadside ditch for the next half mile. He could take the chance that there was a working phone in the run-down house he had passed a half mile back. Or he could hump it across the cornfield, which would take a quarter mile off the distance to the Riordan house, and hope like hell his broken rib didn't puncture his lung before he got there.

He picked his way across the steep ditch and took off through the corn.

~

When Angela brought the president's glass of ice water into the living room, she noticed that the professor was at it again with his handkerchief. This time, though, instead of polishing his eyeglasses, the poor old guy was mopping his brow and his upper lip. She empathized completely, hoping her own deodorant hadn't failed her over an hour ago.

"It's Agent Holland, isn't it?" the president asked, smiling genially as he leaned forward from his seat in the center of the couch and took the tall glass of water from her hand.

"Yes, sir."

Heaven help her, her mouth was dry, her hands were trembling, her heart was pounding like a jackhammer, and she felt this overwhelming urge to curtsy all of a sudden.

"My mother tells me you and Bobby have done a wonderful job, Agent Holland." He aimed a sidelong grin at Mrs. Riordan. "Under difficult circumstances, I'd imagine."

"I'm not difficult, William," Mrs. Riordan snapped. "I'm precise."

The professor chuckled and reached for Daisy's hand. "Your mother is a perfectionist, Mr. President, misplaced in an imperfect world."

"Exactly." Daisy Riordan gave a little snort, then smiled, first at Gerrard and then at her son, before she said, "It's fairly obvious why I'm fond of Gerald, isn't it?"

"I'd say so," the president said.

"May I bring you anything else?" Angela asked, feeling awkward, not knowing how to take her leave and return to the kitchen.

"Not at the moment," Mrs. Riordan said. "Thank you, Angela."

The president glanced at his watch. "Were you planning on dinner, Mother? If so . . ."

"I'm planning on dinner at six-thirty, William, and not a moment sooner, as I told you on the phone. If you feel the need to leave, dear, you'll just have to bolt your food, won't you?"

Bolting sounded good to Angela, so she turned and quietly exited the living room. She still had to finish setting the dining room table and then find a crystal bowl and a way to rearrange the professor's bouquet to make some sort of centerpiece that was low enough so they could all see each other across the table. All that, plus fishing the last of the slimy little lemon seeds out of the carrots and cooking the hell out of the chicken, along with the salmonella, so it didn't kill the president. She wondered bleakly what the prison term was for accidental assassination.

After tonight's trauma, she thought, the rest of her career in the Secret Service was going to be a breeze.

~

Jogging through the cornfield wasn't the stroke of genius or the relative piece of cake that Bobby had originally assumed. He had thought that cutting through the field would easily slice a quarter-mile off the distance to the Riordan house and allow him to get there faster, and he'd figured his only impediment would be the pain in his side. What he hadn't factored in, however, were the perils inherent in a mature cornfield.

He choked on clouds of gnats. He turned his ankle on a furrow, then tripped in a tangle of weeds and took out several seven-foot tall plants when he fell. Acre after acre of the broad green leaves that had appeared so docile from a distance smacked him and slapped him and cut the holy hell out of his hands and face.

None of that mattered, though. And, God help him, the fact that the president's life was in jeopardy hardly mattered either. His wife was in danger. That was all that mattered. Angela was all that mattered.

He couldn't lose her. He couldn't lose her. Not like this. Not ever.

The stalks of corn were little more than a blur as he charged through them, and somewhere in the recesses of his brain he realized that his vision was blurred because his eyes were filled with tears and that the pain in his chest wasn't purely physical, but emotional, too. As if some protective wall, some firewall, some ancient barrier, had shattered inside him. His heart felt raw and exposed and defenseless. It felt vulnerable. Mortal. It felt . . . real.

Ah, God. Suddenly he knew what Angela needed from him, all that he hadn't been able to give. This! Just this! All that he could give now, all that he would give.

If it wasn't too late.

By the time he crashed out of the field not too far from the surveillance trailer, he was soaked with sweat, bleeding from a hundred cuts, and barely able to breathe. They'd probably shoot him on sight if he headed straight for the rear door of the residence, so he hobbled across the back of the property and opened the door to the trailer.

When he walked in, he could see hands automatically moving toward holsters. Doug swiveled around from the bright, blinking bank of monitors, took one look at Bobby, and said, "What the hell happened to you?"

"I've got to get into the house, Doug," Bobby said.

He'd already made up his mind, while he was breathing gnats and being sliced and diced by hybrid leaves, that he wasn't going to inform Doug or anybody else what he suspected was going on inside the house because that would only guarantee a full-blown assault, a fiasco with a score of armed agents racing inside the place, probably panicking the professor and certainly putting lives at risk, not the least of which was his wife's.

Doug was talking into his radio now, his voice calm but clipped, apparently soothing the concerns of agents who just a moment ago had seen a bleeding guy in a tattered suit limping across the backyard toward the trailer.

"I've got to get into the house, Doug," he said again, more insistently this time, desperate for clearance; without it, some hotshot might take him down with a rifle before he ever got inside.

"That's a big negative, Bobby," Doug drawled. "Angela's inside. Everything's going fine." He scowled at his watch. "Dinner's in ten minutes. We plan to have Honcho out of here and on his way back to Washington by nineteen-thirty."

In a casket, Bobby thought bleakly.

"Okay," he said as casually as he could. "Well, I'll just walk around, maybe see if I can make myself useful in the yard or directing traffic or something."

The special agent in charge swiveled back to his monitors and growled over his shoulder. "You just make yourself scarce, son. You're not on duty right now. You hear?"

~⌐

In the living room, Daisy sipped her Manhattan and plucked at her strand of pearls, all the while sneaking small glances at Gerald, who seemed oddly and uncharacteristically nervous as he sat in the club chair adjacent to hers and directly across from the sofa where William was ensconced. Gerald was perspiring so dreadfully that she was certain his handkerchief was wringing wet by now.

It was true he didn't meet with the president of the United States every day, but on the other hand, during his long and successful career, Gerald had to have met with some very powerful and influential men. Of course, he'd never had to ask any of those powerful and influential men for the hand of their mother in marriage. That was, she assumed, what he was planning to do.

She wished like the very dickens that he'd hurry. If Angela had everything under control in the kitchen— Dear Lord, please let her have everything under control in the kitchen!—then dinner would be served in fewer than ten minutes, and Gerald wouldn't have much opportunity to say anything once they were seated at the table. William, even in his high chair, had always had a tendency to concentrate fiercely on his plate during a meal, making any sort of conversation difficult if not impossible.

If it was going to happen, it seemed she was going to have to take matters into her own unasked-for hands, although she was loath to do it, considering that Gerald hadn't officially popped the question. She didn't want to ruffle his bright male feathers or trample on his dignity. Most of all, she didn't want to humiliate herself if it turned out that he didn't actually have marriage on his mind.

She nearly laughed out loud, imagining the look on William's face if Gerald broached the subject of their living together without benefit of clergy.

William was eyeing his watch again.

"Dinner will be served in five minutes, William," she said rather testily, hoping that Gerald would take the hint.

The chicken breasts were perfectly browned, worthy of a photo in *Bon Appetit*, if Angela did say so herself. If they were a tad overcooked, at least they weren't lethal. And, what the hell, the president ate so much rubber chicken at campaign fund-raisers that he'd probably forgotten what tender and moist chicken was supposed to taste like anyway.

The carrots may have gotten a little mushy, but they were julienned to perfection and absolutely glistened in their sauce of butter and lemon juice under a light sprinkling of parsley and lemon zest. She added a tad more salt and pepper for good measure. What the hell.

If only the stupid rice would get done. Angela had worried about burning it, so she'd added an extra cup of water—maybe a cup and a half, she wasn't exactly sure—to the pan simmering on the stove. But now, with just a few minutes to go before dinner was expected on the table, she peeked under the lid of the saucepan again, then cursed the soggy, bloated kernels in their soupy white liquid. Dammit. She needed a sieve.

Just as she was pulling one from a drawer by the sink, she heard the back door open and close, and the next thing she knew, Bobby was rushing into the kitchen. She hadn't expected to see him again. Maybe not ever. At least not here. Certainly not now. Her heart was bounding up into her throat at the very same time that she was taking in his appearance.

He looked terrible, like someone who'd just been run over by a convoy of trucks. Twice. His face and hands were scratched and bleeding. His tie was torn and tattered. His suit was ripped and stained. The left sleeve of both his jacket and shirt had been sliced open, disclosing his tattoo. The little red heart seemed to be beating, wildly. The look on his face was fierce, nearly frightening. His hazel eyes had an almost feral gleam.

"My God!" she exclaimed. "What happened? You're not supposed to be here, Bobby. Does Doug—"

He grabbed her by the upper arms, practically shaking her. "Listen to me. I think the president's in trouble."

"You think—" His pupils were dilated, she realized all of a sudden. He really did look crazed. At the edge of control, which wasn't like Bobby at all.

"Where are they, Ange?" He tightened his grip and really shook her now, nearly rattling her teeth. "Where? Are they in the living room?"

She nodded.

"Who's sitting on the couch?"

"The couch? Who's sitting on the couch? Bobby, are you crazy?" She looked from his wild eyes to the clock on the stove, and watched the bright blue numbers change from six-twenty-six to six-twenty-seven. Oh, God. She batted at him with the sieve. "Let me go. I've got to drain my rice."

"Forget about the fucking rice. Tell me who's sitting on the couch."

"President Riordan," she said. "At least I think so. He was when I was in there a couple of minutes ago."

"Okay. Good. That's good." He seemed to relax just a bit. His harsh grip on her eased, and he didn't look quite so crazed anymore. If anything, he began to look uncertain, even slightly confused.

Suddenly the mixed and muted voices in her earpiece gave way to Doug's clear and urgent tone. "Agent Holland? Angela, do you copy? Is Bobby inside?"

She lifted her arm, spoke a soft "Affirmative," then winced as she heard her supervisor explode.

～

At the moment, Daisy was far more concerned about Gerald than she was about the possibility of dinner being late or even edible. Her erstwhile fiancé was perspiring more than ever and seemed quite uncomfortable in his chair beside her, crossing his legs, recrossing them, shifting this way and that. It was more than mere nerves or proposal jitters, she concluded with some alarm. Even William, who was normally oblivious to everything around him, seemed aware of the man's discomfort.

"Are you feeling all right, Professor?" he asked. "You're looking a little pale."

"I'm a bit warm, actually," Gerald said in a voice that sounded quite feeble. "And a little dizzy. It's nothing serious, I'm sure, but I wonder if I might trade places with you, Mr. President. Perhaps if I could put my head down—"

Daisy's arthritic knees didn't keep her from shooting straight out of her chair. "Get up, William," she snapped. "Get up, for heaven's sake. Let Gerald have the couch."

~

Bobby was racking his brain, trying to decide what to do to insure that everybody got out of the house alive, knowing full well he was being derelict in his sworn duty to protect the president and only the president. In the meantime, Angela was obviously listening to instructions on her earpiece while she looked at him as if she had a big net or a goddamned straitjacket concealed behind her back.

"Listen to *me*," he said, reaching out and plucking the device from her ear.

"Bobby!"

"Listen. Bootsie hired Gerrard to kill the president." When she began spluttering, he said, "Don't ask me how I know. I just know."

"Bobby, honey." Her voice was soothing, as if she were speaking to an overexcited child. "That can't be true. And even if it were, the professor doesn't have a weapon. They searched him before he came in. McCray did a pass with the metal detector. I saw him do it."

"He stashed a weapon last week. The night he threw

the rocks at the window. Mrs. Riordan brought him in. That's when he secured it."

"You're wrong," she said. "That's impossible. Tricia frisked him."

He shook his head. "No. Mrs. Riordan called her off. Remember? Gerrard came inside and sat on the couch. That's where he hid the gun."

She stood there blinking at him now, wanting to believe him, not wanting to believe him. Beautiful in her confusion. The bravest woman he knew. He wanted to pull rank on her and order her out of the house this second. Out to the trailer. Away. He had no choice but to risk her life, though. He figured—God, he prayed—that he was quick enough, agile enough to take two bullets. One for Angela and one for the president. Like Billy.

Billy! The sudden thought of his brother nearly swamped Bobby's brain. He missed him. God, how he missed him, but that wasn't what had been eating at him these past two years since Agent Billy Holland had taken that bullet in the course of duty. It was that he'd never told Billy how fiercely proud he was of him, or how he—the big brother, the one who bullied their way into the world, the one with the brawn and the brass balls—didn't trust his own ability, his own reflexes, his own courage to give it all up in a single moment for the job.

"Bobby?" Angela's voice brought him back into the moment.

It was time to find out. He focused on his wife's worried face, the green mist in her eyes.

"I love you, Ange," he whispered, then he turned her and aimed her toward the hallway. "Gerrard might panic if he sees me, and we don't want him to panic. Go in and tell them dinner's going to be a few minutes late. I'll be right behind you. If Riordan's still on the couch, sit down beside him. Reach under the cushion and see if you can find the gun."

"Bobby, I . . ."

"Do it, Angela."

Well, she didn't have much choice, she thought. Especially when, just behind her, she heard Bobby slide his gun from his holster.

Oh, my God. If he was right—was he right? how could he be right when nobody else had a clue?—then this was some horrible, bizarre nightmare in which President Riordan was about to be assassinated right under the very noses of two dozen Secret Service agents. If Bobby was wrong—please let him be wrong!—it would undoubtedly be the most horrendously embarrassing moment of her life when she plopped down on the couch beside the president of the United States, smiled, and casually inquired, "So, how's it going, sir?"

She heard Bobby's labored breathing at her back. Maybe he was crazy. Maybe the pain in his left side had driven him over some invisible edge. Maybe *she* had.

Then, as they neared the living room, Angela heard Daisy Riordan exclaim, "Don't just stand there, William. Help him, for heaven's sake."

"He's up," she said over her shoulder to Bobby. "Honcho's up from the couch."

They were all up—the president, Daisy, the professor—standing in an awkward little group like three people trying to dance. The president looked dismayed as he stood holding the professor's elbow. Mrs. Riordan looked distraught. And the professor was looking desperate, and staring at the couch, where Angela could see the polished wooden curve of a pistol grip peeking from the cushions.

"Oh, God."

She reached for the gun at her ankle just as Bobby went flying past her.

～

It happened so fast that Daisy Riordan couldn't even summon up a scream. Suddenly Gerald didn't appear ill at all, but angry—all red-faced and wild-eyed and teeth-gnashing—as he wrenched his arm out of William's grasp, then lunged for the couch.

There was a gun in his hand when he stood, when he turned, but it hardly had time to register on Daisy's brain before something, someone, a hard arm, hurled her down.

She was falling, flailing, when she heard the first shot. The second one exploded just as she hit the floor.

～

No sooner had Angela lowered her weapon and screamed, "Officer down!" into her wrist mike than the front door crashed open and a wave of agents raced past her to surround the dazed president and move him briskly out of harm's way.

"But my mother—" William Riordan said as they

swept him past Angela in a human current that flowed out of the room and dragged her with it toward the door.

"Bobby!" she screamed, breaking free.

By the time she reached him, Daisy Riordan held him cradled in her arms. There was blood all over. Gerrard's from her head shot. Bobby's.

She shrieked into her mike again—"Officer down!"— then sank to her knees. She thought she saw where the bullet had hit his arm, then realized it wasn't blood at all but the crimson heart tattoo.

Suddenly something seemed to crack inside her, and instead of tears pouring from her eyes, a hot fury roared through her veins. "Breathe, Bobby. Do you hear me? Do you? I swear to God, if you don't hang on here, I'll kill you myself."

"Do you hear that, Robert?" Mrs. Riordan said barely above a whisper, but firmly all the same. "I'm sure she means it, too. I'd strongly urge you to survive, my dear."

Bobby opened his eyes and looked up at Angela. "You okay, Ange?"

"Ssh. Yes. I'm fine. The president's fine. You're going to be fine, too."

"I'm trying here," he said weakly. "Hard to breathe." Then his gaze flickered farther up toward Mrs. Riordan, and a tiny grin pulled at his taut lips. "You're crying, Daisy," he said.

"I most certainly am not," the president's mother snapped.

"Yes, you are," he said. "Isn't she, Ange?"

"Yes," Angela whispered. "She is."

Bobby closed his eyes a moment, then blinked up at

Daisy Riordan again. "So, tell me," he said. "How does it feel?"

Mrs. Riordan swiped at her wet eyes with the back of her hand. "It feels . . . it feels . . . well . . . not so horrible."

"Glad to hear it," Bobby replied as his meager grin twisted into a grimace. "Because . . . Jesus . . . I'm about to do the same thing myself."

Huge tears slid from the corners of his eyes just before he slipped into unconsciousness.

20

Two weeks later, Angela paced back and forth in front of a hangar at Andrews Air Force Base. Not too far away, Doug Coulter was doing his own motionless pacing by lighting one cigarette after another.

"He's late," she said, looking at her watch for what must have been the hundredth time in the past half hour.

"This isn't exactly what you'd call a scheduled flight, Angela," Doug said. "Relax. He'll be here in a few minutes."

Relax. She hadn't relaxed for two consecutive minutes since Bobby had been shot. First there was the harrowing helicopter ride from Hassenfeld to the hospital in Springfield. The president, countermanding standard Secret Service procedure, had refused to take off until he knew whether Bobby's injury was serious. When he was informed that it was life-threatening, he insisted, with some vociferous assistance from his mother, on diverting the helicopter to the nearest trauma center, where his own blood type had been stockpiled in case of emergency.

During the flight, Bobby could hardly breathe despite the oxygen mask Angela held in place for him. As it turned out, Gerald Gerrard's bullet, which had gone through Bobby's right arm and lodged in the muscle of his chest wall, was of far less immediate concern than the punctured lung from his fractured rib.

When someone in the emergency room had asked, "Who's the next of kin?" Angela had stepped forward and said, "I'm his wife," so adamantly that several heads turned in her direction. That was probably her sole moment of clarity for the next forty-eight hours, the moment she had known for certain that she would always be Bobby's wife, no matter what.

She'd stayed with him constantly the next two days until his condition stabilized, refusing to return to D.C. for a debriefing on the assassination attempt even if it meant her job. And the few times she nodded off to sleep, she woke to find Mrs. Riordan there, holding Bobby's hand, whispering encouragement to him, keeping watch while she kept concerned agents and nosy reporters at bay.

Outside of her own debriefing by agents, all the president's mother would say on the subject of Gerald Gerrard was, "There's no fool like an old fool," but Angela knew the woman was devastated by the turn of events. Her beau had used her to try to assassinate the president, her son. The headless, handless corpse in Boston had been positively identified as Gerald Du-Maurier Gerrard, and the professor turned out to be an ultra-right-wing fanatic named Donald Elvin Paste, who'd been arrested numerous times for impersonating medical doctors or academics or officers of the law, and who'd been threatening the president, among others, for years.

As for her longtime nemesis, Bootsie, the former

belle of Hassenfeld, Mrs. Riordan seemed to blame herself for encouraging the woman's vengeful behavior over the years, and was saddened to hear that in the opinion of the doctors who examined her, it was the recurrence of the tumor in her brain that had probably contributed to Bootsie's ultimate act of vengeance. Mrs. Riordan made certain she was as comfortable as possible in the hospital ward at the federal penitentiary in Marion, where Bootsie was likely to remain until she died.

"There it is," Doug said now, pointing to the plane that was just touching down on a north-south runway. "See, Angela. I told you he wouldn't be late for his own wedding."

"The wedding," she muttered, looking down at the ivory satin suit she'd had to buy in such a rush. There hadn't even been time for alterations, so the sleeves lapped over her knuckles when her arms relaxed. But who was relaxed?

This renewal of their marriage vows was Crazy Daisy's harebrained scheme, her way of thanking her Robert for his courageous sacrifice. And Bobby was either too weak to protest, or else he was in collusion with Mrs. Riordan in her plot to reunite the two of them permanently as soon as Bobby was released from the hospital.

Probably everybody thought she'd change her mind at the last minute and take off for L.A. and Rod Bishop. But that wasn't likely to happen. When she'd finally gotten through to him in Mexico last week to tell him she was moving back to Washington and wouldn't be seeing him anymore, before she could even say a word, Rod had broken down in tears—the wimp!—and confessed that he'd fallen for his leading lady.

The ceremony for the renewal of their vows was set for three o'clock in the Rose Garden, replete now with hundreds of potted white mums and asters. Her parents and an untold number of siblings were already there, she was sure, with their pockets crammed with tissues and white rice.

"This is just ridiculous," Angela said, shoving up the sleeves of her jacket as the Lear Jet taxied closer. "We're already married."

Doug lit another cigarette. "Well, hell. I guess it never hurts to tighten the noose a little every now and then," he said.

~

Bobby didn't remember being nervous before their first wedding, but maybe that was because he and Billy had drained a little silver flask of vodka ten minutes before the ceremony. Or maybe it was because it had seemed like just the three of them—Bobby and Angela and Billy—versus the crying Callifanos. Or maybe it was just because he had been three years younger and believed that everything lasted forever. He knew better now.

He really didn't want to do this. He was still walking around in a haze from the pain meds he had to take. His patience was down to about one-ply, with the press that wanted to glorify both him and Angela, to turn them into poster children for the Secret Service, and with the powers that be at the agency, for encouraging them to do it.

All he really wanted to do was get away for a while with Ange, but he was going through with this wedding because he knew it was important to Daisy Riordan. For some reason she had appointed herself their personal Cupid. She'd spent hours at his bedside, using his cell phone to plan the ceremony, haranguing people all over D.C. It seemed to take her mind off Bootsie and the professor. It might, he thought, be her only way of coming to grips with her own dashed dreams, the ones she refused to discuss. Bobby knew the name of that tune. The one that had no lyrics. He'd practically written it himself.

"You should have waited to put your tuxedo on once we were here, Robert." Mrs. Riordan was clucking her tongue and fiddling with his lapels as they waited to exit the Treasury Department's plane. "Your jacket is all wrinkled."

"Then it matches my disposition," he said.

Her eyes widened perceptibly. "You're not nervous, are you? Or apprehensive?"

"Who me? Nah. I'm used to saying my marriage vows in front of the president of the United States, the First Lady, the director of the Secret Service, and my in-laws. It doesn't bother me one bit."

She got huffy. "Well, if I had thought for one moment that this would be the least bit stressful for you, I—"

"You would have done exactly what you did," Bobby said, grinning. He tipped her soft chin up, forcing her to meet his gaze. "I appreciate it, Mrs. Riordan. So does Angela. It means a lot to both of us. Thank you."

"Well, you both mean a great deal to me," she said, giving one then the other of his lapels a good tug just before a dark scowl crossed over her face. "Dammit."

"What?" Bobby asked.

"Oh, nothing. It's just that I was thinking that when I return to Hassenfeld, the Itos will be back from their cruise. I'm not sure I want those people bowing and scraping around me all the time."

"Move to Washington," he said.

"I can't do that."

"Why not? There's nothing to keep you in Illinois anymore, unless you're planning to visit your pal Bootsie in the slammer." He shrugged. "Besides, it'd be nice having you close."

"Really?" A little more light returned to her eyes.

"Sure. Plus, arguing with you would be a nice break from arguing with my wife," he said, adding a teasingly deferential "ma'am."

Daisy Riordan smiled as if she'd been doing it all her life. "I just might do that, Robert."

~

"Oh, don't let me go just yet," Angela murmured in the back of the limousine when Bobby broke their kiss and started to disentangle her from his arms.

"There's plenty more for later," he said. "I've got to straighten out my shoulder, babe. It's been acting up on me a little."

Angela carefully drew away, knowing that when Bobby said a little, it probably meant a lot. "What can I do? Anything?" she asked, already deciding that one

thing she was going to do was cook outrageously fatten-
ing meals, so he'd put back some of the weight he had
lost in the hospital.

He leaned back against the door and let out a long
sigh. "Marry me," he said. "Again."

"Okay. But other than that?"

"Let's see. Keep your father from killing me with one
of those bear hugs of his this afternoon."

"I've already warned him," she said. "And I've also
informed him that if he starts boo-hooing, I'm going to
stop the ceremony dead in its tracks."

He reached for her hand. "Thanks for doing this, Ange.
It means a lot to Mrs. Riordan."

"She looks happier than the last time I saw her."

"She'll be fine. She might move to Washington."

Angela laughed. "What? Leave beautiful Horsefeath-
ers, Illinois, for this?" She gestured toward the Washington Monument poking up in the distance.

"Well, now that Bootsie's gone, she needs somebody
who's not afraid to twit her a little."

"And that would be you."

He nodded. "I think I'll pass on the orange hair,
though."

"Oh, I don't know. It'd go great with the tattoo."

The sweetest, saddest smile curved across his mouth.
"I've been thinking about Billy these past two weeks.
Let's go out to Arlington tomorrow, Ange. Maybe take
some flowers."

Angela tried not to look as surprised as she felt. Actually, she was stunned. Not once since his brother's funeral had Bobby been back to visit Billy's grave. She'd
had to go alone.

"I'd like that," she said. "You've never—"

"Yeah. I know. I couldn't."

His gaze cut away from hers for a moment, a long moment during which Angela's heart held absolutely still. She could hardly breathe. If he didn't look back . . . If Bobby continued to withhold . . . Oh, God. If the big brick wall was going up again . . .

But then his gaze returned. Warm. Steady. Open. "I couldn't go before, Ange," he said. "It hurt too goddamned much. But I'm ready now."

Yes. Oh, yes. Angela's heart resumed its happy beat.

~

The Rose Garden was almost as lovely in October as it was in June, but unfortunately the timing of events had been out of Daisy Riordan's control. William's staff had done a lovely job on extremely short notice, although personally Daisy would have interspersed lavender or yellow asters among all the pots of white chrysanthemums, if not for variety's sake, then to avoid a certain snow-blind effect from bright October sunshine on so many white petals.

The string quartet was superb, and when they segued from Mozart to *Lohengrin*, Daisy patted William's hand as he sat beside her.

"Good job," she said.

"Why, thank you, Mother."

He looked so stunned that Daisy wasn't sure whether to laugh or cry. It still amazed her that she was capable of tears, and that shedding them seemed to make her feel better rather than worse. "Don't be so shocked,

William. Haven't I ever told you how enormously proud of you I am?"

"No, Mother. You haven't."

"Well, I just did." She patted his hand again. "Your father would be proud, as well, dear."

She turned then and craned her neck to see Angela and Robert walking together down the white canvas aisle toward the mum-bedecked archway where the chaplain of the Senate awaited them. They looked so happy. Robert looked a bit thin, but Angela would no doubt soon be stuffing him with green-speckled egg salad and her peculiar tuna concoction.

Daisy glanced at the bride's side of the aisle, crammed with dozens of teary-eyed Callifanos. She hoped she could hear the service over their wet histrionics. And she hoped, most of all, that Robert would be gratified that on the groom's side of the aisle—in place of his derelict parents and his deceased brother—sat the president of the United States, the First Lady, the director of the Secret Service along with many of his fellow agents, and one very grateful and affectionate old lady.

Now, no sooner had the chaplain intoned, "Dearly beloved," than a chorus of wet sniffles rang out on the bride's side.

Daisy shot the Callifanos a fearsome glare, but it didn't do any good.

She could barely hear Robert's reply to ". . . as long as you both shall live?" And when it was Angela's turn to respond, her relatives set up such a caterwauling that Daisy was tempted to pelt them with a handful of rice. She very

well might have if William hadn't smiled at her and
warmly, firmly clasped her hand.

⟳

"Nice service," Doug said, standing near a tiered bank
of mums at the edge of the crowd, lighting up as he and
Bobby watched the smoothly efficient White House staff
set up tables for the supper that was to follow the ceremony.

Bobby laughed. "You mean you could actually hear it
over all the caterwauling?"

"Those people cry a lot," Doug said with a bemused
shake of his head. "What is that? An Italian deal?"

"Beats me," Bobby said.

They stood there a while, Doug fulfilling his nicotine
requirements and Bobby taking a little break from the
embraces of his in-laws. He kept thinking he ought to be
putting a little pressure on Doug about his reassignment
to a desk here in Washington on counterfeit detail, letting
him and everybody else in the agency know that he
wanted to get back on protective duty as soon as he could
pass the physical. But there was something else bothering
him even more.

"Ange looks great, doesn't she?" he said.

After Doug gave a nod of approval, Bobby added,
"Has she said anything to you about the shooting?"

Special Agent Doug Coulter blew out a long, thin
stream of smoke. "Nope. That was some shooting, by the
way."

"I wouldn't know," Bobby answered almost petu-
lantly. "She won't talk about it. Not to me, at least."

"It's only been two weeks," Doug said calmly. "These things take time, Bobby. You know that."

He did know that, Bobby told himself, at some level of consciousness. The problem was, he didn't seem to be operating on his usual cool and unemotional planes lately. If he really let himself think about their current situation—his and Angela's—the irony of it was almost laughable.

Bobby Holland, the Iron Man, was about to move to a wimpy desk job while his wife had just executed, literally, a perfect head shot that was the talk of the agency, only she didn't want to talk about it, wouldn't let him help her work out her feelings about having killed a man.

Jesus. No wonder she'd been so lonely after Billy died. Not only had Bobby refused to speak about Billy, but he knew now he'd denied his wife the comfort she needed that only he could give. That wouldn't happen again.

~

The president gave them a lovely toast, Angela thought, even though William Riordan's toasts always had the slight suggestion of a campaign speech about them. When Doug raised his champagne glass in their direction and repeated what he'd said to her earlier about the benefits of an occasional tightening of the marriage noose, all the guests laughed and applauded.

Her father's toast, predictably, had been too long and too wet, causing Bobby to squirm in his chair, but Angela loved every tear-drenched second of it. Amazingly enough, however, it didn't bring a flood of tears to her own eyes.

Maybe, she thought, she'd cried so much in Illinois that she'd actually damaged her tear ducts. Severed them or something. Or maybe she was still too emotionally unsettled by the shootings—Bobby and the "professor," both—that she was afraid to let go. Or maybe, even probably, it was just that she was so damned happy to be sitting here with her hand tucked warmly into Bobby's, that crying was completely out of the question. All she wanted to do was smile.

Now, beside her, Bobby squeezed her hand, then cleared his throat, not once but twice, before he tapped a spoon on his champagne flute. She thought he looked a bit queasy.

"Are you all right?" she whispered.

His response was the usual "Oh, yeah. I'm fine" as he rose from his chair and began to thank the president and the First Lady for their valuable time and incredible kindness, saying all the right things so appropriate to the occasion.

She sat there looking up at him, almost not hearing his words so much as drinking in the sight of him, so handsome in his black tux, a little paler than normal after his stay in the hospital, a little thinner, but still so strong and sure and vital. How had she ever left him? The past seemed like a thousand years ago, something horribly sad that had happened to two other people. Not to them.

Tomorrow, when they went to Arlington to visit Billy's grave, that sad past would forever be behind them. It would be tucked properly away in their hearts rather than simply ignored.

Bobby was thanking her family now. Her gaze drifted to his left sleeve, picturing the little red heart hidden there. Maybe for Christmas she'd surprise him with one to match it.

"The last time Angela and I were married," he was saying now, "my brother, Billy, was . . . was best man. I wish—"

She had looked away, toward her parents, but when Bobby stopped speaking so abruptly, her gaze jerked back to his face.

His face! It was all scrunched up, his eyes closed and his lips twisted in a valiant and macho, but unsuccessful, attempt to hold back his tears.

"I wish—"

He absolutely couldn't speak. He bent his head, and his strong shoulders began to heave.

And then Angela did something she thought she'd never, ever do. Not in a million years. She jumped up from her chair, threw her arms around her husband, kissed him and whispered, "Oh, honey. Oh, Bobby. It's okay. Don't cry. Sweetheart, please don't cry."

～

The weather was perfect the next day when they went to Arlington National Cemetery. Indian summer. Texas weather, Bobby thought, with big white clouds pushing across a brilliant blue sky, and a strong, steady breeze rustling the red leaves of the maple that shaded Billy's grave.

They brought a pot of white chrysanthemums from the ceremony in the Rose Garden to place beside the smooth gray granite marker, which had yet to be inscribed.

"It's time we put something on this stone," Bobby said.

Angela rested her head against his shoulder. "I would have done it before, but I didn't know what you wanted."

He stared at the glossy unmarked surface, but all he could picture was Billy's face with a milk mustache and that goofy grin of his. "What do you think?"

"I was thinking," she said with a sigh, "that it might be nice to have William Holland, the dates, and then just the simple word *Brother*. Would you like that?"

Bobby knelt, reached to smooth his hand across the sun-warmed stone. "*I'd* like it," he said, "but I'm not so sure Billy deserves to go through eternity labeled as somebody's kid brother." He looked up over his shoulder. "You know?"

She was quiet a moment. "I know."

"Maybe just his name and the dates, Ange. Or, if we put any word at all, we could put *Hero*."

She didn't answer, and Bobby knew it was because she was crying. A year ago he would have walked away, waiting for his wife's tears to subside. But now he stood, wrapping his arms around her, absorbing her tremors and her tears, all of her. They'd talk later about Billy, about the shooting in Illinois, about sunsets, about everything.

This, he thought, was a moment far more sacred than

yesterday's renewal of their vows. For better or for worse. For richer or for poorer. In sickness and in health.

In silence or in speech.

This was their true beginning.

About the Author

Mary McBride has been writing romance, both historical and contemporary, for ten years. She lives in St. Louis, Missouri, with her husband and two sons.

She loves to hear from readers, so please visit her Web site at MaryMcBride.net or write to her c/o P.O. Box 411202, St. Louis, MO 63141

More

Mary McBride!

❦

Please turn this page

for a preview of

MY HERO

available

in June 2003.

"I don't believe in heroes."

"Holly, for crissake." Mel Klein wanted to tear out his hair. What was left of it anyway after thirty-five years in television news production. "Do you want to be a producer or not?"

He was bellowing. Okay. He couldn't help it. No more than he could keep his blood pressure from skyrocketing. He'd just spent the entire morning with the idiots in charge of programming for the VIP Channel, pleading Holly Hicks' case, practically begging Arnold Strong and Maida Newland to give his assistant a chance to produce a single segment for Hero Week.

One lousy hour out of the seven hundred they were projecting for the coming year. Forty-eight minutes of actual footage if you figured in commercials.

He'd sung Holly's praises, handed out copies of her creatively padded résumé, passed her picture around, and popped in one of her tapes. With over three decades in the broadcast news business, Mel knew talent when he saw it, he told them. Holly

Hicks had a real flair for putting together a story. She could write an opening sentence to nail the average viewer to his BarcaLounger. Her sense of timing was impeccable. Her sense of balance was right on. She had a rare eye and an intuitive appreciation for the blended power of pictures and words.

All morning he'd virtually tap danced on the big teak conference table on the nineteenth floor. He had a headache now, not to mention carpet lint on his knees and elbows from practically prostrating himself between Arnold on his frigging treadmill and Maida in her black leather, NASA endorsed, ergonomic executive chair.

Then, just as he was about to toss his next raise and his firstborn grandson into the bargain, the idiots said yes.

They said yes!

He'd nearly given himself a coronary rushing back to his office to tell her the news. And now Holly—the Holly who'd been on his ass ever since the day she walked into the building three years ago in one of her itty-bitty, primly tailored, "This is how a producer looks" suits—the Holly who wheedled and needled and wouldn't let go of her smoldering desire to produce anything—*I'll do anything, Mel. Anything!*—the Holly who left homemade, but not half bad demo tapes on his desk every Monday morning—*that* Holly was blithely telling him she didn't believe in heroes.

He bellowed again. "Do you want to be a goddamn producer or not?"

"Of course I want to be a producer. It's all I've ever wanted to be." Her chin came up like a little Derringer aimed at the frazzled knot in his tie. "I just thought I should be up front about my prejudices, that's all."

"Fine. Great." He waved his hands like a maniac. "Hey, I don't believe in Santa Claus, but that didn't keep me from producing 'Christmas Around the World,' did it?"

"No."

"I don't believe in capital punishment either, but I still did a helluva job on 'Drake's Last Meal,' right?"

"Right."

"Well, then . . ." Mel Klein planted his hands on the top of her desk and leaned forward, lowering his voice, allowing himself to grin for maybe the third or fourth time in his grouchy life. "You got it, kid."

Her pretty little face lit up. Two hundred watts at least.

"I got it!"

Then—Cut!—the light went out.

"Mel, I think I'm going to be sick."

In the ladies' room, Holly Hicks splashed cold water on her face, then slowly lifted her gaze to the mirror above the sink, hoping to find Joan Crawford staring back at her. Big-shouldered. Yeah. Hard as a diamond. Tough as nails.

Or Bette Davis—even better—with her bold, unblinking eyes.

Madonna would be good.

Instead Holly saw herself.

She shook her head and watched her strawberry blond bangs rearrange themselves in a series of sodden spikes on her forehead. She was hardly big-shouldered. In fact, at five foot three inches, she wasn't even tall enough for her shoulders to be reflected in the glass. As for her eyes, rather than bold and unblinking, they were a pale green, smudged with mascara at the moment, and the left one was definitely twitching.

God. She'd waited her whole life for a chance like this. If not her whole life, then at least since she was twelve. While the other little girls in Sandy Springs, Texas, drooled over Donny Osmond, Holly had been a "Sixty Minutes" groupie in love alternately with Harry Reasoner and Mike Wallace. But she didn't want to kiss them. She wanted to *produce* them. It was why she'd come to New York in the first place.

Not once had she taken her eyes off the prize.

Not while growing up in a house where watching the news was considered a foolish waste of time, where reading was deemed eccentric at best, subversive more often than not. *What's that you're reading, girl? "A Separate Peace"? Some kind of Commie Pinko story, I'll betcha. Lemme see that.*

Not while attending a high school where her nickname was El Cerebro, or The Brain, in a school where beauty and brawn were prized over intelligence, where the football coach was the only Ph.D.

on the faculty, and where her classmates put far more effort into getting laid than getting an education.

Not while filling out reams of scholarship forms each year at the University of Missouri's School of Journalism or practically indenturing herself every semester to the campus bookstore.

Not while working her way east for so many years at so many stations she could have thrown darts at the alphabet and come up with the call letters of at least one of her employers. Not through downsizing, takeovers, cutbacks, drawbacks, freezes, firings, new regimes, old boys' clubs, pink slips, and innumerable *Sorry*s and *So long*s.

Hers had been the great American migration in reverse. Go east, young woman, go east. With her journalism degree hot in her hands, Holly had crossed the wide Missouri and the mighty Mississippi to a station in Peoria, Illinois, where the phrase "entry level" meant being solely responsible for a temperamental, two-pot Bunn-o-matic. Across the moonlit Wabash, in Terre Haute, she graduated to a three-pot coffee machine. Ohio took a while to traverse, and a lot of coffee, from Cincinnati to Columbus to Canton. In Wheeling, West Virginia, she'd actually been Acting News Director for two days before they brought somebody in from outside. She spent a winter in Buffalo that lasted a millennium. One wet spring in Syracuse. Then she'd bided her time in Albany before crossing the Hudson and hitting the Big Apple at the ripe old age of twenty-eight.

Here at the VIP Channel, Holly had finally found a mentor in Mel Klein, a man who not only appreciated her abilities, but who also supported her goals. A man of uncommon generosity in this notoriously cutthroat business.

You got it, kid.

"I got it," she repeated now as her adrenaline surged again and her heart began to race with a weird combination of high-flying excitement and lowdown fear.

"Breathe, dammit." She sucked in a huge breath and held it while she kept her eyes closed. She counted to ten, slowly letting the air out through pursed lips, telling herself there was no one at the station, no one in New York, and probably no one on the planet more ready for this assignment than she was.

Then she opened her eyes, and there she was.

Holly Hicks. Producer.

Hot damn.

"You sure you're okay?" Mel asked her. "You want to take the afternoon off and we'll go over this tomorrow?"

"Not on your life. Are those the production notes for Hero Week?"

"Yep." He slid the folder across the top of his desk, somehow managing to avoid a calendar, a tower of pink While-You-Were-Out notes, an electric razor, three empty coffee cups, and a bottle of Maalox. Bless his heart. Mel's little office was an oasis of friendly clutter in the otherwise sterile chrome and glass headquarters of the VIP Channel.

Holly held the dark blue binder a moment before she opened it, then she read the first page with its list of the five heroes Programming had chosen for the special week. Other than Neil Armstrong, she didn't recognize a single name.

"Who are these people?" she asked. "Who's Al Haynes?"

The springs of Mel's chair creaked as he leaned back. "He was the pilot of United Flight 232. Remember? The plane that pinwheeled down the runway in Sioux City, Iowa, in 1989?"

"Oh, sure. Good choice," she said. Great footage!

"Thelma Schuyler Brooks is the woman who started the music school on the Wolf River Reservation in Arizona, and now has at least one student in every major orchestra in the country."

"Okay." Holly was thinking she'd have to work closely with her sound man on that one, not to mention brush up on her Beethoven.

"Howard Mrazek is the NYPD hostage negotiator who saved all those people a couple years ago during the standoff at the Chemical Bank."

"Mm," Holly murmured as her eyes drifted further down the page. "Who in the world is Calvin Griffin?"

"The Secret Service agent who took the bullet for the president last year. He's your hero."

"Excuse me?"

"He's your hero, Holly. He's your guy. That's the segment Arnold and Maida want you to produce."

"I'd rather do Haynes," she said. She was already imagining how she could use repetition of that fiery runway footage to come up with a really dramatic piece. Hadn't they been in the air a long time, flying touch and go, trying to bring that sucker down? Had Haynes flown in Vietnam? Was the crash footage in public domain? What was her budget? Her mind was going ninety miles an hour, so she was barely aware of Mel's reply. She knew he'd said something, though, because the little office was still reverberating from his growl.

"You're doing Calvin Griffin," Mel said. "You don't have a choice, kid. That's what Arnold and Maida want. Griffin's how I sold them on the idea in the first place."

She glanced down at the name on the page. "What do you mean?"

"I mean because you're both from Texas. Because you know the territory. You speak the language."

Holly wanted to laugh, but it would have come out high and maniacal, like a person being carted off to an asylum. She didn't know the territory. She hadn't been back to Texas in over a decade. Thank God. As for speaking the language, she'd had six months of very expensive lessons with a voice coach in Cincinnati in an attempt to bury her accent. She hadn't said *y'all* in years.

"I do not speak the language, Mel." She rolled her eyes. "When was the last time we went out to lunch and you heard me tell the waiter *Bring me a slab of baby back ribs and a big ol' beer*?"

Her mentor narrowed his eyes. "When was the last time you didn't have to remind yourself not to ask for mayo on pastrami?"

He was right, of course, and Holly could feel her lips flatten in a thin, stubborn line. Why couldn't she have been born to a lovely couple in Connecticut, instead of Bobby Ray and Crystal Hicks of Sandy Springs, Texas?

"Hey. Come on, kid. The accent's cute. Refreshing." Mel's chuckle was just obscene. "Plus it got you the job. Not to mention an all expenses paid trip back home."

"Where I get to interview some good ol' boy who got shot just doing his job," she added glumly.

"Take it or leave it, kid."